G581: Earth

Book 3 of Gliese 581g series

By Christine D. Shuck

Secret of Survival

**Earth, China's Guizhou Province
02.06.2099**

Before Dawn

In the pre-dawn darkness, Jia could hear odd noises. They sounded as if they were coming from the tiny, cramped kitchen. Mama had always hated it, that kitchen, the whole house for that matter, and Jia was surprised that she hadn't wanted to move to Auntie's after she passed. Cheng had told them both that they could have it, and Jia couldn't understand why they had stayed in their tiny house. Cheng's house had been nearly twice as big, something that Xiao Wang had long coveted and envied her younger sister for having.

Jia had asked Mama and received no genuine answer. The older woman had simply muttered about spirits and continued stuffing her face with greasy Chow Fun. She had welcomed no further discussion on the matter.

A sound of glass breaking blasted through the quiet, and Jia jumped up. Mama had been acting weird, well, weirder than normal. Jia's phone lit up as she fumbled for it. It was earlier than she had initially thought, just after three in the morning. What was Mama doing up?

She slipped on her house shoes and reached for the wall to help guide her in the gloom. A light would be too bright, and she was far too tired to have it shining in her eyes. She hadn't fallen asleep until after one, anyway, what with the craziness that was going on outside and all around them. Her neighbors, people she had seen every day of her life for the past sixteen years, were acting as if possessed. A desperate hunger in their eyes as they devoured anything they could lay their hands on or fit into their mouths. It was like something out of a horror movie.

Seeing their next-door neighbor eating a rat raw, that had been the last straw for both Jia and Xiao. They had closed the doors and windows to the house, preferring the smothering, fetid, greasy air to that of the insanity that was just beyond their walls. Mama had locked the door, then insisted on moving the couch against it.

"Everyone has gone mad," she muttered and then headed for the kitchen to polish off the Xiao Long Bao that Jia had made for her the day before.

She had doubled the recipe on Mama's request, and it should have lasted them for days. The large pot had been full to the brim of the tasty dumpling soup, enough to feed a family of five with leftovers. Instead, it had quickly disappeared, the bowls filling the tiny sink and then spilling onto the counter. Jia shook her head at the thought. Mama was eating like the neighbors, like the rest of Guiyang, as if it were a compulsion. Their cupboards were looking bare, and Jia dreaded having to shop later in the morning. She inched her way down the hallway; rustling noises continued to guide her way.

Xiao Wang was seated on the cracked and peeling linoleum floor, the refrigerator door wide open, lighting the small, dingy kitchen in a weak yellow light. The sound of breaking glass had come from the jar of fish sauce on the door. It was now on the floor, shining sharp shards mixed with the dark brown liquid that spread quickly across the floor. Xiao looked up then, her eyes shiny and desperate. Food dribbled down her chin and her hands appeared covered with fish sauce. She paused in mid-lick, her mouth working on processing the salty mess, throat convulsively swallowing.

"I'm so hungry, Jia, so very hungry."

And with that, she reached into the puddle and pulled out a piece of glass covered in sauce. Jia screamed and ran forward to stop Mama, but she was too late. Into her mouth went the piece of glass. And as blood sprayed from Xiao's mouth, and Jia looked at the few pieces of glass remaining, she realized with horror that it was far from the first piece her mother had swallowed.

Jia screamed.

The Road Out

Jia peered out of the window, her stomach rumbling, aching. It had been four days now, and the world around her was silent. Her mother had died there in the kitchen, a pool of blood slowly spreading from her mouth, her eyes sightless and staring. It had been mere minutes after the last piece of glass was consumed.

Xiao's hands were remarkably strong as Jia had tried to pry a piece of jagged and sharp glass from her hand. Her blood had mingled with her mother's and she had screamed over and over as Xiao's body convulsed, her back arcing, the sound of her head slamming against the cracked and dirty floor. It had taken seconds, but each one had felt like an hour.

Jia had sat there, unmoving, overcome by it all, until the sun had risen and Xiao's blood had congealed, her body cold, rubbery to the touch. Jia had covered Mama with her favorite blanket, fingers shaking, tears dripping in great fat drops.

Outside, the bright morning sun had been at odds with the horrifying sights visible from the smudged glass window in the front door. Jia had kept the curtains drawn, the door locked, and the door blocked with the couch. On the first day after Mama's death, the door had shaken and cracked under the pounding of feet and hands. The couch in front of it, however, had held it fast and whoever was on the other side eventually gave up and tried another house. This was repeated time and again on the first day, and again on the second. By the third day, as Jia sat in the gloomy living room, her stomach growling with hunger, there had only been one person who had tried to get in. A neighbor, one she knew slightly, a friend of Mama's. He had scrabbled at the door, called for Xiao and Jia, and cried. She had almost opened the door. She had stood up, grabbed ahold of the couch to hoist it out of the way, when she heard his next words: "I'm just so hungry. So hungry."

Jia was hungry. But it wasn't the same as

what was happening to the others, and she knew it. Why did the virus not touch her? Before the vidcast had stopped transmitting live, the newsvid anchor had described the virus in excruciating detail. The city outside was in a frenzy of consumption, desperate to put food into their bellies, and finally, anything else, food or otherwise, that could fit inside their mouths.

She had watched numbly as the newsvids showed vids of Guiyang residents eating vegetation, small animals, non-food objects, glass and metal, and even chemicals. It made what Mama had done almost tame. She had sat there hunched in a chair, watching the newsvids until a stark black and white viral contagion symbol, the Chinese and English symbols replaced the broadcasts that instructed everyone to stay inside.

She had stayed. The smell of Mama's corpse had grown, and the streets had been quiet, eerily so, for over twenty-four hours now. Jia had slept, poorly, there in the living room, unwilling to go into the kitchen and look for any scraps left from

Mama's rummaging through the cupboards. The flies, how they had found their way inside a closed house was beyond her, were thick and buzzing. Jia could barely stand the smell. Her stomach roiled now, not just with hunger, but with nausea. She had to leave, had to find a way to food, to other survivors. If there were any. The silence was thick, cloying, and overwhelming. She had never felt more alone.

It was difficult to move the couch. She panted, straining to move it. Just days ago, with Mama helping her, of course, it had been easy. It was more than it being just her moving it, and Jia knew that.

If I don't get food soon, I'll die.

And despite her fear, her terror at the thought of stepping into a city empty of inhabitants and life, the urge to survive took hold, and she heaved at the couch again, felt one leg catch on the worn wood floor and gouge a deep scratch in it. *Mama would kill me if she saw that.* And then she laughed. It was small, dry, and sounded as if it were someone else, someone unfamiliar. A bark of sound in the silence.

She shook her head, and the movement caused the world to dance and spots of light to appear before her eyes. She strained, pushing again at the couch, and it moved away from the front door enough for her to slide behind it, unlock the locks, and open it. She pushed again, one last time, and the couch gave way, giving her enough space to open the door further, slide out of the opening and into the bright sunshine overhead.

She blinked, shading her eyes and weaving slightly as she stood upright on the doorstep. The street was empty, preternaturally so. The trees that adorned the tiny front lawns of each house were all denuded of leaves from the ground to over six feet in height. The grass was gone, only dirt and the occasional root showing. Everything looked odd, barren, as if a mad landscaper had removed every last leaf and laid the world bare. There was no sound, not a voice, not the twittering of birds, the sound of traffic, nothing. It was as if the city was empty of its inhabitants, but worse, stripped of every animal and plant as well.

Jia walked down her block, past another, the sickly-sweet smell of rot the only constant. She saw bodies then, scattered, lying where they had fallen, clawing for food, eyes staring, flies buzzing. Jia swallowed down nausea, sick at the sight of death at every turn. It took an hour for her to reach Hequn Road and when she did, she wished hadn't.

The road was littered with bodies, the open-air market where she had loved to share a bowl of Hot Pot with Cheng before he had left for Hong Kong, where she shopped each week for their meals, was in tatters and bodies lay among destroyed stalls, pots, and swarms of green flies.

It was here, however, that she found other survivors. Hollow-eyed and unsmiling, she joined them as they left the city, stumbling as they moved away from the city and into the countryside. In the countryside, there was some nourishment to be found. As day faded to night, Jia and a group of other survivors skinned, cooked, and ate a goat from the remains of a farm. She felt slightly guilty as she sat by the fire and gorged on a haunch of poorly cooked, unseasoned meat. The family that had worked this land were dead, their corpses swollen and rotting in a field 200 meters away. As her hunger pangs subsided, it startled Jia and the others to see jets streaking across the sky. They watched as each of the aircraft dropped their deadly cargo and enormous explosions lit up the sky. Beside her, a young man stared at the fire blooming in a column in the sky.

"They're too late to stop it. Everyone is dead."

"We're not," Jia said, softly.

"We might as well be. They will shoot us on sight, I think. I saw them do it when riots over food broke out." He shook his head. "They're too late. Far too late. All that's left are the dead." His eyes slid over her and towards the city in the distance, the flames reflected in his dark eyes. "They'll come for us as well. Or we will eat ourselves to death, just like the others. We are the walking dead."

Five days later, they stopped on the outskirts of a town. The population sign showed it had been a town of over five thousand people. The wind shifted as the ragtag group of survivors stood on the tarmac, and the smell of decay blasted them. Jia stayed on the road with the others while two of the men walked through the town, calling out. The next morning, one of them was dead, a handful of pills in his hand. He had been the one who told Jia they were the walking dead.

Six Months Later

"Just a pinch, now, Jia." The technician's face was round, kind. "Folks tell me I'm the best at this." She slid the needle into Jia's skin and released the flexible tubing from around Jia's arm.

Jia watched as the blood filled the ampules with a thick red froth. "What do you hope to find?" She said it haltingly. English was still new, and she had been struggling to learn the language for nearly four months now, ever since she had arrived with other ESH survivors to the new city of New Athens.

The woman smiled at her. "You are a

rarity, Jia. And we are doing some genetic testing to find out your profile and see why you, and not any of your other family, survived the virus. AB negative blood in the Asian population is incredibly rare, less than one in one thousand have it."

She filled a second and the third ampule. "We will do a full profile and you can pick up the results tomorrow if you like."

Jia nodded, smiling tentatively in return. "Yes, thank you."

The next day she returned, struggling to remember the words in English to describe what she needed. "I ah, I pick up, um, the..." The woman manning the front desk stared at her and Jia felt embarrassed.

A voice from down the hall spoke up. "Ah, Jia! I see you returned for your lab results." It was the kind technician, the one who had taken such care of her the day before. She had been right. The blood draw hadn't hurt a bit. "Come in, come in!"

Jia heaved a sigh of relief and followed her down the hallway and into a small office. The woman pointed to a chair. "Sit, please. I want to talk with you a moment."

She waited until Jia sat down and then plopped into the chair opposite and handed over several sheets of paper. "What can you tell me about your father?"

"My father? He died five, no, six years ago now. We were not close." Jia toed her chair rung. "I am sorry, I should not say that."

The woman nodded thoughtfully. "You noted here that your parents were both full-blooded Chinese."

Jia nodded, confused. "Yes, of course. Why?"

"Well, according to these results, Jia, your father was not Chinese. He was of European descent, probably from Germany or possibly Austria." She tapped the bottom of the first page. "Those genetic markers right there are quite clear. You are only half-Chinese, which means the secret to your survival was in your genetic heritage. I'm sure your father possesses the AB blood type, and if so, chances are that he may have survived the virus. Have you logged into the Survivor Network yet?"

Jia blinked at her, at a loss for what to

say. Bao Wang was *not* her father? How was this possible? She opened her mouth, then closed it. The words in her head were all in Mandarin, not English. She did not know *what* to say.

The woman looked concerned. "I am so sorry, Jia. This must be a deep shock to you!" She put a hand on Jia's shoulder and squeezed it lightly. "Look, if you need anything, the Survivor Network can help. Not only is it a way to reconnect with family, but it also provides counseling and support groups for people who are still struggling with our new world and reality. I hope you will consider signing up and taking advantage of the services. Who knows, you might even find him."

"Find...him?" Jia's voice sounded hesitant, stretched.

"Your father." She smiled. "After all this, wouldn't that be a miracle?"

Jia walked from the Med Center in a scattered fog, her mind replaying moments of her childhood in a fast loop of memories. Her mother and father fighting, her father staring at her with something akin to hatred, and him never, ever holding her or loving her. She had seen other dads with their daughters. Her friends had loved their fathers, and their fathers had obviously loved them. But hers? She had never understood it and, even as she felt traitorous and unworthy thinking about it, she had been relieved when he had passed away shortly before her eleventh birthday. His absence from their home had allowed it to feel less like living in an enemy camp and more like a home. Even if it was filled with a mother who did not understand her.

She stared at the papers in her hand, shocked at her new reality. Her father wasn't her father. Her father, the only one she had known, the one who lay in a casket deep in the ground thousands of miles away, wasn't her biological father. So... what? Mama had an *affair*? Just imagining it was mind-boggling.

She walked back to the comfortable suite of rooms they had given her in the large apartment block on the west end of New Athens. Here she was alone, free to decorate the walls in a way she saw fit, and eat and live how she wanted. It was such a far cry from living with Mama in Guiyang or the internment camps that she had found herself in for over two months before she had qualified to go to the Reformed United States of America. She sat down on the couch and absentmindedly poured herself some tea as she stared at the papers and pulled up the Survivor Network on her tablet.

She blinked as the screen splashed a message of welcome and prompted her to enter her information. She typed it in and clicked the Search button, hoping for it to match her with someone just as much as she hoped it wouldn't. A moment later, it chimed softly with a match. Her genetic profile, listed in a standard identifier on the papers the technician had given her, had found a match in the system and it displayed a photo next to the details. He lived in New Munich, the report listed, and he had included a request to be identified to any potential genetic matches, which meant that *he* might very well have been looking for *her*. Possibly? Probably. She sucked in a breath and let it out slowly.

A question appeared on the screen: "Notify Genetic Match?" She could log out now, walk away, and never have to talk to him, never meet him. Her finger hovered over the button, hesitating.

Jia clicked it. He was, after all, the secret of her survival.

Anomaly

Lick Observatory
11.13.2099

Stefan sipped his coffee, choking on it as he realized it wasn't just cool, it was stone cold. And what was that black speck? A fly? How long had he had his eye fixed on the array? Far too long, obviously. The blurry image was disturbing. An anomaly. It wasn't an object he expected to see there in the night sky. He couldn't help but stare at it. Apparently, he'd stared long enough for his hot coffee to cool.

He stood up, massaging his already stiff neck. According to the clock on the wall, it was just past two in the morning and the last time he had checked it was eleven p.m. Every muscle in his back and legs complained. He really had been sitting that long, though he couldn't imagine how.

Ms. Frizzle, an ancient Golden Retriever, groaned and shifted in the bed nearby. She was deaf now, and mostly blind. The dog bed was thick and perfect for her old bones. She rarely moved from it these days.

He added the data from his notes into the large tablet, dictating the exact location of the anomaly. Short of Bates, who was holed up in the UP city of Sanctuary, locally referred to as Mirepoix, no one particularly cared. The ESH virus had taken people's eyes from the stars. Earth was their focus now. Well, that and the newly discovered issue of the lingering effects of ESH on the reproductive system. Jim Bates had been a professor, mentor, and, until recently, Stefan's boss. He had been hiking the Appalachian Trail when the virus hit. And now he was one of the rare few Uninfected Persons, which was no stroke of luck.

More like the guillotine hanging above you, just waiting to fall.

There was no cure, after all. No immunity. No survival unless you had the rarest blood type in the world, like Stefan had. And now, as if humanity hadn't been dealt enough of a blow, now those that were left were likely infertile.

Myra, if she were still here, would have had plenty to say about that. Then again, his wife had always been clear about her wishes–she hadn't wanted children. And Stefan had wanted her too much to care, although as the years passed, he had certainly had his moments of doubt. Myra was so kind, so *maternal*, that he had never quite understood her child-free stance. In the end, well, close to the end, he had resented her for it. If only because she was leaving him alone, with no one to hold, no one to love as she withered before his eyes, a victim of a rare form of bone cancer. It had taken her quickly. Just three months from diagnosis to death, but they had been hard ones. Sitting by her side, day in and day out. He had become a fixture first in the hospital and later on a couch adjacent to her bed in the living room of their rental. With its plain, unadorned walls, it had been a place for her to die. Rather than where she belonged, on the mountain, and at the observatory that they both had loved.

She had passed weeks before the world dissolved into chaos. The rumors and whispers of some odd virus causing people to eat until they died, growing into a crescendo in days before she succumbed.

In a sense, her death had been muted, made almost irrelevant, in the face of such a calamity as the world had ever seen in human memory. Not the Collapse, nor the myriad of diseases that had run their course through the world from medieval to present had stood up to something as lethal as the ESH virus. The loss of her—sometimes Stefan felt as if he were the only one who really missed her.

She would have died from ESH if she hadn't already been gone. It was small comfort, really.

After she had passed, quietly, her breath rattling out a final farewell, he had cremated her remains and gone back to the observatory. There on the mountain, high above their ravaged world, he was alone, at peace. And because he was alone, with only her urn as company, he had found himself talking to her as he had when she was alive. Simple, run-of-the-mill things. Those unimportant details that no one but your life partner cared about or particularly wanted to hear.

They had been together for nearly twenty years, longer if you counted those first two years of unrequited crush in high school that resulted in him following her across the country to a strange college and changing his major from art to astronomy. It had worked out, no matter what others thought of the oddity of an art major turned astronomer.

"I'm worn out." His words echoed in the empty room. "The next few weeks are supposed to be clear, plenty of time to figure out what in the world I'm looking at." He glanced at the urn. At first, he carried it everywhere, even on long walks along the mountainside. Somehow, he felt less alone when he did it. Occasionally, if he saw something truly breathtaking, a fiery sunset, a shooting star, or a majestic deer with its full spread of antlers, he would take out a pinch of ashes and let it float in the breeze. In that way, it was as if a part of her spirit accompanied him everywhere.

Sometimes though, the dreams were far too real with her ashes close to him in the night, sitting on the nightstand. He would wake up and think she was still alive, lying next to him. Those were the hardest moments. He had settled instead on giving it a place of honor on the small desk in the observatory. Here she was with him, by his side, as he continued their life's work.

"You keep an eye on it for me, Myra, while I get some rest."

He kissed his fingers and pressed them against the top of the cool metal that housed his wife's remains. "I'll see you late in the evening for more star-wandering."

He glanced at Ms. Frizzle. Her muzzle was shot with white and her eyes, although closed now, were rheumy and clouded with cataracts. She hadn't moved a muscle since he stood up. He figured she would be fine. Leaving her here for the night was better than waiting for her to hobble along the long walk down to the cabin. He left the door open a crack, in case the old dog needed to relieve herself. She was nearly eighteen years old, far beyond her breed's life expectancy, and if he didn't give her an opportunity to relieve herself outside, she was sure to do it there on the observatory floor.

Besides, she'd keep Myra company. Ms. Frizzle had always preferred his wife's company to his own anyway.

Despite his efforts, a large puddle of urine greeted him the next evening, inches from the door. Ms. Frizzle avoided looking at him, her head hanging low as she watched him mop the mess up. Stefan finished up, walked over, and patted the old dog. She couldn't help it, and he knew it. He imagined her waking up in the night, her joints stiff and painful. The door was heavy, so even though he had propped it open with a brick, it had likely been too hard for her to move.

"Old girl, I'm sorry. I should have left it open more." The dog's tail thumped twice and she licked his hand, her soft, warm tongue conveying apologies the only way she knew how. "You are a good girl. Never forget that." The tail thumped again and she lay back down and closed her eyes.

It wouldn't be long now. He hated the thought of it, though. Myra had picked her out when she was a fluffy scrap of a thing, sitting there in a cage with her brothers and sisters crawling all over her. They had been full of teeth and wiggles and sharpness, all while she lay there quietly. She had been a fine dog over the years and Myra had loved her so. She had treated the dog like the child she never had, lavishing her with specially formulated food, toys, and treats, and even costumes each Halloween.

They had a picture of Ms. Frizzle as a

clown, as Beetlejuice from that old film Myra loved so much, and even dressed up as a big yellow bus after The Magic School Bus cartoon they had both grown up watching. The cartoons were ridiculously dated, but Myra had clearly loved them. Whereas Stefan had enjoyed them, Myra had been a hardcore fan. It was where the name Ms. Frizzle had come from.

He set down the dog's bowl, a can of soft dog food dumped into it. They had stopped feeding the old girl dry food years ago and by now, he doubted she had more than two teeth left in her head. Ms. Frizzle's tail thumped, and she slowly stood up and walked over to it and began to eat. *Well, at least she will live a little longer.* "One day at a time, Ms. Frizzle, one day at a time."

The night was clear and as he stared down through the telescope, checking the image on the screen, he zeroed in the distant blur. "Whatever you are," he muttered as he adjusted the controls, "you are new. And you don't belong there."

He spent the rest of the evening taking measurements, logging them meticulously, and cross-referencing all known Kuiper Belt Objects. There were hundreds of thousands of KBOs, likely millions, but most were nowhere near this size. And that was what concerned Stefan most. To be showing up now, where it was, and moving as fast as it had to be, meant that it was something significant, if only he could see it better!

When Ms. Frizzle whined to go out, Stefan was surprised to see that it would be dawn soon. He had enough information to be concerned, but not nearly enough to raise an alarm. Most concerning to him was the fact that he couldn't see Ultima Thule, despite the KBO being in prime viewing position. Known more formally as Arrokoth 486958, the asteroid resembled an upside-down peanut with a wasp-like waist. The larger lobe was 21 kilometers across and the smaller lobe on the opposite end was 15 kilometers across. With an orbital period of around two hundred ninety-eight years, Arrokoth had been classified as a cold classical Kuiper Belt Object. He should have been able to see it. The fact that he couldn't, combined with the presence of a "new" object now heading into this way, was unsettling. He really needed to talk to Bates. He knew from regular messages back and forth that his mentor had been in the process of building an observatory on a mountain with excellent viewing, just a few miles from Mirepoix. Even if the observatory wasn't finished, Bates could take a look at his data and give him some kind of opinion.

He turned to his tablet, the sudden movement causing a muscle in his lower back to spasm painfully, and he reached down to rub it. Sitting all night didn't help. *You need more exercise, even if it is plodding along at a slow pace so an aged mutt can keep up.*

His fingers flew over the keyboard.

Dumas,Stefan@LickObservatory   to BatesJim@SanctuaryTUPG
/BEGIN TRANSMISSION
Anomaly detected heading for home. Possible fracture of Arrokoth 486958? See data packet for measurements and further data. Please advise as to next step.
*AttachDoc
/END TRANSMISSION

Stefan clicked Send, leaned back, and massaged his tight muscles.

"Bates might take a while to respond," he said aloud, his words echoing in the enormous room. "The old man might be working, but more likely he is sleeping. I think he said something about the observatory being several months away from completion."

Ms. Frizzle groaned from her bed in the corner at the sound of his voice. She didn't move, though. The aged mutt was used to Stefan talking aloud to no one in particular.

The data was far from complete. It would take at least a few weeks of study before he could validate any of his suspicions, and possibly a month or two to ascertain whether or not the object would possibly come within range of impacting Earth.

Still, Stefan mused, *being able to see Ultima Thule's demise would be rather thrilling*.

Since its discovery in 2014, and the New Horizons flyby that had sent back detailed pictures, it had long been bantered back and forth as to when the object would break apart. The tenuous connection that the larger lobe, Ultima, had with the smaller lobe known as Thule had brought plenty of speculation as to not if, but when, it would break and what would happen next.

It seemed that they might actually have their answer. Stefan wasn't worried. At least, not really. Not until he had a whole lot more data logged. Space was vast. The possibility of something impacting Earth was so ridiculously small in the bigger scheme of things. He stood up, the vertebrae in his back popping. Nearby, Ms. Frizzle groaned again, her legs stretched and one long claw scraped the concrete floor. She opened one eye and stared at him blearily.

"C'mon, old girl, let's take a little walk, watch the sun come up, and then toddle off to bed."

The dog slowly made her way to her feet, giving a small shake as she stood, wobbled for a moment, and nearly sat down again.

He turned toward the urn that sat on the left side of his desk. "Good night, darling. Keep an eye on that anomaly for me, will you?"

He walked out of the door, Ms. Frizzle limping behind him.

Mirepoix

Sanctuary, Reformed United States of America
01.06.2100

The city was brimming with Uninfected Persons. It gave hope to May as she walked down the last of the muddy streets. The 3D printers had been hard at work replacing churned mud with sidewalks, gravel with macadam, and slowly houses rose in place of the trailers, RVs, and tents. Another month, possibly two, and their new city would rise from the Kansas plains.

Could she even call it a city? The City Council seemed to think so, and they had voted on naming it Sanctuary. Peter thought it was silly, and perhaps it was. Perhaps they should have kept the name Mirepoix, since they had such an international soup of residents here now.

At last count, there were at least thirty different languages spoken and over fifty nationalities. May wasn't sure who had been the first to label the moldering ruins of a Midwestern farm after a soup, but it was that name that stuck.

By the time she and Peter had arrived over three months ago, the town was already called Mirepoix. Their faces had been obscured with fabric masks, and then they were questioned at length, and a fair amount of distance, as to their travels and whereabouts over the past few months.

They had stayed in quarantine, patiently waiting for the full six weeks to pass before being accepted into the Uninfected Persons new city.

May wondered if her grandmother had felt like May did, with the entire world in upheaval during the COVID-19 outbreaks some eighty years prior. Or did she even remember? She had been young, not much older than preschool age. Still, she could imagine her grandmother's generation growing up with the fear of a deadly virus that could shut down the world never too far from their thoughts.

It is a shame we do not carry racial memories; if we did, we could avoid repeating the same mistakes.

May and Peter had been on a dig in Arizona, on the southern edge of the Petrified Forest, when the world came apart. First had come the rumors–nothing to worry about–a weird eating disorder, one that some folks were actually dying from. Then the newsvids had turned grim, advising social distancing, masks, and avoiding any social gatherings. It had been surreal to be sure, especially as they had run low on their food supply and contemplated having to go to town.

Peter had wanted to go on his own, but for May, that was unacceptable. She wasn't a delicate flower, and she didn't need his protection.

Sleep with a man and they think they have to be your white knight and chief protector.

Instead, they had both made the trek into town, only to discover that the tiny town of Tusayan, Arizona, already small to begin with, was now empty of everyone but the dead. It had been a tiny town of less than five hundred, slowly whittling itself down as the newest generations left for Flagstaff or Phoenix and beyond. But now? The bodies were mainly in their homes and

the tiny grocery store was empty of mostly
all foods, the meat rotting in the
refrigerated units. The glass had crunched
under their feet, the way inside of the store
open, a door hanging open.

That had been in late summer. By
October they had made their way
northeast, following the instructions on the
radio to head for Kansas if they had
remained unexposed to the ESH virus.

May was safe, oddly enough. From what
she learned as she listened to the vidcasts
and the radio, her AB negative blood
would save her life if she were to be
infected. But Peter? And all the rest of the
refugees in the barracks that she had
befriended in the past two months? They
would all die horribly.

"May!" Peter's voice called from behind
her, and May forced a smile on her face
and turned to greet him. May had thought
of their affair as short-lived, a summer
fling, before she returned to school. She
had just one year left to finish her degree
in botany. She had intended for the added
classes in paleontology to fill out her
resume, not define it.

But the world crashing down and
disintegrating around them had thrown

them together, for better or worse. Peter seemed to think it was some kind of cosmic sign that they were meant to be together, whereas May was pretty sure it was a cosmic joke at her expense.

"Hey there!" He grinned at her. "I was calling your name and you must have been deep in thought because you didn't respond."

Sure, let's go with that. It's better than me admitting I ignored you the first two times.

College was supposed to be a time for experimentation, freedom, and exploration. Not a "we slept together and now, thanks to ESH, it must be true love" kind of future. And sure, she had encouraged it, she knew she had. She didn't have the family connections he had. Growing up in foster care had hardened her, and she questioned everything. She knew she did. When the world had come apart, she'd panicked, clung to him. After all, it had felt as if they were the last people on Earth. Especially when they had walked through Tusayan, looking for life and finding nothing but death. Not a single soul left alive.

"Sorry, I must have been a million miles

away," May answered, batting her eyes at him.

Peter reached out and touched her arm. She wanted to pull away, wanted to tell him to stop touching her all the time, but she didn't. He liked her. That was obvious. That he seemed to think she was "the one" had her twitchy and overwhelmed. He wasn't her type, not at all.

"There's a new batch of refugees at the gate, and Reese was asking where you were." He pulled her closer, wrapped an arm around her even as she stiffened in response. "I told him I'd find you and have you talk to them."

My blood is both a blessing and a curse.

The inhabitants of Mirepoix depended upon her to provide the safety net they so desperately needed. Because she wouldn't get sick with ESH, they had her meet all new incoming refugees. If any of them had the ESH virus, she would survive contracting it. This meant that they tapped her for gate duty, and the limited amount of contact allowed for those wishing to join the new Uninfected Person's city. The powers that be, such as they were since the government was devastated by the plague as well, kept promising that a vaccine was in the works. Their promises seemed empty.

It has been a year and still no proposed vaccine for the virus.

The 3D printers, cleaned and disinfected remotely, arrived two months ago, just days before Peter and May approached the city. They had begun work—churning out the basics necessary for Sanctuary to rise and house the UPs indefinitely.

Face it, girl, whatever this virus is, however it is mutating, we won't be leaving soon.

She gently disengaged herself from Peter's embrace, ignoring the hurt look on his face. He was sensing her reticence. It had been different on the road than when it had just been the two of them. It had been edgy, even desperately romantic, how they survived together, just the two of them. But it wore thin, eventually. She wasn't ready to settle down, to commit to Peter.

He's sweet, kind, but he's not the one.

"Right, well, I'd better get over there."

His hand fell to her arm, sensing the widening gap between them. "Dinner, later?"

May scrunched up her face. "If I'm delayed, eat without me. I'll catch the last rations run or some snacks that were just airdropped." She pulled away from him, and Peter's hand fell back to his side. There, that look, he was like an open book. Her stomach turned. She didn't want to hurt him. She really didn't, but she didn't feel the connection. It had been fun, exciting even, but it was over. She just didn't know how to tell him that.

She waved at him, her pathetic attempt to disengage from him gently falling flat as she turned on her heel and jogged back toward the front gate. Walls of thick steel had surrounded the entire city, twenty feet high, with razor wire on top. It stopped people from entering, and from leaving. It was necessary. At least, that's what the people in charge said. The only way in or out was through the front gate.

Although the term front *gate infers that there is also a* back *gate, and there is not.*

The massive steel doors were the last bastion of defense. Beyond the opening was a maze of razor wire with armed sentries in towers above. It was an ugly view. It felt as if they were in a violent backwater town instead of a sanctuary, but it kept the ESH positive out, and that was important. On the last leg of road, Peter had been ready to turn back, especially after he took in the menacing sentry towers. A series of low-slung, prefab buildings had welcomed them in, all of them staffed by people in hazmat suits and the full respiratory gear. From one building to the next, would-be inhabitants found themselves poked, prodded, and tested– often at the business end of a carbine. They weren't taking chances, after all. The people here were uninfected, and they planned on staying that way until they developed a vaccine.

And it was here in front of these gates that she could finally enter, with Peter and a handful of others by her side, into the safety of Mirepoix.

She couldn't think of it as Sanctuary. The name Mirepoix was firmly embedded into her brain thanks to the extraordinarily cute Matthew, whose French accent made her wiggly in the knees. He was taken, however, claimed by a bone-thin, pinch-faced girl, Lilou, who spoke little or no English and looked as if she were surgically attached to Matthew's hip. She glared at any girl who dared to come within five meters of Matthew and seemed especially antagonistic of May.

I'll find out what "fille américaine sale de demi-sang"[1] means. I know *she isn't saying anything nice!*

May's father had been black, her mother white. That much she had learned from her birth certificate, and nothing much more than that. Her skin was a warm mocha color, and most didn't seem to mind, but occasionally she ran into the racists. The look on Lilou's face was clear, even if her words were in French.

Just my luck that here, in this UP city, I would end up face-to-face with some white-bread bitch who fears losing her man to me.

Matthew, Lilou, and two large Greyhound busses full of European tourists had wound up here, isolated, thousands of miles from their homes, on the last leg of their tour of Middle America. And here they had stayed until the newly formed Terran United Planetary Government had stepped in and offered them protection from the outside world. From the stories they had shared, it had happened just in the nick of time. How they had avoided infection was mind-boggling when May thought about it. They had stayed together, working the farm, the owners absent and likely dead from the virus.

That had been some dumb luck. From what Matthew explained, a full half of the French contingent grew up on farms outside of Moulins. As the news reports had spread, and people became increasingly concerned, roadblocks were erected and cities locked down. The soldiers at the roadblocks had ordered their busses to turn around, to leave, although there was nowhere to go. A few wrong turns, and eventually they had ended up in the middle of Kansas, with prairie stretching as far as the eye could see. The first abandoned farm they found had become the base of Mirepoix, and more refugees had quickly joined them.

And here she was, with Peter, and nowhere left to go.

Although, technically, I could leave here. I'd be safe unless the virus were to mutate again.

Back in the '20s, that was what had made the coronavirus so damn scary. Just when they thought they had an effective vaccine, the damn thing had mutated. It had changed the world, if only for a short time. And the current fear on everyone's mind was the question–could the ESH virus mutate to include AB negative blood types too? And that was what had stopped May from leaving. It would be just her luck if she left this uninfected place and found herself in a mutated virus hotbed. Besides, they had shut her college down. They had shut down New York City, bombed the bridges and tunnels that led out into the surrounding boroughs. Word was that the Big Apple would never reopen. The cities quickly filled with the dead. Now the future was in new cities rising to take the place of the old. They were prefab, white-spired, ultra-modern, and they planned to take the scattered remains of humanity into the new century and beyond.

May reached the gate and waved up at the guards. The doors slowly opened, groaning as they did, and she slipped into the outer perimeter and entered the nearest low-slung prefab building on the right. She donned a hazmat suit. A new batch of refugees, three of them, waited in a room beyond. They had passed the forty-five-day mark and were clear of any symptoms. Their faces, tight and weary, showed little expression as she explained she would assign them bunks in the communal living space that a majority of Mirepoix's inhabitants were currently sharing.

"The 3D printers are working at capacity, and we expect you will have more permanent housing assigned within the next twenty days, give or take a day." She looked them over. "You all wish to stay together?"

The woman wasn't much older than May, and the child who clasped her hand couldn't possibly be her own. The woman was far too young. From the way the girl was clinging to the woman, she doubted the girl was related to the older man, either. The man stole a glance at the woman before asking, "Will it slow our chances of getting housing if we don't?"

May smiled and shook her head. "No, not really. We just need to tell the printer what size home to produce. Currently, the 3D printers limit us to two-, three-, and four-bedroom models. For those not already in familial groups, we advise separate housing."

I haven't told Peter that I requested a two-bedroom unit independent from him. I'm not looking forward to that discussion.

The man looked relieved, whereas the

woman's mouth compressed in a thin line of disappointment and hurt.

Perhaps she had been hoping for more—an instant family complete with child and husband. Huh.

May settled the three refugees in the northwest barracks on the second level. By the time she left them, the man had requested a one-bedroom unit for himself and May noted it in the tablet she carried with her.

No happily-ever-after pandemic-style for the woman. What about me? How do I tell Peter I don't see us staying together?

It wasn't a conversation she ended up needing to have. Instead, two days later, Peter exhibited the classic symptoms of the ESH virus. His temperature rose slightly, to 98.6 from his baseline norm of 98.2. Even within the relative safety of the city walls, everyone was monitored closely and their temperatures taken three times daily, right before meals. When it stayed at the elevated temperature and his appetite increased, well, by then it was too late. Too late for Peter, and too late for the rest of Mirepoix. The ESH virus spread like wildfire thanks to Peter, who was assigned shifts at the cafeteria after he hurt his back lifting the airdropped cargo.

How had he become infected? It was never clear, but likely it had come from the airdrop. They disinfected all incoming cargo both at point of origin and upon arrival, but the ESH virus was virile, aggressive even, single-minded in its mission to find new hosts. Whether it had mutated enough to survive the disinfecting spray, or a spot had been missed, no one ever really had a suitable answer. They isolated Peter immediately, and May too, in the glassed-in prefab next to him, but it was far too late to make a difference.

In the years to come, she wished she could scrub her mind clear of the memories, erase what she saw from her organic data bank, and go back to the pre-virus world she had lost. Her reluctance to stay with Peter, her wish for independence and adventure, all of it subverted and dulled by what unfolded over the next few weeks.

It was Matthew who came and released her from the isolation room when it was clear there was no longer any need for her to be there. His eyes were red from weeping, and his long, delicate fingers shook. It took several tries before he got the lock open and when he did, May hadn't known whether to come outside or invite him in, so she had simply stood there and stared at him.

His eyes finally focused on her. They were alone, surrounded by the dead. There was no sound, except the raucous calls of the crows that flew overhead in lazy arcs.

"Elle est morte. Ils sont tous morts.[2]"

"I'm sorry, Matthew, I don't understand." She stepped forward and took his hand. It was cold, and she closed her hands over his to warm them, to comfort him perhaps, or just to touch another. "I have AB negative blood. Do you as well?"

Matthew just stared at her for a moment, his eyes sliding over her as if he were staring at a stranger.

"On devrait être morts aussi.[3]"

He pulled his hands from her, reached into his pocket, and pulled out a black handgun.

May stepped back, heart suddenly jackhammering in her chest. "Matthew, no. Please put that down."

He stared at her. The cute, artistic college student with the disarming smile had vanished.

"Fuir le. Maintenant.[4]"

He stepped to one side, gestured with his free hand towards the door, and May wobbled past on shaky legs.

"Fuir!" Matthew shouted, and May felt a surge of adrenaline. Her legs transformed from wobbly sticks barely able to hold her to machines that powered her journey away from the isolation chambers towards the front gate on the opposite end of Mirepoix. She had made it halfway when she heard a single gunshot ring out. She didn't turn around; instead, she ran faster.

Translation:
1. American girl dirty half-blood.
2. She's dead. They are all dead.
3. We should be dead too.
4. Run away, then. Now.
5. Run!

By the Light of the Moon

Lick Observatory
01.09.2100

Stefan stabbed the End Call button and glared at the Comm in his hand. Just two rings, and then it went dead. This had happened every time in the past week that he tried to call Jim Bates, and it was getting old. Especially considering the data he had collected over the past twelve weeks.

Bates had gotten back to him the day after he had sent the initial email, while he was sleeping, and the transmission had been waiting for him when he awoke that evening. The old man had been cranky, frustrated. The observatory had experienced several delays.

It was to be expected. Nearly everyone's focus was on rebuilding. The cities were unlivable, not just for the Uninfected Persons, but for everyone. Nearly one year later, the smell of death still hung in the air. It had created hazardous living conditions as bodies rotted in the streets and in houses. In many of the larger cities, the dead had even affected the water supply.

Bates' plans for an observatory took third place to creating a safe environment to sleep, live, and exist in. And the UP cities had it far worse. They had to start from scratch *and* not involve any ESH-positive survivors, to touch any part of the materials necessary for the creation of the buildings, sewers, or supplies of any kind.

No matter the protocols enforced, the ESH virus remained highly contagious and exceedingly lethal. Several UP encampments had fallen to the virus before they learned this painful lesson.

After receiving several terse emails from his former boss, Stefan had learned not to ask for status updates on the new observatory. From the sound of it, the project was on indefinite hold as Sanctuary's population continued to grow.

The changing weather patterns over the past century had included record-high water levels thanks to a majority of the world's glaciers melting by the mid-21st century, and that had led to additional changes in storms. From what Stefan understood of the area, Lick Observatory had never seen such damaging electrical storms until the past three decades. Outside, one was raging right now and the air itself felt as if it were alive. He could feel it crackling with energy. Ms. Frizzle whined on her bed, and when Stefan did not respond, she slowly levered herself off of the soft cushion, limped slowly over, and nudged him with her muzzle, positioning her body so that she could lean against his legs.

Her wet nose pushed against his fingers until he automatically threaded them into her fur. She felt greasy, and she smelled. How long had it been since he had given her a bath? The thought came through, bounced about, and then flitted away as he scowled at the screen on his tablet, the data in neat little rows.

He hated the fact that he was over 1,500 miles away from his mentor and friend. He wanted to sit in the same room as Bates, exchange ideas and data without the fear of giving him this terrible virus. He had spent the last few months, hell, most of the last year, alone on this mountaintop.

How could a tiny, blurry light be so dangerous? And yet, the data was incontrovertible. Ultima Thule had broken apart, and part of it was on a collision course with Earth.

There was, of course, the planetary defense system, a series of automated missiles designed to target and destroy any kind of incoming object larger than one kilometer in diameter.

"Destroy" isn't the right word, however, Stefan thought as he continued to stroke Ms. Frizzle's lank fur. Outside, the lightning flashed and the dog and man both flinched as a loud boom of thunder fractured the air. All the lights went black and the ever-present hum of machinery ceased.

"The lights will be back on in no time, Frizz," Stefan said, more for his own comfort than the dog's. "Meanwhile, we might as well head to bed, huh?" Ms. Frizzle whined; her body occasionally trembling. The lightning flashed, lighting up the small windows and the doorway, which he had left open for Ms. Frizzle to come and go. As a flash lit up the doorway, he noticed it was in vain, however. A large puddle had spread just feet from the door, and it was not rainwater. Stefan sighed. "Poor girl." His fingers rubbed the ridge of her skull and on down her spine. It was protruding in several spots, and he could feel the outline of her ribs underneath his fingertips. She was losing weight. How long had this been going on?

He rose, stretched, and walked to the door, skirting the puddle of urine. He'd clean it up later, during the day. For now, it was time to get some sleep. Tomorrow he would try again. By then the power would be back up. He needed to talk to Bates. This was a development he had never dealt with before, and there was a chain of command. Or at least there had been once. He whistled to the Frizz and set out down the steps and into the rain. The water fell from the sky in a heavy shower, stronger than the water-saving faucet in his bathroom. Stefan squinted, tucked his head down, and picked up his pace. Behind him, Ms. Frizzle whined and fell slightly behind. She struggled to keep up.

"Come on, old girl. Get your hiney moving!" he called, and she limped faster, giving one sharp bark of complaint as she did. The living quarters were barely two hundred feet away, small, 3D-printed, poured concrete living quarters guaranteed to stand for one hundred years, possibly more. From what he had heard, it had survived over three massive wildfires that had decimated the vegetation on top of Mount Hamilton over the past fifty years. Likely the building would be here long after he was gone. He left the door unlocked, for there was no one to lock it up against, especially not now.

Ms. Frizzle limped behind him and finally caught up as he stopped and held the door open for her. She creaked over to the soft dog bed, managed a half-hearted shake, and slowly lowered herself into it. He doubted she would have made the journey outside in the storm if he hadn't urged her to. He liked her company, though. Even if she wasn't able to lever her old bones onto the bed any longer.

Better that way, he thought as he watched her lick her wet fur and groan her way into position for the night. *I don't think I could stand the smell. I really need to give her a bath.*

The flashes of light were the only source

of illumination. Stefan pulled off his clothes and settled into the bed.

The new day dawned, but instead of sleeping through most of it as he normally did, Stefan found himself awake. The power was still off, the air conditioner silent, and the air was now hot and thick. It reminded him of Missouri, where he had lived for the first two decades of his life before being lured away with the promise of the stars and a beautiful woman who loved them even more than he did. The summers there were hot and muggy. It was January, however, and he was shocked at the massive changes in weather. It was winter, time for snow, and shouldn't he be snuggled under a pile of covers instead of sweating right now?

He reached for his tablet and swore when he saw it was nearly out of juice. *Damn batteries aren't the problem, Stefan, you are—always forgetting to recharge the damn things!*

All he had to do was remember to place it on the charger. Hell, the chargers were scattered throughout the facility—by his bed, at the desk inside the observatory, even in the kitchen. It was almost as if he had a brain malfunction. He could never remember to keep the things charged, despite the batteries lasting for well over a week with heavy use.

He puttered about the residence, tired and grouchy. Ms. Frizzle whined at the door and vanished as quickly as her old bones could trot her out to the tree line. She could sense his mood and wanted nothing to do with it. As the sun shone through patches of clouds, he cleaned the dishes, washing them by hand in cold water, mumbling under his breath as he did so. He hadn't pushed for solar. Damned if he had just taken the grid for granted, despite the hell that the ESH virus had unleashed, causing instability in every basic function of life that most people took for granted, including an already outdated and overloaded electrical grid.

When he finished with the kitchen, he began working on the rest of the small house, shocked at the level of mess he had created. There was no one else to blame. Just him and Ms. Frizzle. The old mutt sure hadn't put his clothes on the floor, although she was happy enough to inch her way across the floor and lie down on them.

Within an hour, despite the water being

cold, and the inability to do anything more than hand-wash and then dry his clothes on hangers hung in doorways, his living quarters looked better than they had.

He hiked down the road to the power station by mid-afternoon and realized then that the power would not go back on. The blackened remains of the small station had been struck with a massive bolt of lightning. It had caused a fire and melted several of the key pieces. No electricity, and no way to charge his tablet, meant that if he wanted to tell anyone about a potential killer asteroid headed towards Earth, he was going to need to go down the mountain.

"Shit." He walked around the circumference of the fenced power station. How had he missed the fire last night? Oh yeah, the downpour that soaked him to the skin in seconds. That was likely also why he never smelled the smoke from the fire until he was less than one hundred yards away.

Since Myra's death, he had been quite content to hide away here, like a hermit on a mountaintop. He had even asked that a drone deliver all of his supplies, citing the poor road conditions as an excuse to not see anyone. And while the twisting, one-lane road was poorly maintained and dangerous, it had been less that and more a wish to see no one. The act of interacting with other humans seemed tedious and took more energy than he felt necessary. Myra had been the more outgoing of them, but even she had avoided most social situations. Together they had been all the other really needed. And now with her gone, and the world outside of this lone mountaintop focused on rebuilding, there was little that would induce him to journey down from the top of it.

A killer asteroid, however, that was something that demanded action. Like it or not, he was going to have to go down, contact Bates, and make sure that the powers that be knew of the terrible danger. By his estimates, they had at least four and a half years before impact. Surely that was enough time to adjust its course, or if necessary, blow it into hundreds of far smaller pieces. It would make a spectacular meteor shower if they pulled that off. And if not, well, the alternative did not bear contemplating.

Ultima Thule, Arrokoth 486958, whatever you wanted to call it, was large, in a "crash into the Earth and it's the end of humanity" kind of way. And considering that the meteor that wiped out the dinosaurs was around that same size, life on Earth in four plus years could look rather grim.

He looked down as Ms. Frizzle limped her way to his side, sniffing the remains of melted plastic and wire, and whined. "We have to go down the mountain, girl. No other way about it."

Stefan should have left then and there. The sun was already hanging low in the sky, and by the time he had dithered about, gathering his tablet, organizing the data, and more, the stars were emerging as he loaded up in the Jeep. Autocars were all fine and dandy on decently paved roads, but the winding and deteriorated blacktop that circled around Mount Hamilton was past its prime. It would've stopped an autocar dead in its tracks with all the cracks and potholes alone.

This was fine with Stefan. He hated the autocars. They had certainly had their share of glitches and malfunctions. Sure, those had been decades ago, but he had often joked with Myra that if astronomy hadn't caught his interest, then he would have been hard at work on a time machine to take him back to the 19th century where he was sure he belonged.

Coaxing the elderly pooch into the Jeep was difficult. When she was a pup, she had loved car rides, but as time took its toll, she had ceased to find joy in hanging her head out of the window as the Jeep made its way down the treacherous path to civilization far below. He considered leaving her there, but there was no telling how long it would be until he returned. It could be just an overnight stay, or it could be days.

He picked her up and hauled her to the car, the dog stiff in his arms. He'd bathed her when she returned from her jaunt into the small forest, but with only cold water available, her fur still felt oily to the touch. He levered her in and then gave her one last shove onto the car seat, her claws catching in the upholstery as she tried to turn around and jump back out. "No, girl. Stay. Stay!" He shut the door in her face and she gave a sharp bark of displeasure, then disappeared from view, scooting down into the passenger footwell, no doubt. His hand was on the door latch when he remembered Myra's urn. He fetched it from the observatory, his feet moving unerringly toward the desk and scope in the middle of the room. The sky was darkening and more stars had come out as he tucked the urn under his arm and strode back to the Jeep. The tablet and corresponding handwritten notes and more were already in there, and he gently placed Myra's remains on top before starting the Jeep and heading for the road.

The first hairpin turns were steep and difficult, and Stefan could hear the engine complain as he slowly drove through them. The way would be clear for at least ten minutes until they hit another set of hairpin turns that were the worst of the journey. As he made his way through the first set, he shook his head at his own foolishness. "I should've left earlier." The words had barely left his mouth when he came out of the last curve and saw the moon hanging full and bright in the sky.

Ms. Frizzle whined from her spot on the floor and he looked over at her. "Don't worry, Frizz, we've got clear sailing for a while. And by the light of the moon, we'll make it down in no time."

Two things happened simultaneously in the next moment. Ms. Frizzle retched and they hit a large pothole. Myra's urn flew up into the air, turning as it did. A flash of silver in the bright moonlight.

He should have let it fall. It wasn't as if it would come open. The screw-on lid was tight, hard to turn. Perhaps it was the fear that it would fall on Ms. Frizzle, already sick in the passenger's footwell side, old and fragile. The urn was heavy, after all. All of those second thoughts ran through his mind as the Jeep bucked and jerked, and he pulled hard on the wheel as he reached to catch the urn in midair. He missed catching it, and the Jeep responded quicker than he expected, the two tires on the right jumping away from the pothole and over the edge of the road at the precise spot where the guardrail had fallen away in the recent rain and mudslide. The next few seconds seemed to stretch out impossibly long as his heart climbed up in his throat. The moonlight lit up the steep edge and the trees far, far below. There was no time to correct. The Jeep bucked, heaved, and then fell, two wheels catching on an outcropping and setting it to spin in the air. Stefan had just enough time to register that the urn he had tried so hard to catch was now headed straight for his head. It struck at the same time as Ms. Frizzle yelped in fear, and the world went black.

It was a kindness, really. The Jeep rotated once in midair and then, hundreds of feet later, crashed to the valley floor, igniting into flames with a dull "whoomp." The rush of air and gas and spark sent flames shooting into the air as the Jeep, its human and canine occupants, and the data the world so desperately needed to see, ignited in fire.

Missed Message

Earth
02.14.2100

In the days following the deaths of his family, if it hadn't been for Greta, Willem would have pulled the trigger and ended his sorry excuse for a life. Anja was gone, and with her, their three beautiful children. And today, of all days, it felt especially painful.

This time last year on Valentine's Day, he had taken Anja for a day away, leaving Greta in charge of the children. Back then, the ESH virus was merely an assortment of odd, disconcerting news stories.

Having no children of her own, Greta adored Jonas, Lisl, and Luca. She spoiled them rotten. Willem and Anja had returned from a date night out only to find that his big sister had baked butterkuchen, his favorite dessert. The children had helped, judging by the flour speckled on their cheeks, arms, and clothes.

Eight weeks later, Greta had stood by his side as four caskets, an adult-sized one for Anja and three smaller ones for the children, lowered into the ground. They had held each other upright and sobbed, Greta's arms around him as protective then as she had been when he was small. Through his tears, Willem had seen at least six other funerals underway, the clumps of mourners dotting the cemetery. He had been lucky. Just two months later, all funerals were canceled and the overwhelming number of bodies had been slated for incineration or burial in mass graves. If they buried them at all. Months later the smoke from the crematoriums darkened the skies. At least he had a place to visit his family. Most didn't have that.

And then, in early fall, Greta had suffered a stroke. No doubt from the stress. Everywhere they had turned, the world was disintegrating around them. Willem dropped everything and sat next to her bed for three weeks as the doctors, already overwhelmed by the ESH virus, ran their tests.

He was there for her in the end. She never came out of her coma, never stirred to wakefulness, and the doctors had given Willem absolutely no hope that she would recover. The stroke had been massive, ravaging her mind as the ESH virus had ravaged countless others' bodies. She was merely a shell, a meat sack that held no hope of recovery. He had sat with her, watched as they removed the life-sustaining equipment, and counted the hours until her body slowly figured it out. There was no one left in mission control, no personality, no spark, nothing to distinguish her from the basic organic soup.

The Greta who had read to him when he was small, the one who had fiercely protected him from bullies at school and held her tongue when she saw him spit out his vegetables into his napkin and later held his babies with happy tears running down her face–Greta was gone. Only her body remained. It had taken sixteen hours and eight minutes for her body to figure out what everyone else knew. In the end, her pulse uneven, and with a few rattling breaths, it had been over.

By then the world had changed. New

Munich had risen from the ashes of the old, and Willem had sat by his sister's bed while the world had moved on. Life does that. It keeps going, rudely, even in the face of such unimaginable loss. Life claws and tears and fights its way forward, immune to sorrow, ignorant of anything but survival.

Willem left the hospital and went home, ignoring the white spires that were quickly emerging in what had been acres of plains and forest outside of Munich. The massive machines could practically run themselves. There were few humans present, and Willem remembered an antique hardcover he owned and had read cover to cover several times in his youth. *Battlefield Earth* was a sprawling, thick monster of a book. Near the end, despite humanity having been nearly wiped out entirely, only thirty-five thousand surviving worldwide, they had taken back their world from the Psychlos, become an interstellar power to be reckoned with, and other species had built them vast cities on the planet that just sat there, waiting for humanity to catch up and repopulate the Earth.

Willem drove past the site of New Munich and imagined that this new world was not so much different from that of the Earth depicted in *Battlefield Earth*. Would there ever be enough people to populate these cities once more? Would he ever walk down the street and experience the press of people on all sides, scurrying about their business, and fight for space to breathe, to walk? He had hated it, but now, irrationally, he missed it.

Willem had moved his family to the woods and away from the choking press of humanity, but not so far away that they couldn't experience it in smaller bursts. They had spent an untold number of weekends at Viktualienmarkt, sipping coffee while the children ran through the market and begged for pastries. He remembered also stopping by the nearly two-hundred-year-old Glockenspiel at Marienplatz before spending an afternoon at Hellabrunn Zoo. Their children had stood and gaped as the ancient clock with its intricately carved figures moved through its motions.

The image of an empty city built just 32 kilometers from one filled with the dead kept returning to his thoughts as he finished the last leg of the drive, a length of tree-dappled narrow road that ended with their stone and wood house. It was empty now, except for Mufti, a five-year-old mutt and a barnful of half-feral cats that Lisl had named. Their names had died with her, and now, after several months of neglect, they were completely feral. They ran from him, disappearing into the shadows, hissing in fear when he brought them food.

The leaves, mostly green before Greta's stroke, were now awash in red, orange, and yellow. They fluttered from the branches and washed over the road, kicked up in the air in brilliant bursts of color as the autocar drove over them. The air had a sharp chill to it.

As the car had slowed to a stop, Mufti trotted around the side of the house, his pink tongue hanging out, panting. Willem hadn't shaved the dog's fur last year like they normally did, and the poor dog had looked hot and miserable. Even now, in the chill of mid-February he looked warm. He greeted Willem, sniffing his hand and his pant leg thoroughly before whining and turning away. Mufti had been Jonas' dog, his eldest son's constant companion since Willem had brought home the ball of fluff after they had moved from the city to their forest home. It had been a promise kept to his son. Jonas had mourned the loss of his friends in their tightly packed apartment building in the city, and bitterly resented leaving them. The dog had helped. Soon Jonas and Mufti were exploring the woods and the stream that ran close to their house, and he had made friends with other children. Mufti had been Jonas' constant companion, which had eased Willem's mind, and kept his wife Anja from worrying when the boy disappeared for hours at a time in the thick forest.

Willem ran his hand through Mufti's thick fur. The dog whined and pulled away long enough to sniff at the car, as if expecting Jonas to jump out of its recesses, full of energy and ready to play.

"Tut mir Leid, junge. Ich weiß, du vermisst ihn. Ich vermisse ihn auch.[1]"

The dog had butted his head against Willem and accepted another head scratching before walking off, his tail limp, dejected.

The house was a mess. Dishes piled in the sink, bottles of Jägermeister scattered about, and he'd started smoking again, a habit that Anja had hated. Here in the house, it had felt wrong, so he sat outside on the porch, but eventually it had followed him inside. Now, plates with old food, crusted and moldering, shared space with piles of ashes and cigarette butts. The house smelled rank, and he was thankful that the dog hadn't starved while he was away, likely thanks to a ripped-open bag of cat food, the remains of which were fluttering in a light breeze on the sheltered front porch. He had found cat food at the local store. Not dog food, but then again, supplies were low, erratic, and so one settled for what one could find. Most, if not all, the factories had shut down. Only the factories that were run entirely with automation had survived the pandemic and the results had been pretty immediate. Fresh meat was in short supply, but cat food? There were loads of it. He had received a call about Greta moments after arriving with a bag of cat food, dumped it on his front porch, slit it open, and ran for the car. That had been more than three months ago. He had continued to scour the countryside for kibble and simply dump it on the porch for the feral cats and Mufti to scavenge from. By the looks of the most recent bag, Mufti had a couple of days before it ran out.

Poor dog. You're stuck with me, and

what do I do but ignore you?

He walked into the house. He left the door unlocked all the time now. Not that it mattered. Few had survived the virus, even here, and fewer still came out this far. Willem had heard the stories of houses being stripped of their valuables, but that had been in the immediate vicinity of the city and its suburbs. And if they wanted something of his, fine. The only things of true value were gone, buried in four coffins, with only a single headstone to sit and mourn at. There had been no time for more, no labor force, no…anything in the months that had followed. Just him and Mufti and weekly visits from Greta, who made the drive out of the moldering city she was watching rot from the inside out, as she tried desperately to somehow keep him from wasting away as well.

And now Greta was gone too.

His phone chimed in his pocket and he reached for it, reading the message. It was the same message that had been sent twice per week for the past five weeks. Greta's cremation was complete and her ashes were ready for him to pick up. He deleted the message, lay down on the couch, and closed his eyes.

There is no one left in this world who I love, or who loves me in return.

It didn't seem possible, and yet, here he was. Just ten months ago, he had a wife, three beautiful children, a sister. And now? No one. He wasn't the only one. He knew that. He kept repeating it to himself. Across the globe, was there a single survivor who didn't have the same sad tale? And why was he here? Why did he keep breathing, keep eating, and keep going? For what? What was the point of it all?

He slept then. The light left the sky, and Mufti, with nowhere in particular to go without Jonas, settled on the floor near the sofa and slept as well.

Willem ignored the random buzzing of his phone for weeks. The atomic battery that kept the damn thing charged was nothing next to the titanium case that protected it from the dozens of times he tossed it away from him. Mufti, with nothing better to do, seemed to think this was a fine game of catch. He would watch the phone sail through the air and land, then spend seconds, sometimes minutes or even hours, retrieving the thing as it continued to chime with unread messages and calls.

Every morning, Willem woke with the same question in his mind. The question was a simple one, borne from grief and loss and loneliness. He thought of it as he made his breakfast. Or if it was late enough, he'd simply open another bottle of Jäger and take a pull off of that and consider it. Each night, the question remained unanswered, which was an answer in itself. At least for the moment.

The days were followed by weeks and then months. It was February when a knock came on the door. Willem came to answer it, Mufti at his side. The dog wagged his tail, eager for new company, anyone other than a boring old drunk. A small box was held under the arm of a young man. He stood there, thin, unsmiling, and held out a tablet towards Willem.

"Unterschreiben Sie hier, bitte.[2]"

"Was ist das hier?[3]" Willem asked.

"Persönliche Auswirkungen von Greta Grunsfeld,[4]" the man answered, and waited for Willem to finish signing before he retrieved the tablet, handed him the box, and walked away without another word.

Willem watched as the small van

backed out of the driveway, turned around in the thin scattering of snow, and drove out of sight, carrying the only human he had seen in nearly four months.

Mufti gave a disgruntled woof and turned around, heading back toward the warmth of the house. He looked disappointed. Willem stared at the box, then carried it inside to open it.

He sat down on the only clear spot of the couch to open it. It was from the hospital where Greta had spent her last three weeks. He had missed taking the personal effects when he left, and now the hospital was making sure that they returned them.

Inside was a zippered, clear plastic bag with Greta's jewelry. Their mother's wedding ring, which Willem remembered Greta sliding tearfully onto her right hand after the funeral. He had been fourteen, and Greta had been eighteen when their parents had died in a freak accident, caused when a drunk had overridden his autocar settings in order to drive himself. And drive it himself, he had done, straight into Mama and Vater's car on their way home from a dinner out.

Next to Mama's ring was a bead

necklace Lisl had gifted her aunt just a week before Willem's perfect little girl died alongside her mother and brothers. In addition to the zippered plastic bag was Greta's phone. He lifted it out and Mufti's ears twitched forward. The dog looked hopeful. It had become quite the custom to throw his phone, and the dog never seemed to tire of it. But it was the words that crossed the screen that caught Willem's eye and stayed his hand.

Survivor's Network: Sie haben eine genetische Übereinstimmung! Unsere Aufzeichnungen zeigen eine genetische Übereinstimmung von 28% mit Wang, Jia. Klicken Sie hier für weitere details.[5]

A genetic match? Willem stopped and pressed the open key on the screen. It flashed and then requested a password. He guessed and keyed in his birth date. Even now, Greta's passwords were predictable. A second later, he was in the Survivor's Network app and staring at the screen, dumbfounded, reading a message from a Jia Wang.

He pressed the button and read the message in English, and then pressed the translation key to see it again in German, sure he was misreading it. He wasn't.

Somehow, some way, if the sender was truly who she said she was, he had a daughter. Xiao, his first love, a girl with warm brown almond-shaped eyes, soft-as-silk skin, and a fiery love of art, had given birth to a child. *Their* child.

Willem's eyes moved back through the words on the screen again. Jia. The photo of her on the screen caused Willem's heart to wrench in his chest at the memory of the love he and Xiao had shared—both alone on the shore of a foreign country—both in New York, far from home, from family. Xiao, bright-eyed Xiao, both thrilled and nervous, so far from home. She had been ready for something different after a childhood with a repressive father and emotionally distant stepmother. As for Willem, he missed Greta, but it was also the first time they were apart, and it had been a change that was needed, for her to move on with her life now that her little brother, her charge and responsibility, was now an adult. And for him, a chance to spread his wings and fly.

RISD had been that and more for Willem and Xiao, and their love had blossomed those first two years in classes together. When Xiao hadn't returned at the end of the second-year summer break, it had devastated Willem. Worse, Xiao had cut off contact, saying nothing past a non-specific "family obligations are such that I cannot return" message and then said nothing more. After a year of moping, of staring at his tight bank balance and wondering if he could fly to the city of Guiyang on credit, he finally gave up and did his best to move on. He had dated, nothing serious, for the rest of his stay at RISD until he received his master's degree and moved back to Germany. It was in his first year back in Munich working for the Neue Pinakothek that he had met Anja and fallen in love again.

How could he not have known? How could Xiao have kept this from him? That he had a child, a daughter, all these years and knew nothing?

Mufti growled at him, his eyes firmly on the phone, tail wagging impatiently.

"Tut mir Leid, junge. Diesmal nicht.[6]"

Instead of throwing the phone, his fingers danced across the screen as he composed a message in return. He stopped before sending it, looking at the date of the original message. It had come in on the day of Greta's stroke. Had she known about Xiao? Or had she suspected it where Willem had not? Had she read this message before her stroke?

He imagined his sister lying in that hospital bed, caught in the rift between life and death, hovering there, stuck in her mind, damaged irretrievably by the stroke, unable to tell him what she already might have known. That he had someone left in this great, empty world. That he wasn't alone, after all.

And worse, that Jia had not received a reply. Not for four long months. What must she think? His thoughts flitted to Xiao, and for a moment he had hoped, however fleeting, that perhaps she too had survived.

No. She couldn't have.

His mind flashed back to a blood drive at the college. She had been A negative blood type. He could see the shiny card in her hand. Xiao, his first love, had to be dead. But Jia, this child he had never known existed, she was alive. Somehow, she had survived the firebombing of the major cities and a civil war that China was still struggling to recover from. Somehow, she had made it all the way to the middle of old America, to one of the new cities. He read the words aloud, scarcely able to form them, to calm his mind long enough to say the English words out loud. And here, in this empty house, with only ghosts of the love he had experienced whispering in his ears, the words felt like hope as they bounced off of the empty walls.

"I am not sure how I am related to you or Mister Grunsfeld, but I would like very much to speak with you. You are the secret of my survival. Jia."

Willem clicked on the Reply button and hoped with all of his soul he wasn't too late.

The question that had faced him every day since he returned, alone, without Greta, had remained unanswered, hanging before him. The question had been simple… *Is there any reason I should still live when my family is gone?* And he finally had his answer. Jia. She was alone, too. And it was time that he met her.

1. Sorry, boy. I know you miss him. I miss him too.

2. Sign here, please.

3. What's this?

4. Personal effects of Greta Grunsfeld.

5. Survivor's Network: You have a genetic match! Our records show a

28% genetic match with Wang, Jia. Click here for more details.

6. Sorry, boy. Not this time.

A Place Known as Home

Earth
04.19.2100

Jia stood in the terminal outside of New Munich, heart pounding, mouth dry. Her eyes cast about, examining the faces of strangers. A few digital photos were not sufficient. Everyone looked the same to her, and she found herself afraid she would not recognize him and somehow miss connecting with the man who she shared half of her genetic heritage with. Despite the months in the refugee camps in Guizhou Province, and the last few weeks in New Athens in America, she felt more nervous than she ever had before in her life. It was one thing to chat via the web, another to meet in person, even if

Willem Grunsfeld was her biological father.

"Jia." A familiar face swam into focus. He was out of breath, panting even, and he beamed at her. She noticed a tiny gap between his upper front teeth that was just like hers. "I went to the wrong gate. So sorry to keep you waiting."

She stared at him and then smiled back; her fears forgotten for the moment. Here he was, her father, flesh and blood, standing before her.

He looked nervous. "May I, is it okay for me to, you know…" His voice petered out and he opened his arms, a look of hope on his thin, bearded face.

She had sat on the hypersonic for the past two hours trying to imagine how this meeting would go. She had told herself rather sternly that she would keep her distance, that this man was her father by biology only, and that they barely knew each other. Reality, however, was a different matter. Here, standing before him, she couldn't help but feel her heart leap in response. When was the last time she had been hugged? Mama had always been so stern with her, so traditional. And Mama's husband, who she had thought of as Father, he had never been affectionate, never wanted to spend time with her, ask about her day, or listen to her speak. Mama had shushed her at mealtimes, sent out to play, and kept Jia away, rather than annoy the man who she had thought was her father.

In retrospect, after months of consideration, Jia was certain that Bao Wang had known he wasn't her father, just as Mama had known. A thousand times since, she had wished she could ask Mama why she had never spoken of it. Why had she never told Jia the truth? And she wished she could ask Father as well. Perhaps Willem, who stood before her waiting for her response, could shed light on her beginnings, to explain why her mother had married Bao, and why Willem had never stepped forward until now.

She stepped forward and felt his arms fold around her. She nestled her head on his right shoulder and gingerly encircled his body with her own. He smelled foreign and so…*different*. She fought off the questions that crowded her brain, demanding answers. There would be time for it. They had the rest of their lives to speak of such things.

When they separated, his pale blue

eyes glittered with unshed tears. He smiled again. "You are beautiful. I see so much of your mother in you."

Mama? Little round, angry Mama? Jia's smile was uncertain until she remembered a picture of Mama holding her as an infant. In it, Mama was young, barely older than Jia. Beside her, Bao had stood, his back ramrod straight. Mama had looked exhausted, her face splotched, shadows under her eyes. And of course, Jia herself had been in the photo as well, her skin scrunched and red, a dark thatch of fine, downy black hair on her head, the rest of her, out of sight, swaddled in a blanket. She had looked as all babies look, squished, and rather unfinished, as if they emerged half-baked from the wombs. Mama had a small smile on her face, Father none, and Jia's infant self was fast asleep, exhausted no doubt by the bright new world she found herself in.

How many times had she thought of that photograph in the last six months and wondered what her parents had been thinking? Had Bao Wang known she wasn't his? He had to have. And yet he had still married Mama.

Is that why he was always so cold to

me?

"Come, come, we have a long drive ahead of us." Willem's words shook her from her reverie. "Do you have any other bags?" His words were in English, with a little accent.

"Yes, I have one bag checked." She nodded, and he pointed.

"We will go this way then." As they walked down the long terminal, he turned to her again, his blue eyes warm. "Have you eaten? Are you hungry?"

Jia shook her head, realized it wasn't an answer, and replied, "I am not hungry, thank you." In reality, she hadn't eaten since last night.

This morning, long before the sun's rays had kissed the horizon, she had stared at the contents in her small refrigerator and felt her stomach clench. Nothing had felt right. Not the tea she tried to force down her throat, nor the packet of crackers they had offered her on the flight. The nervousness she felt had transformed her stomach into an inhospitable place, and even now, in the early afternoon, she preferred the lightheaded feeling. Somehow, it made her feel in control, something that was still new, almost addictive.

"Okay, well, after we get your bag and my autocar, we could stop in New Munich for an early dinner before heading to my home. It is remote. I do not live in the city." He smiled. "A peculiarity, I know. But I prefer to be alone these days, ever since..." His voice petered out. "Well, you know."

She knew he had married, that he had a family and that they died from the ESH virus. He had said as much. He had not, however, said anything more about them, and she had not wanted to ask. The wounds they all carried were tenuous things–scabs on their hearts. Scratch them, and they would bleed.

Jia nodded. "Yes, you sent pictures. Your home looks beautiful." She searched for something more to say. "Peaceful."

Willem nodded. "Yes. I think you will like it. Many of my favorite pieces are there."

He frowned then. "I forgot to ask, but are you comfortable with dogs? I have one, and..." His voice petered out and he bit his lip.

Jia smiled. "I love dogs. My mother never let me have one, but a friend of mine had the sweetest Pug when we were in primary school. He would follow her to school and wait by the gates for her every day."

Willem blew out a breath. "I think that you will like Mufti. He is very loyal."

They continued down the terminal in silence. In one of the first emails they had exchanged, he had mentioned he was an artist, and a sculptor. It was something that had occupied her dreams in the days leading up to the visit. She had researched his work extensively and found that he was very talented and had studied at RISD, the Rhode Island School of Design. What had been even more shocking had been when she learned Mama had been a student there as well.

Willem Grunsfeld's career had been a long and storied one. He was talented in multiple disciplines—from sculpture to painting—and in the past decade had created multi-sensory pieces that were smelled, heard, viewed, and in one case, *tasted*. The art nerd in her was clamoring to see his work in person, to put her hands on it and breathe in the artist's essence. The other part of her longed to find a connection between this stranger and her own surprising survival. The ESH virus had killed everyone she knew. Willem, despite being unaware of her existence, had saved her life through the gift of his DNA, his blood. That he was also her biological father was a gift she was still unwrapping.

The air was cool, but the sun shone brightly overhead. The skies were clean now, cleaner than anyone could have thought possible a year ago. The factories, nearly all of them, remained silent. The traffic, if there was any, was silent. The autocars ran on renewable solar and charging stations were everywhere. The Earth had responded to the absence of humans in remarkable ways, and birds and wildlife had exploded everywhere. Here in the hills of Germany, Jia stared out at the unfamiliar trees and rocks, absorbed in the brilliant colors of spring.

"You like it, yes?" Willem's voice startled her out of her reverie.

"It's beautiful here, yes," Jia answered.

"You speak English well. Do you have your mother's knack for languages?"

Jia stared at him in confusion. "Mama spoke other languages?"

Willem's lips curved up in amusement. "Oh yes. Mandarin and Cantonese, of course. Also, English, German, and she was soaking up French so that she could read *Candide* and *Les Miserables* in their original format." He laughed at the memory. "Xiao was quite the purist."

Jia shook her head. "I did not know. I never even saw her reading anything at all, much less the classics." A sudden fear stole through her. Could he be remembering someone else? Perhaps he just liked Chinese girls and had forgotten Mama, maybe substituted her with someone else. Maybe he had been one of those boys who played the field. Maybe that is why Mama had returned and married Bao and never told Jia. It couldn't be Mama he was talking about.

Jia glanced at Willem. His face had fallen. He stared off in the distance, not really seeing the landscape that surrounded them. The autocar hit a small pothole, and the car lurched. "No? The Xiao I knew read voraciously. Between her love of books and languages, she was a talented artist. Surely that was something you saw. Her sculptures were exquisite." He smiled, his teeth a bright white. "It was your mother who got *me* into sculpture, after all. After you contacted me, I looked for her work, but I found nothing. No records of her art anywhere."

Jia's heart fell. Surely there had been a mistake. He couldn't be talking about Mama.

"Did you know other Chinese girls there at RISD?" she asked, unsure how to phrase the question best.

Willem stared at her for a moment, his face perplexed, before a look of understanding replaced it. "You think I am remembering someone else, yes?"

Jia couldn't meet his eyes. She shrugged. "It is, how do you say, hard to sight. Mm, no, not sight, *see,* yes? My mother was, well, she was not happy, and not, mm, not an artist."

The sadness was back in his eyes. "Jia. She was at one of the most prestigious art schools in the world. Of *course* she was an artist." His smile had vanished and his fingers strayed to a chain around his neck. "It has been nearly twenty years, but I have never taken it off." He pulled it from his shirt and removed it and handed it to Jia. "She made it for me. It is a miniature, done in metal, of a sculpture that stands outside of the ruins of Austin, Texas commemorating the rebuilding of the nation after the Collapse in the early part of last century. She had the winning design out of over twenty thousand entries."

Jia took the piece in her hands and examined it carefully. She knew it instantly, recognized it from her studies of the Reformed United States monuments in her newly adopted country. She still couldn't believe it. How could this possibly be Mama? Willem was describing a stranger, someone that Jia had never known. She turned the piece around; her fingers felt a small etching, and she peered closer at the inscription on the back.

"Oh." She could barely speak. Mama had always written her name distinctively, a flair on one line that was not standard. And here, in this autocar, thousands of miles from home, she found her chest tighten. The Chinese characters were tiny, and she wondered how in the world Mama had got them just so, but it was, without doubt, in her mother's hand.

"I never knew," she whispered. "How could I not know?"

Willem's hands were warm on hers as he gently retrieved the necklace, replacing it on his neck. "She never spoke of home," he said, "never. And after two years together in school, she just," he sighed heavily, "she never returned from summer break. No matter how many messages I sent. I imagine she was pregnant with you and that…" He shrugged, a hitch of the shoulder that betrayed far more pain than he was comfortable expressing. "…she didn't want me to know."

A maelstrom of confusion and pain whirled within her. Willem didn't strike her as a careless, uncommitted baby daddy. He had obviously cared for Mama. Why in the world would she not have told him? What could have possibly been a good enough reason to not return to RISD, to her lover and the father of her child?

The answers she sought; she would never have. They vanished in the fireball that had consumed the city of her birth. There were no answers, and likely there never would be.

The slowing of the autocar interrupted her thoughts. She had been so wrapped up in their conversation, in this sudden mystery of an artistic mother she had never really known, that she had not noticed the forest fall away and the clean lines of New Munich appear.

Tall white buildings shining in the bright spring sun, their clean lines curving tall, reaching for the sky. They were like those in New Athens, and Jia had heard that the same architect created the designs for all the new cities. There were differences, though. And obviously, they had gone to great lengths to create a diversity in design that gave each city a unique look.

The autocar wound its way to a nearby parking lot and stopped. "We walk from here," Willem said. "But you can leave your bags. I reserved the autocar only for us. It's just a few blocks to the north, but they reserve everything beyond this point for pedestrian use only."

They stepped out of the autocar, and Jia breathed in the clean air. A year since leaving the city of her birth, and she still marveled at the cleanliness of the air in cities. Guiyang had been hazy, thick with smog and pollutants, despite the myriad of clean air acts that China had passed in past thirty years. She had spent the first seventeen years of her life with itchy eyes and near-constant allergies, even in the winter. It had been a shock to realize that it was the air quality that made her nose run, eyes burn, and throat perpetually sore.

Even the refugee camps had been better, although the sorrow that filled the air had its own taste. The camps had housed thousands of mourning survivors, with little or nothing to their names, their families torn apart. It had tinged everything with a bitter taste, one that hadn't left her mouth until she set foot in North America.

The streets here were pristine. Not a trash wrapper or errant weed existed. Everything was new; nothing looked worn or out of place. In that way, New Munich and New Athens were the same. As a small group of children ran past the two of them, shouting in German, it reminded Jia that not everything was alike. New Athens had very few children, but it was predominantly English-speaking. Jia had learned English quickly, and by the time she had landed in New Athens, the voices were no longer gibberish, but filled with recognizable words and phrases. She would get the gist of what was being said in small snatches which sprouted in the days that followed.

As they walked, Jia sniffed the different cooking smells emanating from nearby. She missed home the most at mealtimes. She had yet to eat anything that reminded of her of home since her long journey to the RUSA. Until now.

As they rounded the corner, Jia sniffed again, her eyes widening and a smile creeping onto her face. She looked over and realized Willem was watching her with a pleased smile pulling at the corners of his mouth.

"I thought you might like a taste of home," he said, nodding towards their destination. The smell of the Sichuan pork was mouth-watering and somehow smelled even better than she remembered.

Jia grinned at Willem. "Thank you, that is very kind. I much like that."

An hour later, she sat back, groaning. She had eaten enough food that it made up for any of the skipped meals, and then some. Willem chuckled. "You remind me so much of your mother, Jia. She was as thin as you and had a terrifyingly enormous appetite. I could barely afford a meal out with her. Starving student and all that. Thank goodness for all-you-can-eat buffets."

Jia shook her head ruefully. "The mother I remember was not skinny, not at all. I had better watch out. Or I'll end up as round as her someday!"

Willem laughed out loud. It was the first time she had heard him laugh, and a current of happiness surged through her. This man wasn't a stranger. Even after a few hours together, she could see the kindness inside of him. It made her happy to hear him laugh. Especially because he had the look of someone who had stopped laughing long ago, maybe even forgotten how.

The laugh ended, but the smile stayed. "Would you like to look around the city, Jia? Or shall we save that for another day and head home?"

Home had a nice ring to it. He hadn't said, "Shall we go back to my house?" He had called it "home" as if it were hers as well. No place had been home. Not since Guiyang. Not since Mama died.

"Maybe another time you could show me the city? For now, home sounds nice."

He nodded. then snapped his fingers at the server and asked for the check. Jia hid a smile, wiping her mouth clean. She liked the sound of the word as it rolled off her tongue.

Home.

While it Burns

Earth
04.20.2100

"Fall back!" the captain screamed as the flames roared. May's skin was tight, hot, and she stumbled back with the rest of the firefighters. The gear hung on her body, growing heavier every day. The horizon glowed, a steady, creeping line that occasionally flared, flames shooting into the air as the fire line advanced and took yet another structure, and another and another.

"The entire damned state is going to burn to the ground," Joe, a tall hunk of a man standing next to her spat in disgust. His face was dark, creased, and she had stuck by his side, just as the captain had instructed her to. They had pulled out of Pasadena, flown northeast to Glendale, and from there they had fled to Bakersfield.

It didn't matter where they went, or what they did, they wasted their efforts on the massive conflagration. It was a firestorm from hell and it had barreled through Los Angeles, mindlessly consuming the remains of the city and most of its sprawling suburbs. It felt as if the hand of fate were upon them all. It seemed intent on obliterating what was left of humanity's presence in one of the more populous cities in America. As if the stink of death weren't enough, the El Niño winds now reclaimed the land and burned it clean.

May had walked out of the remains of Mirepoix and volunteered on the front lines of the fires less than two weeks later. She wanted to do something, anything, other than look at the faces of strangers in New Athens and remember how it had felt to watch everyone she knew die.

The twins who had slept two bunks over. Maggie, who reminded her of her art teacher in high school, warm and caring. She had handled all the newer city members, arranged for their housing and more. Peter. Matthew.

May still had nightmares about Matthew. When he had pulled out that gun, she was sure he meant to use it on her. She couldn't stop thinking of him. Immune. Sleep-deprived and mourning the loss of that skinny, rude girlfriend of his. Could she have helped him? Stopped him, perhaps? It bothered her. The image of him standing there, gun in hand, alone. As she struggled to help fight the fires that were consuming nearly 75% of the state, May found herself lost in reimagining the scenario, as if it were possible to rewrite history. In it, she imagined herself reaching out, not running in terror, her hand closing over his and pulling the weapon from his hand. "Fuir" meant run. He had wanted her to leave, but she should have stayed.

"Denning!" Joe's hand grabbed her arm. "Get a move on. Cap said to fall back!" She nodded and matched his steps, trotting a little to keep up. Joe was nearly seven feet tall and when he stretched his long legs into a ground-eating stride, May found herself at a jog, straining to keep up.

Joe reached out a hand to help her up into the nearest Huey. Behind them the fires roared and growled, the air blowing hot and dry. May could barely hear the heavy whine as the helicopter's blades rotated.

"Belt up! It's going to be rough!" the co-pilot hollered. May fumbled with the restraints. They clicked into place as the helicopter rose from the ground and the doors shut, cutting out most of the smoke.

She could see a line of helicopters rising into the gathering darkness and they rose into it, the smoke from the fires engulfing them for a few terrifying seconds before the Huey rose high enough to escape and punch through the blackness into a startling brightness. She hadn't seen the sun in days. It was obscured by the thick haze.

"Where to now?" she asked, but Joe just shrugged. He didn't know or particularly care and, really, neither did she. It was something to do, this firefighting. It was better than sitting around and thinking about the billions of people dead from ESH and the rotting cities.

Here, the dead burned just as easily as the houses they had once lived in. She settled back in her seat and closed her eyes. They burned as if they, too, were on fire. The eyeballs themselves felt desiccated, much like the rest of her exposed flesh. The heat from the flames, the punishing winds, it was exhausting.

It was the rough landing that woke her hours later, and Joe squinted at her in the gloom. May blinked, disoriented. It had been full daylight, and now it wasn't.

"You were out for hours," he said. "Talked a lot in your sleep. Was Matthew someone close?"

He asked it like he knew the answer. She could see it in his face. Hell, it wasn't hard to figure out. When she joined up, Captain James had told the group she came from Mirepoix. She had seen a few pitying glances, but in the end, everyone there had a sad story to tell.

"No." She glanced outside at the artificial lights that lit up the airport. It was an unfamiliar one, not the base of operations they had been operating out of for the past three weeks. It was also free of the acrid smoke she had become so used to smelling.

"We're in Vegas. Well, the outskirts. Smells better here than it does in the city," Joe said, catching her look of confusion. "They're shutting down the firefighting divisions." He picked at a blackened nail, scraping the soot away. "They got the last citizens willing to leave out of the path of the fires and now we wait for the rains to come. Nothing else will make a difference."

May shrugged, disengaging her harness. "So now what?"

"Now you go back to New Athens, kiddo. Find yourself a cute guy, have babies, rebuild the population."

May realized the helicopter's blades were still spinning. And Joe was still in his harness. "Wait. What the hell is going on here, Joe?"

The older man met her eyes. A look of pity stole across his face. "New orders from President Chen. They signed the National Recovery Act into law last week."

May looked at him and shrugged her shoulders. He might as well have been speaking Greek.

"I'm guessing you don't pay attention to the news much, do you?" Joe commented. He reached up and scratched a soot-blackened ear and the fingernail he had just cleaned was filthy and black again. "The National Recovery Act is pretty fucking broad. It addresses conservation of resources, orders the construction of the new cities, and makes it mandatory for survivors to become residents of them. There's orders for the conservation of art across the world, especially in places like the Met, in New York, where they have flooding and hurricanes further damaging the building. And if that wasn't all enough, it also requires all women of a certain reproductive age to get work of a safer nature."

May blinked at him. "What the hell does that mean?"

"That means they don't want a healthy, possibly fertile young woman like you risking her life fighting fires." He gave her a crooked smile, "You are a resource now, Sweetheart. Time to conserve you for more important things that men can't do."

May stared at Joe, her mind cycling. She looked out the windows again and saw only one other, a woman from one of the other teams. They had met, briefly. Laura, that was her name. She stood there, her uniform off, just her jeans and a shirt. She looked cold and pissed off. Which was definitely akin to the emotions rising in May, her chest and stomach hurting.

"Just because I have a baby factory in me, I get bounced? What the hell, Joe?" She thought of staying put, refusing to go, but from the look on Joe's face, and the co-pilot behind him, that would not fly.

Joe lifted his hands, palm up, as if in supplication. "You hold the keys to the future of humanity, girl. It's out of my hands, out of Cap's hands. Hell, get yourself knocked up, and it's Easy Street for you, the way they are talking."

May's jaw worked silently. They were tossing her off and sending her back to one of the new cities to *have babies*, like she was some brood mare. And Joe was selling it like it was okay.

"Fuck you, Joe." She stood up, yanked off her hat, her coat, and shimmied out of the heavy uniform pants. She ignored his outstretched hand, jumped down to the ground, and walked away from the helicopter without a backward glance. To hell with all of them.

The other female firefighter wasn't alone now. Two soldiers stood as escorts. The taller of the two soldiers nodded at May as she approached. "May Denning?" She nodded, and the soldier pointed towards the low-slung building in the distance. "If you and Miss Ames will accompany us, there's a flight waiting for you two."

A few moments later, May had her choice of seats. The large passenger jet could seat two hundred passengers easily.

Instead, perhaps one-quarter of that number sat scattered throughout the plane. Some were in their thirties, others younger, and there were more than a few teenagers. A handful of female soldiers clustered together, their faces a mixture of anger and resentment. The only males on board were the two soldiers that had escorted May and Laura onto the plane, and the two pilots who disappeared into the front of the plane once May sat down in her seat.

As the plane pulled away from the airport and headed for the runway, the screens overhead splashed the seal of the Terran United Planetary Government along with the words "Please Stand By."

As the plane oriented itself on the runway and sped up, the fasten seatbelts sign came on with a soft chime, and the video played.

Madeline Chen, the widow of RUSA President Gary Chen, appeared at a podium. May had seen her plenty when her husband was campaigning for the election in May's senior year of high school. They had made a stop in Philadelphia and her school sent the top fifty academically gifted seniors to one of the campaign speeches. Madeline looked the same as May remembered. She was tall and thin, her red hair straight, long, nearly to her butt. She smiled and looked directly into the camera now. It felt as if Madeline was looking straight at her when she spoke.

"Over a year ago, the ESH virus devastated our world. It killed the young, the old, the healthy, and the sick. It did it with little discrimination and it did so mercilessly. Nearly nine billion men, women, and children have died. Every single one of you has known loss, heartache, horror, and death firsthand."

May's mind flashed to Peter, to Matthew, and the rest of the denizens of Mirepoix. She couldn't help but remember the long road there, of seeing empty towns that reeked with the sickly-sweet smell of decay.

"We have survived so much, but now we stand on the precipice and face yet another challenge. The ESH virus didn't just rob us of our families, our friends, neighbors, and co-workers. It has also threatened our future as a species." Madeline continued, her voice steady, her face grave. "What we have left of the world's leading minds is hard at work on the problem, but they have explained to me and the other members of the Terran United Planetary Government just how crucial the next few years will be for our future. The ESH virus affects us, all of us, at a basic reproductive level. Since the virus, miscarriages have skyrocketed and the teratogenic effects of the virus on our unborn babies, and even newborns, have made themselves known. We are on the brink of extinction as a species, and we must fight this invisible war with every ounce of energy and dedication possible."

Madeline stopped, looked down at her notes, and then stepped away from the podium, her willowy frame displaying a slight bump along her abdomen. Her hands splayed across it, gently cupping the edges of her swelling abdomen.

"I take my duties as President of the TUPG, and that of a woman of reproductive age, very seriously. Our world, our future, depends upon it. And I'm prepared not only to do what it takes to ensure the long-term survival of humanity, but also model the behavior I would hope to expect from you. In war, we have to sacrifice for the greater good, and make no mistake, we *are* at war. We are at war for our very basic survival as a species. Each of us must make a choice of whether we will step forward and embrace the future of our race. I am stepping forward to do my part and I am asking you to do so as well."

Madeline's eyes glittered with unshed tears, her hands now both firmly over her tiny baby bump.

"The road ahead is difficult. But I implore you to make the right choice, to make the *only* choice right for the future of humanity. Together, we will find a way for humanity to thrive and rise again. Together, we will create a future worth living for."

The screen returned to the TUPG seal and then went blank. May stared at the black screen. The plane was in the air, its nose still pointed up as they rose into the air. A girl a few seats away crumpled the handout a male flight attendant had just handed her and twitched nervously.

"Did you hear they banned abortions? *Banned them.*" Spit flew from the girl's mouth as she enunciated the last two words. "Worse, no more birth control at all. Nothing. Like it's the goddamn Middle Ages or something." Her nails were ragged, bitten to the quick. "They want us to all get knocked up and have babies, whether or not we want them."

A mousy-looking woman in her early thirties on the left of May shrugged. "It's better than cleaning hotel rooms and serving drinks to assholes that want to grab your ass all the time. I hear that the *Dollars for Babies* show is the real deal. You have a baby and they set you up with a nice, new house. And if you don't want to raise the baby, well, there are plenty of women who won't be able to carry to term, so they're cool with you just dropping a kid and moving on." She reached for a glass of soda the flight attendant held out to her. "You don't even have to have sex with a guy. They've got plenty of sperm banks."

"And that makes it okay?" spat the twitchy girl. "That's fucked-up."

"No," the mousy woman said, glancing at the needle tracks on the twitchy girl's arms, "you are. And if you can't stay clean, they'll toss you out on your ass."

May shook her head as the flight attendant, an older man, possibly in his late forties, smiled and offered her a bottle of water, which she accepted. "That's nuts. They can't do that. They can't *make* us have babies."

"They…*can't* expect us to just be okay

with this."

The mousy woman shook her head. "Where have you *been* in the last few months? They've been talking about this for *weeks*. Thanks to the lack of scientists and researchers, all dead of ESH, they think it might be decades before we figure out how to combat the infertility caused by the ESH virus. Human women are only fertile for approximately twenty years; after that the birth defects and miscarriages quadruple, and that's on top of the high numbers already in motion because of ESH. It's our *duty* to have children."

"Hooey, that bitch sure has been drinking the Kool-Aid," Twitchy Girl muttered, nibbling at one of her fingernails. "The fuck I'm going along with this."

May sat in silence, the water bottle unopened in her hands. Its surface was cool, beaded with sweat, and she was thirsty. She didn't open it, though. Her thoughts were consumed with the future in front of her. She could think of nothing else.

A future worth living for? Just how many babies are we talking about?
She stared at the brochure the flight attendant had handed her with the bottle of

water. On the front it read "Official International Recovery Act" and from what she could tell, it was as comprehensive as Joe had warned. She paged through it, words leaping out from the pages. The part that caught her attention was the section entitled "TUPG Children First Act" which felt like anything but that as she read the words behind the words. The world government, with Madeline Chen at the head of it, had just passed the most restrictive set of laws in the history of women's rights. And she, May Denning, raised in foster homes since her single mother died of leukemia when May was nine years old, seemed to be stuck in the middle of it. Her life was no longer her own.

Herr Grunsfeld

Earth
04.22.2100

Jia stretched and yawned. Her body told her it was the middle of the night, but the light outside said differently. The time difference between New Athens and Willem's beautiful wood-beamed home in the woods was seven hours, and she was still adjusting to it. The first day that they arrived, she and Willem had talked well into the night until he was yawning and rubbing his eyes. The next day had been a quiet day, filled with a long walk through the woods. There were no other neighbors, not now. The woods were not as quiet as Jia had imagined they would be. Instead, there was the constant rustling of creatures in the brush and thick undergrowth, birds singing and flying, the hum of insects, and the gurgle of a nearby stream that their path seemed to follow no matter where it curved and dipped.

Mufti had been her constant companion, sticking by her side, never leaving. He had stared off into the underbrush many times, his tail straight out behind him, one foot tucked up near his chest. Each time he did that, she would stop and try to see what he saw. Sometimes she spied a bird, or a squirrel, other times it was nothing but thick brush.

They had eaten a simple meal that evening. Jia noticed the wide variety of Chinese food staples Willem had stocked in the refrigerator. As they ate fluffy, steamed baozi filled with vegetables and barbecue pork, Jia finally asked, "Where you did find this?"

Willem looked up; his mouth full of food. He looked anxious. "Is it not good?"

"It is, how you say, delicious. Very good. Traditional. But how you know? You not read Mandarin, right?"

He shook his head. "No, only a few words that your mother taught me. I went to the only Asian store in 200 kilometers. I told them about you." He smiled self-consciously. "And I asked them to recommend the foods that you might like."

"Thank you, Willem, you are…" Her chest had felt tight and she hesitated, then continued, "You are kind to me."

It was the next day that she finally asked about his children. Their pictures, along with his wife, a plain yet happy-looking woman, were everywhere.

The moment she asked, she wished that she could take it back. Willem had prepared a heavy German breakfast of boiled eggs, dense rye bread with slices of ham and gouda cheese. He paled slightly and glanced at the portrait of him and three young children rolling in the grass. Jia recognized the trees in the distance; the photograph was taken outside on the back lawn.

He set down the large serving plate full of food, rubbed his hands on a towel tucked into the half-apron tied at his waist, and reached for a cigarette and lit it, taking a deep drag before he answered. Jia's nose itched from the acrid smell.

He noticed and put it out. "Sorry, it is an unpleasant habit. I took it up again this past year." He waved his hand in the air, walked over to the back door, and opened it before sitting down across from Jia. He handed her one of the family portraits.

"Jonas was the oldest. He is, was, ten, nearly eleven. Then Lisl, she was five. We had trouble conceiving after Jonas. Then Luca, well, he was our surprise. He had just celebrated his fourth birthday when the virus hit. Anja, my wife, she went first. I think perhaps it was her work at the clinic that did it. She likely brought it home the month before they shut everything down. She died fifteen days into lockdown. The kids followed behind her just a few days later."

He said it evenly, emotionless, as if reciting a recipe or presenting evidence at a trial. His eyes told a different tale, however. Tears filled his brilliant blue eyes. They spilled over, fell down his cheeks, and dripped from his neatly trimmed beard.

"Lisl, she was the musical one. Dance, singing, musicals," he said and then let out a brief laugh. "Beautiful. Such a pretty child. Pretty inside too, you know?" His right hand strayed to his heart. "A kindness that knew no bounds."

"Jonas, he was good with his hands. He uh…" Willem's hands pantomimed whittling. "…made wood figures. Bears, penguins, even a princess for his sister. I buried her with the princess. She carried it with her everywhere." Willem's voice was thick, full of emotion. "He was a good boy, a protective older brother. And Luca, well…" The man's tears fell faster as he said, "He was just so small for his age, but always smiling. Luca was a happy boy."

Jia could feel tears on her cheeks as well. They had been her brothers, her sister. How often had she wished for siblings growing up in the house, with Bao glowering at her and Mama so unhappy, so negative? Just someone, anyone, to have by her side. But there had been no one. How different her siblings' lives had been here in this house. She imagined them rolling, tumbling, laughing, and playing. Bare feet twisting in the grass, following the rough trails, playing in the stream, and living in a house filled with love. She envied them this life, but more than that, she wished she had been able to share some of those moments with her half-brothers and sister.

"I'm sorry, I shouldn't have asked," Jia said, brushing at the tears. She stared down at her plate until Willem reached over, gentle fingers cupping her chin, and raised it up to meet his eyes.

"I'm glad that you did, Jia. They deserve to be remembered. They were special, beautiful children, and I miss them every day," he said simply. "I only wish that you could have met them, known them as I did. I wish I had known that you existed, even if Xiao did not love me as I loved her, even if she chose another. You are still my family, Jia. You had brothers, and a sister, and they would have loved you."

A rough, calloused finger brushed away one of her tears. "But we have now. And that will have to do. Yes?"

"Yes." She had nodded.

He had smiled at her then, just a small one, before turning his attention to heaping her plate with meat and eggs.

"Eat, eat! And I will take you to see New Munich. There is an art museum there that I think you will like."

They spent the day in the state-of-the-art museum. Willem had neglected to tell Jia that he was the director, something that became all too apparent within moments of their arrival. As they entered a massive egg-shaped building, a plump, middle-aged woman approached. "Herr Grunsfeld, Ich wusste nicht, dass du heute reinkommen wurdest![1]"

He held up a hand. "English, if you please, Klara. This is my daughter, Fraulein Jia."

Klara smiled widely. "Oh, of course, my apology, yes? Well come, Fraulein!" Her accent was heavy, her English tentative, drawn out. "We not expecting you today, but is good you are here. We are preparing for the new gallery, Herr Grunsfeld. Would you like to inspect it?"

Willem nodded, and Jia followed. When she had first learned that Willem lived outside of New Munich, which was only 20 miles from the ruins of Munich, she had grieved over the Alte Pinakothek; it was one of the oldest galleries in the world and housed a significant collection of Old Master paintings. She had feared that Munich had been firebombed, as had far too many cities to count. It allayed only slightly her fears when she learned Munich had not burned. The unsatiated hunger and madness that the ESH virus created in humans had caused all manner of death. After reading about a family who had died from consuming a Monopoly game board, or another who had drank embalming fluid, who knew what ESH-addled art-lovers might do?

Willem quickly answered her unspoken question as they moved towards the new gallery.

"*The Burning of Troy*, by Elsheimer, received significant damage during the second wave of the ESH virus," he said. "We have it in the basement restoration room," he said, smiling at Jia. "It is still worth seeing if you are interested."

Jia's eyes widened. "Oh yes, yes, I would love to see it all!"

"We have been assembling the works by floor. As visitors ascend to the top, the pieces become more and more modern. They dedicated this floor to the fifteenth century," Klara added, as they passed by Lippi's *Annunciation* and Durer's *Lamentation of Christ*. Jia's steps slowed. She nodded in automatic response to Klara's words, her eyes fixed on the priceless works of art around her.

The elevator was glass, and it moved silently. Jia would have thought it was standing still were it not for the floors that flashed by at a dizzying speed. They emerged into a wonderland of kinetic sculptures and sharp lines. Jia was less excited about this, but she stayed silent and drank it all in. The Alte Pinakothek had obviously enlarged its holdings significantly. She could feel Willem's eyes on her, and when Jia turned to meet his gaze, he spoke.

"There have been significant salvage efforts going on throughout the world, more than just what was inside of Alte Pinakothek in the old city," he said. "They have recently put me in charge of seeing these works safely added to the collection here, as well as in several other new cities."

Jia was about to ask him more, but they arrived at the new gallery, and Willem's attention moved from her to the work happening around them.

"If you will excuse for a moment, Jia." He stepped away from her before she could respond and strode into the fray. "Nein, nein! Der Warhol geht nicht an diese Wand! Es sollte stattdessen hierher gehen![2]"

The woman, Klara, stepped closer to Jia. "He has been very, how you say, anxious, before you arrive. Very happy to see you, Fraulein." Her eyes were a warm brown. "I knew him from before virus. I was a, participant, no, uh…" She paused, searching for the right word. "Volunteer?

Yes, that is the right word. I love the art and Herr Grunsfeld was very kind to me after my Felix died. I can see you also love the art. Such good that you find Herr Grunsfeld, Fraulein. He is a good man; he needs some happy in his life, yes?"

Jia nodded. "Thank you, Frau Karla, I love art. Very much. I am glad too, that I have found him. I did not know of him for most of my life."

Karla nodded sagely. "Yes, yes, I hear of this. It is, how you say, shocking? He was very, very, erm, startling, yes?"

Jia nodded, her eyes tracking Willem as he pointed to several other pieces and re-arranged the layout of the new gallery, gesturing and nodding, occasional short bursts of German as he stood in the center of the exhibit, turning slowly in the space.

"Frau Karla, is Herr Grunsfeld the Director here at Alte Pinakothek?"

Karla looked at her and shook her head. "Oh no, no. I am the Interim Director, for now. It is a very, hm, demanding job, but no, Herr Grunsfeld only comes here once a month, maybe twice."

Jia frowned. "But he is positioning the art."

Karla laughed then. "Fraulein, he is the

Chief of Staff for the Arts and Antiquities division of the TUPG. He reports personally to Madame President Chen, and he directs the reclamation projects and preservation efforts across the globe. When a man of his knowledge and experience wants to place the art in an exhibit a certain way, you let him. Yes?"

Her father was the *head* of the TUPG Arts and Antiquities Division? Jia reeled with the knowledge. He had said nothing about it. Nothing at all. Her mouth worked, but no words came out. She felt a bit like Alice in Wonderland. She'd fallen down a rabbit hole into a world of wonder. A good one, however. She was pretty sure there were no mad queens waiting to request her head.

She spent the next few hours wandering the massive structure, with Willem checking in on her frequently as he handled various administrative tasks. It was well past noon when Karla tracked her down and insisted Jia eat some lunch. She had been staring at Rubens' *The Fall of the Damned* for nearly an hour, drinking in the details of the painting, when Karla's hand startled her out of her trance.

"Herr Grunsfeld would like for you to

meet him in the atrium on the second floor, Fraulein. Come, I will show you."

The older woman led Jia into a beautiful atrium. They had lined it with living palm trees and a flowing fountain. There, at a table in the middle, sat Willem. He smiled up at her as she and Karla approached. There were already three plates on the table.

"Sit, sit. I ordered for both of you."

Jia sat across from him. Karla took the next chair over. "I found her with the Rubens, Herr Grunsfeld."

His smile grew wider. "Ha! I knew you would enjoy that one." He leaned forward and whispered, "It is one of my favorites."

As they dug in, a young man who wasn't much older than Jia approached Karla. "Direktor, es gibt eine neue Sendung in.[3]"

Karla nodded and flicked her fingers at the man. "Ich werde für einen Moment da sein.[4]" Then she turned to Willem and Jia. "Forgive me, I must go. Herr Grunsfeld, please let me know if you need anything else. Jia, my dear, well come. I am happy to meet you. I see you again soon, yes?"

Jia nodded and returned the older woman's kind smile. "Vielen Dank.[5]"

Karla beamed and as she turned to

Willem. "Sie ist von innen und außen so schön, Willem.[6]" She disappeared through a side door.

"What did she say just then? Did I mangle saying 'thank you' to her?" Jia asked, panic rising.

Her father laughed and reached out to pat her hand. "No, you said it perfectly. She said you were pretty. Inside and outside. Karla is a wonderful woman."

Jia felt relieved. "That's what she said about you."

He looked surprised. "She did?" When Jia nodded, he smiled softly. "So, what do you think of the art, Jia? Which areas have you been in and what are your favorite pieces so far?"

Jia launched into a rambling monologue of her morning, from the Murillos to the Durer and all points in between. Willem seemed content to listen to her talk, only occasionally interjecting a question or comment and Jia realized with shock that her soup had gone cold while her sandwich had disappeared from her plate, tiny bites of it firmly wedged between her focus on the three Van Goghs and a critique of Emanuel de Witte's *Portrait of a Family*.

She realized it was nearly two in the afternoon and her face flushed. "I have been talking and talking and talking!"

Willem laughed, a tiny gap between his two front teeth showing. "I enjoy listening to you. It reminds me of how passionate Xiao was."

Jia felt sorrow wash through her. What had happened to Mama? Why had she chosen to marry Bao instead of returning to Willem? What would her life have been like if Mama had gone back had told Willem that she was pregnant?

As if he could read her thoughts, Willem said, "I think I know why she never told me, why she married your father."

"Bao was never my father; he despised me," Jia answered reflexively, a flush of anger darkening her cheeks. "Sometimes, I think Mama did too. And knowing what I now know about her artistic talents, I can't help wondering if I was the reason. She was so unhappy, so bitter."

"I am sorry for that, Jia," Willem responded, his voice quiet and sad. "I have my memories of Xiao, and they are beautiful ones. I only hold the sadness that came from losing touch with her, of wondering why she never came back and why she said nothing to me about you. If I could take the loneliness from you, change history, I…" He stopped and stared at the crumbs on his empty plate. "But I guess that would mean wishing away my sweet wife and children as well." He leaned back and sighed. "I would still wish a different childhood for you, Jia, one in which I would have been your father. I envy Bao those years."

Tears gathered in Jia's eyes. "You barely know me."

"This is true. I know you only from a few genetic reports, some pictures and emails, and the last two days." He nodded. "But I *know* you, Jia. I can see who you are. You are worthy of love. Of good things."

He reached out and took her hand in his. Again, she could feel the callouses on his fingers, a sign of the artist that transcended the fancy title he held.

"Stay here. Stay here with me, or if you are not comfortable living in my home, I can find you your own studio and apartment here in New Munich. I would like…" He took a deep breath and raised his eyes to meet hers. She could see he was nervous and afraid she would refuse him. "I would like to be a father to you if it is not too late. I would like to have a daughter. To make up to you, if I can, these lost years. Will you stay?"

Jia had lain in the guest bedroom of his house each night, staring at the ceiling in the darkness and imagining what it would have been like to call Willem's house her home, to know him as her father, to have grown up laughing and wrestling on the lawn with two brothers and a sister. Instead, the cramped two-bedroom house with a gruff, angry father and a perpetually bitter, miserable mother. That had been her childhood. She sat there in the bright atrium and thought of how it would feel to be in Willem's house, not as a guest, but as his daughter. This pale, blue-eyed stranger who was kind, thoughtful, and, honestly, a better father than she could have ever hoped for.

Neither of them could unmake the years before, but they had the rest of their lives to make tomorrow different.

"Yes. I would like that very much."

Translation:

1. Mr Grunsfeld, I didn't know you were coming in today.

2. No, no! The Warhol doesn't go to this wall! It should go here instead.

3. Director, there is a new shipment in.

4. I will be there for a moment.

5. Thanks.

6. She is so beautiful inside and out, Willem.

We Need Better Drugs

Earth
04.22.2100

May didn't want to argue, she just wanted the drugs. The man in front of her was talking and talking, and she wasn't hearing a word. Didn't care, really. Her skin itched. It felt as if she had bugs crawling underneath it. Lexie, the twitchy girl on the plane, sat next to her. She shifted in her seat and glanced around the room, squirming.

It had been two days since they had scored anything, and May could see that Lexie was far worse off. No surprise there. From what the girl told May, she'd spent the last three years indulging in heroin daily. Her work at Fantasia on the Vegas strip had paid for her habit, and her long black gloves, Lexie's signature look, had covered the track marks. She'd talked about the topless dancing in a dreamy sort of way when high and avoided the subject when sober.

"I never put out," she had confided to May. "I did this whole dominatrix routine for special clients in the back. They got to look all they wanted but not touch. Perfect for me," she said, her gaze sliding down to center on May's cleavage. "Girls are more my thing, anyway."

Landing in New Athens had been a surreal experience. The newly printed buildings and perfectly placed streets had reminded May of Mirepoix's aborted start, and she had been more than happy to take off with Lexie when the minders had turned their backs at the airport.

It wasn't as if they were prisoners, but it had been clear that they expected the women on board the plane to be good little citizens and listen to the government. Or, as Lexie had said, "Shut up, spread our legs, and let the doctors inseminate us like we're goddamn brood mares." Lexie had hitched her backpack higher on her bony shoulder and flung her straight blond hair over one shoulder. "I grew up in Kentucky on a stud farm. They can paint it a pretty color and call it saving humanity, but I call it bullshit."

And May had followed her to a section of the city that remained unfinished, empty, with half-built buildings and plenty of dark corners. They had scraped the last of Lexie's dope out of a tiny, wrinkled plastic baggie, and May had sailed into the night and marveled at the stars. She hadn't minded Lexie's hands groping her, not at all.

The weeks that followed had been an interesting mix of opportunity and deprivation. Without agreeing to join the ranks of motherhood, they didn't have assigned bunks or official places to stay. However, there were barracks, rows and rows of transitional housing provided for free. A simple fingerprint allowed you access to a clean bed and bathroom any night of the week. There were also public cafeterias that dotted New Athens, providing food free if you didn't mind the propaganda overload. Pictures of Madeline Chen and her baby bump were everywhere, and Lexie scoffed when she glanced up at the enormous poster of her on one wall, along with the message: *What Sacrifice Will YOU Give for the Greater Good?*

"Sacrifice this," Lexie had said, holding up her middle finger at the poster. "I hear she's had a miscarriage already. They don't talk about *that*, oh no. No one does." She slurped up her spaghetti. A spot of sauce landed on her cheek, and she ignored it.

"One girl at the club got knocked up, miscarried, and damn near bled to death. But the powers that be don't want to mention that, or that pregnancy damages your body, that it wears shit out. You want to have a prolapsed bladder? Have kids. Want to lose a tooth or two? Have kids. And don't get me started on what the little shits are really like. That same girl at the club? She had a four-year-old. Snot all over his nose, whining and crying, when I came over with some junk for us to party down with. Hell, if she hadn't slipped some Diphen into his food and knocked him the hell out, I would've had to do something drastic."

May had eaten her spaghetti, fingers tearing into the fresh bread, and reached for the pitcher of water. She could see several others sliding away from them, eyes nervous as Lexie's voice ratcheted up in volume. She'd scored more heroin three nights before, but they were down to the bottom of the baggie, and she was already getting agitated.

"Don't drink that. I hear it's drugged." Lexie said, her voice louder than ever.

A thin woman at the far end of the table with dark circles under her eyes openly stared as Lexie pushed the pitcher away from May and down the table. The liquid sloshed in it.

May couldn't help it. She snickered. "And what, you don't enjoy being drugged?" The contradiction seemed ridiculous. Lexie was fine with injecting heroin, but not okay with drugged water?

Lexie snarled. "They do it to keep us quiet, complacent. So that we do what they want. Eat what they tell us to eat. Live where they tell us to live. Get pregnant and go on *Dollars for Babies* and collect prizes for being nothing more than a sow." She turned towards the staring woman and said, "That's a mama pig, in case you didn't know, you dumb cow."

The woman turned away.

"It's supposed to be all-natural," May

muttered and stared at the water. Some of it had flown out of the pitcher with the force of Lexie's push and landed with a splat on the shiny white table. It spread in a small puddle, wetting a stack of napkins.

"All natural, my ass," Lexie snapped and scrunched up her napkin before she began shredding it methodically into ribbons.

May could feel more people turning and staring. Their eyes made her feel itchy, uncomfortable.

"Let's get out of here." She had stood up, and Lexie had followed. A low murmur of voices followed them out to the street.

It had rained the night before. Apparently, this part of the country was prone to spring storms and tornadoes. May had grown up on the east coast, in cities that stretched from New York to parts of northern Florida in one unending arc. They all had names, and they all touched each other, individual cities in name only, a densely populated mass of humanity breathing down each other's necks. At least they had been. Here, in flyover country, the ESH virus had wreaked havoc as well, but at least the air was clean, free of the stink of the rotting cities. May figured she would gladly trade that for a few tornadoes. Still, she was here because some soldiers shoved her onto a plane and flew her here. It put a real damper on the concept of freedom.

The tall, thin man standing in front of her was blocking her departure from the cafeteria. As she made to move around him, he reached out a hand.

"Wait, Miss…" He might have said more, but Lexie was already surging forward.

"Fuck off, Mister."

And that would have been that if he hadn't spoken up again. "I can get you more of what you've been using, if you like."

Lexie stopped in mid-stride, turned, and flashed the man a look. "Oh yeah? And what is it I need?"

He smiled then. Said nothing. May gaped at him as he turned and walked away from them both, heading towards the eastern edge of town.

Lexie flashed a look at May, shrugged, and followed. Drugs were in short supply in this pretty new town, and Lexie cared far less about her safety than she did about scoring her next hit.

May, who had spent the past few days in Lexie's company and knew no one else, followed. After twenty minutes of walking, they had left New Athens behind and found themselves ushered into a building that looked like a cross between a barn and a church. Lexie had glanced at May, muttered, "They sure as shit better not try to save my soul," and followed the man inside.

And there they sat, along with dozens of others as a younger, rather charismatic and good-looking man in his twenties began talking to them about how it was the end of humanity.

May sat silently as the presentation droned on. She wasn't sure what to believe, but she could feel the last of the drugs leaving her system and, after days of regular use, the need for it was there, pushing at her consciousness, demanding she pay attention.

When they paired everyone off in smaller groups, she found herself on the spot. Now she had to say something. The bright-eyed, nervous woman who was leading their group of four was staring right at her, expecting an answer.

"I, uh." May tried to remember the question. "I guess that uh…"

"Sure, yeah, we're all done for. Agreed.

No future, got it," Lexie interrupted, her chair rocking on the different legs, as she sat, tapping impatiently with her fingers clenching the sides of the bucket seat. "Look, you guys going to hook us up, or what?"

May stared at the wall hangings scattered around the inside of the building.

NO FAMILIES

NO CHILDREN

NO FUTURE

Scattered fragments of the presentation came floating through her mind.

The ESH virus had robbed humanity of our families, stolen our ability to breed, and cemented the future.

That was the basic message, and it was hard to argue with it. The woman, her name tag read "Stella," was reiterating what the young man had said during his presentation.

"They are building these cities, but there's no one left to live in them. They tell us we all have a duty to bear more children, but they aren't telling us the truth, that a visionary who understood humankind's time on Earth had ended *created* the virus. *This* is the natural order."

The older man, the one who had led the

way to this strange place, returned. He handed them a clipboard, first to Lexie and then to May.

"If you'll just sign here." May blinked at the perfectly ordinary gesture and signed her name, Lexie following suit.

He placed a small packet in Lexie's hand and pointed to a hallway on the far side of the room.

Lexie examined the packet in her hand and whistled, a smile melting the tense look from her face. She grabbed May by the shirt and pulled her over, giving her a smacking kiss on the lips, and then pulled May to her feet.

"Let's go!"

Hours later, May found herself on an operating table in a dark, windowless room. Above her, a bright light was practically blinding her. She tried to sit up and realized she couldn't. Her arms and legs barely wiggled in the restraints. She blinked in the harsh light. Where were her clothes? Her clothes were gone, replaced by a hospital gown that was tied in the front and, from the breeze in her nether regions, that was all she was wearing.

The last thing she remembered was following Lexie down the hallway and into a small room. Lexie had pulled out her kit, prepared the heroin, and loaded it into the needles. May remembered Lexie's lips on hers as the rush of the drugs hit her and then nothing else until now.

She pulled against the restraints, and a voice from the shadows made her jump.

"Relax, dear."

A white-haired, rotund woman came into view. She smiled.

"The doctor will be done with your friend in a few minutes and then we will get started."

"Get… started?" Her words felt mushy, awkward. Her brain was fuzzy from the drugs. And it felt different from the other stuff she'd done with Lexie since arriving in New Athens. "Where's Lexie? Where am I?" She tried to wiggle out of the bindings, to get loose. Her anxiety was rising.

I should have never followed Lexie here.

"Yes, dear. With the procedure." The woman patted her shoulder. If she meant to reassure May, she was failing miserably.

"*What* procedure?" May demanded, now squirming and fighting her bindings. "Look, you need to let me go."

As the woman opened her mouth, an enormous boom shook the building.

Shouts and the sound of running feet and more booms followed immediately after. It sounded as if the building were under assault. May fought against the restraints even harder.

"Oh! Oh my!" The older woman ran to the door and opened it, peering out into a well-lit hall. "I'll, uh, I'll be right back." And with that she disappeared out of sight, leaving the door to swing closed behind her.

"On the ground! On… the… ground… *now*."

When the soldier burst through the door, his weapon drawn, May nearly peed herself in fear. Whatever the hell was going on here, she wanted out. The soldier swept the room and then hit the Comm patch on his uniform. "I've got another one in the second barrack. Intact. Over."

His eyes swept over her like she was a farm animal. Did she see contempt? It sure as hell looked like contempt to her. He set his assault rifle down and pulled a blade from its sheath at his waist. May's face must have shown her terror because he took pity on her, raising his hands with the blade still clutched in the right.

"Hey, I'm not going to hurt you. I'm just

going to cut these restraints off of you, okay?"

May forced herself to nod and the second her ankles and wrists were free, she shot off the table and backed away from the soldier. She nearly jumped out of her skin when the door flew open yet again, revealing a man and woman in scrubs, both with the New Athens Hospital crest on their shirt pockets.

"Miss? We are here to help you, if you'll let us," the man said and nodded to the woman. She took the approach from the right around the table while he went left.

May felt trapped. The soldier blocked the only exit, and these two would not let her go. "Miss, we're trying to help you. These No Future cultists are butchers."

"I just want to leave. I don't want to be here. I'm not part of this," May said, desperate to get away from every one of these people.

Why did I follow Lexie here?

It was a dance, one that she couldn't win. When she took her eyes off of one, they advanced closer, and May could see that the woman held a syringe. Whatever was in it, May didn't much care to find out. They moved closer and then, well, then it was too late to get away. The woman jabbed the needle into her arm and with her heart hammering away, the sedative slammed through her. May's knees buckled beneath her.

"Let's put her on the gurney; we can wheel her back to the detention center." May could hear the man's voice from a distance. "We were too late for the other one. They took everything, even her uterus. Left her to damn near bleed to death on the table too. Rick's working on closing her up now and she's stable."

"This one has track marks," the woman said, her voicing echoing down the long track of May's dwindling consciousness. "She'll need to detox."

"A little clean living works wonders, given the right circumstances," the man answered and then May knew no more.

The next time her eyes cracked open, she was in a bed, alone in a room. The room was clean and white. Beside her bed was a small dresser and she could see her clothing neatly folded on top, her shoes lined up on the floor below. Other than that, and a chair, the room was empty. No restraints, no IV or medical machinery. She lay there in the hospital gown, covered with a blanket. This was no hospital bed. It also wasn't a standard bed. She sat up and stared at her surroundings. The bed was a thick pad that sat on a raised shelf of sorts. Almost as if she were in a prison or a psychiatric unit.

Which is exactly where I am—either in jail or a psych unit.

The door buzzed at that moment, and a woman entered. She wore scrubs and gave a perfunctory smile. "I see you have woken up. The sedative was necessary, you understand. We didn't know you and you certainly didn't know us." She pointed to the chair next to the bed. "May I sit?"

May nodded silently, and the woman sat down with a sigh. "Brand-new everything, but they still haven't figured out how to make floors easier to walk on. I've been on my feet all day processing the group they brought you in with." She slipped off one shoe and massaged her foot.

May watched her, her unease slipping away slowly.

"I'm Ollie, by the way. Ollie Duvall. And before you ask, it is because my mother loved the oleander tree and I won the name lottery, thanks to her. No one in my class, my generation, or pretty much anyone in this century shares my name. I never had to worry about being confused with one of a dozen Angelas or Marys." She laughed then.

"I'm May, May Denning." There was something comforting about this woman, and May, who normally had a hard time connecting with strangers, found herself drawn to her.

Ollie met her eyes. "It's nice to meet you, May, circumstances notwithstanding." She groaned, slipped the one foot back in its shoe, and repeated with the second foot, sighing as she did. "Your friend, Lexie, is asking for you. She's just down the hall and still recuperating from what they did to her."

"What exactly did they do to her?" May asked, her heart rate increasing as she remembered waking up on the gurney restrained.

"What they would have done to you, May, given another half an hour." Ollie's lips formed a grim line. "It was a good thing the New Athens police raided the building when they did. She required a transfusion from the blood loss. The doctor fled mid-surgery and left her there, bleeding out."

May remembered the conversation she

had heard right before she lost consciousness. "They took her ovaries and uterus, didn't they?"

"Her fallopian tubes as well." Ollie sighed. "A standard signature of the No Future movement. They remove the entire package except for the penis in the men."

"I didn't know who they were," May said, feeling ill. She wasn't ready for kids, not at all, but that didn't mean she wanted to take it all out. After all, things could change in the future, get better maybe. That she had been on that table and helpless to stop them was terrifying.

Ollie nodded. "I talked to the soldier who found you; he said as much." She sat back and set her hands on her stomach, her eyes meeting May's searchingly. "May, I need to ask you a question. I need to ask you if you knew that you are pregnant."

May blinked, the gears in her brain grinding over the words.

Pregnant. Are, not was, not have been, but are *pregnant.*

"Um... I'm... what?"

Ollie's lips twitched into a half-smile. "Scans show gestation at right around seventeen weeks."

Seventeen weeks. That's just over four

months.

May felt sick. She'd done drugs, heroin, Nocdon, whatever she could get her hands on. Her entire body folded into itself. It was Peter's child, and hers, and what had she done to it? The image of a child twisted and deformed floated behind her eyes.

I've been poisoning an innocent baby. Hurting it before it ever has a chance at life.

Her face must have betrayed her agony. Ollie reached out a hand, reassuring.

"May, your baby is fine. More than fine. He's healthy, and he has AB negative blood as well." She shrugged her shoulders, her smile widening. "Most pregnancies are failing, but yours is thriving, May. You can't know how rare that is right now." She squeezed May's hand.

May's mind was awhirl with fear, guilt, and something else–a small, yet joyful hope.

"You're sure? I haven't hurt him?"

A son. I'm having a boy.

Ollie took both of May's hands in hers. It felt like a memory. This woman was different, nothing like her mother, and yet, somehow, it felt the same.

"I won't lie to you, May. He may face

challenges. Heroin causes premature birth, low birth weight, and there can be complications such as placental abruption during the pregnancy. But as soon as we realized you were pregnant, we did every scan, and he shows no evidence of birth defects; he's even on track for weight and length." She smiled wider. "Any day now, you will feel him moving around in there. A little flutter here and there. Like butterfly wings."

May blinked at Ollie, tears welling up in her eyes.

A child. My child. Peter's child.

"And the virus? It won't hurt him?"

"We tested his blood, and he is safe. He was exposed to the virus in the womb and his blood type keeps him safe." Ollie's answer was reassuring. Just what May needed. "You are due on September 25th."

September 25th. The 23rd was Mom's birthday.

Tears welled up in May's eyes. "Ollie?"

"Yes, May?"

"Will, will you help me? I need to get off of the junk but I'm going to go into withdrawal. I'll get bad soon, maybe tomorrow at the latest, and, and I need help." The tears splashed down onto their entwined fingers.

Ollie's fingers tightened on hers. "May, look at me." May looked up, met Ollie's kind gaze, her features blurred thanks to May's tears falling like rain. "I'll help you. I promise I will."

Extinction

Earth
05.18.2100

"Thank you for meeting with me, Madame President." Mireille Marcelin was beautiful, young. Her dark hair, loosely gathered in the back, had a blue-black sheen to it.

Madeline reached out and clasped the younger woman's hand. "I hear you are the newest member of the TUPG Council. I hope that is going well for you."

"Thank you, Madame President. It is, how do you say, a learning curve, but I am swiftly catching up."

Madeline smiled. "Sit, sit."

Madeline nodded to her assistant, who placed two cups of tea down for Madeline and Mireille. The younger woman lifted the cup to her lips and sipped as Madeline sat down opposite. Mireille smiled. "Ceylon, my favorite. It is a taste of home."

"Home is far away these days," Madeline answered, sipping from her own cup as her assistant set down a plate of beignets. "Your work with the Council has kept you away for a while now."

Mireille, like Madeline, had inherited her place on the Council. Her father had been the head of the European Union until his untimely death from ESH a year earlier. The vacuum of power was a tenuous thing. It had strained countries to the brink of collapse. China was in the middle of a civil war, most of the Middle East was in chaos, and Asia reported pandemonium. The infrastructure was gone, and most had never had to deal with it or understand a world in which politicians and law enforcement no longer provided structure and the rule of law. Many of the new wave of politicians were like Mireille, younger family members, widows, and widowers.

"It has." She said nothing more, and Madeline could tell the young woman was eager to begin. Mireille's fingers twitched against the fine porcelain of the teacup. Madeline suppressed a smile.

"Please, proceed."

Mireille set down her cup, sat up straighter, and pressed a button on her tablet. The viewscreen at the front of the room flashed to life. "As you can see, this is a graph of the effects of the ESH virus on our population. We started 2099 with over eleven billion human beings on Earth. By the time ESH had spread to all corners of the globe, the census reported 14.5 million survivors, approximately eight hundred and fifty thousand of those are the Uninfected Population, although that number is difficult to gauge since the UPs are extremely averse to any outside contact." She tilted her head and shrugged. "Understandable, really, especially when you consider Mirepoix."

Madeline winced. Mirepoix had been a disaster. They had been so sure they had effective protocols in place for the food drops and supplies. Despite all of their efforts, the ESH virus had found a toehold and spread like wildfire through the burgeoning UP city. Only five of them had walked away, all with AB negative blood. Within a year, two more had died of suicide. Every time they thought they had a handle on safety protocols, the ESH virus proved them wrong, and none of the research in finding a vaccine had yielded any positive results. It didn't help that they had lost the most brilliant minds in the world to ESH and that those who remained had no one left to test their vaccines on safely. The images of Mirepoix, the first UP city gleaming and new, and now filled with the dead, remained fresh in her memories.

Madeline shook her head, as if doing so could shake loose the guilt she felt after seeing the bodies. "Please, continue."

"Right. Sorry." Her fingers moved again, and another graph appeared. "This is the breakdown of ESH positive survivors. It follows the standard population pattern that was already in place since ESH does not show any proclivity towards a particular set of age or gender groups."

"Right. ESH infected and killed indiscriminately, and only those with AB negative blood survived," Madeline added.

"Exactly." The girl nodded. "Here you can see that there was a significant decrease in population for the age five and under category. As well as the seventy-five and older age bracket, which was due not to the disease, but extenuating circumstances."

"Such as lack of care and resources."

Many small children had died with their parents, even if they themselves were immune. The breakdown of everything from city services to the electrical grid had spelled doom for countless innocent young children. The aged and infirm also died in droves, from lack of city services, violence, and even suicide.

"We also have the SHTF scenario that caused even more deaths–simply due to lack of care, accidents, breakdown of government and city services."

"Yes, I'm familiar with all of this," Madeline said, wondering whether she had made a mistake in agreeing to this meeting. Perhaps Mireille did not understand how demanding her position was, and how little time she had for reiterations of what she already knew.

The girl nodded. "Yes, ma'am, I know, but here is the part that no one wants to talk about. We are fighting against extinction, Madame President, and we are losing the battle." Her fingers danced on the pad in front of her, and the screen on the wall changed to yet another graph.

"These are the suicide rates broken down by age group. Prior to the ESH virus, suicides held steady at fifteen per one hundred thousand. The red shows where we are now in terms of suicide per one hundred thousand population versus what we were at the beginning of last century, shortly before the Collapse."

Madeline stared at the graph. "This can't possibly be right! It means an increase of…"

"Of over 500 times pre-ESH levels. Yes." Mireille nodded; her face solemn. "Worse, over 60% of these suicides occurred in a population that is still within the reproductive age parameters. We are losing a full one-one tenths of one percent of our population to suicide alone *each month*, and that isn't including the suicidal gesturing, or increased risk-taking we are seeing in a population that has become more and more depressed. Alcoholism and drug use have skyrocketed. Accidental death has tripled, and we *need* these people if we are to survive as a species. We need them *healthy*. The last thing we need is a crop of drug-addicted, fetal alcohol syndrome, disasters on our hands. And that's what we will have if we don't change the way we think of child-bearing and the next generation."

"Break it down for me. How many are of

child-bearing age?"

"In the ESH positive population?" Her fingers moved over her pad in a blur. "Right at 16% of our population. Which figures out to just over two million women, aged sixteen to forty years." She stopped and stared at the screen. "This might seem like a lot, Madame President, but that doesn't consider other factors, such as the 12% of women who are *naturally* infertile, the teratogenic effects of the ESH virus and its high rates of sterility, and finally, as if we didn't have enough working against us, the *willingness* of the fertile population to reproduce."

"And homosexuality, that's a problem as well, isn't it?"

The girl waved her hand dismissively. "No, not at all. The studies have disproved the whole 23% of the population myth. It hovers around 5% and is irrelevant."

"How so?"

Impatience flashed for a moment over the girl's face. She looked at Madeline, opened her mouth, then stopped, perhaps realizing she had almost spoken her mind to the leader of the world. She swallowed hard, then frowned slightly as she struggled to form a more polite answer.

"With in-vitro, and the mandatory donation legislation passed recently collecting eggs and sperm of every TUPG citizen upon the age of sixteen, we have no lack of genetic material. What we have is a shortage of *hosts*. We cannot *force* women to carry babies, and it is becoming even more apparent that many are choosing *not* to have them for a growing list of reasons."

Madeline remembered the horror she had felt as she read *The Handmaid's Tale* not once, but many times, until the cover bent and the pages slipped from the spine. It had been old to begin with, an antique paperback, faded and worn, on her family's bookshelf. Madeline struggled to remember the author's name for a moment. Margaret…something. In *fiction*, you could force women to have babies, but in real life, in a free world, not so easy.

"What is truly concerning is a movement that arose among the ESH positive survivors in China and Japan," the young woman added. "The Meiyou Weilei cult in China and Mirai Ga Nai in Japan are growing at an alarming rate. And not just in the Far East. Recently we have seen a sharp spike in membership of No Future, an end-of-days cult here in the RUSA and variations around the world. And with those spikes come a corresponding drop in pregnancies." She shook her head and bit her lip. "Each day there are reports of the cults growing and the birth rates, such as they are, plummeting. We have another twenty years to turn this around, and if we don't, well…"

"What are you suggesting?" Madeline asked. She could feel a headache taking hold.

"Madame President, we need to take drastic measures."

Madeline threw up her hands. "We have enacted the incentives in the new cities that Drs. Aaronson and Brooks suggested. We have that ridiculous birth lottery, financial incentives, even that insipid *Dollars for Babies* program—how much more drastic do we need to be?"

Mireille's face grew grave. "I know you are against some of the more, how should I say, *stringent* measures, but the future of the world is at stake."

Madeline laughed bitterly. "The world? No, the world will go on, albeit happily without us. I think you mean the future of humanity may be at stake. A century ago, we were facing overpopulation, war, and a scarcity of resources. Not that long ago, we compared ourselves to cockroaches and everyone thought we could withstand anything, even our own foolishness."

A silence stretched out between them.

Finally, Mireille spoke, choosing her words carefully. "If we don't raise the birth rate, humanity, and its current diversity, is doomed. The Council has looked at every option available to us and frankly, the No Future cults, in whatever form they take, are no better than a cancer. They are recommending we remove these cultists from the general population."

"And do what, exactly?" Madeline snapped.

"This." Mireille handed her a holo disk. Madeline pressed her thumb on the green button and watched as an ad for Bliss popped into view.

"Feeling down?" a woman's voice asked. "Do you often feel that your life is not what it should be? We can help! Bliss is safe, non-habit-forming, and composed of all-natural ingredients. Our proprietary herbal supplement will help you see the future of our world in a whole new light, put a spring in your step, and hope back in your life. Rediscover joy and hope with

Bliss!"

Madeline shook her head. "You cannot seriously think that people are swallowing this drivel. Herbal? All-natural? After the ESH virus, everyone is twice the cynic they used to be."

Mireille shrugged. "It won't matter, not to the No Future cultists. We remove them from the general population, put them in centers where they cannot spread their infectious outlook to others, and add Bliss to the water. We end up with a built-in, controllable breeding population."

Madeline stared at the young woman. "They are *people;* they have rights!"

Mireille cocked her head to one side. "No, they are subversives. They aren't content with choosing not to reproduce, oh no. They spread their poisonous outlook to others at the worst possible time. We have a window of ten years, maybe fifteen, and then the number of women capable of reproduction falls precipitously. These dissidents aren't just deciding for themselves; they are affecting the future of the entire human race."

Madeline's mouth worked as she fought the idea that Mireille was presenting. "We still have the Uninfected Persons, there are plenty of them, and more than enough to help jumpstart humanity again."

Mireille shook her head dismissively. "The UPs cannot stay here. We must send them on to Zarmina's World. It is no longer a choice. They *must* go. Eventually our containment measures will fail and they will die. Mirepoix wasn't the first disaster, and it won't be the last. We have two human races now–the UPs and the ESH positive–and we must behave accordingly."

Madeline stared at Mireille. She was barely more than a girl. "How old are you, Mireille?"

The girl stared back at her. "I'll be nineteen next month, Madame President." She paused, her eyes dark, brooding. "I've been trying since last fall."

"Trying for a *child*?" Madeline said, her mind whirling with facts and figures and the shock of it all.

"All miscarriages. Four now. The Eurasia Coalition has introduced legislation that will make it mandatory until we can iron out the kinks with the artificial wombs."

Madeline blinked at her. This girl wasn't talking out of the side of her mouth, she was embracing it wholeheartedly.

Hours later, Madeline stared at herself

in the mirror, inspecting her willowy frame. She had listened to Mireille's revolutionary ideas. Ideas that bordered on fascism, on control to a level she would have found horrifying in any other place and time.

But here and now, what is the world if not horror unending? Do I sit by and let humanity die?

She had issued the orders to retrofit two existing spaceships for at least some of the UP population to leave Earth. They were going to Zarmina's World, whether or not they liked it. Earth was and might always be a place of death and destruction. She had agreed to the Bliss—both the placebo pills and the surreptitious addition of the drug to the water supply. It would provide an interesting social experiment—who would accept the pills and who would refuse?

Mireille had suggested it all. She had pointed out that most of the population would fight the Bliss pills, which was the reason for adding it to the water. They had to achieve higher saturation and stop the suicides. It would give people the illusion of choice. They would believe that they still had control over their own bodies. It might prevent further loss of life and less fear of antisocial behavior.

A population drugged into submission, into acceptance, and a pleasant simulacrum of happiness. Is it more important that they live? Controlled and drugged, but alive?

To do it, to pull it off as Mireille had described it, she needed to lead the way. The girl hadn't danced around it like most would. Perhaps Mireille's young age was a blessing–she had no patience for the complicated dances that most politicians learn before progressing further than city alderman. She had straight-up said it.

Mireille had looked Madeline in the eyes and said, "You must serve as an example, Madame President, that women will follow throughout the world."

Madeline frowned, "I've tried. It didn't take."

"Try again, and keep trying. The people will respond to your struggles, the women will want to emulate you. And just imagine if you are successful, Madame President, you will serve as inspiration to so many!"

Gary had never wanted children. Neither had she, not really. Babies smelled of sick and bodily fluids. Her sister Jacqueline had given birth to two, no, three. She hadn't met the youngest. A boy, if she remembered right.

It was a stark reminder that ESH hadn't just killed people. It had killed the infrastructure that protects people. Two months into the pandemic, her sister, had taken an overdose of pills after losing her husband and three children to the virus.

Two months after that, she had taken the oath of office, vowing to protect the Reformed United States of America and serve as acting president. By then there had been almost no one left in the halls of the White House. Politicians died just as easily as the rest. With ESH, it didn't matter how expensive your health coverage was. Unless you had AB negative blood, you were dead. No exceptions, no mild cases. You simply died.

Madeline tried not to think of the dead that filled the cities and highways. The reek of burned flesh still served as a terrible memory of what that had been like, and how necessary the new cities had become. She had moved quickly, decisively, and when the world needed a central, united government; she had stepped forward. As President of the Terran United Planetary

Government, she had a duty, to protect her people, to guide them, and hopefully to inspire them. If that meant trying again and again, so be it. She would do it.

Women have been doing it for thousands of years. I can do my part and hopefully pull other women back from the brink at the same time.

Her tablet, sitting on the sink nearby, buzzed with an incoming message. She had four more meetings to attend before dinner and two more this evening.

No rest for the weary nor the wicked.

She reached for the tablet.

A Study in Sculpture

Earth
06.08.2100

Jia was so deep in her work that she didn't hear Willem until he was a few feet away, his feet bare in the grass. The summer had jumped in on the heels of spring, but here in the forest, the hot sun filtered through the thick shade of the trees and the only thing to take her from her sculpting were the insects that buzzed by her ears, inquisitive as the woodland creatures that crept through the underbrush a dozen meters away.

Mufti lay curled up nearby, the perfect model for her new piece. Since Jia had arrived, the dog had followed her everywhere, and she in turn had been delighted. The night before, the mutt had even crept up and laid down across her feet. She hadn't had the heart to make him get down, no matter how hot her feet got.

"It is coming along nicely," he commented and handed her a damp rag.

"Thank you." She wiped a majority of the clay from her hands and took the cup he was holding in his other hand. The scent of jasmine crept up her nose. "The new tea came in!" She flashed her father a smile. "My favorite!"

He nodded. "Just like your mother."

He sat at the small bistro table a few feet away, and Jia joined him. "Thank you. This is wonderful. I woke up with an idea this morning and couldn't wait to get started."

"I can see that." Willem's eyes slid over her pants and Jia looked down, realizing they were inside out.

Her face flushed, and they both laughed.

"You know how it is!" she retorted, still laughing.

"Indeed, I do." He broke eye contact, staring at his cup. The last two months together had taught Jia plenty about Willem, including his mannerisms. There was something on his mind, and he wasn't sure how to say it.

"What is it?"

"Hm?" He lifted his eyes to meet her gaze.

"What's going on? You have that look like you need to tell me something, but you aren't sure how to say it."

He raised his eyebrows in surprise. "You know me far too well." He set the cup down and drummed his fingers. "I have to fly to New York."

Jia blinked. "New York is flooded and filled with rotting corpses."

"That it is, but it also has the Met."

"I thought it had burned!" Jia exclaimed, leaning forward. "And suffered at least a partial collapse. Were the reports wrong?"

"Apparently so. They recently charged the team that inspected it with over two hundred counts of conspiracy to commit art theft. They had cleared out the entire first floor. Rumor has it they hoped to sell it on the black market." He sipped his coffee. "Well, minus the east wing, which truly was a complete loss." He ran a hand through his hair. "The Degas they had there was exquisite. The loss was, well, you understand."

"And now they want you there to curate it?" Jia asked.

He nodded. "Yes. I'd ask Karla to come with me, but she is busy here with the last Escher found at Het Paleis."

Jia thought for a moment, sipping her tea. "How long will you be gone?"

"Several months at the very least. They are also excavating the Museum of Contemporary Art after the El Niño wildfires decimated the area and collection. It's a near total loss, but they are hoping to get an opinion about some pieces before giving up entirely. And President Chen asked me personally to see if I could provide help. Apparently, her family donated several pieces there a few years back." Willem looked tired, not surprising when Jia considered how much work he would end up doing himself rather than farming it out like he should.

"I could go with you," she offered, a small streak of hope rising in her. "I could help."

The look he gave her said it all, but then he frowned. "Are you sure? Your work here is…"

"My work here can wait," Jia interrupted. "And besides, the chance to visit the Met?

I've wanted to go there since I was a little girl!"

He smiled then. "You are a lifesaver, Jia. Thank you."

"Es ist nichts, Papa.[1]" She had been practicing German, but it was the last word that brought tears to the older man's eyes. He said nothing, just reached his hand out and tucked her black hair behind one ear.

"Ich liebe dich, Jia.[2]"

Jia put away her sculpture, wrapping it carefully in moistened sheets, followed by bubble wrap, and even more sheets. She packed her bag and then his as Willem made a flurry of calls back and forth, half in German, half in English. By late afternoon, the house was closed and ready for their departure. They had dropped Mufti off at Karla's, and a private ultrasonic jet was waiting for them at the airport. Two hours later, the skyline of New York appeared. It was altered beyond anything Jia had expected. The past two years had not been kind to the Big Apple. Several of the iconic skyscrapers lay open to the elements, their windows shattered. It made them look as if they had rotting or missing teeth. The city stunk. It had been more than a year since the ESH virus shot through the city, infecting millions of New Yorkers, and killing almost all of them. What it left wasn't pretty. The flood controls that had been instituted nearly fifty years before as the sea levels began rising had flooded in several areas. Humanity was a little shorthanded on engineers right now, and in the dead cities, there was not much call for them to save the buildings. The Met, however, was a unique case. Jia could see the sump pumps spraying brackish water, large hoses that sent the floodwaters away for blocks in every direction. It was a losing battle, from the looks of it. The waters stopped just a few feet short of the top of the stone steps leading to the front doors of the massive building.

Jia now understood why they switched at the airport to a helicopter. There was little or no way to get to the Met, unless one *wanted* to swim in fetid waters filled with rotting dead and a plethora of opportunistic rats. The roof was reinforced and the steel beams stretched across the nearby streets to other rooftops or windows, depending on what was nearby.

A TUPG ambassador, seated next to the pilot in the front, turned towards Willem and Jia. "It's just a precaution, mind you, what with the flooding; everything was settling a bit. The beams are just there for everyone's safety."

It didn't feel reassuring, not at all, but then again, here was a chance to save priceless works of art. Jia looked at her father, her face alight with excitement.

The Met. I can't believe I'm here!

Willem glanced over at her, and his mouth quirked up at the edges. He patted her hand as the pilot gently landed on the roof. It wasn't empty as Jia had expected. Instead, there were different levels, as well as shrubbery, on the top of the building. In one corner was a large Gothic-style house.

"The *Psycho* house," Willem commented, seeing Jia staring at it, "They meant for it to be a temporary installation, but then there was the Collapse and the Second American Civil War and it ended up a permanent piece after the artist died in the war. It's seen better days."

Jia thought he wasn't far off-base. It *had* seen better days, but if it were nearly a century old, she was impressed at its staying power. "It's open on two sides, just a frame really, like the original." He looked out the other window. "Time to get to work,

I see." A group of people congregated a few yards away, next to a large doorway. "Are you ready?"

Jia nodded and took his hand when she climbed down from the helicopter, careful to bend low. The blades circled at a terrifying rate of speed. When they had reached the others, the ambassador who had shared the helicopter with them introduced each of the others, his voice impossible to hear over the roar of the helicopter. Moments later, inside, Jia stared at the walls and floor. They had filled it to the brim with objects d'art, from fashion to sculpture, photography to paintings. There was barely room for them to all stand clustered closely together.

Mackenzie, the ambassador, caught her eye. "We cleared whatever we could from the lower levels and moved it up. In hurricane season, the water has risen as high as the ceiling on the second floor. And it looks as if we might have a Category Two heading our way next week."

Willem nodded. "Well then, it looks as if we have our work cut out for us. I'd like to go to the lowest unflooded level and then assess from there, yes?"

The ambassador caught the eyes of

several of the group, and they nodded. "Mr. Grunsfeld, I will leave you in capable hands. The team here is excellent, as I am sure you will discover. Let me know what you need, and we will do whatever is necessary to save the art stored here. It is our heritage, after all. Donna," he said, pointing to a bottle-blond standing just to his right, "will assist you with everything you might need while you are here in New York. That includes lodging, food, anything at all."

"Thank you, Roger, I appreciate it." The ambassador ascended the stairs, and moments later they could hear the helicopter taking off.

Willem clapped his hands together, smiling brightly. Jia hid a smile. Willem was uncomfortable with groups and crowds, but he hid it well. "Time to get to work. Donna, if you will lead the way." The woman nodded, and they inched forward, following her lead while avoiding stepping on or running into any of the piles of priceless art around them.

The overwhelming stink of the city rotting around them faded slightly as they descended into the massive building. The distinct odor of linseed oil and lacquer replaced it and Jia found herself at a loss for words as they descended into a world of art-filled wonder. Within these walls were treasures beyond measure. Jia drank it all in, ignoring the other smells of decay and death that filled the city with dank, dark floodwaters below. She accidentally stepped backwards onto someone else's feet and immediately jumped away, apologizing as she turned to see dark, almond-shaped eyes and jet-black hair on a young man who appeared to be in his mid-twenties. He grinned at her; his perfect teeth flashed white as he reached out a hand to steady her.

"Careful, you nearly put a heel through the Rembrandt." His accent was American, but his face was Chinese.

Willem's hand landed on Jia's shoulder. "Trust you to find my star intern moments after we land, Jia." He smiled at the young man. "Eaton, it is good to see you here!"

"Good to see you, Herr Grunsfeld," the young man responded, grinning even wider.

"This is my daughter, Jia Wang. Jia, Eaton Ngai."

"Herr Grunsfeld's course on sculpture in '98 changed the course of my studies,"

Eaton said, his hand still on Jia. "It is a pleasure to meet you, Jia." Jia liked how warm it felt against hers. She could feel her cheeks flushing red.

"Are you in charge of the sculptures, Eaton?" Willem asked, a bemused smile on his lips, clearly noticing Jia's response to Eaton. "Jia is focusing her studies on sculpture recently; perhaps she could assist you in the cataloging and packing of the Asian and South American exhibits."

"Her help would be more than welcome." His grin was warm, friendly, and Jia couldn't help but smile, blushing as she did. His good looks were giving her butterflies in her stomach.

"Excellent! Jia, if you are comfortable working with Eaton, then I will try to find you for a bite of lunch in a few hours, yes?"

Jia nodded, unsure whether she was more excited to be handling the priceless sculptures or to spend time with the handsome Eaton Ngai. Perhaps it was Eaton's easygoing manner, so different from the intensity of the boys in Guiyang. He was American through and through and shared his family's history with her as they worked through an exhibit of Mayan burial urns. Jia quickly learned that Eaton was third generation Amer-Asian, and yet he spoke Mandarin flawlessly.

"My father insisted upon it, so that I didn't forget my roots," Eaton said, his hands cradling an urn with four small skulls sculpted around the large central figure of a jaguar standing on two feet, paws outstretched. "I can manage the basics in Cantonese, but not much past that, unfortunately." He handed her the urn, smiling, and Jia felt the butterflies in her stomach again. She managed a half-smile as she cradled the urn in her gloved hands, noting the tiny imperfections of the vessel.

"I speak both, and I'm happy to help you learn, if you ever want to." She placed the piece in the box, nestling it in the packing material and double-checking that the tag on the urn was the same as the box.

"I just might take you up on that, Jia Wang." She looked up to see Eaton staring at her. She looked down immediately. Americans might not be as intense in some ways, but in others, well. His hotness was turning her into a bundle of nerves, and she feared she would drop something priceless if she didn't get herself together.

"What about you?" he asked, trying to

make eye contact.

"Me?" Jia responded; he was so close to her, she felt as jumpy as a cat.

"Yeah, what's your story?"

"I, uh, I grew up in Guiyang." She patted the packing material into place and sealed the box.

"Guiyang? The one that was firebombed?" Jia glanced up to see his eyes wide, curious, the smile wiped from his face. She nodded. "And you got out." He looked embarrassed. "Sorry, Captain Obvious here. But how?"

Jia shrugged. "I just walked out. I was on the outskirts of a farm, a couple of kilometers out, when the bombs fell."

His eyes were warm, his voice earnest. "I am happy that you survived, Jia. If I may ask, what was it like?"

She shivered, remembering the emptiness, the trees denuded of bark, and of leaves. Every piece of greenery gone. Every animal, even the birds, consumed by the virus-riddled citizens. Her neighbors, her friends.

Eaton frowned. "I'm sorry. I shouldn't have asked that. My British friends would say 'Bad form, Eaton!' Please forgive me."

"No, no, it is all right. The question took

me back there, for a moment, though."

In bits and pieces, between packaging humanity's treasures, she told Eaton about watching the city fall, her mother's death, and then, months later, her discovery that Willem was her biological father.

"The secret to your survival," Eaton said, "I like that." He pulled off his white cotton gloves and reached out and did the same to hers. He smiled then and took her hands in his. "Will you come to dinner with me?"

Jia stared at their entwined fingers, barely trusting her voice to stay even. "I should eat with Willem."

"I'll invite both of you, then. My mother would love it. She used to run her own restaurant; it's how she met my father. She misses having people to cook for. I keep telling her to leave stinking New York and move to one of the new cities, but she won't leave while I'm still here. She cooks and cooks and there's never enough people to feed all the leftovers to. Say yes, Jia."

Jia agreed, and as she did, her tablet beeped with a notification. "I must go, it is Willem asking me to meet him in the American Wing Cafe?"

"I know just where that is," Eaton

answered. "I'll show you the way. It's easy to get lost here if you don't know your way around."

Several flights of stairs and no less than a dozen twists and turns through other massive halls filled with workers and priceless art, and they arrived at the American Wing Cafe on the first floor. Jia spied Willem at a table at the far end of the room and waved at her father. He smiled and beckoned both of them over, pointing to the two empty seats across from him.

Willem's smile looked rather smug when he asked Jia how her morning had gone. It stayed there as she described the Mayan funerary urns and the skulls that had surrounded the jaguar standing upright.

Willem nodded, his glance straying to Eaton, who had brought them all several plates of food to share and was passing out silverware and napkins while Jia spoke.

"The jaguar is second only to the snake god in religious importance in the Mayan gods' pantheon. I knew you would enjoy the exhibit."

He nodded his thanks to Eaton and tucked into the food, which mainly consisted of prepackaged foods. This was not surprising, considering their surroundings. Through much of the city streets surrounding the Met, the black waters continued to rise. New York City, once referred to as the Big Apple, was now rotten to the core.

Eaton, in between bites of beef hash, asked Willem if he and Jia would join him for dinner. Willem's gaze wandered back to Jia, and he saw her blush and nod quickly to his unspoken question.

Willem's lips twitched, bemused. "We would enjoy that very much. Jia has been enduring my pitiful attempts to recreate some of her favorite meals with boundless patience, but I know she will appreciate your mother's cooking far more."

Eaton grinned happily in response. "My mother will be very pleased."

The afternoon flew by after they finished lunch and returned to work. By the time the lights flickered in a quick on-off, on-off pattern that signaled the end of the workday, Jia and Eaton had finished with the entire Mayan exhibit and were ready to move on. She had spent the day laughing more, and talking more, than she could remember since her cousin Chang had left for Hong Kong. *Dear Chang*. Her heart panged at the thought of him.

Dinner that evening was full of laughter as Eaton's mother, a bright-eyed, round woman with liberal streaks of gray threading through the black, kept spooning more and more food onto their plates.

When they arrived at the Brooklyn apartment, the helicopter landing on the roof, Eaton had led the way down one long flight of stairs and into the penthouse.

"My father was from a wealthy family, but my mother never felt comfortable with it all. She insisted on keeping direct control of her family's restaurant after my grandparents retired. She had me washing dishes at ten and waiting tables by my mid-teens. I guess you could say that I was raised in both worlds."

Lisa Ngai had placed her hands on Jia's cheeks and kissed her forehead, beaming, and clearly happy for the additional mouths to feed. She had shot a glance at Eaton as well. One that looked not dissimilar from the one that Willem had given Jia when he saw her standing at Eaton's side.

She dug into the food, happy to be eating something that reminded her of her childhood. Lisa Ngai was an excellent cook.

1. "It is nothing, Papa."

2. "I love you, Jia."

Creche Baby

Earth
08.15.2100

Julie Lynn Aaronson stood when Madeline arrived, the doctor's face beaming as she closed the distance and grasped Madeline's hand.

"Madame President, we have someone for you to meet!"

She bounced on her toes and beckoned Madeline over to the tiny bundle held by Janelle Brooks' adopted daughter, Karen. The girl bounced a small baby in her arms. She met Madeline's eyes for a second, smiled tentatively, and then looked down, focusing on the infant.

"You did it," Madeline breathed, fascinated by the infant's tiny size. The baby had a thick head of silky black hair and the child's eyes drew her in, a moth to the flame. She stepped closer.

"Thirty weeks gestation, yes." Julie's eyes sparkled and the older woman sounded positively giddy. "She is off the charts."

"She?" She didn't look up. The baby's gaze was steady on her. She was so small, but she had a presence about her. Madeline found herself locked in a staring contest with the newborn. The baby's eyes were a brilliant blue, the limbal ring a dark, midnight blue, which then brightened into a blaze of yellow, orange, and red near the pupil.

"We named her Primina," Janelle said quietly. "It means 'first'."

"Appropriate, to be sure." Madeline stared at Janelle. "You have concerns, Dr. Brooks?"

Janelle and Julie exchanged glances, and Janelle shook her head. "No, Madame President, I'm just tired. Primina is very active."

"I imagine she is, even at just thirty weeks gestation. That's definitely premature, am I correct?"

"Yes, in normal cases, it would be." Janelle seemed to choose her words carefully. "However, the artificial wombs seem to accelerate the process. Although Primina is early, she is also rather advanced, which is not what we expected."

"How so?"

"She is one week old today, but she has held her head up since two days after bir… er… removal from the artificial womb. And yesterday she turned over on her own a full three months before most children."

Madeline and Primina stared at each other. "That's impossible. No child is that advanced."

"Yet here she is."

Madeline broke eye contact with the baby and turned to the researchers. "You're here to ask for more."

Julie didn't hesitate. "Yes."

"How many?

"Five hundred, along with a support staff of at least that number. There is an empty medical center in New Phoenix that could easily convert into a production lab and care center."

Madeline blinked. "Five *hundred*?" You have *one* and now you want five *hundred*?"

"Actually, we have seventeen more. Her other sisters will join Primina in short order, especially now that we see how quickly they advance once removed from the artificial wombs."

Madeline stared at Julie, her mind spinning. She turned to Janelle. "And you, Dr. Brooks, what do you think of all this?"

The younger scientist looked at her partner, then back at Madeline. "It's necessary. We need to move forward on these experiments *now*. Not to put too fine a point on it, but there are very few researchers who can do what we can do, and many of us don't have decades upon decades left to live."

Madeline had a feeling of disquiet, of unease. Something was not being said.

"Send me the specs. I'll review them and give you a decision soon."

"Thank you, Madame President."

Madeline spared another glance at the baby girl swaddled in Karen Brooks' arms. Her eyes tracked Madeline. The child was unsettling.

Moments later, in a small conference room, she met with her aide.

"Aiden, what do we know about Kavu?"

Aiden shook his head and ran a hand jerkily through his hair. He didn't meet her eyes. "They confirmed a breach. A computer analyst damned and determined to see his wife and child again." He cleared his throat. "He had contact with a busier section of the city, the open-air market, and potential exposure to dozens of UPs. We have quarantined the east side, and they are reviewing all CCTV feeds to ensure everyone exposed is now quarantined."

"I see." It would be days, possibly weeks, before they would know for sure.

If only they had agreed to the iDent chips.

The UPs had been difficult to reason with. It was understandable. They were rabidly afraid of contracting the virus, and for good reason, ESH remained stunningly infectious. The iDent chips, injected subdermally, allowed the TUPG to monitor its citizens whereabouts, as well as their basic health. But the UP leaders had been leery of them, concerned that the chips could introduce the ESH contagion into their population.

It had been a hard enough fight to get them into the new cities, built entirely by automation. And now dozens may have been exposed and infected. All because of one lonely husband.

"Keep me updated."

"Yes, Madame President."

There were circles under his eyes. There usually were. He turned to leave her.

"And Aiden?"

"Yes, ma'am?"

"I won't need anything else tonight. Get some sleep."

He nodded and left the room.

Madeline sat in her office and stared out at the dark sky and soft lights of the city below. It was nearly midnight, and the city was quiet, only a few autocars moving along the streets.

She closed the folder abruptly, remembering the latest report on women of childbearing age. Earlier this year, they had stood at 1.5 million women capable of reproduction. Thanks to increased testing, scores of other women declared infertile, aging out of the safe range for pregnancy, and suicide rates that followed on the heels of skyrocketing miscarriages and fetal death—the number of fertile women was now closer to seven hundred thousand, possibly less.

Artificial or not, against nature and all of that bullshit, humanity ran the distinct chance of being eradicated from the universe.

As the leader of the TUPG, she had to do something about it. And damned if she wouldn't. She pressed the call button on her desk and the door opened within seconds.

Aiden waited for her to beckon him to her desk. "Sorry, Aiden. Just this one last thing and then please call it a night. I need you to call Aaronson and Brooks and tell them to proceed."

"Yes, ma'am."

She was going to keep humanity alive, whether they liked it or not.

But something in the back of her mind worried her.

What was Dr. Brooks not *saying? It felt as if she was holding back somehow.*

The thought troubled her. They were descending the slippery slope by experimenting with humans and artificial wombs. Would they soon be a free fall on the road to hell?

These thoughts continued the next day as Madeline faced her bevy of advisers, all of them with their own agendas, their own opinions of how she should proceed in the months to come. Although the TUPG Women First Act was intended for the entire world, it was far from widespread. Most of North America and Europe were on board, but that still left nearly all of the Middle East, Africa, Asia, Central and South America, and those still scattered through Australia, New Zealand, and the Pacific Islands. China was its own disaster. The land was vast, but its population centers were now home to millions of rotting corpses. The rest of the country had dissolved into chaos and civil war. It was more fractured now than it had been before the Chen dynasty, over fifteen hundred years ago.

There were doomsday cults springing up faster than the TUPG could squash them, and the suicide rate was at an all-time high. Jack Hesper presented the newest figures just two days prior, showing that the rate had shot up from a pre-ESH average of twelve per one hundred thousand to a devastating two per one hundred. It was an increase of over 150% and as the infertility rates continued to rise, so did the suicides.

"We need more than just North America and Europe on board, we need to pass legislation making suicide illegal," Loren argued, his nose turning red. He was broad-chested, heavy, and his nose and ears turned red the more passionate he became.

Jeff laughed. "What resources do you think we have, Loren? We can barely contain the doomsday cults, most of the West Coast of North America is burning, half of the East Coast is under water from the last hurricane, China is, well, a scattered mess of city states and fiefdoms, Africa is too large for any of the TUPG troops to even contain, much less control, and frankly, unless we plan on putting the entire population of Earth in padded rooms and feeding them gruel in straitjackets, I'm pretty sure that the suicide rate will not get better."

Loren bristled at Jeff's derisive tone. "Fine, *you* come up with a solution then."

Jeff slumped in his seat. "I wish I had a solution." He threaded his long fingers through his hair. Unlike Loren, who sported a bald pate, Jeff had a head full of hair. The white hairs were quickly taking over what had once been a raven black. "I just can't see how passing more laws is the answer."

Dinah spoke up. "There are plenty of law-abiding people in the world. They might not agree with a law, but they will follow it if it is in effect." She shrugged and pointed a blood-red talon in Jeff's direction. "Laws work. We need more of them."

His lips tightened into a grim expression. "We will have to agree to disagree on that."

Jack spoke then. "I believe we should pass the legislation. If it saves a hundred, maybe even a thousand, then it is worth it. We are fighting a war for the survival of our species. Anything justifies that."

"Anything?" Jeff barked. "How about helmets in bathtubs then? I hear they are pretty damn dangerous. And are you sure we should let our constituents have medicine or sharp knives around? Maybe we should just confiscate all rope, and hell, shoelaces while we are at it."

The rest of the meeting would have devolved into further bickering–Jeff holding his ground against the rest–if not for an aide rushing in with the latest news, a suicide pact that had decimated the remnants of a large refugee camp outside of Seattle. Three hundred and fifty-two men, women, and children were dead. The newsvids were already flashing images of the corpses in the streets.

Madeline signed the anti-suicide bill and

asked grimly, "As for the media showing these graphic images, I want it stopped. In fact, I think the bill needs an addendum restricting the media from covering these stories. We have only to look at our own history here in the former United States to know that the more the media focuses on isolated incidents, the more frequent they become. School shootings, for example, in the early part of last century. If the media hadn't allowed those graphic images to go viral, it wouldn't have inspired other unstable adolescents to open fire on their teachers and fellow students."

She stood up. "Work on it, muzzle these vultures. I never want to see those kinds of images on the mainstream news again."

Her advisers' voices rose instantly, ratcheting upwards in volume before she could exit the room, already arguing. Jeff's was loudest of all.

Aiden followed, his stride matching hers. "Are you alright?"

Madeline didn't answer. She was too busy wondering if she had done the right thing signing the bill. Seeing those children, though, their bodies contorted, stiff, unmoving. It made her sick to think of them dying.

"Is there any update on Kavu?" She wanted to hear good news, even as her stomach twisted in anticipation of what Aiden would say in response.

"Not yet." Aiden flashed her a look. "But we've been down this road before, ma'am. You and I both know how it ends."

The UP city of Kavu would fall. All because of one lonely husband. Over four thousand souls, a mere handful of them with AB negative blood. The rest would die. It was as simple as that. The citizens had been notified and lockdown measures initiated, but the chances of it saving their lives were unlikely. Kavu would fall, and Earth would lose thousands of Unaffected Persons.

"We have to get them off of Earth, Aiden. It's the only way we can be sure of the UPs safety."

"I agree, ma'am. The Nostradamus is well under way in orbit. Another six months and we can send over ten thousand people to Zarmina's World."

"I just hope that there are ten thousand UPs left by that time, Aiden," Madeline said, her face grim. "I'm so tired of death everywhere I look."

Aiden reached out a hand and laid it on

her arm gently. "And how are *you*, ma'am? After the last mis…"

Madeline cut him off. "I'll be fine. The doctor says I need a month to recover and then I will try again."

Aiden frowned. His handsome face looked grim, concerned. "Are you sure, ma'am? It doesn't all have to be on you, you know."

Madeline stepped away from her closest aide, her hand on the door of her suite. "Yes, it does, Aiden. The future of humanity is at stake. Every child matters." She slipped into her suite and said, "I need a half hour to rest; give a knock when it is time for the next meeting."

The concern in his eyes as she closed the door was touching, and it felt bittersweet. In another time or place, Aiden could have made a skilled lover. Perhaps, in another year or two, things might change between them and she could have that. She had loved Gary and always been faithful to him, despite a myriad of temptations. But he was gone. Madeline missed the touch that comes from a partner, the intimacy. However, she had a world to save, and humanity needed her. That was the only relationship she was prepared to have.

Encrypted

Earth
09.11.2100

Madeline sat up, pulling her robes closer. It had been the requisite time for her to lie prone, with her hips slightly elevated per the doctor's instructions, and now she had to get back to business. She had a world to save, after all.

It had been exactly six weeks since her second miscarriage and here she was, trying again. Was there any point? She wasn't sure, but her popularity had risen over seven points since a series of infovids released. They felt ridiculously overly done to Madeline, dramatic shots of her standing beside an empty crib, a hand on her flat stomach. The words appearing on the screen, "I'm doing my part. Are you doing yours?"

When she had first seen the clips, she'd felt ill.

"Seriously? This is what they think will work? Guilt trips? Blatant manipulation?"

Several of her advisers had persisted, pointing out that they were fighting a war for the survival of humanity. Only one had dissented. Jeff Bonovich wasn't politically correct. Hell, he wasn't even political.

"Humans are no better than cockroaches. Don't worry, humanity will survive." His voice had been the lone voice of reason, outvoted and overruled by the cacophony of the others. The statistics won in the end. Especially after the infovids were released to a test audience who had responded well. Whether or not it was a guilt trip, people cared more that even the president of the Terran United Planetary Government would step up to the plate and endure miscarriage after miscarriage in the name of the greater good.

Ever wonder if Jeff is right?

The thought flitted through her head as she slipped off of the bed and reached for her clothes. She had three meetings this afternoon and a dinner full of delegates to soothe. The new policies were now in effect worldwide, and there were plenty of people who weren't happy.

Jeff was right about that as well. It is government overreach. But what other choice do we have? The next decade is critical to humanity's survival.

Her suit was form-fitting and made of a silk blend. She had three dozen tailored maternity suits in the far closet, just waiting for her body to fill out. She had purchased them after the first positive pregnancy test, so certain that the IVF treatment would work. It hadn't, of course, and after the second miscarriage, she had asked for her attendant to move them to the far closet and closed the door. Now, for the third time, hope flared in her.

Is it too much to ask that I might actually be a role model to others? An inspiration, even?

It would take a successful pregnancy for that. And successful pregnancies weren't what they once were thanks to the ESH virus that still flowed through their bloodstreams.

A knock sounded at the door.

"Come in," Madeline called as she slipped the suit jacket over her shoulders and slid into her heels. The added height, besides her five foot ten-inch frame, helped when dealing with fractious diplomats and politicians. They weren't used to women looking them straight in the eye.

"Madame, there is a classified report from the Mars colony that has come in. Your eyes only," Kate said, a small frown on her face.

"Classified?" Madeline's eyebrows raised in surprise.

"Yes, ma'am, we received it on an encrypted channel. A Lieutenant Ethan Livingston is waiting in the atrium. Shall I send him into your private office?"

"Yes, tell him I can give him five minutes." Kate nodded and slipped back out of Madeline's bedroom; the door closed whisper-soft behind her.

The meetings couldn't wait. Well, at least not for long. Five minutes to find out what in the world warranted a classified report from Mars when there were only half a dozen people left on the planet. How had anyone even known *how* to send the transmission?

Madeline checked her reflection carefully in the mirror and brushed on lipstick and headed for her office, which was next to her living quarters.

"Lieutenant Livingston?"

The young soldier standing at attention snapped out a salute, and Madeline nodded in return, settling into her office chair after she gave his hand a firm shake. "I understand you have some information for me?"

"Yes, Madame President." He pulled a data drive from his front pocket and placed it down on her desk. "The data drive gives coordinates, and the estimated size and date of impact. I gave it a once-over, and it appears legit, ma'am."

"Impact?" Madeline frowned, reaching out for the data drive and turning it over in her hand as if that would somehow cause it to reveal its secrets. "Impact into what?"

"Into Earth, Madame President. The remains of Ultima Thule, which appears to have suffered a fracturing event or collision which has propelled a chunk of asteroid towards Earth."

"A chunk of asteroid? Exactly how large is a 'chunk,' soldier?"

"Fourteen kilometers in diameter, give or take a kilometer."

Madeline struggled to visualize that in terms of damage to Earth.

The lieutenant added, "It is equivalent to the asteroid that struck at the end of the Cretaceous period, and the estimate on that one was eleven kilometers in diameter."

"The one that wiped out the dinosaurs?"

"Yes, ma'am."

Madeline blinked at the lieutenant. After all that they had been through, with over 99% of the population of the world dying, was this man really telling her that there was a killer asteroid heading their way?

"There are hundreds of near misses every year." She felt silly saying it. Obviously, this asteroid would be one of them.

"Yes, ma'am, there are. This, however, is a credible threat. I ran the data that the Mars colonists have collected through the asteroid-tracking software and it scores a 9 to 10 on the Torino scale."

"Which means what, exactly?"

He grimaced. "Best-case scenario? Widespread regional devastation capable of producing a mega-tsunami that could threaten surrounding land masses for thousands of miles."

Madeline's eyebrows arched. "That's the best case?"

The man nodded. "Yes, ma'am. Worst case, well, we go the way of the dinosaurs."

"An extinction-level event?"

"Yes, ma'am."

Madeline leaned back in her chair. She was sure that Kate would knock on the door at any moment now. The meeting was with the vice-presidents of Europe and Asia, where several UP cities were located. The question of what to do with the UPs and how to protect them adequately continued to be a problem. The vice president of Asia Minor was chafing at several other recent TUPG edicts and he was a pain in Madeline's rear, anyway. They wouldn't wait forever, though. She had to get to the meeting before he dug in like a tick and began stirring the pot like he had in last month's meeting.

A deadly asteroid is heading towards Earth and this guy isn't suggesting it will miss. Not at all. He's saying it will *hit. And when it does, it could send human civilization the way of the dinosaurs.*

She realized she was sitting there, her fingers interlaced before her mouth, just as Gary used to do. This was impossible. They had dealt humanity one hell of a hit with the ESH virus. Hell, the virus was an extinction-level event all on its own. And now this soldier was telling her that an asteroid was going to hit Earth?

"How did they see it and not anyone on Earth?" Madeline asked.

"I couldn't say, Madame President, other than we've been rather absorbed with things on the surface, and less on the stars."

"Where?"

"I beg your pardon, ma'am?"

"Where is it going to hit?"

"We don't have that data yet. We won't. Not the way it is wobbling. It's turning, end over end, at a rate of over 14,000 kilometers an hour. And that number will only increase once it enters Earth's gravitational pull."

Madeline closed her eyes. By now, the Asia Minor vice president would take full advantage of her absence to peddle his own ideas on how they needed to save Earth's population.

"Forgive me, Lieutenant, but I'm skeptical. Incredibly so. Asteroids this size are charted and tagged and watched. And they have been for over a century. If there was an upcoming threat, those tracking systems would have notified us."

Lieutenant Livingston nodded. "Yes, ma'am, they would have, *if* it were a normal trajectory. But this is, from what Liu Fong, the astronomer stationed at the Beijing Science Station, said, this results from a collision. Ultima Thule smacked into something else, something unknown, and in doing so, the collision sheared it in half. The force of the collision sent part of the KBO deeper into the Belt and…"

"KBO?"

"Kuiper Belt Object, ma'am. The other piece, the bigger piece, is heading for Earth."

Madeline inhaled deeply, battling to stay calm, to keep her anxiety levels at a reasonable level.

"And when is it due to impact?"

The lieutenant tried to summon a smile and failed.

"Well, that's about the only good news I've got, ma'am. They projected the remnants of Ultima Thule to impact in the second or third week of August 2104."

"That's the *good* news?" Madeline asked.

"Yes, ma'am. It means we've got time. Not a lot, not enough for everyone. We have just under four years to get as many people as we can off Earth.”

She tapped a small button on her desk and only a few seconds passed until there was a low knock and the door opened.

“Lieutenant Livingston, this is Isa Netanyahu. I will leave you in his capable hands. Isa, please double- and triple-check the lieutenant’s info and get back to me as soon as you have confirmation.”

She stood. “I have a meeting to attend, one that I’m late for.” She reached out her hand and shook the lieutenant’s hand. “I hope you are wrong, Lieutenant Livingston. In fact, if I were a person of faith, I would pray for you to be wrong. We have all suffered enough in the past twenty months.”

Livingston grimaced. “I have never wished so much to be wrong, either, ma’am.”

Madeline left her Chief of Staff of Science and Technology standing in her office with the lieutenant and promptly pushed the entire discussion out of her mind. The key to being effective in leadership is letting go of what you can’t control, or of what you don’t have answers to at the moment, and focusing on one challenge at a time. Her challenge right now was simple—she needed to get to her meeting and work through the concerns the men had with the rioting. Her advisors showed that the rioting was in response to the recent removal of three children from a woman who pled guilty to heroin trafficking a year earlier.

"It was a simple case of safety for the children," Loren McClellan had sniffed, his mouth pursed in disapproval, "and we have provided a better home for them."

It didn't help that the mother had committed suicide shortly after the final hearing that had removed all visits and remanded the children, now in three separate homes, to the permanent custody of their foster parents.

"Somehow, despite the overwhelming evidence of neglect and child endangerment," Loren continued, "a few rotten apples have taken this as an affront to the rights of parents. A drug trafficker, no less!" He picked at a piece of lint on his otherwise immaculate suit and flung it away with a manicured hand. Madeline frowned.

"Wasn't there a question about whether the father of her youngest child had forced her into it?"

Loren waved the same perfectly manicured hand dismissively. "Pft, they will say anything, do anything, just so they can live their lives however they please. She lied, of course."

Vice President Tao Zhu knitted his fingers together. "What's done is done. Lies or no lies. It matters not. I need additional troops to deal with the situation."

"And you will have them, Vice President," Loren groveled.

Madeline suppressed a flare of anger. Loren had been one of her late husband's advisers, a minor one at that, but the virus had changed the landscape of their world in more ways than one. Loren had always been good at positioning himself to his own best advantage. In the chaos that followed Gary's death, Madeline had gathered anything familiar, and that had included Loren McClelland. Occasionally she questioned whether that had been the best choice.

She cleared her throat and Loren, his focus turned back to her, showed a millisecond of panic. "Erm, I…"

He had put her in a terrible position. Troops were extended, limited, and taxed.

First, they had the challenge of combining multiple forces into one—not just here in the former RUSA, but internationally. It wouldn't do to send all American troops to the site of the riots. In fact, it could only exacerbate the situation. The newly formed TUPG had many challenges before it, of which, combining hundreds of different countries together, along with their armed forces, was but one facet. The RUSA had a better history than the USA had. The RUSA were far less meddling, especially as their position on the world stage had taken such a beating during The Collapse in the earlier part of the century.

Currencies, customs, rule of law—it was shifting, and every three steps forward, it felt as if they slipped two steps back. Progress had been slow. And now Loren had promised Zhu troops, when there were other conflicts in other cities, as well as the civil war still raging in China itself.

She forced her face to relax, to smile. "Yes, of course the TUPG will help with the riots, Minister Zhu, just as I'm sure you will find time to provide the infovids my team has asked for repeatedly. All hands-on-deck, so to speak. When can we expect those infovids?"

Zhu had repeatedly stalled at creating a similar series of infovids that were pro-life and modeled the behavior and life choices they so desperately needed to see in the remaining population. And considering that Asia Minor had the worst reproductive rates post-ESH, his reticence was a thorn in Madeline's side.

Zhu's face betrayed his frustration, and then resignation. If he wanted her help, he was going to have to compromise. It was his turn to be put on the spot.

"Erm, yes, that was, I meant to, hm…" His smile looked forced, all teeth. Madeline thought he looked as though he would have been happier biting her than smiling at that moment.

"Excellent! I have a crew that will be happy to come to you, Minister Zhu. They can return on the flight with you, in fact." She hid the rush of dark joy she felt at twisting the Chinese ambassador's arm and obtaining the videos he had drug his feet for so long on.

They took the rest of the meeting up discussing a rollout of experimental vaccines and a report on the UP city established 20 miles outside of Madrid using the new remote drones and carrier units.

In the back of her mind, however, the thought of an asteroid rocketing towards them was never far from her mind. Nor was whether the latest IVF treatment would work. Would she finally be able to model the actions the infovids were promoting? Would she lead her world as more than someone who was all talk and no action? Would instead she be able to show the women of the world the message they all needed to see so desperately–that of life, new life, growing inside of them before it was too late for them to bear the future of humanity?

Abruption

Earth
08.19.2100

May stared at the blood on her hand in confusion. She sat there on the toilet feeling light-headed, her abdomen twisting in pain. Her head pounding. This wasn't normal labor; no one had said anything about bleeding heavily during labor pains.

She hadn't felt well since yesterday, and Ollie had fussed over her this morning, checking for fever, her eyebrows knitted in concern.

"Perhaps I should call in, take the day off."

May had waved her off. "I'm fine, really. Just a little dizzy and I think maybe I'm getting contractions or maybe it is those Braxton-Hicks things again."

"Even more reason for me to call in."

"Ollie, I'll be fine. All the books I read say that the first pregnancy is the longest. If I'm in labor, you'll know soon enough!"

Ollie had relented and went off to work after making May promise she would call her on the Comm if there was any change.

The last three months had been the best months of May's life. She could say that honestly, without reservation, if not without a small amount of guilt. Those years before Mom had died, what she could remember of them, were riddled with trips to the hospital, stays on stranger's couches, and then straight into the foster care system. But here in New Athens, pregnant with her baby, once May had made it through the withdrawal from the drugs, she had gone home with Ollie.

It had been unusual. May saw the looks on the others' faces as they looked at her and back at Ollie. She had tensed up, stopped in her tracks, ready to do battle. She knew it wouldn't matter. She'd open her mouth and piss someone off and then they would just flat-out say it.

"That one will be nothing but trouble." It was what folks had been saying her entire life. From the first foster home she had found herself in, just hours after her mother had passed away in the hospital, she could hear the whispers. "She's too old to be adopted."

"She's quiet, that one. But not the good quiet. I expect she will be trouble," her foster mom had stage-whispered to a friend as May walked to her room days later after the funeral. Standing there, waiting to be discharged from the hospital all these years later, it felt as if nothing had changed. May opened her mouth, ready to give them all something to talk about, but Ollie had squeezed May's arm and ushered her down the hall, May's backpack slung over her shoulder.

The house had been identical to the rest there in New Athens. Clean, sparse, and filled with light. Ollie had pointed to May's room and told her to take her time settling in. Now that she wasn't itchy and twitchy and feeling like she had ants under her skin, May had found the room to be a little boring, but safe, reassuring. Perhaps it was the small vase full of wildflowers, or the new tablet, loaded with books on prenatal care and what to expect when expecting. May had smiled at the silky pajamas in a deep blue satin that sat neatly folded on her pillow. She had told

Ollie once that blue was her favorite color. And on a walk outside of the hospital, they had admired the wildflowers flourishing in the prairies that surrounded the eastern edge of the city. These things she had shown an interest in, Ollie had provided. May walked to one corner of the room and saw an easel, assembled and ready for use, a rainbow assortment of acrylics assembled in a box, along with a stack of blank canvases. How long had it been since she had painted? High school, and her art teacher Miss Swan. She had let May stay after class and paint, long after most students had fled the school for the comfort of their homes, their families, their friends – none of which May had. Miss Swan had been different. She had been like Ollie, patient, kind.

It was here in this house, living with Ollie, that May had found a rhythm that made sense, that kept her happy and calm and changed her entire outlook. When she had first learned that she was going to have a baby, the thought of the junk she had put into her body, the *poison,* it had filled her with such self-loathing. It had taken days for her to even imagine *keeping* the baby. Abortion was illegal thanks to the International Recovery Act, and it wasn't something she would have even considered anyway, but for days all she could think of was getting clean so that she could bring her child safely into the world and then give him away. May knew it wasn't as if there would be a shortage of hopeful adoptive parents. She had asked Ollie, the only person on the floor she felt she could talk to, or confide in, and Ollie had looked at her and simply nodded.

It hadn't been until the fifth day or so, when May emerged from the worst of the withdrawal symptoms, that Ollie had asked her, "May, have you considered keeping your son?"

May had burst into tears. It was a huge gush of waterworks, and body-wracking sobs. Ollie had gently put her arms around May and held her until she recovered enough to put into words her fears and guilt.

If it hadn't been for the older woman's steadfast belief and support, May wasn't sure she would ever have imagined that future. And yet, when the question had come during a standard OB/GYN appointment in her sixth month, May had said the words, "I'm keeping my baby." The doctor had simply noted her response in his notes and told her she could get dressed. She had gone home to Ollie's house trembling at the thought.

"Words, when spoken out loud, can change the course of our lives," Ollie had said, a smile on her face. "You will be a wonderful mother, May, I know you will."

Ollie's belief in her was steadfast, and May had found the parts of her heart scattered in the wind after losing her mother and all the years in foster care, finally knitting together. Ollie felt like a mother to May. It was what she needed, desperately, as her body finally showed that she was one of the lucky ones, a woman who could, despite the teratogenic aspects of the virus, carry a child to term.

As the months dragged on, they had assigned May round-the-clock protection. The ESH virus had stripped far too many women of the ability to carry a baby, and after eighteen months of data, this continued to be the case. As if seeing over 99.6% of the population die from it wasn't enough, the inability to bear a living child often broke those already traumatized by loss. Suicides had skyrocketed, but so had crimes against pregnant women. It had caused such alarm and concern that now protective details were assigned to all pregnant women in their third trimester.

It had changed the dynamic of their peaceful little house. But, as Ollie had reminded her, it was necessary. Right now, Ryan was on duty. He was May's favorite. Ryan often had dinner with them just before his shift ended. May suspected Ollie was doing her best to play matchmaker with them.

She stared at the blood and groaned as another deep lance of pain tore through her abdomen and into her lower back.

No, this is definitely not *normal.*

A soft knock at the door came then. "May? Are you all right in there?"

Her body convulsed in pain and she cried out in response, a wordless, keening groan.

The door flew open, and Ryan took in the blood that had dribbled across the floor before she sat down. He slapped the Comm unit on his uniform.

"I need a rush on a bus to 529 Surrey Street!" he barked and yanked a fluffy towel off of the bar, wrapping it around May. His Comm squawked back, but May was too busy staring at the gush of blood that was staining the toilet bowl and her clothes to notice.

"Oh God," she whimpered as another lance of pain hit while she stood with Ryan's help, her body sagging against his.

"Hang in there, May, I'm going to stay with you the entire way." Ryan's voice was calm, reassuring. "Let's get you out to the living room."

"Ollie. I need…" Another wave of pain. "Please get Ollie!"

The next few hours were a frantic rush of medical personnel, lights, and the pungent scent of antiseptic. By the time Ollie arrived at her side, out of breath from running, they were prepping May for an emergency C-section.

"We have a twenty-year-old pregnant female, at approximately thirty-nine weeks gestation, and a placental abruption," the doctor announced to the room as he shoved his sanitized hands into gloves and nodded to the anesthesiologist. "Maternal blood pressure is eighty over forty, baby's heart rate is reading as 80bpm. We need to move on this, people."

He leaned close to her. "May, we're going to get your baby out now and get you stabilized. Hang in there."

A nurse moved to usher Ollie out, but May wouldn't release the death grip on Ollie's hand.

May barely noticed an unspoken conversation flit between Ollie, the nurse, and the doctor before the doctor shrugged and turned his focus on the emergency C-section.

May shivered as they cut her open. Not because she could feel it, but because she knew they had sliced her open, an incision cutting through skin, muscle, and more to get to her unborn baby, who was still inside her now-hemorrhaging uterus. She could feel them rooting about inside of her and, even though she wasn't in pain, thanks to the epidural, the experience was terrifying. Placental abruption. Women and babies *died* from it. She could die. *He* could die.

I did this. This is my fault.

It wasn't until she heard the thin cry of her son that she felt any hope return.

"You have a son, May. He's beautiful!" Ollie whispered in her ear.

"Blood pressure is seventy over thirty, Doctor." The nurse's voice held a note of fear, and May thought for the briefest moment that perhaps she should still be afraid.

But her eyelids were heavy, leaden, and she was fading, from consciousness, from the world, the voices and sounds, the bark of the doctor as he called for a transfusion, all of it slipped away as the darkness rushed in to claim her.

When May's eyes opened again, the room was unfamiliar, dim, and with far less medical equipment. She realized they must have moved her to a standard room. At the far end of the room, she could see Ollie curled up on the couch, a blanket over her thin shoulders, fast asleep.

The rest of the room was empty. No bassinet.

He's supposed to be here with me.

She sat up and was halfway out of the bed before she gasped in pain. It wasn't loud, but it was enough to wake Ollie, who sat up with a start. "Oh honey, stay there. I'll come to you."

She hustled over to May's bedside as May gasped at the angry slash across her abdomen. The sight of it, the dark red, nearly black line sealed with a partially clear glue or gauze, made her feel ill and the pain was deep, aching. Ollie pressed the Call button, her eyes dark with concern.

The response was just as swift. The hospital was new, just like the rest of New Athens, and there were few occupants and plenty of staff on hand. A nurse appeared, her long, black hair pulled back in a side braid that fell over one shoulder and down her back. She had high cheekbones and a hawkish nose.

"Awake, I see. And no doubt needing something for the pain." She advanced with a syringe at the ready.

"No, I..." May held up one hand as if she could fend off the woman in her weakened, pain-riddled state. "I don't want them."

Ollie slipped a warm hand around May's cold one and said nothing, just squeezed her hand.

The nurse paused and exchanged a glance with Ollie.

"My baby. Where is he?"

"He's in the nursery right now, May," Ollie answered, but her tone betrayed her. There was something she wasn't saying. There was something wrong.

"It's best for all involved," the nurse said. Her tone sounded cheery, but there was no smile on her lips. "After all, Miss Denning, you just underwent major surgery and suffered significant blood loss. You need your rest." She moved again towards the IV bag.

"I don't want that. Please. I just want to see my baby."

"May." Ollie's tone was muted, her face drawn. "The TUPG authorities have moved to assume custody of your baby. Recent expansions to the International Recovery Act allow for this. They looked at your history, health, and drug use, and they are considering the placental abruption that you suffered directly related to your use of heroin. They are considering termination of parental rights, May."

"No! I didn't know, and when I did, I stopped!" May's eyes filled with tears. Her abdomen ached, and her heart felt like it would burst. She had come so far, felt happy, for the first time in a long time.

It was all for nothing. I shouldn't have hoped, shouldn't even have wanted to be a mother. What kind of mother could I be?

And yet, she wanted it so badly. She had dreamed of her son. Of what it would feel like to hold him in her arms, to watch him take his first steps. The thought of that being taken from her hurt worse than anything she could imagine.

She sagged into the bed, deflated and

devastated. They were going to take her son and there was nothing she could do about it.

"We will fight this, May. I will stand by your side and we will fight this together." Ollie squeezed her hand and reached for a nearby tissue box before turning to the nurse. "May has the right to see her son and to establish a parental bond until court convenes in this matter."

The nurse looked distinctly uncomfortable. "I'm following TUPG guidelines, Mrs. Duvall. I'm just doing my job."

Ollie stood up straight, and said in an even tone, "We have committed atrocities under the auspices of others just doing their jobs—I'm sure you don't wish to be lumped in with them. May can't run away from here; the girl can't even walk right now. She isn't a flight risk. And you know me, Asta, I would never let harm come to that innocent little boy. But as a licensed psychologist, I can tell you that May's recovery, and her infant's son's emotional well-being, are depending on you being human, and letting a mother see her son."

The woman crumbled in the face of Ollie's argument and she strode away, out of the room and down the corridor. Moments later, she reappeared with a bassinet on wheels, and May cried again as Asta gently placed the baby in her arms.

"Oh, Ollie. He's *perfect.*"

The older woman beamed, her own eyes sparkling with unshed tears. "He is indeed, my dear. He's perfect and healthy. They said he had a perfect score on the Apgar." She reached out and caressed his hand gently before she spoke to Asta.

"I will vouch personally for his safety here in the hospital room, Asta. And I'll duke it out with Doctor Hendricks in the morning."

Asta looked distinctly uncomfortable with this. "Ollie, I really don't think…"

"Asta, look at them. There is nothing more natural, and you have got to see that."

"Damn it, Ollie." The woman threw up her hands. "Fine, but you better make sure nothing happens. The social worker will be here tomorrow to pick him up and put him in emergency foster care until the court hearing. I'm already going to get an earful from Social Services on this one." She walked out, shaking her head, and closed the door firmly behind her.

Ollie watched her go, and then pulled a chair up next to May's bedside and leaned in close.

"May, do you think you can walk?"

"What?"

Ollie spoke softly. "They are going to take your child, May. Unless we get you out of here, tonight."

May felt her heart rate increase. "But Ollie, you said that they would schedule a court date, and, and…" Ollie met her eyes and slowly shook her head.

"May, honey, I've been watching the news. Everything is getting locked down. Everything, everyone. They're panicked about the rise in suicides, the infertility and sharply decreased birth rates, about the future of humanity. I've seen the measures they will pass in the next few weeks and they are… well, they're *Draconian*." She shot a glance toward the door and then dug into a bag she pulled from under the bed. "They have a list of non-conformers–drug use, any kind of neglect or abandonment, hell, if someone had an abortion–those are all grounds for removing a child and putting that child in the care of the TUPG, to be raised as the government sees fit."

She laid out a shirt and pants, a uniform, on May's legs. "I need you to get dressed in this. If you can walk, just two hundred feet, out that door at seven minutes past midnight, then I promise you, you won't ever lose your baby. But if you stay here, it won't go well for either of you."

"But you said…"

Ollie hugged her. "I lied, May. To get her out of the room. To give you this chance. There is a shift change in thirty minutes. You put this outfit on and then pull your hospital gown over it. You walk out when I tell you to. I'll be right behind with the baby."

"He's tagged, Ollie. So am I." May held up her wrist and they could both see the rainbow flash of the Identichip embedded in the hospital wristband. The baby's chip was there too, around his right wrist.

"I called in a favor. When you and I walk through that door, and down the hall, it won't register. We will cut them off once we get out of the hospital and on the road. I have a place outside of the city where no one will find you, May. You and your son will be safe and you will be together. If that is what you want, then I need you to get dressed now.”

May nodded. She handed her son to Ollie, who sighed with happiness as she held him in her arms.

“Have you decided what his name will be?”

May nodded, and winced as she slid off of the bed, wishing to hell she had accepted the pain meds. The action gave her a moment to turn away from Ollie and gather her panicked thoughts while she wrestled the pants on. The idea of fleeing from the hospital with her newborn son seemed insane and frightening and final

“I thought of Aaron, and Peter, but…” She pulled the shirt on, nearly passing out. She felt like they had pummeled her inside and out. “But I want it to be special, really special.”

Ollie waited for her to speak, and she fumbled with pulling this hospital gown back in position. “I, uh, I remembered all those walks we went on, outside of the hospital, at the edge of the forest. And I remember how my mom always used to take me on walks in the forest and talk about the old man of the forest and you said that the name Silas meant a man of the forest? I thought that would be a good name. Because Mom was, well, she was my mom, and she loved me and you, you seem to, I mean, I think of you like that. As a mom. I mean, I know you aren't my mom, but you cared enough to bring me to your home, and where would I be without you? I mean, when Lexie died, and you made sure there was a service and everything. So, I just thought, Silas, because it just fit."

May finished dressing, turned around, and saw Ollie's eyes filled with tears. They ran down her cheeks, and she did not wipe them away.

"Silas."

May blinked, suddenly scared that she had done something terribly wrong. "Yeah, I mean, is that okay? Did I say something wrong?"

Ollie managed a smile, which was at odds with the tears running down her cheeks. "No, May, you said nothing wrong. Quite the opposite." Her eyes tracked to the clock on the wall. "Back in bed, my dear, I'll drape another blanket around you. They will be back to check on you once more before shift change."

May did as Ollie instructed and as the older woman draped the blanket over her shoulders, May asked, "Ollie, how long did you know, that they would try to take Silas from me?"

"From the beginning, May. I saw where things were heading, but I wanted…" The older woman's breath caught, the tears still shining in her eyes. "I wanted for you to feel safe and loved and cared for. I had even found a midwife to handle the labor and delivery. To help get you out of New Athens. There are cults like No Future, and there are zealots who are taking away freedom under the guise of saving us from ourselves, and then there are people like me, who believe we must find a middle ground."

May thought about that for a moment. "So, there are others?"

"Yes. Ryan is one of them; he's waiting outside the hospital as we speak." The revelation made May's heart jump a little. She had liked Ryan before this, but now even more so.

"And someone on staff here? Someone in Tech?"

"Yes, his name is Samuel. He is like a son to me. He would say that I saved his life a few years back." Ollie smiled. "The truth is more that he found a reason to live.”

"Ollie, why did the name I chose make you cry?”

Ollie’s tears slid down her cheeks again, and she reached out and stroked Silas’ cheek. “Because I had a son named Silas once. He loved the forest. So will your Silas. We will all be safe there.”

Fire from Above

Earth
09.23.2100

Madeline tried to relax as the ultrasound tech spread the jelly over her still-flat stomach. It was warm, but Madeline hated being touched by anyone, especially strangers. Still, there was a damned good reason for it. The ultrasound could detect the positioning of the fetus and tell Madeline if she was indeed pregnant.

The teratogenic effects of the ESH virus evidenced early, although what they could actually see at just twelve days of pregnancy was questionable.

It will probably end in miscarriage, as the first two did. Don't get your hopes up.

It was simply the optics of it all. The entire world would see her on their vidscreens. See her doing her part, submitting to whatever IVF procedure was necessary to create life, to deal with the disappointment of her inevitable miscarriage, and to try again.

The polls showed an increase in her ratings, despite the Draconian measures that were still causing riots around the world. Many disagreed with her choices and her rulings, but her very public attempts to become a mother inspired a greater number.

Dinah Sterling, one of her advisors who Gary had often described as a consummate politician and a snake in the grass, had gushed over the spike in ratings. "Your re-election should be guaranteed at this rate, Madame President! Just imagine what you can do to save our world!"

Madeline's mouth twisted into a frown, and the tech paused. "Are you in any discomfort, Madame President? Should I give you a moment?"

He was young, perhaps mid-to-late twenties, and he was already balding. He had a nervous tic as well, one that caused one eye to squinch up at odd intervals. She wondered if he was nervous because he was dealing with her, the interim ruler of the TUPG, or if he was like this with everyone. She shook her head and beckoned him to continue.

Dinah Sterling was a brown-nosing suck-up, but she was also manipulative and dangerous. Shortly before her husband had contracted the ESH virus, he had shared his suspicions with Madeline that Dinah had inserted herself in an investigation that ended up bringing down a congressional representative who had snubbed her. She was vicious with anyone she perceived as a danger to her own little corner of power. And yet, in the days following Gary's death, Madeline had seen no way out of adding Dinah to the advisory council. Her connections were vast, and necessary, in the vacuum of power left.

"I can't see much yet, Madame President," the tech said, interrupting her train of thought. "But for now, everything looks as if there are two gestational sacs in place and developing."

Madeline always found it interesting *how* things were said. The tech had avoided any words like "normal" or "pregnancy," but that wasn't unusual in today's emotionally wrought territory. The doctor had implanted three fertilized embryos, and two had made it this far. Madeline had learned plenty in just a few months of trying. One thing she had learned was that the ultrasounds of today, compared with the ultrasounds of the earlier part of the century, were night and day different. The technology had improved by leaps and bounds.

The ultrasounds had dutifully recorded the tiny fetuses for her first two pregnancies. The detail had been good enough that she had stared at the images, wondering if these babies would look like her or like the great unknown, the male subject who had provided sperm. Each time, they had implanted her with three embryos. The first IVF treatment had yielded just one successful embryo that replicated successfully. That pregnancy had lasted nearly twelve weeks. The second IVF treatment had resulted in two embryos implanting themselves on the uterine wall, but one had disappeared by the end of the fourth week and the lone remaining embryo had lasted only three weeks after that. With this third round, the doctors had suggested a different donor, and Madeline was fine with it, even as the doctor dithered about, concerned a different ethnicity might put her off. She couldn't care less if the sperm donor was purple-skinned. The picture of the donor, with his rich chocolate-brown skin and bright white teeth, made her smile in return, a rare thing these days. He had fathered five successful pregnancies since the ESH outbreak. Four had given birth, and one was due any day.

A baby was a baby, and it was the optics that mattered more to Madeline than the color of the skin. Although Dinah, upon hearing about it from God knows where, just had to mention that having a child of "African lineage" would improve the optics for the "voters of color."

Whether Dinah was right, the idea of Madeline's future child's skin color improving Madeline's chances of re-election struck a discordant chord inside of Madeline. She soothed it away with the thought…

This pregnancy will end in miscarriage, just as the first two did.

A soft knock at the door to her suite came as the ultrasound technician was wiping the jelly off of Madeline's stomach. Madeline glanced at the clock. It had to be Isa. The ultrasound had taken longer to conduct than expected, and Isa Netanyahu had requested time in her schedule today to present his findings. Madeline had done her best to put the thought out of her mind of an extinction-level event hurtling towards Earth through space. In fact, she had managed to not think about it for the last three or four days, until the message had popped up informing her that her morning meetings were being altered to fit him in.

She took the towel from the ultrasound technician and flapped a hand in his direction. The room she was in was her own medical suite, complete with all the machinery and equipment necessary for her should she require bed rest, additional imaging, and much more. He exited through a different door, scuttling away now that his job was complete.

Madeline sat up, slipped her tunic down, and cleared her throat. "Come in."

Isa entered, waiting for her to leave the medical suite and walk into the small conference room and sit down. He bowed slightly. "Madame President." The look on his face said it all, and Madeline could feel her anxiety rise. She brought one perfectly manicured hand up to her mouth, a habit she had worked so hard to eradicate resurging in her. She wanted to tear each nail with her teeth down to the quick. Instead, she set her hand on her lap and gave Isa a nod. "Good morning, Isa. You have reviewed all the data?"

He nodded, sighed, and slid into the seat across from her. "I wish I had better news, ma'am, but I don't. I didn't just rely on the data from Mars; I assembled an independent team to look at the incoming object, run through different scenarios, and they all point to the same answer." He ran his hand through his hair, tugging at the sides, his hands curling into fists. "The largest part of the KBO known as Ultima Thule, well, multiple pieces actually, but most of it comprising a section that is approximately 14 kilometers in diameter, is without question on a collision course with Earth. At present, it is impossible to deduce the angle of impact, but with something as large as this, it will cause devastating damage no matter where it lands. What we don't know, and won't until approximately six months before impact, is at what angle it will approach."

Madeline frowned, confused. "What do you mean by *angle*?"

"I've prepared a presentation to better explain it." Isa pressed a button on his tablet. The overhead screen sprang to life with an image of an asteroid slamming into the Earth. It showed a troupe of brontosaurus staring at an incoming ball of light.

"The asteroid that wiped out the dinosaurs was a one in a million fluke," Isa said, and clicked to a graph. "It came in at a 60-degree angle to Earth. This was literally the *worst* angle. It ended up tossing debris hundreds of miles into the air, rocking the planet on its axis, and causing an impact event that carried so much force it obliterated everything within 1,000 miles of impact. The wave of fire that followed caused the dinosaurs' blood to boil, and researchers estimate the debris blocked the sun for at least eighteen months and likely up to ten years, causing a mini-Ice Age."

He clicked through the slides as they showed first an invisible ring of destruction, then another of fire, and finally the last. The image of Earth from space, plunged into a new Ice Age and covered in ice.

"And there's no way to determine what angle it will impact?" Madeline asked, her stomach churning.

Isa shook his head. "No, not until it is much closer."

"And you are absolutely sure that it will impact Earth?"

"Yes, ma'am, the numbers don't lie." His eyes were red-rimmed, and he looked exhausted. "I've gone through them, I've had three separate teams go through them, and every single one has come to the same conclusion. Azrael *will* impact Earth. And when it does, it will rain fire from above, the likes of which make the ESH virus feel like a walk in the park."

"Azrael?" Madeline asked, arching an eyebrow.

Isa met her gaze. "Azrael is the angel of death in Islam and some Jewish traditions. He transports the souls of the deceased after death." He shrugged. "I suppose if you were to split hairs, Azrael wouldn't be the best choice. He doesn't *bring* death; he simply is the vehicle for those already deceased."

Madeline closed her eyes. The weight of the world was upon her shoulders. The responsibilities felt so heavy, and she could feel a wave of exhaustion rising and pulling her out to sea. Sometimes it felt as if she and the other survivors were the ones who were dead. Their bodies and minds simply hadn't figured it out yet, and so they kept going.

"We have to put everything we have into escaping Earth, Madame President," Isa said, and she could hear his fear. "We must build as many ships as possible, put as many in Cryo as possible, and get off of the surface of Earth before Azrael arrives. Nowhere on Earth is safe."

Nowhere was safe. That was all too clear after the virus escaped Earth and decimated the lunar colony, the three space stations, and Mars. Yet somehow, she had to save as many people as possible. Suicide rates were already at unheard-of highs, and now this? What would happen when the survivors learned of the incoming threat? How many of them would choose suicide rather than fight to survive yet another devastating future?

Madeline's eyes flew open. "Tell no one. I need all the people who took part in the fact-checking held until we can devise a strategy for dealing with this. Tell me you can do that for me, Isa."

She grasped his hand, holding on in desperation. She felt ill. They had all lost so much.

"Ma'am?"

"We need a plan in place before we can release this information. A *plan*, Isa. Otherwise, it will be a catastrophe. As it is, the suicide rate has risen to 500 times the levels pre-ESH. Five hundred times, Isa! Think about that!" The thought of so many choosing death rather than face the reality of their new, fractured world was unsettling. "If we don't have a plan ready for them, how many will die out of sheer hopelessness?"

"Ma'am, we won't be able to save *most* of the people left on Earth."

"That's just four years from now, Isa. How many children could be born between now and then who might not get the chance to live?"

"Ma'am, there are nearly 14 million people left on Earth, over 3.3 million of which are children. We can't even save all of them. It would leave us with a population of entirely children, with no moral compass or guide."

"We test them. All of them. Figure out which ones are more likely to reproduce successfully. We save the Uninfected Persons, send them to Zarmina's World.

We find a way, Isa!" Madeline was trembling, her emotions already frayed from the pregnancy, from the news of the asteroid. She set her jaw and stared at the man, her height matching his. They stood eye to eye. "You shut up anyone on the teams that verified this info, keep it quiet, and work on a plan that will save as many lives as possible. You will do this, and when we have a solid plan in place, we will tell the world."

She turned on her heel and then walked away from him before she lost all semblance of control.

The Truth

Earth
11.01.2100

The newly formed committee had many suggestions for destinations for the hundreds of thousands of refugees to escape to. They were in luck. For once, there was a plethora of spacecraft to choose from. The ESH virus had hit in the middle of a renaissance of space travel. There were at least two dozen spacecraft already in use and several large spacecraft in various stages of being readied for extra-solar missions. And the committee, formed in secret, had been working hard to narrow down the possibilities. They linked in to Madeline's chambers now via her tablet.

"What do we know about Kepler?" Patrick Gaines, who looked to be in his late twenties and had a shock of orange-red hair and freckles, flicked through his notes and responded.

"Um, Kepler 438b, yes, the D.O.V.E. probes that were deployed are still transmitting information, but we have learned a great deal. Gravity isn't a problem, but the average temperature is 3 degrees Celsius, and that means domes."

"Colonists will live in domes on Mars for the next three centuries; it's doable. Add it to the list."

"Ma'am, the Kepler 438 system is nearly four hundred and seventy-three light years away. It will take one hundred and forty-two light years, well, one hundred fifteen with the improvements to the warp drive, to get there!"

"Keep it on the list. We have to keep our options open."

Patrick nodded, his fingers dancing on the touchscreen.

"Kepler 62." His fingers froze, and he looked up at Madeline. "The colony ship was over 75% complete when the virus hit. Are we going ahead with that mission?"

Madeline shook her head and rubbed her eyes. "We need to be examining all destinations, but so much could go wrong on a generational ship. Especially with such a distance, it will take nearly four hundred and fifty years for them to arrive. *If* they arrive at all!"

One of the younger members of the team spoke. "Perhaps Tau Ceti f?"

Patrick shook his head. "The presence of a far higher magnesium and silicone ratio has confirmed that there are far higher levels of ferropericlase."

"In layperson's terms, if you please," Madeline asked, wearily.

"Sorry, Madame President." He chewed on his lip and then said, "Ferropericlase is less viscous, or resistant to flowing. The hot, yet solid, mantle rock would flow more easily."

"And this means what?" Madeline pressed, trying and failing to modulate the frustration out of her voice.

"Um, that the surface is quite unstable, Madame President. Gliese 581g, er, Zarmina's World, has several massive volcanoes. And here on Earth, well the Yellowstone super-caldera has shown us just how bad it can be with its partial eruption in late 2072, but Tau Ceti f? It would be a challenge to find an area that didn't have volcanic activity. The D.O.V.E.

probes registered tectonic activity that was off the charts and actually captured the formation of two new volcanoes before we lost several probes to eruptions."

"And we already learned that Tau Ceti e is far too hot *and* the gravity would be nearly twice Earth's," Madeline said, her fingers tapping the report. "The heat is one thing, but the gravity would be too much for long-term colonization goals."

Patrick nodded. "Unless we are willing to bioengineer humans, something that is decades away, if even acceptable."

As far as Patrick knew, those words were absolutely true. Genetic tinkering, after learning that the ESH virus was bio-engineered, had become an unacceptable option for most of Earth's population. But it wasn't decades away. It was here, now. And she had okayed Aaronson and Brooks to tinker with eighteen human fetuses and then gave the go-ahead for hundreds more bio-engineered humans. The decision had appealed to her at the moment, but now? The thought of even allowing research in that field was political suicide. Perhaps she should shut it down.

Madeline stared at the touchscreen, but her mind was elsewhere. Silence filled the room, and minutes ticked by.

Patrick gently brought her back. "Ma'am?"

"Sorry, Patrick, where were we?"

"Shall we cross Tau Ceti off of the list?"

"Yes."

His fingers danced again, clicking and typing. "That brings us to Trappist One, just forty light years away. I have the final D.O.V.E. reports assembled and collated."

Madeline perked up. "I've been waiting for this!"

"The initial fears that the three Trappist planets, planets e, f and g, with the best Earth-like environs had all lost their atmospheres. This was true of planets f and g, but with Planet e, thanks to the D.O.V.E. probes, it is the opposite."

He tapped on the tablet in his hand and the screen on the wall displayed raw footage of a probe sliding through thick clouds before breaking through into a world that looked quite similar to their own.

"This is Planet e, the smallest of the three. The planets are all tidally locked, and this planet is no exception. It is a rocky planet, and as you can see from the D.O.V.E. probes, it has an atmosphere, water in liquid form, and land masses over approximately one-third of the planet. The marine life is, erm, robust."

The dense clouds obscured the sun overhead, and the seas roiled with life. A large, long tentacle that moved impossibly fast interrupted the image of a large, bulbous creature floating on the surface. It had come close, too close. Madeline felt her body jerk away in response.

"The planet has multiple life forms that may prove problematic and certainly hostile. Several, like the one just shown, appear to be massive, bigger than the largest marine mammals we have here on Earth. The one we saw was approximately 52 meters long and exceeds 80 meters, if you count the reach of those tentacles. Compare that to the largest Earth life form, the blue whale which measures in at 27 meters. All the larger life forms appear to be predatory, or at least aggressive. We lost one-third of the probes to attacks. We would need to ensure the colonists had adequate protection, shielding, and defensive weapons if settling on Planet e. This would significantly affect the number of colonists we could carry since the shielding alone would take up far too much space. And then there are nutritional supplements that would need to be imported with them, as they do not exist in any known quantities on the planet."

"I see." Madeline's stomach churned.

"Madame President, we face a plethora of unknowns here. Zarmina's World is the least among them. The Calypso is a year away from dropping out of warp and just over three years away from arrival. It will be at least a few months *after* Azrael's impact before we will know if all is well on Zarmina's World and that it is truly habitable." Patrick twisted the ring on his left hand around and around. "I think we are better off focusing on what we have and know—the space stations, the Lunar colony, and the Mars colony. We know Cryo is safe and effective, and with the advances in solar collector technology, we can harvest adequate power, even on Mars, to power large numbers of Cryo units. We could take the chance and put at least one-quarter of the Uninfected Persons on a ship bound for Zarmina's World and park another one-quarter to one-half on the Moon, at least until we know more."

Isa spoke then. "I agree with Patrick's assessment, ma'am. And I think it is time for us to tell the world the truth. Come what may. They deserve that much from us.”

Madeline closed her eyes, tried to will a sense of calm through her body. They had no suitable solutions, but Patrick and Isa were right.

“Fine.” Her words sounded clipped. “We turn all exploration ships into Cryo facilities. Pack as many people as possible onto them. Re-open the Lunar Colony, send ships to Mars, and prep others for a trip to Zarmina’s World if we get a confirmation on the successful establishment of the first colony. Patrick, I’d like for you to head that task force.”

She stood up, and she felt heavy, as if the entire world, or what they had left of it, rested on her shoulders. “Isa, schedule a press conference for tomorrow. It’s time to tell the world.”

She couldn’t bear to eat breakfast the next morning, despite the array of choices her chef provided. Part of it was the tiny creature still growing in her womb, although she held little hope in that endeavor. The first two losses had lessened her expectations considerably. At six weeks, her stomach roiled each morning, and she was miserably ill until mid-morning. Of all of their scientific advances, morning sickness was still an issue.

Madeline rested a hand on her tiny baby bump. So small, so delicate, so easily lost. This is what the new world was—loss and more loss—as if the hits would never stop coming. She forced down three bites of egg, cooked to perfection, just as she preferred, the rich flavors of herbs registering but bringing her little joy.

"Toast, ma'am?" Aiden appeared at her side. "Or crackers? My wife always preferred the salted crackers when she, well…" His voice died away.

Madeline pointed to the seat next to her. "Please, sit down. And good morning."

Aiden managed a smile as he took his seat. "I have the notes you asked for, ma'am."

Her tablet pinged. A file, along with a virtual stack of index cards with brief descriptive bullet points, appeared on the screen. Madeline pushed a bowl of fruit towards him and reached for a piece of toast, fighting the nausea she felt. The bites of egg roiled about in her otherwise empty stomach.

"Thank you, Aiden." She scanned the

notes. "Perfect. It will keep me on track. Try the blackberries. Chef told me they just came in this morning. They are my favorite, but right now the thought of tasting them sets off my gag reflex."

Aiden reached for a small plate and loaded it with fruit. "My wife," his voice caught, "Allison, she was miserable with morning sickness with each of our children. Believe it or not, her diet for the first three months of pregnancy was comprised of salted crackers and peanut butter. Thank God for vitamin supplements."

"I think I would have given up after one," Madeline said. Her insides churning, she pushed the plate away, staring at the fruit with longing and frustration.

Aiden's smile was brief, bittersweet. "Allison loved being pregnant; we ended up with a religious exemption and we had five, three boys and two girls." He looked away. "None of them inherited my AB negative blood, however."

She reached out, placed her hand on his. She had lost Gary and her sister, as well as her sister's children. Her parents too, as were Gary's. "I am so sorry, Aiden."

He nodded and pulled away, spearing one of the plump blackberries with his fork.

He ate it, his eyes distant.

"Do you think it's worth the effort?" she asked. "These laws and measures? I wonder, sometimes, what Gary would think of all of my machinations, desperate to save humanity. What would he think of Azrael, coming to end us, the last humans on Earth? What do you think your God thinks of it all?"

Aiden coughed and reached for some water. "The religious exemption was for Allison; she was the believer in our family." He shook his head, coughed again.

"I had assumed you were a practicing Jew."

"No, I…" He coughed again, his face turning red, his voice rasping. "I was an agnostic, and now…an athe…ist." He wheezed now, his fingers pulling at the top button of his pressed white shirt as he continued to cough.

Madeline stood, alarmed. "Aiden, are you alright?"

The man shook his head, still coughing, his face now darkening to a shade of purple. His wheezing was more pronounced, labored. "No, I…" Another fit of coughing and he was on his feet, wobbling, his skin flushed to his hairline and spreading down his neck along with white blotches. His mouth opened and foam gushed out; his eyes were bloodshot and bulging.

She hit the communicator badge on her chest so hard her hand stung. "I need medical help in my quarters immediately!"

Aiden wobbled again, swaying as he coughed and gasped for air, his fingers scrabbling at his throat, the veins in his throat standing out, a look of terror etched on his face. The door slammed open and an entire team of people poured through her guards and medical personnel.

"He just began coughing and struggling to breathe!" She felt her security detail's hands closing on her arms and she wanted to resist, to stay. Aiden had been at her side from the beginning, had served Gary when he was president, and had mourned his wife and five children in silence, never once mentioning them until now. How could she know so little about him?

Aiden collapsed then, and the medical personnel swarmed around him as Madeline's detail pulled her to the safety of her inner chambers.

"It's protocol, Madame President, until we know what happened," Adam, a slim man with a grip of steel, said. The double doors that led from her bedroom were now closed, but she could hear them working on Aiden. It sounded as if his airway had closed and they were fighting to get a breathing tube down so that he could breathe.

Adam kept a hand on her, as if he feared she would bolt through the doors to be back at Aiden's side. And she wanted to, that was for sure, but the questions were already creeping up, and that stopped her in her tracks. What had caused Aiden's coughing? His inability to breathe? It had come out of nowhere.

An hour later, nerves frayed, her heart heavy, Madeline stood before a host of reporters and cameras, their lights bright and harsh against her pale, freckled skin. Whatever she did, she couldn't let them see her afraid. Whoever had poisoned the blackberries had intended it for her, not Aiden, and she had fought hard for her protective detail to step aside and let her conduct the press conference. She would not live her life in fear, and she would show those who had meant her harm that she was alive and healthy, despite them. Her hand strayed to her belly, to the tiny life that had rooted there and still survived, at least for now.

"Citizens of the Terran United Planetary Government, I come to you with grave news. I will not sugarcoat it, but I urge you to have faith, whether it is in God or our ability as humans to survive insurmountable odds, to believe that we will find a way past this new threat as well."

She stopped and took a sip of water, trying not to remember how Aiden's face had looked as he fell to the floor. She needed to focus, to give the world hope in the face of terrifying news.

"As if we have not all suffered enough from the loss of loved ones from the ESH virus, we now find danger of an entirely different kind hurtling towards us. A chance collision in the blackness of space, over 400 billion kilometers away in the Kuiper Belt, has fractured a Kuiper Belt Object known as Ultima Thule. One large piece, possibly as large as 14 kilometers in diameter, is heading towards Earth. I received confirmation yesterday that it is on a collision course with Earth. It brings with it a destructive power that could mean the end of civilization, the end of *us* if we do not take action, *now*, and without delay.”

The cameras clicked away, and Madeline paused, took a breath.

“It is far away, billions of kilometers, but it is coming. And we must do everything we can to prepare for its arrival. We have just under four years to find a way to survive the impact, and I promise you, we *will*. As I speak, a team is being assembled to combat this threat. We hope to fracture it or shift its course in order to mitigate or avoid impact entirely. But that isn’t enough. We must prepare for impact.”

She took another sip of water. The glass was cold. She struggled to swallow; her throat tight.

“This asteroid has the power to destroy life on this planet. But we *can* survive, and we *will* survive. By both digging down, under the ground in shelters of stone, and lifting ourselves up and out of Earth’s gravity to the Moon, space stations, Mars, and Zarmina’s World.”

“If the ESH virus and this asteroid have taught us anything, it is this: We can no longer limit ourselves to Earth. Humanity must expand to other worlds, other solar systems, and we must travel through the darkest reaches of space. We must decentralize, adapt to different biospheres and environments in order to never face the threat of extinction again."

The press murmured, the cameras flashed, and she could feel their fear, their anxiety rising. Whatever they had expected she would say here at this press conference, it hadn't been this.

"We must set aside our differences. We must stop rioting or arguing over the resolutions passed, and focus on working together to create the life ships and Cryo units that will save as many of us as possible. We must dig into the mountains and launch ourselves into space. We must *survive*."

Madeline felt her voice gather power, certainty, as she stood before the cameras, before her people, her world.

"Humanity, and its survival in the years to come—that's all that matters right now. Each of you, *each of you*, carries within the capacity to save untold hundreds, even thousands of your fellow TUPG citizens. This is not the end of our world, it is the beginning of a challenge, a fight for the survival of our species. Will you rise with me? Will you meet this challenge?" Her voice rang across the room. "Set despair and fear aside. It has no place here. Instead, step forward, and together we will forge our survival in the fire to come."

She turned on her heel and walked away then, even as the reporters, shocked by the news, found their voices and called after her. She could hear their frenzied questions as the door quietly shut behind her.

"Adam? Is Aiden…" She looked up into her bodyguard's eyes. He shook his head.

"I'm sorry, ma'am, he passed just as the press conference began."

Her heart ached, even as her anger rose. Aiden had been a good man. He hadn't deserved this end.

"Poison?"

Adam shrugged. "It had all the signs of it, but they are conducting an autopsy as we speak. They are also testing the fresh fruit and investigating the origin point."

Madeline closed her eyes; she could feel a headache gathering strength. "I need to rest. Ask Jack to clear my schedule for the next two hours. I don't care who calls me, they will have to wait."

Adam nodded. "They have readied your emergency quarters downstairs."

Madeline blinked in surprise. "Why?"

"Protocol, ma'am. We have a suited team in your quarters taking samples of everything. Then they will disinfect and sterilize the suite. Meanwhile, you will stay in the bunker."

She blew out a deep breath, her headache ratcheting up to a steady, painful thump. "Right. Lead the way."

Sleep did not come right away. Instead, Madeline endured a thorough examination from her doctor, who took skin scrapings, blood samples, and more.

"So far, so good," she said, after using the ultrasound to find the fetal heartbeat. "I'll give you something for that headache that will be safe for the baby."

Madeline's doctor was a tall Amazon of a woman with pale-blue eyes and black hair liberally threaded with silver. Madeline, used to towering over other women and half of the men, felt small in comparison.

"Thank you."

The woman paused. "Aiden was a good man. He will be missed."

Madeline nodded, her throat closing, her eyes burning. She heard, rather than felt, the injector whoosh, a dose of medication delivered painlessly to her shoulder. Within seconds, she could feel her body relax and the pain from her head fade. She relaxed into the bed. The room in this suite was identical to the one ten floors above, but she could still tell the difference. It smelled slightly different. Not bad, just…different.

Like a heavy wave, exhaustion rolled through her, and Madeline closed her eyes. She needed an hour or two to just process it all. To surrender to sleep and not have to picture those last moments with Aiden and his fear-twisted face as he struggled to breathe.

Missing You

Earth
01.29.2101

"Come to New York. I just checked flights and there's one leaving New Munich tomorrow at ten a.m." Eaton smiled up at her, his handsome face framed in light. He was standing on the roof of his building, the stars arrayed in the night sky behind him. "I miss you. And its Chinese New Year, Ma is going all out."

Jia sighed, a cup of coffee in her hand. Outside, the world was still dark. But she had woken up early, missing Eaton and New York, and even Ma Ngai, as Eaton's mother had insisted Jia call her.

It had been three weeks since they left, but it had felt like forever.

Outside, the world was blanketed in snow and it was bitterly cold. Not that New

York was much better, but at least the cold had helped with the smell. The Met, as well as the private art collections of a half-dozen billionaires, were now empty, and soon the rotting city would be abandoned completely.

"How is Ma?" Jia asked, changing the subject. She couldn't just jump on a plane; she wasn't rich, and she certainly wasn't important, not like Willem.

"She's busy telling me I need to move to New Munich," Eaton said, rolling his eyes. "And she still refuses to leave New York."

"I hear that Genesis and New Athens are both hopping. She could open a restaurant there and feed everyone her amazing food."

"Why don't you come here and tell her yourself? She won't listen to me, but I bet she'd listen to you." Eaton grinned, and then stifled a yawn. "Come on, come back to New York." He wiggled his eyebrows. "Ma will make you char siu and I'll show you the Empire State Building."

It was Jia's turn to roll her eyes. "I've seen it…twice. Both times were with you."

A wide grin spread over his face. "I remember."

Jia blushed. A crusty old caretaker

caught them in a compromising position in the elevator the second time through.

Eaton had unlocked a playful side of her, one she hadn't allowed herself to indulge in before. She had found it both exciting and shocking, and struggled with the side of her that was obedient and studious. She wanted Willem to be proud of her, but she also loved exploring the crumbling, rotting city with Eaton by her side. Their first tentative kiss had quickly led to far more delightful experiences. The past seven months had been full of joy, adventure, and love.

She clutched the coffee mug to her chest and took a sip. She felt torn. She wanted to spend time with Willem, but she also missed Eaton. The thought of spending Chinese New Year with him was especially appealing, and she knew Lisa Ngai was hard at work cooking and baking for the event.

Chinese New Year was an important holiday, after all. She had cleaned the house here in the woods outside of New Munich, almost on automatic. It was what one did, after all. She had swept away any ill fortune in order to make way for any incoming good luck, although she was hard-pressed to imagine how life could be any better than it already was.

She had Willem. Having a true father-daughter relationship for the first time in her life was something that gave her a reason to smile every day. And then there was Eaton, who she had fallen hard for. She had Ma Ngai ready to fill her full of good food and cluck over her anytime she visited, and art surrounded her. Of all the things that could have happened to her, and all the losses behind her, it was all an outcome more beautiful than she could have imagined.

Not even the shocking news of the asteroid hurtling towards them dimmed her happiness. She had years left to worry about it and right now, on the cusp of a new year, she felt only happiness and contentment.

Jia sipped again from her cup, letting the silence wash over her. Eaton was good with silence, something she appreciated. Most of the Americans she had encountered when she arrived in New Athens felt compelled to fill the silence, but not Eaton. Their time together, in person or through the long-distance video calls, had been filled with long silences. He waited, one eyebrow raised, as she sipped at her coffee.

"Say you will come for the Chinese New Year."

The floorboards creaked, and Jia turned to see Willem shuffle into the living room, yawning. Like Jia, Willem rose early, often before the dawn. He leaned down and kissed the top of her head.

"Good morning, Jia," Willem croaked. "Eaton."

"Guten morgen, Papa," Jia answered.

"Guten morgen, Herr Grunsfeld," Eaton said, grinning.

"I think we can make the drive to New Munich in time," Willem said, settling himself in his favorite armchair, a cup of black coffee in his hands. "I heard the roads being cleared last night, and there's only been a few flurries of snow since midnight. I'm happy to drive you."

"Papa, are you sure?" Jia nibbled on a fingernail. "I don't want to be a bother."

"Bother? The last thing you are is a bother, daughter. You need to get out, do something fun, not waste your time with an old man like me," Willem scoffed.

Jia laughed. "Papa, you are not old."

Willem groaned theatrically as he put his

feet up on the thick wood coffee table. He was wearing the thick wool slippers she had gifted him for Christmas. "So *old*." He groaned again.

They all laughed.

"I'll schedule the flight and send you the information, Eaton," Willem said, "But only if you promise to ask Mrs. Ngai to send some of her char siu back with Jia when she returns. I need her back by the end of next week for an art showing." He frowned, then sat forward. "In fact, why don't you come here as well, Eaton? And bring Mrs. Ngai, I think she would enjoy this exhibit. I'll arrange the tickets for all of you. Once your mother sees the sparkling city of New Munich she may never wish to leave."

Eaton's eyes sparkled. "I'll do that, Herr Grunsfeld, thank you!"

Later that day, Jia felt as if she had left one home, only to arrive at another.

Spending Chinese New Year with Eaton and Ma Ngai was better than the childhood celebrations at home in Guiyang. No brooding father scowling from his chair in the corner, no overbearing Mama scolding her when Jia didn't put the tablecloth on just right. She felt a pang of guilt at the thought, and sadness as well. Mama had turned away from happiness so long ago, that she wouldn't have accepted it even if it had been within her grasp.

Lisa Ngai was the de facto leader of the last Chinese Americans in the city and she had gathered them to her, her vivacious energy drawing them in. The mood was joyous, and Lisa Ngai's restaurant was filled with red, the color of good fortune. There were banners on the walls that featured intricate paintings and poetry. Festive scrolls littered the long dining table, a dozen smaller tables were shoved together, and paper lanterns hung from the ceiling.

Jia's face hurt from smiling so much, and her throat was sore the following day from talking to so many people. Even a petite young Asian-American girl who kept glancing at Jia and Eaton, watching the two of them together with a combination of longing and envy, did nothing to dampen her mood.

Ma Ngai stuffed them with jiaozi and niangao and a dozen different spring rolls and fish entrees. Jia was uncomfortably full as they climbed up to the top of the building where Eaton had set up the roof for the Lantern Festival. Normally, it would be in the streets, but the streets of New York were flooded. Instead, dozens of lanterns had been lit, lighting up the large, flat roof with candlelight that flickered magically in the night air.

Jia felt in her pocket for the envelope stuffed full of "lucky money" that Ma Ngai had pressed into her hand. She sighed and felt Eaton slide his arms around her. He nuzzled her neck, which tickled, and she giggled and squirmed. His grip tightened.

"Wait, the best is yet to come," he breathed in her ear. Seconds later, the shrill screech of the first of the firecrackers sounded as it shot into the sky and exploded in a bright bloom of red and gold. Voices cheered. There were at least twenty of them on the roof, laughing as each new explosion lit up the sky with color. Red with gold sparkles. Blue, green, even silver. Beyond that was the brilliant night sky so full of stars. Jia leaned back into Eaton's arms, feeling safe, loved, and happier than she had felt in a long time.

"I love the stars," Eaton whispered in her ear, and his warm breath tickled. "We never saw them before. Too much light pollution, I guess."

The city was enormous, but it was also mostly dark now. An empty city filled with relics of the past did not need light, after all. New York, with its hundreds of thousands of buildings filled with corpses, was decaying swifter than anyone could have imagined. Already buildings were capsizing thanks to the floodwaters. It sometimes felt to Jia as if the city itself knew it was doomed. That without people, it was no longer a necessary thing. She couldn't help wondering what the place would look like in another ten years, or twenty, as the floodwaters continued to wreak havoc.

Then again, she thought, *will any of us even be here in ten more years? Or twenty?*

Her thoughts strayed to the threat of the asteroid, still years away from them, but a grave danger to the fate of their world. Nothing was for certain. Not their world, nor their survival, not even the ability to have children any longer.

She pulled Eaton even closer. Here, in his arms, this is where she wanted to be. Here, at this moment, she was happy. The rest would work itself out, somehow, some way.

A Mother in Name Only

Earth
06.08.2101

It felt rather anti-climactic–these past thirteen months of failure after failure and then walking on eggshells through her first, second, even her third trimester. The baby she had fought so hard to keep in her womb was finally here, and Madeline felt nothing.

No connection, no rush of endorphins filling her with love, no reaction when Ireti cried, nothing. The girl wriggled in her crib, her eyes a startling blue in her milk-chocolate skin. She held Madeline's gaze and cooed. Was she smiling at her? Or was it simply gas?

Madeline couldn't remember at what age that changed. She knew almost nothing about babies past a few awkward moments holding her sister's babies. Jacqueline would have been able to tell her exactly when the genuine smiles began. But her older sister was gone, and Madeline couldn't ask her. She felt foolish asking anyone else.

Jacqueline had understood her more than their parents had. She would have known how unprepared Madeline was for motherhood. She imagined her sister swooping in and gathering this tiny baby in her arms. She had always known just what to do with little ones, instantly mothering them and calming them. Madeline, instead, held them stiffly, sure that at any moment they would begin screaming, which they usually did.

During her pregnancy, which only became real to her in the second trimester as she felt the baby move inside of her, she had wondered if Ireti would be different. Would her own child have a connection to her outside of the womb? Would she know Madeline was her mother? Would there be a bond between them?

So far, it hadn't happened. Ireti was nearly a month old now, and there had been nothing but wails that irritated Madeline, similar to nails on a chalkboard. When Ireti cried, Madeline's skin would prickle, her hairs standing on end. It was unpleasant, and her first instinct was to thrust the child into anyone else's arms but hers and run in the opposite direction. It felt like a fight against her nature to stand there and make the inane soothing noises as her infant's distress climbed exponentially.

Soon now, Ireti would begin to fuss and Madeline would step back and allow the nanny on duty to swoop in. Thank goodness Madeline's small army of advisers had intervened in the first week after Ireti's birth and suggested a milk bank and a handpicked group of nannies, guaranteed to serve Ireti's every need.

Running a world was no slight matter, and as president of the Terran United Planetary Government, Madeline Chen had her hands full. She was lucky to get six hours of sleep without an emergency erupting somewhere around the globe. From El Niño-spawned wildfires in California to the newest drought in Ethiopia, it all landed on her doorstep.

Caring for an infant was not something

she had experience with or any interest in. Just because she had done what over 90% of childbearing virus positive women could *not* do—carry a child to term—it didn't change the fact that Madeline was a mother in name only.

The three miscarriages that had preceded her successful pregnancy were nothing now. It was a drop in the bucket, par for the course, a fact that her medical adviser and personal physician had reminded her of last week when inquiring if she would consider trying another round of in-vitro fertilization.

As if bearing one child was not enough of an incentive for my fellow survivors. I'm not a brood mare, I have a planet to save!

One of the four nannies assigned to her stood just feet away, waiting for a signal from Madeline, or the slightest peep of distress from Ireti herself, to scoop up the infant and give her all the love that Madeline could not bring herself to give.

The virus left fourteen million souls on Earth. Of those, nearly one million were UPs, Uninfected Persons, guarded carefully against the possibility of infection from the ESH virus. The rest of the population, all ESH-positive survivors, were quickly becoming desperate.

Children are our immortality. Without them, my people are lost.

The high rate of infertility, miscarriage, and fetal death had driven the suicide rate sky-high even before the news of the massive asteroid, and now they were seeing suicide rates skyrocket past the 500 times pre-ESH levels.

Ireti ceased her cooing. Sensing no response from her mother, the infant's face wrinkled, her mouth puckering as if she had tasted a lemon. And slowly, taking her time, a robust wail finally issued forth.

The nanny darted forward, a look of apology on her face as she stepped up to the crib and leaned in, a wordless song on her lips as she scooped up the tiny creature into her arms.

"There, there, little one!"

The infant's arms waved, her back arched, and she yowled theatrically, as if it were her calling, something to embrace. Madeline watched dispassionately. Not that she didn't *like* the baby, this life form that shared half of her DNA. It was that she just had limited experience, only her nephews and nieces, to practice on. She had never babysat, never interacted with a smaller child, except in those rare visits home to see her family. There, Jacqueline's children had grown up overnight, transitioning from squalling babies to curious children and the eldest in their teens before they were felled by the virus.

Her parents had groomed Madeline to step onto an international stage—and she couldn't remember that stage ever having included plans for the next generation. For Madeline—raised to seek power, understand political machinations, and blend in seamlessly in the higher circles of government—children were… confusing.

"Would you like to hold her, Madame President?" the nanny asked, and Madeline struggled to remember her name.

"No, not now, thank you…"

"Maureen, ma'am."

"Yes, of course. My apologies, Maureen."

"Not at all, Madame President. You are busy, after all."

Ireti calmed in the woman's arms, nestling close against the woman's ample chest.

"She likes you; I think."

"Babies love being held, and I think I could hold her all day long." Maureen sighed, moving up and down in a rocking, soothing motion. The baby hiccupped and Madeline smelled the sour milk before she saw it. She moved back, trying to not let her distaste show, but she could see that the nanny noticed. A tiny frown passed across the woman's face and disappeared.

"She has such a beautiful name, Madame President. What does it mean?"

"It's Yoruba for 'hope'," Madeline answered, trying not to breathe through her nose.

Maureen smiled widely, patting the baby who had soiled her shirt, seemingly without a care in the world. "So appropriate! Where is Yoruba?"

"It's a who. An ethnic group of Nigerians. Ireti's sperm donor was a Yoruba."

"Well, it's lovely."

As if she could sense Madeline's discomfort, she turned and checked the clock. "I imagine Ireti will be ready for a bottle and a quick change right about now. Do you mind?"

Madeline gave a wave. "Carry on. I'll be busy for the rest of the day in meetings. I leave her in your capable hands."

The day passed as most of them did, in a frenzied rush of meetings with advisers, reports, and policymaking. Madeline loved it. When Gary had been president of the Reformed United States, she had been stuck firmly on the sidelines, relegated to choosing china patterns, entertaining the wives, and even some of the mistresses, while Gary sparred with the other leaders of the world.

She had been envious of him, she knew that now, and perhaps even better suited for this life than he had been. Certainly now, her perspective as a woman, despite her lack of maternal instinct, had served the world well. There were scores of women who loved her. She read their missives each evening, handpicked by Jack from the thousands of messages that came in every day.

The challenges, the twists and turns of the world she found herself responsible for, even the uprisings provided a surge of excitement. Not everyone was content with her rule, not everyone was at peace with the changes the Terran United Planetary Government had put into place.

She was pushing radical agendas, and

despite the emptiness of their planet, and their dwindling numbers, many fought the changes at every turn.

She understood it. She wondered what Gary would have thought of this new world. She was promoting polygamy–ensuring that women had multiple partners and a wider exchange of genetic material. Last week's announcement, that of rewarding those women who were more successful carrying healthy children to term with additional financial and social rewards, had generated controversy, especially in the remnants of the Reformed United States.

Enough critics of social reform survived the ESH virus and still think they are in the 21st century.

These changes to the status quo were often met with angry rhetoric and, sometimes, threats. Most of the population believed in her, had voted her in for her life term, but there would always be the malcontents and naysayers.

Jack, her adviser, appeared at Madeline's side. "Madame President, Doctors Aaronson and Brooks are here, ma'am."

"Thank you, Jack, please show them into the atrium." He nodded and disappeared.

Madeline stood up from her desk and smoothed her suit, brushing an errant hair from it. Her body hadn't fully recovered from bearing Ireti, but it was close. If they hadn't bigger things to worry about, like the survival of the human species as the remains of Ultima Thule approached, she would have already submitted to another round of IVF. It was important to model the behavior she wanted to see in others. But her pregnancy with Ireti had been difficult, if only because the act of growing a child was exhausting work, and she needed her full focus on saving as many of her people as possible.

The atrium was a brisk walk—the corridors busy with aides rushing about. Jack had informed her that there was a breach in Vive, a new UP city outside of the fire-bombed city of Paris. There was an operation going on there to remove a virus-positive individual, as well as enact the standard quarantine procedures.

The atrium, normally bright with indirect light, was gray. A late-season storm filled with torrential rains pummeled the city. The clouds above were so dark that the sensor lighting that typically turned on at dusk was alive and glowing. In her monthly missive, Dr. Aaronson had mentioned that she and Dr. Brooks would return with Primina, but the baby was nowhere to be seen. Instead, Aaronson and Brooks flanked a young girl.

The child stood still, and it was her stillness that felt off. Different. It was both attractive and repellent at the same time. Madeline struggled to pull her eyes away, to smile and greet the two doctors.

Primina's sisters had joined her over the next two months, all but two, who had died unexpectedly in the artificial wombs. The five hundred genetically engineered embryos that Brooks and Aaronson had planned had experienced failure after failure. The artificial womb technology could not be replicated, thanks to losing its team of creators to the ESH virus. Somehow, despite all the documentation, the new models failed to bring an embryo to full-term, or even the thirty-week mark. Madeline had kept up on the doctors' regular updates, but the technology loss she had feared, one that her adviser team continually harped on, was already happening. They had lost far too many brilliant scientists to the ESH virus, and those left were traumatized and often suicidal.

Droplets glistened in the trio's hair. Madeline could smell the damp, earthy odor that accompanies rain. She missed being outside. There was always some meeting to attend, and she could not remember the last time she had stepped outside of the vast, multi-spired building. How she missed walking in the rain in California, where lightning was rare. Here, on the Midwestern plains, one stayed inside during a storm as electricity strobed the air and thunder boomed, shaking even the most deep-seated of buildings. The power of the storms was inspiring, but she wished she could see the gentle rains of her youth.

"Dr. Aaronson, Dr. Brooks, I see you have not escaped our stormy weather." She clasped Julie and Janelle's hands before turning to the child in between them. "And who is this?" She smiled brightly at the girl, who returned her gaze with little emotion. Her eyes showed the same spectacular fire entwined with a dark midnight blue limbal ring, edged with gold, orange, and red. She was thin, her black hair long and neatly arranged in a braid that fell halfway down her back. The child had a preternatural calm, and her direct gaze was unsettling.

"I remember you," the child said, tilting her head and staring at Madeline.

"Wait." She looked up at the doctors, incredulity spreading across her face. "This can't possibly be…"

Julie Aaronson nodded. "Yes, Madame President, this is Prim…er, Syn, Syn Travani. She recently requested, well, all the girls requested, the freedom to name themselves."

Madeline stared, and the girl stared back.

"How is this even possible?"

Less than ten months ago, Primina, or Syn, as she wished to be called, was an impossibly tiny baby and now she was, well, far bigger. Madeline struggled to guess at what age the child looked to be.

If Jacqueline were here, she would know.

Dr. Brooks leaned down and made eye contact with the girl. "Syn, if you will sit on that couch over there, Miss Janelle and I need to speak with the president."

Syn nodded and walked over to the seating on the far wall of the atrium, sat down, and pulled a tablet from her jumper.

A few flicks of a finger and then she stilled, her head bent, eyes focused intently on the screen.

Julie Aaronson stepped closer, her voice lowering. "She's currently reading vintage science fiction. She especially enjoys a juvenile series by Robert Heinlein written back in the 1950s."

Madeline stared at the girl, so composed. The child wasn't even wiggling as she sat there, her finger occasionally tapping to move to the next screen.

"She's not even a year old."

"She is ten months old today, as a matter of fact," Janelle added.

"Explain, please."

Julie nodded. "Schwarkopsky, the creator of the artificial wombs, wrote at length on the potential for accelerated growth inside of the wombs, and out. His formulas pointed to a need for gene manipulation that would open the door for it inside of the womb, but he died before he could test it out at length. We knew that farm animals, even monkeys, seem to mature at a quicker rate, but we didn't expect this. This is unprecedented."

Janelle spoke then, her voice low, almost urgent. "They barely sleep. Of all the girls, Syn is the oldest, of course, and they typically sleep around three hours per night on average. Their growth rate is off the charts. Nearly five times that of a normal human child. Most are reading, like Prim…er, Syn. And it shows no sign of slowing down. At this rate, we are looking at puberty by year three and adulthood by year four."

Madeline found herself at a loss for words. The girls would be adults by the time the asteroid entered the atmosphere. The thought of it boggled her mind, and she stood there, alternating between staring at the girl as she read, and gaping at the doctors. Finally, she remembered herself and the original goal for these genetically engineered children.

"And their fertility?"

"We won't know until puberty," Julie answered, then smiled. "But at least we won't have to wait an additional nine years for answers."

Janelle Brooks spoke again, her eyes troubled. "There are, *issues*, however."

Julie frowned at her partner, her mouth turning down in disapproval. "They are too early to concern the president with yet, Janelle."

Madeline zeroed in on Janelle. "Go on."

Janelle glanced at her partner, swallowed, and said, "Well, the sleep patterns are a concern, obviously. But it is their behaviors that are, well, unnerving. You may have noticed the lack of, well, childishness." She paused, her gaze straying to her partner.

Julie sighed, shrugging. "Go on."

"As babies, they never cried. Sure, it has been exhausting, especially with their lack of sleep, but when awake, they just lay there, eyes tracking, taking in everything, until we thought of putting in the educational screens on the ceilings."

Madeline nodded. "Yes, I seem to remember that in the reports. And that led to early language development."

Dr. Aaronson snorted. "Early, yes, that's one way of putting it. By Syn's fourth month, she was using the telegraphic speech you see in two-year-olds, and by the end of that month, full sentences."

"Why was this not expanded on more in your reports?" Madeline demanded.

Janelle Brooks visibly squirmed, discomfort written all over her face. "I actually talked Julie out of it. I was… I was afraid you would shut the study down, and we were still so certain that the newer iterations of the artificial wombs would work, but they didn't. They failed miserably, over and over, and then, well…" Her voice petered out.

Dr. Aaronson spoke up. "We weren't sure how you would react. And, Madame President, I saw it on your face when you first walked in. Syn and her sisters, they have that effect on people. I will admit that, being around them, day in, day out, it never stops being unsettling. They are different, fundamentally so, from other children. In fact, I would go as far as to say that they *aren't* children, and never have been. Their emotions, their reactions, it's all so…*different*."

Different. Unsettling. Yes, those are all words I would use to describe that child.

Madeline thought of Ireti, lying there in her crib, tiny, cooing, *normal*. She stared openly at Syn Travani, who continued to page through her tablet, reading at what appeared to be an accelerated pace, her finger rapidly stabbing the page-advance button. *No fairy tales or* See Spot Run *for these children*.

"I am sorry, Madame President, we should have told you sooner." Janelle

Brooks' voice betrayed her growing distress at Madeline's silence.

What have we done? What have I done, allowing this experiment? Thank God, there are only fifteen of them. The discontented, if they learned of this, would riot in the streets and demand I resign.

"Well, you've told me now," Madeline said, forcing a smile to her lips. "And we will stay the course with Syn and the other fourteen girls. Any other children, however…"

"Say no more, Madame President," Julie Lynn answered quickly. "These fifteen we have will give us enough data to process for the rest of my life and beyond."

"And you will keep me apprised of all developments from here on out," Madeline stated.

"Yes, ma'am."

Madeline could see Jack enter on the far side of the atrium, not too far from where little Syn Travani sat. From the look on his face, it was time to end the meeting.

"I'll look forward to your complete monthly reports, Doctors." She nodded brusquely and turned toward her aide, stepping away from the doctors.

"It's Vive, ma'am," Jack said as they

moved out of range. "It's fallen to the ESH virus just like Kavu did."

Hours later, long after meetings had taken her into the deep darkness of night, Madeline thought of Syn's unsettling gaze. It filled her dreams that night with nightmarish images of half-human, half-machine children. That, and blood, so much blood.

When Joy Returns

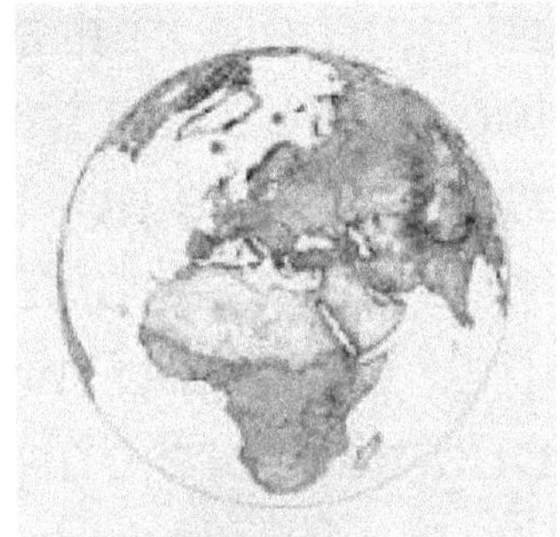

Earth
04.19.2102

It was the list that reminded Madeline and filled her with shame. A list of children, all of them under the age of ten. Seeing it had reminded her of Ireti and the fact that she couldn't remember the last time she had checked in on her. Had it been four days? Five? Maybe longer?

The list had arrived while Isa and Jeff and the rest of the committee had battled it out. Who to take, who to leave behind when the asteroid fell to Earth? Hand-delivered, it had included the signatures of nearly one thousand parents.

Each of them had pledged to stay behind as long as the committee guaranteed each of their children a Cryo unit on one of the lifeships. Five hundred children were on the list, with nearly a thousand adults and caregivers pledging to remain on Earth and die in the hell storm that was coming. It was not the first such list, and it certainly would not be the last. The committee members raised their voices, fighting to be heard, while Madeline's thoughts were only of Ireti.

She was a beautiful baby and was developing well, healthy and happy, with the best of care. A small army of nannies and other staff were on hand to make sure her every need was cared for, and Madeline wasn't worried about the girl, not like that. After all, Ireti had a space reserved in the Cheyenne Mountain Complex, as did Madeline. There they would wait out the violence done to the Earth in relative peace, their futures far more certain than a majority of the people left on Earth. Madeline had made her preference clear, choosing to hide below the surface instead of exposing herself and Ireti to spaceflight and the complexities that accompanied such a journey.

What bothered Madeline was that her place in Ireti's world was an unnecessary one. Yes, she was her mother and yes, Ireti recognized Madeline's face, just as she did a dozen other faces. But there was no connection, no expressions of love, no emotional response. Shared blood and DNA bound Madeline and her daughter, nothing else. When the nanny handed Ireti over, Madeline would sit awkwardly in a rocker and stroke her child's skin, stare into her eyes, or try to talk to her. The little girl would smile, even gurgle, but she did the same for anyone.

Only Ayomide Batan, the Yoruba nanny, had broached the subject, her eyes cast down as she did. "If you could visit more, ma'am, I'm sure Ireti would respond better."

Madeline had nodded and handed the baby back to Ayomide.

"Please forgive me, Madame President, if I spoke out of turn. Your duties, they keep you far busier than I could imagine."

Madeline had waved a hand dismissively. "Please do not worry about speaking your mind, Ayomide. I do not hold it against you at all."

She had slipped away then, wondering if she was damaging her only child simply by being who she was. As leader of the

Terran United Planetary Government, she hadn't had time to breastfeed, or even to pump, and there was a planet to save, after all. The needs of the many outweighed the needs of one small, helpless infant. And while she had become a role model for many women, and a surge of pregnancies had followed Ireti's birth, along with a spike in miscarriages, she was truly a mother in name only. She had served as a vessel, nothing more, and she struggled with that reality, the question of where she fit into her daughter's world a constant niggling itch in the back of her mind.

In less than six weeks, Ireti would be a year old, and Ayomide had already informed her that the baby might take her first steps before the official day. The only reprieve she felt in all of this was the decision to reverse course in the past six months and no longer promote pregnancies. Pregnant women couldn't go into space. The g forces it required to escape Earth's atmosphere had already triggered several miscarriages. Soon, pregnancy could be a death sentence. How the tables had turned!

The argument at the table before her cut

through her thoughts.

"Five hundred motherless children? Are you insane? Do you have any idea how difficult it will be for them without their parents and what a drain on resources it would be post-impact and recovery? They won't be able to build cities, drive cars, or perform surgeries—they will be helpless for a decade or more!" Dinah Sterling squawked.

"So much for maternal instincts," Jeff Bonovich commented, grimacing as he tapped his stylus on the table.

"Oh, and what would you suggest, Jiminy Cricket?" Loren McClellan snapped, and Jeff laughed. It sounded bitter.

"Jiminy Cricket? What, because I have a conscience?" Jeff scoffed. "Color me surprised, McClellan, that you would have ever loved such idealistic stories in your youth. I don't know if I can even imagine you as a child. And believe me, I wish I didn't have a conscience. Maybe then it would be easier to just deny these people out of turn. They are desperate to save their children. Can you blame them?"

He turned to Madeline then, his eyes asking. He wanted her to weigh in on such an argument. She knew he did. Jeff was desperate for someone to see what he was seeing. And she did, even as she also saw the truth in what the others were suggesting. They were in a terrible predicament. The children they had pushed so hard for were now the most expendable. A post-ESH world needed children, lots of them. A post-Azrael world would require adults with very specific skillsets. They needed mechanical engineers, farmers, social scientists, city planners, production specialists, grease monkeys to handle repairs on reams of robots and machines, and programmers. They needed doctors, and an army of therapists and pharmacists to keep the population going through the hell of first a virus and now an asteroid killing everyone they loved. And of course, they needed children as well, but what good were children if there weren't enough adults to handle the basics of re-establishing a human society? What would the generation after such a group of parentless children look like? Would there even *be* a next generation?

Madeline understood the turmoil in Bonovich's mind. She felt it in hers as well. They had to balance all of this. And balance it in the face of imminent destruction was impossible. It felt overwhelming, and it sat at the back of her throat like a lead ball.

The weight of the world had never felt heavier.

"Tell the consortium there will be no deal," Madeline said, and Dinah smiled at the far side of the table. "We have to ensure we have the proper mix of adults and children, and that we have the necessary numbers of men and women capable of recreating our world once the Earth has recovered from the impact."

"So, no lottery?" Loren asked, frowning as he tried to envision how this would work.

Madeline grimaced. "We will hold the lottery, but first everyone must provide qualifications and they must be verified."

"Verified how?" Jeff asked.

"Through educational records, years of experience, whatever." Madeline shrugged. "We must also take childbearing potential into consideration. And we should run it similar to how World Geographic did when qualifying the crew for the Calypso."

"So, if you haven't gotten a chance at education, at life, you die?" Jeff asked, his lips thinning, his expression grim.

"We are talking about the survival of humanity, Bonovich, try to keep up." Dinah smiled again. Madeline thought Dinah's teeth looked sharp, carnivorous.

That woman would eat her own children if it kept her alive.

"Enough mollycoddling. If they have skills that are useful, we keep them, and if they don't, then they are redundant."

Jeff ran a hand over his jaw. "I can think of nothing as worthless as a politician, Dinah."

Madeline winced. She certainly could be considered expendable in that case.

Dinah gave a small gasp and glared at Jeff. "You would cut off your nose to spite your face, Bonovich." She straightened in her chair. "Besides, I'm of childbearing age and I've proven my worth in that department."

"Your son is sixteen, being raised by your sister, and hates you, Dinah," Jeff commented sourly. Dinah opened her mouth in shock, her beady eyes narrowing.

"My duties here…"

Madeline interrupted, "Enough." She looked around the room. "Enough. If you think that after all we have done here that we are exempt, think again. Pull the protocols from the World Geographic records and we will meet again on Thursday to discuss what alterations will be necessary to the mission requirements. We will include families, just as they did, and I look forward to your thoughts on what other requirements we might need to change. This needs to be implemented soon, as do the medications necessary for ending lives. We can't leave millions on the surface to die in agony without some kind of merciful ending. I want to hear what our options are for a drug that is easy to administer and one that will cause no pain or discomfort."

She stood, gathered her tablet and stylus, and adjusted her suit jacket. It was becoming loose on her, the excess pounds from her pregnancy melting away in the daily stresses of trying to save a dying world. She nodded at Jeff and the others and left, marching down the hallway, with her bodyguard Adam matching her stride for stride. A few steps behind her was Jack, now her top aide after losing Aiden. They had never found the people responsible for the poisoned berries, no matter how hard they had searched. It had been a jagged little pill to swallow, the idea of Aiden's death unavenged. He had died because of her, eating food intended for her, and he haunted her dreams at night.

"Cancel my next meeting, Jack," Madeline said, and he sped up slightly to walk by her side.

"It's with Isa. He has an update on the latest retrofitting for the Sana. He thinks he can manage an expansion module, several actually, that will attach in orbit and increase the Cryo storage by 20%."

"Tell him to go ahead with it. I'll meet with him tomorrow if he still needs a face-to-face."

"Yes, ma'am." Jack's stylus scribbled away on his tablet, the script bright against the dark surface.

Madeline turned left at the end of the corridor and headed for the nursery. "Please arrange for my lunch to be brought to the nursery, Jack. And then take an hour for yourself."

Jack smiled wryly at that and thanked her. Just like Madeline, an hour alone was a luxury he simply didn't have. Likely, he would spend it catching up on her correspondence.

His hair, which had been a dusting of

salt in his jet-black hair at the temples, was now a shock of white invading more and more territory. The dark circles under his eyes seemed permanent as well. All of this in less than two years of service. Madeline had taken to avoiding the mirror as often as possible after the first white hairs had sprouted at her temples. This job was not for the faint of heart.

She approached the nursery door and Jack nodded and headed away down the corridor. Adam stayed by her side, holding the door open with one hand as his gaze took in the sunny, well-lit room. He nodded to her, and Madeline slipped past him. He took a seat near the door.

Ireti was just waking up, one tiny fist rubbing at her eyes, and she grumbled, sleepy and discontented. The door had interrupted Ayomide Batan mid-song, and she smiled and continued it. The words were unfamiliar, but the tune was bright and cheery.

Nitori l'otito ni wura
Iyebiye ti ko ṣee ṣe pataki
Eyi ti o ntan ati didan
Ni awọn ọjọ ti o ṣokunkun julọ ti igbesi aye

Tutu awọn irora wa ti o jinlẹ julọ
Idaduro wa lailewu nipasẹ awọn iji lile ti
igbesi aye
Ki a le tàn ninu goolu gara

Ireti's grumble disappeared, and she smiled then, her tiny teeth gleaming white and perfect. But the smile wasn't for Madeline, it was for her nanny, who returned her charge's smile with one that spoke of warring emotions. Love, of that Madeline was sure, but also something else. Something Madeline couldn't quite read on the Yoruba woman's warm, kind face.

"Ireti, your iya, your mama, is here to see you!" She smiled at Madeline and bowed her head. "Ma'am."

"The song you were singing, Ayomide, it was lovely," Madeline said and reached out to caress Ireti's hair. Her child smiled at her shyly before turning away and burrowing into Ayomide's ample bosom.

The nanny's eyes widened with distress. "She just woke up and is still tired. I am sorry, ma'am."

Madeline's hand dropped away. "No, no, it is nothing. Don't worry, Ayomide, she feels safe with you, and that is good. It is as it should be."

In her heart, she felt a kind of relief. She never really knew what to do with Ireti. Should she cuddle her? Sing songs? The last time she had visited, she had tried that, but she couldn't even remember the words to any lullabies.

"It is a Yoruba lullaby," Ayomide said, returning to Madeline's question, one hand stroking Ireti's back. "Mother is gold, a treasure untold," she said and then hummed the song again under her breath.

Madeline sat down on the couch. "It's lovely. I can see that Ireti likes it."

"She is a wonderful baby, ma'am. I so enjoy my time with her." Ayomide was one of three nannies, and Madeline had noticed that Ireti responded better to her than any of the others. The same was obviously true. Ayomide had a way about her, one that Madeline envied. She was, undeniably, a mother, through and through. Her soul spoke of it.

Ayomide smiled at Madeline. "Would you like to hold her?"

"When she is ready, yes. But for now, she looks content in your arms, Ayomide. Tell me," Madeline said, changing the subject, "what does your name mean?"

"My name?" The woman smiled. "It means 'when joy returns.' I was the only girl after five boys and my mother was so very happy. She finally had the girl she was hoping for."

"Ireti means hope, as I imagine you know already."

"Yes," Ayomide said, nodding, "very appropriate."

"Did you have children before, Ayomide?" Madeline suspected she had, but Aiden had handled most of the hiring before he died.

The hand that rubbed Ireti's back paused, and she nodded slowly, her eyes dark with emotion. "Yes, ma'am, I had two children. One boy, one girl. They died with their father early in the outbreak. The children were both immune, as I was, but their father was not. My Bankole was a good man, kind and patient, but the virus turned him into something I could not recognize." She paused, gently gathered Ireti, and handed her to Madeline before continuing.

"I think about that day often. What I could have done different. Had I known what would happen, how the hunger would overtake him, I would have sent him out to the store instead. Or taken our sweet children with me." She stared at her empty hands. "But I didn't take them with me, or send him out for food. I didn't do that."

Ireti was calm in Madeline's arms. She reached up and touched Madeline's face. Her fingers were so tiny, so perfect. Madeline gazed at her baby. This child was half her, half an unnamed Yoruba sperm donor, and she tried to find herself in the tiny features. Did Ireti have her eyes, her lips? Would her baby grow as tall as her or be shorter?

Madeline glanced up and caught the look of adoration, of love, on Ayomide's face.

"She is perfect. Exactly what my aching heart has needed," Ayomide said. "It is so easy to love her."

"Yes," Madeline echoed, "Babies are so easy to love." But her heart felt nothing. Nothing at all except unease and bewilderment and uncertainty. She could command armies, make decisions that affected millions, and prepare her world for untold destruction–as long as no one asked her to take care of a baby. That she felt absolutely hopeless at.

She didn't resist as Ireti slid from her

arms and crawled away from both women to play with a jingle-filled ball on the floor. And later, as she made her excuses and slipped from the nursery, Ireti did not even notice her departure.

She walked down the hallway, Adam matching her stride for stride.

Ireti deserves better, Madeline thought. *Somehow, some way, Ireti deserves love. She deserves a mother who will care for her above all others.*

Live Your Life

Earth
01.07.2104

Willem sat in the darkened family room, the photo album still in his lap. Jia had left early to spend the day with Eaton and his mother after a weekend spent celebrating Willem's birthday. The moon rose in the dark night sky and he still sat, unmoving, caught in the web of memory.

Outside of the house, a wolf howled. Willem thought of Mufti, dead two years now; he had always howled back at the wolves. Jia had been devastated when the old mutt passed away; the two of them had been inseparable.

This house had seen so much laughter, so much life. Would it still be standing in seven more months?

Beneath his fingers rested the photos,

an anachronism from the past. With everything backed up to the cloud, it had seemed silly. But Anja had insisted on placing the order and printing out hundreds of photos of their family. She had placed them in these books and filled a shelf with them, each divided into a handful of years.

He could view the photos any time on his tablet, but these photo albums felt more real. As if the actual existence of a photograph trumped something held in digital format, something he could touch.

Jonas, their eldest, he would be fifteen, almost sixteen now. Willem tried to imagine what his boy would have been like as a teen. He had always been so serious, so lost in his studies, that he neglected other things. He had spent most of his childhood with his nose buried in a book. Jonas' quiet ways had convinced Willem that this was how all boys were until Luca had come along. Willem's youngest child had been a hellion, a spitfire full of energy and running and mud. God, the mud. At four, he had liked nothing better than to sculpt animals, castles, anything, as long as it was with the thick, dark mud by the creek.

Willem smiled into the darkness at the

memory of his wife threatening to hose their youngest child off in the yard if he kept tracking mud into the house.

Sandwiched in between had been Lisl. Small-boned, delicate, ethereal. In some ways, Jia reminded him of Lisl. Imagining her at ten years of age felt like an impossibility. The thought of her at Jia's age, well, she would be five forever in his mind.

He hadn't wanted to live in the wake of their deaths. His three beautiful children, his loving wife, all taken from him, leaving him with nothing and no one except Greta. How he had managed to not kill himself when he lost Greta, he still marveled at. He had come close.

Thank God I didn't end my life before I found Jia's message.

Willem hadn't known what to expect from a nearly full-grown child. Especially one who had grown up believing another man was her father. Somehow, Jia had slid into his life, and he into hers, without friction or discomfort. As if it were meant to be.

His tablet beeped, a reminder appearing on the screen.

He didn't have to look at the message; it

was the same as three days ago. The Masa Depan Bumi lifeship was departing in two weeks, and he and Jia had a place on it. He just had to send a reply.

Yet he delayed. His position and experience as Madeline Chen's Chief of Staff of Art and Antiquities had given him a place on board, just as his position had allowed for one more, an acknowledgment that he had a child left to save. All he had to do was respond yes, and then he could report on January 20th along with Jia, and they would enter Cryo. They would be sent to the lifeship and head for Mars. There they would sleep, likely for years. The asteroid would slam into Earth. The resulting devastation would include a blistering ring of death followed by a deep freeze because of the detritus in the atmosphere. It would mean a mini-Ice Age that froze most of the life on the planet for up to ten, maybe fifteen years.

He would be no older, and Jia would be with him. He could resume his life as curator of the world's art.

But at what cost?

The chances that Eaton Ngai, or even his mother, Lisa Ngai, would have a place aboard the lifeships was infinitesimally small. If Jia hadn't been his daughter, she would have had to take her chances with the lottery. They were taking the best of the best. The polymaths, the mechanical geniuses-the ones who could rebuild the world after Azrael had reduced them to ruin and wiped the world clean.

To take Jia with him meant ripping her away from the man that she loved. Willem saw the way she looked at Eaton, and how he looked at her. Willem had loved her mother like that. Anja too, although it was different. Anja had become the mother of his children and the backbone of their family.

Here he was, sitting in the darkness, consumed with memories of the children he had lost, visiting the past, afraid to consider a future that didn't include Jia dying or living with a broken heart.

He reached for his tablet, punched the numbers into the device, and put it to his ear as he waited for someone to answer.

"No, I'm not calling to verify. I have a question. Yes," he said, nodding. "Option B?" He waited. The person on the other end spoke fast, and his grasp of English was barely up to the task. "Yes, of course, thank you."

A few more questions and answers back and forth, and Willem thanked them again and hung up. He couldn't save them both. And for that, his heart hurt. Lisa Ngai was a treasure, one who deserved to live through the end of the world. But he knew she would accept the choice he had made with grace and joy, knowing Eaton would survive. Lisa, Willem, and millions of others–they didn't get happy-ever-after endings.

Jia had given him a reason to live again, and now it was time to return the favor.

The crunch of gravel under the tires of an autocar broke the silence an hour later. The door, unlocked, opened with a blast of icy January air and Jia turned on the lights, flooding the room with a blinding brightness.

"Papa, you are still awake. I saw all the lights off and was sure you had gone to bed," Jia said, as she pulled off her winter boots and hung her heavy winter coat in the closet. Her face still held the memory of Eaton. She was happier in his presence; Willem saw how she lit up whenever Eaton drew near. She drew closer. "Why are you sitting in the dark?" Her gaze fell on the photo albums, and she bit her lip. Her smile faded away.

"Oh, Papa."

"It is a good thing," he said, attempting a smile, "that you have given me these years, Jia. Years I don't think I could have endured without you." He cleared his throat. "We need to talk."

A bright sparkle on the ring finger of her left hand caught his eye. "I see congratulations are in order. I am happy for you, Tochter."

The smile returned to her face. "Eaton said that he asked you first." Her grin faltered. "What is it, Papa? What do you need to talk about?"

"About your future. And Eaton's."

Her eyes slid away. The sword of fate hung above them all. But for those who had only an infinitesimal chance, or none, there was little talk of what would happen when the asteroid came. The TUPG had announced that once the astronomers could predict *where* Azrael would impact Earth, they would provide transportation for as many as possible, helping citizens to flee the impact point and, hopefully, to a location capable of survival in the aftermath.

There were few places on Earth capable

of long-term survival, but the equator held the best hope. As long as they weren't too close to the ocean. To speak of it, though, when there was little or no chance of access to the lifeships or underground bunkers, was verboten.

"The Masa Depan Bumi lifeship is departing in two weeks, Jia. It will go to Mars and it will stay there until Earth recovers. This might be two years, or it might be ten, but everyone will be in Cryo. No time will pass for you."

"For…*me*?" Her warm brown eyes focused back on his.

"For you, for Eaton," he answered.

"I don't understand." She was biting her lip again, and her hands trembled in her lap.

"I think you do, Jia. I made sure that they registered you as my child with the TUPG and formally recognized you as my sole surviving issue two years ago. That meant that everything that is mine is yours, and because of my status as Chief of Staff, there were certain perks, a place on the lifeship for me and for my daughter."

"And you secured another seat? For Eaton?" Hope sparked in her eyes.

"In a sense, yes."

She frowned in response to his words. "Papa, what did you do?"

"I did what any parent with a choice would do, Jia. I made sure that my daughter, and the man that she loved, would have a future together. The TUPG is allowing Option B, although it is not a well-known fact, and Option B allows me to exchange my seat for someone I feel is better suited. In this case, Eaton."

"But Papa, what about you? You would be alone! Here on the surface, unprotected!" She slipped off the edge of the couch and kneeled on the floor next to his chair.

Willem reached out and caressed her soft, blue-black hair. It wasn't straight, like her mother's. Instead, it had a wavy aspect. Some of him had come through. His wavy hair, his height. Some part of him would remain beyond his own death. His tiny glimpse of immortality lay within this beautiful girl and the love that she had found in Eaton.

"Jia, meine Liebling, it is time for you to live your life. The lifeship, it will be a mere blip, and when you wake, a new Earth will await you. It will be a place stripped clean, ready for you and Eaton to fill with your beautiful children. Perhaps this house will still be standing. A place for you to return to."

"But Papa, *you* won't be here!" She lifted her head, and he could see the tears sliding down her cheeks.

"I don't belong in that world, Jia. I belong in this one."

"But Papa, surely there is some way for all of us to go. I will not leave you."

Outside, he heard the howl again. This time, it had company. A second howl, different from the first, possibly younger?

"Listen, Jia. Listen to the wolf." They sat in silence and listened to the wolves howl. "I think that the first one is male, and he is calling to a female. Perhaps to join him? They are not much different from humans, wolves. They want a connection, community, a mate, and family."

Jia's face was wet with tears. They dripped off her nose, her chin.

"Papa, I don't want to leave you."

Willem nodded. "I know." A moment passed. "But Jia? When the day comes, you *will* board that lifeship. When you do, I will know my life has meant something and that some part of me will live on forever."

Days later, he drove with Jia to New

Munich and visited Lisa Ngai. It had taken some doing to get her out of New York, but the failing electricity had sealed the deal. Two years ago, Lisa and Eaton had moved to New Munich. Lisa promptly opened up another restaurant just down the street from the art museum and Eaton and Jia were inseparable–working together, eating at Ma Ngai's restaurant, and the two families had grown close.

There, in the back, after the eatery had shut down for the night, Willem shared his plan with her and Eaton. The round-faced, perennially smiling woman had seized his hands in hers and nodded, unshed tears filling her eyes. Her grip had been painfully tight. Eaton was her only surviving child, just as Jia was his. He knew how she felt. Their two children had fallen in love at the end of the world. But they would survive. Safe on the surface of Mars, over 54 million kilometers away, they would sleep. Through the devastating impact, and the mini-Ice Age that would follow, they would be safe. Lisa Ngai's eyes glistened. "Through them, we live."

Two weeks later, he stood by Jia's side and watched as she lay back, clad only in a tank top and shorts. The wedding ring that had belonged first to his mother and then to Greta twinkled on her left ring finger. The technician handed him the tablet to sign. It was the last step in the process as he handed over his entry plus one on the lifeship to his daughter and new son-in-law.

Jia trembled, her grip on his arm tight, fingers shaking. "Papa, I don't want to leave you."

"Mein Kind, you aren't. You carry me here," he said, pointing to her heart, "and here." He placed a thumb on her forehead. "And I carry you as well. For the rest of my life." He moved his free hand from his chest to his head. "Thank you for finding me, Jia. Thank you for giving me hope and love when I thought I had no reason to go on."

He nodded to the technician, who began the IV, the drugs that would slow her heart, and induce the first step of the Cryo process dripping into the tubing that snaked down to her right arm. Jia's eyes fluttered.

"I love you, Pa..." Her eyes slipped closed; the last word unfinished. And Willem suddenly remembered Lisl's favorite story, a vintage picture book titled

Guess How Much I Love You. He had never asked Jia about her favorite childhood story.

"Ich liebe dich auch, mein kind. Zum Mond.[1]"

He watched as they inserted her body into the Cryo chamber, the readouts double-checked. The technician nodded and gave him a thumbs-up. Willem watched as her Cryo chamber slowly trundled along the track, finally disappearing into the distance.

Three days after that, he watched the Masa Depan Bumi leave Earth with Eaton and Jia safely tucked away in their Cryo chambers.

"What now?" asked a somber Lisa Ngai as she watched the contrail disperse into the sky.

Willem laughed. "I hadn't really thought past this moment. I guess I'll travel a little. There are some places in the world where art really can't be salvaged–the cities of Petra, Pompeii, to name some. I want to go to as many places as I can and take in the wonders." He looked down at her. "Would you join me?"

She blinked and looked up at him in surprise. "Yes. I would like that very much."

1. I love you too, my child. To the moon.

I, Virus

Earth
05.17.2104

"Huh." A young woman's voice echoed in the large room, pulling Tobias from his work. He had been so lost in his work that he hadn't even heard her come in. His focus had been on the microscope, where he was observing a mutation in progress. This mutation, understanding it, was key in overcoming the effects of the ESH virus on the human reproductive system. It was something Tobias had been hunting since he first laid eyes on the virus in Julie Lynn's lab.

A girl stood just inside the doorway, ogling the pictures that covered the walls. She was whip-thin, yet muscular. Her jet-black hair was buzzed a few millimeters from her scalp on one side, the other half longer. It looked spiky and disheveled, and it covered her eyes and obscured her face. Her clothing was functional and worn. She wore black, heavy-duty cargo pants and a shirt under a thin utility jacket. It wasn't an affectation. Each of the pockets bulged and looked worn, almost tattered. Her clothing spoke of hard work in unfriendly places. Then there were her tattoos, which covered her hands, arms, and even her neck. She looked out of place, especially here, in the sterile halls of the research building. The city itself was an advertisement for conformity, filled with bland, clean streets, simple lines, and, except for the parks, an agonizing lack of color.

"Viruses," Tobias said, gesturing to the colorful panels on the walls.

"What?"

"Those are viruses." Tobias smiled. "As seen under an electron microscope, but still."

"They're beautiful. I've…never seen anything like it."

Tobias' smile grew wider. Here was a girl after his own heart. "Are you new here? Attending classes? I've never seen you before."

She shifted the box in her hand and brushed at an errant strand of hair, avoiding eye contact. "I, uh, no, I was told to deliver this piece of art to you. You are," she said, reading the label, "Tobias Price Aaronson, right?"

A piece of art. Tobias' heart thumped hard in his chest. It could only be from one person.

"I am, yes."

"Well, then this is for you." She held the box out towards him, a pinched, unhappy look on her mouth. He took the box gently. "It's very delicate, by the way. You will need these." She handed him a pair of white cotton gloves.

"Yes, I know, thank you." He set the box down on the table and put on the gloves before he reached for a scalpel, cutting through the tape, easing the box open. He opened the envelope gently and took a moment to read the brief note before he began removing the packing peanuts.

She stepped forward, her own hands now covered in cotton gloves, reached in, and pulled out first the middle piece, a carved ivory water dragon with waves and coral carved below, then the wide wood base, and set them both out. "It is from early in the Qing dynasty, most likely from the mid-17th century."

Tobias turned his attention back to the girl. There was something about her that felt familiar. If he could only get a glimpse of her face, especially her eyes, he was sure he would know where he had seen her before.

"You certainly know your art history. Do you have a special focus or interest?" He set the puzzle ball down gently onto the middle piece, making sure it was steady in its position.

The corners of the girl's lips twitched. "I've always been partial to the Masters, but lately I've been working on the Uffizi Gallery in Florence and it has been quite an education."

"So, you're on Salvage detail?" Tobias looked her up and down. The salvage operations were going on around the world, in varying states of desperation. There weren't enough people for the work, and certainly not enough volunteers. Sure, they were rescuing the greatest treasures in the world—but doing so while surrounded by contaminated floodwaters. And the cities were dangerous now, between the armies of feral dogs and cats, to the armies of rats and other vermin. The sea levels, which had been rising because of global warming for decades, were now encroaching on most coastal cities, affecting the very foundations of the buildings themselves.

Humanity was getting a crash course in just how finite a world they lived in. Without constant care and upkeep, even after just a handful of years, buildings were crumbling. Without proper winterizing, pipes had burst, damaging buildings further. The fluctuations of the seasons on empty buildings with no electricity, no heating and cooling, caused far more damage than anyone had expected.

"Yes." She scuffed her foot on the floor, opting to stare at the puzzle ball instead of meeting his eyes. Her lashes were thick and dark. She was pretty, with just the right amount of exotic and eclectic. He wished she would look up so he could see her eyes. It felt as if she was doing everything she could to avoid eye contact.

"That is incredible. The treasures you are helping preserve, it's, well, it's desperately needed." Tobias couldn't help wondering why a girl of prime breeding age was working in such a place. With the age of consent lowered to fourteen, seeing a girl his age was a rarity. And the crews were usually all male. The toxins, poor conditions, and dangerous surroundings reserved the salvage work for those not able to bear children. With humanity's extinction in the next four decades thanks to the ESH virus and its teratogenic effects, the breeding program his adoptive mother had helped put into place was now a dominant rule of the land, even now, with a humanity-ending asteroid heading their way.

She shrugged, her eyes on the ground. "I should probably go." She stood there, her face betraying an obvious reluctance to leave the objet d'art in his hands.

"Wait, when are you flying back?" Tobias felt drawn to the girl for reasons he didn't completely understand.

"On the transport tomorrow evening. They don't have many flights to Florence these days." She said it deadpan, and he laughed in response, stopping short as he finally glimpsed her eyes. She corrected the mistake immediately, but he had seen the flash of the distinctive eye color in that millisecond mistake.

A creche baby. So that's why she won't

make eye contact. And why she is in Salvage. I wonder if she remembers Julie or Janelle.

"I uh, I need to go." There was panic now, just under the surface.

"Wait!" Tobias reached out, grabbing her hand. As he did, he felt a wave of terror run through him, fear of rejection warring with uncertainty. The creche babies weren't known for their social skills, or for their ability to relate with others.

She flinched, and he dropped it instantly. "Wait, please. I can see you like art. Perhaps you would like to see more of nature's art?" He smiled at her. "I specialize in viruses."

She had stepped back, ready to flee. Tobias held still, pointing to the walls. "I have more in my lab. Would you like to see?" He wasn't ready for her to disappear yet.

"I, uh…"

"Come on, I've been staring into microscopes all day and could really use a break." He smiled, meeting her gaze. She stared back; the blue of her irises interrupted by the flares of fiery orange circling her pupils.

"What's your name, anyway?"

"Syn Travani." He didn't let his surprise show. He had seen her once, when she was barely three days old. Her name had been Primina back then. Julie Lynn and Janelle had kept him and Karen away from the creche babies. Except for the one time Janelle insisted on taking Karen with her and Julie Lynn to meet President Chen, more for optics than anything else, he and Karen had been kept away.

I'll play dumb. No one remembers back that early in their lives.

"As in original sin?" he asked, teasing.

"As in, *synthetic*," came her factual response.

He blinked. "All right, Syn it is. Let me show you my favorite virus." He reached for the remote and paged through it, the pictures on the wall flashing in quick succession before he found the one he was looking for. The body of the virus was a round, pleasing shade of blue covered with long tubules in green and gold.

"What kind is it?" Syn asked, captivated by the image.

"The herpes virus, which we still are working on eradicating. Actually, a genetically modified herpes virus and another virus, pseudorabies. The EcoNu researchers combined them to create what ultimately mutated into the ESH virus."

She nodded slowly, tolerating his presence. "What does the ESH virus look like?"

Tobias smiled. "I'll show you." He clicked through the images and then paused. "Wait, would you like to see it in action?" That earned him an apprehensive stare. "What I mean is, it's here, on a slide. Would you like to see it?"

An almost imperceptible nod in response.

"Great, come this way." He took her hand, and she tensed for a moment before allowing him to pull her to a large microscope structure that covered an entire desk. "This is an electron microscope; it uses a beam of sped-up electrons as a source of illumination. Look."

She leaned in, hesitant at first. "Oh, wow! That is amazing!" She continued to stare at it, unmoving, enraptured by the microscopic virus guilty of wiping out over 99% of the world's population.

Tobias watched her, fascinated. The creche babies, the first, and only, generation of babies to be born from the artificial wombs, were rare. He had glimpsed them when they were first removed from the artificial wombs. There had been a long row of them, preternaturally quiet, the fiery orange corona encircling a ring of blue in their eyes, barely moving in their clear plastic cribs. A year later they had been child-sized, each the size of a five-year-old, and then pre-teens by the end of the second year. It was that which had bothered his adoptive mothers the most, the accelerated growth induced by one of the other researchers in charge of the project. When they had objected, they had been removed from the project, something that had devastated both women, especially Julie.

"It isn't worth the cost–we can't play God," Julie had once said, tears in her eyes.

Many people didn't consider them to be human, which was ridiculous. Syn's cells were as human as his. Yes, she looked like a young adult now, despite being just shy of four years old. They had considered the experiment a failure, shoved it under a rug. He frowned. Some had died under mysterious circumstances. Others had simply disappeared.

"You're a creche baby, aren't you?" Tobias asked, gently.

Her body stiffened, and she said nothing, pulling away from the microscope, staring at the floor. A quick nod of the head was her only answer.

He remembered that another oddity had emerged, right before Julie and Janelle were kicked off the project. The creche babies seemed to evidence behaviors typically seen on the autism spectrum— none of them had ever shown the typical need for affection. Instead, their silent regard had skeeved-out plenty of their caretakers. Tobias remembered his adoptive moms discussing it, both concerned that the children were not developing naturally due to the environment they were being raised in, and then later suggesting autism.

It was as if the act of developing in an artificial machine womb had robbed them of something vital. The artificial wombs had been a horrendous failure.

"I should go," the girl said, but her body language betrayed her indecision.

"Are you hungry?" Tobias asked, realizing that he hadn't eaten lunch or breakfast. It was, unfortunately, a common occurrence.

"Um…"

His stomach rumbled loudly, and Syn's eyebrow raised in response.

Tobias could feel a blush of embarrassment climb up his face. "I uh, forgot to eat today."

Syn's mouth quirked up on one side. "I forget all the time."

"Great, let's grab a bite from the cafeteria."

It was a short walk to the cafeteria from the lab, and since it was mid-afternoon, there were no lines to deal with. A scattering of researchers sat at other tables, preoccupied with eating and reading from medical journals. Syn surveyed the room in silence before she dug into her own food with little fanfare.

Tobias could see that she was used to being alone—everything from the way she had reacted to him in the lab to how she ate, quick and efficient, eyes downcast. "What was it like?" he asked, "Growing up as a creche baby?"

Syn shrugged. "What's it like being human?" The defensive tone was obvious.

"You are as human as I am." That

earned him a direct stare. He could get lost in those eyes. The sunfire in her eyes flared and pulsed.

"How did you end up with a priceless Chinese puzzle ball from the 17th century?" she fired back.

Tobias smiled. "You brought it to me." He laughed at the annoyed expression on her face. "Okay, okay. Actually, Julie Lynn Aaronson, my adoptive mother, inherited it from her mother years ago. She knew how much I loved it and willed it to me before she died last month."

His chest felt tight. He still couldn't believe she was dead.

The girl blinked. "Wait, your mom is *the* Dr. Julie Lynn Aaronson?"

"Well, yeah. She and Janelle adopted me after I lost my parents."

Syn blinked. "Dr. Janelle Brooks? They were *married*?"

It was his turn to act defensive. "Got a problem with lesbians?"

"What?" Syn looked confused for a moment. "No, no, not at all. I mean, I've just heard those two names all of my life. I remember the time they brought me to New Athens to meet President Chen. I just didn't know they were also *together*."

"Yup, they sure were." Tobias nodded, smiling. "I was there for some of the initial trials, although they kept me and my adopted sister, Karen, away from most of it." He grimaced at the memory of late nights and dark circles under Julie Lynn's eyes as the wombs failed again and again after Primina and the first batch of creche babies were born. "And then we were both off to boarding school by the time you and the other creche babies were more than a couple months old. I was there when you were born, you know."

"Hatched."

Tobias blinked. "What?"

She hitched a shoulder. "I've always thought it was closer to hatching than birth." She gave a half-laugh and stared at her food.

He laughed too.

She isn't like what they described. Not at all.

"You never answered me." She looked puzzled, so he clarified, "On what it was like growing up."

"It sucked. I didn't understand human emotions, at least, not for a long time. It was hard to relate, and then there's the nasty reality that normal humans kind of suck as a species." She picked at her green beans, shoving them around with her fork.

Tobias laughed again. "My uncle used to say that too."

"Did you lose them all? Your entire family?"

"Well, not my uncle. He was already on his way to Zarmina's World by then. So, I guess in a way I lost him first. My mom and dad died within days of each other, and I was on my own in a refugee camp. They had rounded up survivors, mostly kids, and taken them to this camp where I met Julie Lynn." He shrugged, stirring his tea. "She took a shine to me and when they wanted to send me on with the other kids, she told them no."

"And now you research the ESH virus."

"Well, I'm almost fourteen, and I'm advanced in some studies." He shrugged and grinned. "Don't ask me to diagram a sentence. I barely know what an adjective is, but science has always come easy. I'm interning in a work-study program right now, but yeah, the goal is to eradicate the ESH virus." He paused for a moment, then stared at her, making eye contact. "And you salvage works of art. Have you spent much time in New Athens? I could show you around."

"No."

"No, you have spent little time in New Athens? Or no, you don't want me to show you around?"

She stared at him and stood up abruptly. "Thanks, Tobias."

"For what?"

"For treating me like I'm human."

He frowned in confusion. "You are human, Syn."

She laughed again, although he could detect an edge of bitterness in it, and placed a warm hand on his. He stared at it for a moment, admiring the intricate design tattooed over her skin, before looking up and meeting her eyes again. They pulsed, the sunfire corona around her iris flickering and flaring again. She looked like she wanted to say something more, but then bit her lip and shook her head.

He felt a sharp pang of disappointment when she pulled away from him, walking out of the door without another word. By the time he had dumped his tray, she had disappeared from sight.

"I hope I see you again soon, Syn Travani," Tobias murmured under his breath as he headed back to the low-slung, organic structure that served as his laboratory.

He couldn't stop thinking of her as he stared into the microscope.

Dinner Talks

Earth
05.27.2104

"Honestly T, I'm trying to understand this, I really am."

Tobias rolled his eyes at his friend. "Let it go, Gavin. I just… I just had an off day."

"An off day?" Gavin stared at him, then guffawed. "An off day and you get a lowly 95% on a test, boy genius. You got 71% on this, *seventy*…"

"Yeah, I can read, Gavin."

"And the note from Berkowitz…"

"Yeah, I read that too."

"I mean, you got a fever, T?" His friend reached out and felt Tobias' forehead, a smug grin belying his solicitous tone. "You're feeling a little hot there, you know, hot for…"

"You aren't going to let this go, are

you?" Tobias growled.

Gavin laughed as he threw himself into the armchair in their shared living room. They were roommates, study partners, and best friends. It was no surprise that Gavin was the first to know about Syn, especially since Tobias had spent every evening of the last week talking to her well past midnight after tracking down her contact info.

"I'm just proud of you, T, rooting for you, and all that."

Tobias waited for the other shoe to drop. Gavin wasn't mean-spirited, but he followed the party line. It didn't take long.

"I mean, I get why you are into her, she's hot in a non-human kind of way."

Tobias felt anger wash over him. Syn was different, that was for sure, but every part of her was human and he would not let anyone, not even his best friend, throw shade on that. She had received enough bashing in her brief life already. He opened his mouth, but Gavin had seen the look on Tobias' face and beat him to the punch.

"T, I'm sorry, that was absolutely not okay." His friend held up his hands wide. "The girl is hot, and human, and…"

Tobias felt his tablet vibrate in his

pocket and he pulled it out to read the notification.

"Shit, I totally forgot about dinner tonight."

"Dinner?" Gavin echoed, frowning.

"Yeah, with Janelle and Karen."

"Aren't they in Genesis?"

"Yeah, it's virtual," Tobias answered, distracted as he cast about for the remote for a few moments before giving up. "NARA, connect main screen to Brooks, Janelle in Genesis City, Mississippi."

The screen lit up, blinked twice, and NARA's voice intoned, "Establishing connection to Brooks, Janelle. Please stand by."

Moments later, he could see his adoptive family, what was left of it, now that Julie was dead, on the screen. Janelle looked haggard, still, despite the bright smile she had plastered on her face. The dark circles under her eyes betrayed her lack of sleep. She had taken Julie's death hard. They had only had a few years together, but the loss had taken its toll. Karen smiled at him, spied Gavin in the background, and waved.

"Hey, T, who's that cute girl there?" Gavin asked, knowing full well who Karen was. She giggled and blushed in return, and Gavin's face assumed a look of mock surprise. "Oh my, that can't be your little sister, T! What a fox!"

Karen's cheeks bloomed with red and she stared at her plate, already filled with food.

Janelle nodded towards the two young men. "Good evening, Tobias, Gavin, good to see you both." Her eyes strayed to the empty table and her chest heaved in a silent sigh.

"It's leftover night here." Gavin sprang up from his seat. "And I'm the one in charge of meals tonight, Doc, so I best get to it." He disappeared into the small kitchen, and Tobias could hear the crashing of dishes as his roommate tried to save the day.

"How are you?" Janelle asked, her smile slipping. Tobias had never felt more thankful for the distance between them. Neither Janelle nor Julie Lynn had been typical mom material, but they had certainly tried hard. Julie had been more relaxed, more willing to let Tobias figure things out on his own. She had been the one to advocate for him when he set his eyes toward the ground-breaking course on virology at the college campus that had opened in New Athens. And when their work had kept them in Genesis, she had been the one to suggest the work-study program.

Janelle tried too hard. It worked out okay for Karen—she'd lost her parents when she was just shy of six years old and Janelle's overprotectiveness was what the girl needed. For Tobias, not so much. He had chafed at her efforts. His parents were dead, and his uncle some twenty-two light years away. Losing his family had been hard, really hard, but Julie had intuitively understood his need for space and steadied Janelle's reactions. Without her, all Tobias could feel was judgment and disapproval.

Typically, Tobias and Gavin ate at the cafeteria. But it appeared Janelle had expected something different. Gavin was on it. From the sounds emanating from the kitchen, it wouldn't be long until they had an eclectic smattering of leftovers to nosh on.

"Sorry," Tobias said. "Work ran late, and I forgot about dinner."

Janelle frowned. "I thought you only had class on Tuesdays."

"I was running an experiment and wanted to check on it," Tobias lied smoothly and turned to Karen. "Hey, Squirt, did you get my last email?"

Karen looked up and grinned at him. "The mega-pack of *Chronicles of Kanoodle*? Yes!" Tobias had loved the books as a kid and read the 25th, and last, in the series right before the ESH virus had unfolded. Finding the series again after he had moved to New Athens had made him smile. He had sent the first book to Karen and received a message from her two days later asking for more. The series was funny, dorky, and he had known she would love it. Karen was a quiet kid, even quieter than he had been, shy too. But she had a sense of humor once she got to know someone. It was in hiding, with Gavin bouncing about in the background, but it was still there.

"All right, all right," Gavin said, holding several clamshells full of steaming food. "I've got tater tots in this one, fried chicken in the big one, and mac and cheese in the little one."

Tobias avoided looking at Janelle. He knew she would have a scandalized look on her face. "Yeah, I'll grab the broccoli beef. It was on the bottom shelf."

Fried foods, no vegetables–the next thing he knew Janelle would sign him up for a fresh greens box complete with a juicer. Never mind that the end of the world was going to be here in less than three months. He was betting his next care package would be a shit-ton of vegetables and fruits he didn't know the names of.

A few seconds in the microwave and the broccoli looked wilted, while the beef was bubbling. He returned to see Gavin plonk a half-eaten piece of chicken on his plate while aiming his famous heart-melting smile in Karen's direction.

"Dude, did you seriously take a bite out of that chicken and then put it on my plate?" he hissed at Gavin. His back was to the screen, but Karen must have heard because she gave a little snort and giggled. Gavin just shrugged, blinked, and reached for the broccoli beef.

"I'll take some of those healthy greens you got there, Roomie. Hey, Karen, you and Janelle have got to come to the city for the 4th of July. I hear rumors that there is going to be one hell of a party and the fireworks will be off…the…hook!"

Janelle frowned. "I had heard nothing

about 4th of July celebrations. There weren't any last year."

Gavin shrugged. "I know, I know, it's an antiquated holiday and all that. Especially after the Collapse and Reformation, but here in the city, I guess they figure folks need some way to blow off steam. Impending doom and all that."

"And still no word on the passenger manifests for the last of the lifeships?" Janelle queried.

Tobias shook his head. "They're playing everything close to the chest. Right up to the last minute. Way I hear it, they hope to add another half million Cryo units to the Moon but they're having trouble with the solar array." He shoveled a forkful of food into his mouth and reached for the ketchup, missing it as Gavin swiped it away.

"Tick tock, tick tock," his roommate noted, winking at the screen.

Gavin wasn't worried. And for good reason—his acceptance in the bunker was guaranteed, just as Tobias' place was. They had both passed an essential hurdle six months earlier. Both were in good health, young, educated, and involved in a work-study program. Gavin was helping construct the Cryo units, whereas Tobias was on the fast-track doctoral program. The world would need virologists and scientists and, thanks to Julie Lynn's mentoring, he was more than qualified.

Tobias had just retrieved the bottle of ketchup and shoved a handful of lukewarm tater tots in his mouth when Gavin announced, "Well, when are you going to tell them about your girlfriend, T?"

He choked at that, and bits of food sprayed out. Tobias glared at Gavin before glancing at the screen. Janelle's face looked concerned. "Is she scheduled for the lifeships or the underground bunkers?"

"Well, of course she is. I mean, I'm sure she's on one or the other, Janelle."

"Oh?" The way she said it caused an unsettling twist to his stomach. *Syn would have mentioned it, wouldn't she? If she would not be on the transport?*

"I mean, she's a creche baby. Primina, well, she calls herself Syn now." He saw Janelle's expression turn dour as her head shook from side to side. His stomach twisted again.

"Tobias, they are all infertile. All of them. They won't have qualified for the lifeships or the bunkers." Janelle pushed her half-empty plate away from her. "Once we realized they were infertile, President Chen ended her support of the program, and the Committee removed us from the project."

"I know," Tobias said, panic rising, "I was there."

Janelle continued, "They went off the rails… Some of the Committee, the loudest ones, actually thought the girls weren't human, despite all evidence to the contrary. Their behaviors, the autistic tendencies, and their abnormal growth rate, all of it, worked against Syn and the others. That she and a handful ran away from that place before that terrible fire was a miracle, Tobias, but there is no way they will let any of them into a lifeship. And they certainly won't be considered for a place within the bunkers. I am so sorry."

Tobias was on his feet before he even realized it, his chair falling backwards, anger coursing through him. How could he not have known? How could he not have asked? Here he was, so certain of his own safety, his own future safe within a lifeship or a deep mountain that he couldn't even consider what it was like for someone who wouldn't have that.

"What the hell is wrong with them?" he

bellowed. "This is bullshit, Janelle!" Gavin was on his feet as well, his playful act gone, dread replacing it. His roommate reached out and put a hand on Tobias' shoulder. Tobias shrugged it off and glared at the screen. "Do something, Janelle. She deserves a chance."

Janelle blinked, her throat working. "Tobias, they won't listen to me. They wouldn't even listen to Julie Lynn, not after the Incident."

The Incident had involved not just the removal of both Julie Lynn Aaronson and Janelle Brooks from the team, but a highly suspicious fire barely two months later that had killed most of the bio-engineered children and destroyed the facility they had been staying in. President Madeline Chen, once so interested and invested in the venture, had stopped accepting meetings or responding to their messages.

Goddamn politician, Toby seethed. *She probably* was *behind it.*

Janelle looked haunted.

"Tobias, if I knew of any way to help, I would. Please believe…"

A prolonged set of chimes interrupted Janelle, and the screen blinked and reshaped to include a box in the right-hand corner. The text on the screen read "Breaking News" in bold red text.

Seconds later, the TUPG newsroom appeared, along with Tierra Stevens, a familiar, trendy news anchor. She had handled puff pieces before the virus, and it had made her career standing on the bones of the dead as she quickly became the lead newsvid reporter on the ESH virus. Tobias despised her. He suspected that she loved tragedy, absolutely loved it. *Like a dog loves rolling in shit.*

"Breaking news out of New Athens, where a woman, disguised as a service worker, overpowered a member of President Chen's personal staff and confronted the president for a few moments before President Chen's security detail took her into custody." Tierra's eyes were bright and shining.

Tobias thought her face betrayed barely contained glee. Plenty of things had changed in the past five years, but the news was still the same. *If it bleeds, it leads.* He could see Janelle's mouth moving, but whatever she said remained unheard as the newsvid continued, overriding all devices.

"The president is unhurt after the three-minute confrontation and the intruder has been identified as Alana Malting, a twenty-three-year-old recovering drug addict who lost custody of her young son after the Child Protection Act passed in April 2100. Malting has an arrest record detailing more than a dozen arrests over the past four years. She was also recently charged with criminal trespass, stalking, and violating stay-away orders regarding her son's adoptive family."

The news anchor's face faded, and the box displayed the TUPG flag, along with the TUPG seal, "Together we stand strong."

The box then faded away, and the screen resumed its full display of Janelle and Karen. Janelle had pushed her plate away in disgust. "First someone poisons her closest aide with poison intended for her, and now this. I'm surprised they haven't shot off a dirty nuke towards New Athens."

Gavin's happy-go-lucky façade vanished. He had firsthand experience. He had lost his father to the ESH virus, and his mother to the Child Protection Act when his mother, whose bipolar disorder was normally well-controlled with medication, broke down in the wake of her husband's death. Child welfare authorities had swooped in and removed him from her care, expediting the termination of parental rights and making Gavin a permanent ward of the court. As he had once shared with Tobias, "No one wants older kids. They only want babies, so they can pretend that those babies are theirs and theirs alone. You don't get to pretend a fourteen-year-old's parents don't exist."

Gavin muttered, "I wish that Malting woman had shot her. Or that the president had eaten those damned poisoned fruit instead of her aide."

Janelle gasped, leaned towards the camera, and whispered, "I know you don't mean that, but you can't say things like that, Gavin. Nor you, Tobias." Her gaze flicked to his. "It is easy enough for them to monitor everything we say. You don't need to give them any fuel to deny your place and call you subversive." She straightened up, sat back down, and pulled her chair up to the table. "Let's finish our dinner, shall we?"

Tobias sat down heavily in the chair. Anger, hurt, desperation raced through him. He took a bite out of habit, then chewed and swallowed. Suddenly everything tasted like cardboard. He forced himself to eat more. Janelle kept the discussions on safe topics and avoided mention of Syn again. He did his part, nodding, answering her questions, and all the while his mind was spinning. Syn would not get on a lifeship or have a place in the bunkers underground. How could his world have been so full of the "haves" and so devoid of the "have nots?" How could they justify these choices? How the hell did President Chen and the rest of those people sleep at night? Who were they to tell Syn her life wasn't worth saving, especially after they had given her life in the first place? And now they wanted to abandon her?

Long after the dinner ended and Janelle and Karen's faces faded from the screen, the questions continued to roll through him. That, and desperation. Surely there was some way to save her. Surely there was someone he could talk to, some deal that could be made. That question, and the thought of her lost in a fireball of destruction, kept him tossing and turning late into the night.

Reading of the Names

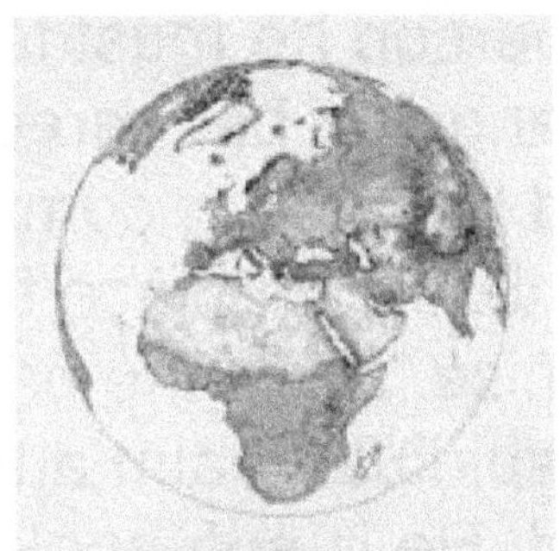

Earth
06.30.2104

"Citizens of the Terran United Planetary Government. Brothers. Sisters. Mothers. Fathers. Children. Today we stand on the edge of the precipice. And we must all be ready to face the challenges yet to come." Madeline's voice was clear as it rang across the world. Right now, her face appeared on every screen, every tablet, every communication device across the world. The transmission interrupted every other function, overriding conversations, movies, and more—all so that one message could reach as many of the citizens of the TUPG as possible.

"According to one Muslim tradition, forty

days before the death of a person approaches, God drops a leaf from a tree below the heavenly throne, on which Azrael, the Angel of Death, reads the name of the person he must take with him. He is not an angel to be feared. He is kindness, and brings joy, comfort, and inspiration to those who face their imminent demise. He is the bridge between the spiritual realm and the material world. He is soft-spoken, patient, meticulous, and unobtrusive."

She paused, swallowed past the dryness in her throat, then continued, "We stand at the edge, and all that has gone before has prepared us for what is coming now. The end of our world is at hand. The last of the lifeships will depart in the next few weeks, ensuring that humanity will live on. Our scientists can project the angle of impact now and it is worse than we had hoped. In exactly forty days, on August 9th, 2104 at approximately six p.m. GMT, Azrael will impact the Earth at a sixty-degree angle. The last asteroid to impact Earth at this angle brought about the end of the age of the dinosaurs, who had reigned on Earth for over one hundred sixty-five million years."

"Some of these ships will return, when it is safe to, whether that is in two years or ten, or even twenty. And in a few moments, you will know if we have selected you for those lifeships, or for a chance at survival here on the planet, deep under the Earth's surface, when Azrael comes to collect those left above."

She stopped, took a sip of water, swallowed, reached inside herself for the strength to say what came next.

"From the moment we are born, our end is foretold. All living things must die, some sooner than others. We know the time and day of our death, thanks to Azrael, but this will not be the end for all. Our world will survive, and it will recover. And when it does, there will still be humans left to populate it. For those who are not on the lifeships or underground bunkers, we will provide a humane alternative. We have sent shipments of Danake worldwide and it is available to all. It is simple and painless and takes effect in less than ten minutes."

Madeline paused, took a breath, and set her notes down. She didn't want to read the messages from the acting pope or leaders of the Christian coalition. The people could read those online if they chose. Those leaders' assurances to their followers that God would not condemn them to purgatory or hell or damnation for taking their lives using the drug were already well known. She didn't need to say it again. Instead, the truth of how she would end her life needed to be shared. Just as she had given birth to a child in order to model the proper choice for her people, now she needed to model yet another behavior. Her people, her world, they deserved to know the truth.

"I have made choices, pushed through laws, and so much more hoping to save humanity. Some of those choices…" Her voice wavered as she continued, "Some of those choices I would take back if I had the chance to do it over. But know this, my actions have always been in service of humanity. My duty has been to care for the people left in the wreckage of the world that once was. I cannot take back my choices, or my actions, but I can offer the only thing that I have left, and that is my life."

She took another sip of water, set the glass down, and forged ahead.

"I will not be on the last of the lifeships. I will not join those of you who seek refuge beneath layers of rock and earth as Azrael approaches. Instead, I will take my place by the sea and watch the Angel of Death descend on the planet and the people whom I pledged to serve. I will make my stand and accept the fate that so many of you will share with me. I will be strong. And I ask you to be strong as well."

She could sense movement to her right as Jeff stood up from his seat, his face no doubt full of shock. This was not part of the script, and she knew they would try to talk her out of it, especially Jeff.

"For centuries, leaders have sent others to die in their place. Through war, through peace, in times of hunger, and in times of plenty. But what makes my life worth more than yours? Nothing. I belong here, on Earth, with the others. And I have made my peace with that. I urge you to make your peace as well. If your name is not read, if you do not receive the summons to the lifeships or to the dozens of bunkers we have spent the past four years constructing, then I urge you to join me in peace and acceptance. And when the time comes to take the angel's hand and accept your end, I hope you will do so, knowing you have done the best that you can. I can't help but think that God will understand."

She looked into the cameras for a moment, tears blurring her sight. "Spend these last few weeks in peace, in love, and strength." And before they could stop her, even as the buzz turned into shouts and questions, Madeline turned and walked away from the lectern. It was a cacophony of sound.

Her strides were long, ground-eating, and she sensed Jeff's presence, his breathing, as he caught up with her, one hand finally connecting with her arm.

"Ma'am, please."

"I think that, after all we have been through, Jeff, that you might call me Madeline." She maintained her fast pace, the hallway a blur of shocked faces. As the hallway ended and intersected with the enormous atrium, she turned down another hallway and Jeff matched her stride for stride.

"Fine, Madeline, please, can you stop for just a moment?"

They were approaching her personal quarters, which also connected with Ireti's nursery. Adam was waiting there, the rest of the security detail just steps behind her.

She glanced behind and past them. Sure enough, Jack was on his way as well, his face pale, concern written all over it.

Madeline sighed, stopped, and waited for Jack to catch up. "Why don't we take this inside, hm?"

The first room was a large sitting room, and she led the way, sat down on the plush armchair, and waited for the others to sit. Adam let the door close behind them, the rest of the security detail vanishing as the door closed softly.

"Ma'am, erm, Madeline, what in the hell?" Jeff asked, his face pale. "Why did you tell the world you would…"

Madeline held up a hand. It felt like an effort to do so. The exhaustion she felt at constantly going, fighting to stay afloat and to save more lives, was a constant drain on her reserves.

"You won't talk me out of it. Not you, Jeff, nor you, Jack, nor anyone else, for that matter. I will *not* get on a lifeship and leave Earth and I will *not* hide underground while millions of people die."

"The people need a leader, ma'am," Jack inserted, leaning forward, steepling his hands in front of him as if in prayer.

"Perhaps." Madeline nodded. "Yes, I'm

sure that they do. But it will be time for those who do survive to pick a leader who can rebuild our world from the ruins. I don't want that to be me." She wiped at her eyes, thought of the millions who would die in just forty days. "I've done enough damage, don't you think?"

"Damage is rather a strong word, ma'am," Jack persisted.

Madeline laughed then, bitterly. "A strong word? My God, Jack, I've spearheaded laws that have taken children from their parents, forced women to bear children when they had no interest in parenthood, and created a dystopian nightmare—all in the name of saving our world. If Azrael wasn't so damned determined to finish us, what kind of future will I have created?"

"You are doing this out of guilt?" Jeff asked. A myriad of conflicting emotions ran across his face.

"No, no." She raised her hands and shrugged. "I'm not *needed* anymore. Not for whatever comes next. The lifeships, the bunkers, they hold our future. And I'm… I'm the past. I'm part and parcel of what came before. A bastion of the old regime. They don't need me. And honestly, really, I am the face of the government who took their choices away."

"Ireti needs you, ma'am," Jack's voice was gentle. "A child needs her mother."

Madeline sighed and shook her head. "Ayomide is more of a mother than a nanny. Ireti adores her, *loves* her. And I have planned for Ayomide to adopt her."

She grimaced. "Remember the Child Protection Act I signed in March 2100? Because I do. I remember it every day. Most especially I remember the part that said, 'The best home for the child will take precedence over biological connection.' And that has never been truer for Ireti. She's *happy* and *loved* with Ayomide. I'm little more than a stranger."

She stared at her hands, her fingers, and remembered the thousands of documents she had signed over the past five years, three weeks, and one day since she took an oath of office first as the president of the Reformed United States of America, and later as the sole remaining world leader left alive in the chaos that followed the ESH virus. The countless number of lives she had affected, even destroyed, through the legislation that had stripped women of their rights and torn their children from them.

Someone had to take responsibility. And why not her? *God knows, the others came up with the ideas, but I was the one who made it happen.*

Night had fallen by the time Jack and Jeff left her quarters. They had tried every argument, and she had poked holes in every one of them. She made her mind up. Just as the world had needed her to be the face of the mother, now it required the face of the crone. Her time of influencing others, manipulating them into doing what she believed was best for the world, was over. And that night, after signing the adoption papers in front of three witnesses—Adam, Jack, and Jeff—she had fallen asleep and slept deeply for the first time in years, her heart finally at peace.

Other Father

**Earth
07.05.2104**

"Hey! Um, knock, knock! Are you Tobias Price by any chance?" The voice was unfamiliar, jarring, to Tobias. He was in the middle of picking through the last of his belongings from the apartment that he and Gavin shared. He was due back in Genesis to see Janelle and Karen off on board the Esperanza. After that, he was to report to Cheyenne to continue his research into the ESH virus and its sterility-inducing aspects. At least, that was the plan. It was one he had been fighting internally ever since the broadcast five days earlier. His tablet had pinged the notification but all he could think of was Syn. Knowing she wasn't joining him at Cheyenne, or that she had anywhere of safety to go, had jolted him out of his safe little world. Why did he get to survive, and she didn't?

Tobias, startled out of his reverie, turned and blinked. He had expected a soldier. The military was handling most transport and security for the refugees. Instead, it was a young man, not much older than him.

"Are you Tobias Price?" the man asked impatiently.

"Uh, yeah, I am. What can I do for you?"

"Communique from a Daniel Medry." The young man held a thin wedge in his hand. "Thumbprint access only."

"Thumb… For what?" He stared at the tiny device, befuddled.

The guy shrugged. "I'm just the courier." He held it out towards Tobias, waiting.

"My uncle is on a spaceship, headed for the Gliese system," he said, feeling stupid.

The guy raised his eyebrows, gave Tobias a once-over. "Huh, I'm betting you got a golden ticket out of here, you lucky bastard. Me, I'm waiting on the transports to the equator." He gestured with his free hand. "You going to put your thumb down or just stand there?"

"Oh, sure, sorry." Tobias reached out

and pressed his left thumb against the reader. It emitted a friendly chirp and turned green.

"All right, it'll unlock in a second and if you could sign here, I'll be on my way."

Tobias signed his name with a stylus the young man dug out of his jacket and then pressed the OK button. They both stared at the wedge. It flashed green three times, clicked, and then opened to reveal a small memory stick nestled inside.

"Alright, golden ticket kid, here you go."

Tobias picked up the memory stick, staring at it in bewilderment. It barely registered when the guy disappeared. Tobias just stood there, in the living room of his open, and empty, apartment and stared at the memory stick. Finally, it clicked. The ship had dropped out of the trans-light speed and flipped around in January 2102, nearly two and a half years ago firing its engines to begin an agonizingly slow deceleration process. The D.O.V.E. probes, sent over sixty years earlier, had dropped relays, hundreds of thousands of them, over the journey to the Gliese 581 system. With the relays in place, and the Calypso no longer out of contact now that it was out of trans-light speed, it had scooped up the messages from Earth and also, apparently, sent some of its own.

The memory stick was tiny, far too small for the feelings that swirled inside of Tobias. Uncle Dan had been his favorite. Small wonder there. His uncle had spoiled him with gifts, fed him junk food and tons of sugar at every opportunity, and been a great guy to hang out with. There had been little use thinking of him, not with him so far away, but Tobias had dreamed of him more times than he could count. Most of the time, the dreams were memories. Of watching the stars through a high-powered telescope Uncle Dan had given him for his seventh birthday, all the presents his mom and dad had given him paling in comparison. Or learning to ride the vintage skateboard that Dan had bought with his own money when he was a teenager and given to Tobias for his ninth birthday. Mom had been hot about that; she was convinced Tobias would break every bone in his body "on that monstrosity."

And until Uncle Dan had left, Tobias had been sure he would be an astronomer or an astronaut. He had stared into the telescope every night after his uncle left, dreaming of a day when he could follow him to that distant star system. That is, until the ESH virus had descended upon them. Once that had happened, well, the stars didn't matter, not after that. The only thing that mattered was saving humanity from extinction. Julie Lynn's arrival in the refugee camp had changed his life once again, and the dream of following Uncle Dan to the stars had died. Now Tobias hoped to do that by defeating the virus, and by rekindling humanity's ability to reproduce without the endless miscarriages and fetal deaths.

His uncle had learned, possibly for the first time, that Tobias' parents, Uncle Dan's brother- and sister-in-law, were dead, that Tobias had been one of the lucky survivors. If you counted losing your parents and unborn sibling to a nightmare virus as luck.

What would his uncle have to say? Tobias felt rooted to the spot. He tried to calculate the time that it had taken for this message to reach Uncle Dan, and the time a return transmission would take to arrive. What did he know of the Earth that was? Did he know about the killer asteroid? Of the infertility?

Finally, he closed his hand gently around the memory stick and turned toward his rucksack, digging his tablet out of the zipped pocket. He dug it out, waited for it to power up, and slipped the memory stick into the port. The screen flashed, a wait symbol appeared, and then Uncle Dan appeared on the screen. He was thinner than Tobias remembered, but otherwise, the same.

"Hey, Toby." The man on the screen smiled. It wavered there, uncertain, and his eyes clouded over momentarily. "Bear with me, this is, uh, this is harder than I thought it would be. But I've been thinking of you, pretty much every day, since we heard the news." He looked off-screen for a moment. "The days are pretty hard to judge here. No sunrises or sunsets out in space, but we dropped out of trans-light speed on January 13th, 2102 Earth time and learned about the virus a couple of days later. It really shook us."

He paused, rubbed his hand across his forehead. "Stupid, I know, understatement of the year. I just can't... Even now, I can't wrap my head around it. I don't know what I'm doing, Toby, or if I should even reach out now."

The screen jumped and blinked, and Uncle Dan wore a fresh shirt. "Okay, yeah, I'm back. Sorry, kid. I want to do this right, you know? You deserve that much." He winced. "You deserve a hell of a lot more, but you ended up with me."

He held up a screen covered with handwritten numbers and equations. "I've been trying to figure out how old you will be when you get this, so I don't treat you like you are still nine. The way I figure it, it takes around twenty-four months to get, or receive, a transmission from Earth. It won't be immediate. If I send it soon, you'll be getting this around July 2104. Shit, kid, you'll be nearly fourteen years old."

Daniel looked away, wiped his eyes. "I looked for you." His voice changed, caught. "I looked for your mom and dad. Every day, after my shift was over, I dug through the transmission packets. It was a shit show."

He laughed, looked up at the screen, and Tobias could see the moisture glistening in his uncle's eyes. "I think I'm safe swearing in front of you. Your mom would have gutted me like a fish if I'd slipped up when you were younger." He ran a hand through his hair, and Tobias suddenly wondered how they showered in space.

"You'd think there'd be a way to organize the damn things. But no. It was like a slow slog up shit mountain. And the not knowing, that was the worst part of it. I know it was nothing compared to actually being there, having it happen all around you, but believe me when I say there were days when it was too much. I couldn't mentally stand to see another name, read another headline. We were all off our feed, clothes hanging loose, sick and depressed. We were watching the end of the world and helpless to do anything." He waved his left hand impatiently. "I can see you now, 'Get to the point, Uncle Dan.' Sorry, kid. I guess I don't know what the hell to say other than, I finally found you. In some goddamn refugee camp, and later an document that Dr. Julie Lynn Aaronson had adopted you."

He smiled suddenly. "Julie Lynn is the twin sister of the Calypso's Acting Captain. How crazy is that? Our world is smaller than we might think." He winced then, and Tobias could see his uncle regretting his word choice. The world was definitely smaller now than it had been in centuries.

The screen jumped again, and Uncle Dan's shirt had changed again. He had to have recorded this over a couple of days. This time he was sporting a five o'clock shadow. His eyes had gray shadows under them. Tobias couldn't remember his uncle ever looking so haggard.

"Sorry, Toby, it's been a couple of days and I just, well, I'm here now and I'm going to say what I need to say and get on with it, okay?" His uncle reached for some water, gulped it, and closed his eyes as he swallowed. "I fucked up, Toby. I should have never left you. I should have never listened to Janine back in early '90 when we first learned she was pregnant. I should have faced the music; I should have stepped up and told Luke the truth and I should have done the right thing."

Tobias paused the recording. Suddenly, his chest felt tight, his pulse elevated. Exactly what was Uncle Dan trying to say? What did he mean about facing the music? His finger hovered over the play button. Did he really want to hear what Uncle Dan was going to say next? The not knowing was worse than whatever was coming, and his finger finally landed on the play button once again.

Uncle Dan leaned closer to the screen, his voice hitching. "Family is everything, and what I did was inexcusable, but I hope that after I tell you the truth, you will forgive me."

Later, once the video had ended, Tobias sat rooted to the spot, mouth slack, mind spinning. He began piecing through every memory of his uncle, and of his mother's interactions with him. Mom had always been so disapproving of Uncle Dan, and yet, Tobias thought he could remember tenderness as well, when no one was looking. In some ways, it all made so much sense, and in others, he was so angry, so lost and hurt, that he wanted to scream.

He sat there in the empty apartment as the bright afternoon sun gave way to shadows and slipped below the horizon.

There was only one person in the world who Tobias could think of to talk to. One person who would truly understand how he felt. She had been betrayed, too. If not by family, then by those who had brought her into the world. Was it really that much different? He dialed the number, and it rang three times before Syn answered, her voice hesitant.

"I thought we agreed it would be best to

not talk any longer. Aren't you due to go to Cheyenne?"

"I need to see you."

"Tobias," she sighed softly, "I don't think it's a good idea."

"I'm not getting on that ship, Syn. I'll tell you why in person in four hours. Meet me at the airport?"

"Tobias, what…" He ended the call and punched the Do Not Disturb function on his phone. When he missed the transport to Cheyenne, he may or may not be missed. He wasn't going to take the chance. Only the thought of Syn was in his mind and, with it, the ability to do the right thing. That was the parting message that Daniel had left him with. It was one that he was determined to follow through on. Family was everything, but Janelle and Karen were safe, and Syn was more important to him than he had ever thought possible. Doing the right thing, that meant finding a way for the two of them, him and Syn, to be together.

And he was banking on his golden ticket status being important enough to get them into the Cheyenne Mountain Complex.

Five hours later, having practically stolen a flitter, he landed in Florence and taxied the flitter over to Syn's whip-thin frame.

"Tobias, you had Do Not Disturb on your phone. I couldn't get through. I've been calling you for hours. Janelle called every five minutes until they strapped her to a gurney and shoved her and Karen in Cryo."

"I don't care." He unstrapped himself from the cockpit and climbed out, pulling her to him. She froze up. Touch was difficult for her, even with him, and it took her a moment before she slowly relaxed in his embrace.

"Tobias, I…"

"Just listen, okay?" he interrupted, and pulled away from her. "I found out something today. Something I would have known if I'd paid a whit of attention to blood type, and something that perhaps I knew deep down all along. And I'm angry—God, I'm angry—and I'll tell you all about it, but first, I need you to get in the flitter."

"Why? Where are we going? You know that there is nowhere that is safe, right?" She stared at him, took his face in hers. "Why would you give that up for me, Tobias? Your life is important, it has meaning, it's…"

"No more important than yours is, Syn. Engineered or born, you are human and you deserve a family."

Her face wobbled. "I can't have children, Tobias. They tested us, remember?"

"I'm your family, and you are mine. We'll get the artificial wombs worked out, or we'll adopt. We'll make it work. You'll see."

She laughed, but there were tears glistening in her eyes. "They won't let me in!"

"Yes, yes, they will. Now get in the flitter. We're going to Cheyenne."

"You are nuts, you know that, right?" She brushed away tears, secured the five-point harness into place, and pulled her dreadlocks back from her tattooed skin. He could see she had gotten a new one. It peeked out from the top of her tank top above her heart, and her skin around it was raised and red.

"You got a new tat," he said once the flitter was in the air, the destination programmed into the autopilot. "Can I see it?" He found her tattoos as fascinating as he did her.

Syn flushed and turned away, biting her lip. "I'll show you later, maybe. But seriously, Tobias, what do you hope to accomplish? What happened today?”

"I found out my father is alive.”

Syn frowned in confusion. “You said you saw him die, along with your mother in the early first waves of the ESH virus.”

“Yeah. I did. Or at least, the guy I had always thought of as my dad. My biological dad, Daniel Medry, my Uncle Dan, was his half-brother. And Daniel Medry has AB negative blood.” His hands curled into fists. His emotions were all over the place as he felt anger, hurt, and more. The thought that Dad, or who he had thought of as Dad, hadn’t even known that Tobias wasn’t his. That Daniel and Mom had been lovers, that they had conspired to hide it from Luke, Daniel’s own brother, and from Tobias as well.

“I worshiped him, Syn. I really did. He was the cool uncle, the guy who picked me up and took me to skate parks, fast food, and bought me crazy-expensive stuff. I wanted to fly away with him to the stars. I was going to do it, too. I talked about it for months after he left. And then the virus came. I saw what it did to my parents, my neighbors, *everyone*.” Anguish bled through, and Syn rested a warm hand on his arm, gently squeezing it.

"He left us. He left *me*. How could he do that?"

Syn's hand was steady on his arm, and she was quiet, just letting him talk. He filled the next four hours with stories of Uncle Dan, and his mom, and Luke, the man he still considered his dad. By the end, when his voice was cracking and his throat was dry, and there were no more stories to reminisce about or reasons to continue to rail against a man who had provided half of his DNA, she cleared her throat.

"I'm ready to show you my tattoo now."

She met his eyes and pulled her shirt down, displaying the words etched permanently in ink on her skin.

"Astra inclinant, sed non obligant," Tobias read aloud, a smile slowly curving his mouth up.

"The stars incline us; they do not bind us."

"You remember?" she asked.

He grinned. "How could I forget?"

The night after she left and returned to Florence, they had stayed up all night and talked over their phones. She had found it written along a low wall in a private rooftop observatory, taken a picture, and sent it to him. The tattoo artist had perfectly replicated the script from the photo. Tobias leaned over and kissed her impulsively. He had certainly wanted to do that more times than he could count.

Her fiery eyes looked surprised, even pleased. Seconds later, she frowned.

"Tobias, I need you to promise me that when the time comes, you will go inside of Cheyenne Mountain, with or without me."

He stared back at her, wondering if he should just lie. There was no way he was going to do that. He would not leave her to die outside. They would both walk in there, or they would die together. The world didn't yet know just how important Syn Travani was, but they would. He would show them.

A moment passed. "You won't promise, will you?"

He shook his head. "I'll lie to you if you really want me to, but no, where you go, I go, Syn Travani. All the way to the very end."

Two weeks ago, Janelle had tried to tell him he was too young. That at the tender age of thirteen nearly fourteen, he couldn't possibly know what love felt like.

He had nodded and made the sounds of agreement Janelle had expected. But no matter what Janelle said, he knew how he felt about Syn, and nothing they said was going to change that. He was going to get Syn into Cheyenne before Azrael fell to Earth, and that was that.

Nowhere is Safe

**Earth
07.19.2104**

Jack stood outside of the conference room, his handsome face grim and unsmiling. He strode toward Madeline, meeting her a dozen steps from the conference room door. "He's tossed out his entire team, twice. He insists on doing this himself and he's not in a good place, ma'am."

"I see."

Jack opened his mouth to speak again, and Madeline held up a finger. "Let me talk to him."

The conference room smelled of sweat and old coffee. He'd tacked the walls with handwritten notes, indecipherable equations, and what looked like geometry on steroids to Madeline's unpracticed eye.

She winced as much at the smell as at the convoluted equations on the board. It was mid-morning, but her Chief of Science and Technology had been at this for days, not hours, and seemingly without a break.

Isa Netanyahu was standing, pencil in hand, staring at a long equation, one that threatened to overtake the long west wall. He looked lost in thought. There were stacks of papers littering the long conference table behind him. The far end of the table was stacked with empty cups and plates.

"Leave the coffee and get out," he said, his back still turned. Madeline waited for him to turn around. He finally turned, barking, "I said…" His eyes were bloodshot, his hair greasy, and his clothes wrinkled and stained with coffee. Isa was one of the more distinguished members of her advisory team, and usually the most well-dressed aside from perhaps Loren McClellan, who spent more money on clothing than some of her advisers made in an entire year. Madeline remained convinced that Loren, if put in a time machine and dropped into the late 18th century, would have felt perfectly at home with lace cravats and high-heeled shoes.

Isa's eyes widened. "I'm so sorry, ma'am, I thought you were one of the staff."

Madeline smiled. "I heard that you have been in here awhile, Isa, and I thought it would be best to come and check on your progress."

The man's face crumpled in anguish. "The fragments will enter the atmosphere at varying rates of acceleration based on their size and their proximity to each other in one case, and the rate of spin on the other." He threw up his hands. "If only I had left the damn thing well enough alone."

Isa had spearheaded the move to put the fledgling Asteroid Defense System into practice, with disastrous results. Based on what they knew of Azrael, and its rotation rate and incoming speed, it had seemed like a decent gamble. Send the drones to meet it, explode the charges at precisely the right moment, and voilà, problem solved. Or if not solved, vastly eased. The asteroid would have fragmented into enough smaller pieces that, upon entry into Earth's atmosphere, it would have burned most of the mass away. It would have still been one hell of a light show, but the damage would have been regional and minimal. What they hadn't counted on was connectivity issues. In later analysis, the main relay had failed after the first transmission. This initialized the first charge, but not the rest. This resulted in only a partial fracturing. Instead of one 14-kilometer hulk, they now had four or five pieces heading their way, the largest of which was nearly 10 kilometers in diameter. A significant difference from 14 kilometers, but still far too large.

Isa blamed himself, of course. Which was ridiculous, but Madeline understood why he felt that way. He had been in charge of the mission, and the mission had failed to stop Azrael from impacting the Earth. Now he needed to determine where each piece would fall and when.

Madeline chose her words carefully. She needed Isa; she needed his expertise, and he had already tossed out every assistant she had sent his way. The man needed sleep, and a shower, and after that, she needed answers. The bulk of humanity left on Earth was unprotected. If the impact points were identified, then those who had to take their chances on the ground could be transported to an area of relative safety. She needed to relay that information as soon as possible to the world. They had so little time left. Just twenty-one days remained.

"Isa, I need you to listen to me for a moment. I need you to rest. To take a shower, eat something, and sleep." She held up a hand as he objected. "One day, to recover, to screw your head on straight, and to allow the others back in the room so that they can help you. The world can wait one day, Isa. But you, you haven't slept in over seventy-two hours, and you will help no one by giving us incorrect information. Go. Clean yourself up in the guest suite down the hall and I'll have my chef prepare a proper meal for you. Tomorrow will be soon enough for an answer…the next day, even."

"Madame President, I…" She had never seen her Chief of Science and Technology in such terrible shape. Even his skin appeared gray and washed-out.

"It's not a request, Isa." Her tone was firm, steel sheathed in velvet. "This will wait."

Isa looked as if he were about to argue, and then his shoulders sagged. "Yes, ma'am."

Adam stood by her side and watched

Isa totter out of the conference room. Whatever energy he had while facing her vanished. He now moved slower than an octogenarian.

Madeline leaned close to Adam. "Get the doctor to give Isa something to make him sleep. I don't care how it's done. Spike his food if you have to. We need answers, and Isa needs to be in top form to give them to us."

The transports were standing by to help move hundreds of thousands of people to whatever sanctuaries could be found. They only needed to know what parts of the world to avoid. Isa could tell them that.

The next morning dawned with darkened skies and an unexpected cool front, thanks to a hurricane moving through the Caribbean and threatening to come on shore and wash away the crumbling remains of New Orleans. The hurricane was large, so it was little surprise that they felt its effects so far inland.

As Madeline walked down the hall, she saw Isa hard at work in the conference room. It smelled better. She had instructed the staff to not touch any of the papers, and just clean. They had, and now it smelled faintly of flowers, and there was a fresh pot of coffee on the small table in the corner, still half full. Isa turned to greet her as she walked in, his dark eyes brighter, his skin no longer gray and haggard. He had shaved as well, and the older man managed a small smile in her direction.

"Good morning, Madame President." Madeline grimaced, then smiled in return. No matter how many times she had asked him to call her Madeline, he insisted on the honorific. Here, now, in the last days of her office, of her life, it seemed onerous.

"Isa. You rested. You look better."

"Yes, ma'am. Thank you. I've been up since a little before dawn and I have some information for you. Not all of it, but some."

"Excellent. Please proceed." She reached for an empty cup and filled it with the steaming-hot coffee. Sumatra blend, her favorite. She walked over to the newest drawing on one of the whiteboards that lined the walls.

"I had already identified the impact point for the largest piece. I just needed to recheck my figures." He looked embarrassed. "I had made a mistake in the fifth equation that you can see here." He pointed to a scribble that reminded her of Egyptian hieroglyphics. "It was sending me round and round. Once I had a decent rest, it was as clear as day." He shifted to a massive map that appeared on the far wall. He pointed a laser towards a tiny chain of islands in the Pacific.

"My calculations show that the 9.1-kilometer piece will impact the main island of Hawaii here near the Kapapala Forest Reserve, give or take ten miles north or south. It will cause catastrophic destruction of the Hawaiian Islands. Ma'am, there will be nothing left. Worse, it has the likely possibility of setting off a destructive chain of volcanic eruptions up and down the Ring of Fire." He gestured his pointer in a broad arc that outlined the active volcanic range and ran both north into Alaska and south into Central America and further. "And of course, the tsunami, well, mega-tsunami, will affect all the surrounding continents. Most especially Japan and China, and of course the Americas and down to Australia as well." His hand drew a long red circle around the impact point.

Madeline sucked in a breath. "Any chance it will miss and hit the ocean instead?" She remembered them discussing this in the strategy meetings as a possibility. Evidence shows that water impacts, while destructive, have less effect, both short term and long term, than a land impact.

"I ran the numbers three times and messaged a colleague; he's getting the same answer." Isa ran his hand through his hair. "I wish I were wrong, ma'am, I really do."

"And the others? The smaller pieces? They are still large enough to cause damage. Any ideas where they will impact?"

"Yes, ma'am. There are hundreds, possibly thousands of pieces, but we have five objects of significant size that we need to worry about. Those are what I've focused my calculations on, the big one that will hit Hawaii and then the following in order of size." He ran his fingers across his tablet and the wall displays flashed and morphed to another map of the world, one that showed a large red circle around the doomed Hawaiian Islands and smaller circles that dotted a smattering of sites around the world.

"Here is impact point two, a 2-kilometer piece that will impact the Alps." He pointed to it and the simulation showed an impact radius significantly smaller than the first.

"Here we need to worry about ejecta and adverse air pollution. The city of New Munich will need to be evacuated entirely."

The map rotated slightly and zoomed in on the southern edge of Europe and northern corner of Africa. "Here is impact point three, a 1.2 kilometer in diameter piece that will impact the Strait of Gibraltar." He winced. "This would be a limited event except for La Palma. It is a volcanic island in the Canary Islands archipelago. It has long been dormant, but it is unstable. The impact of such a large piece will cause enough tectonic destabilization that the entire western flank of the island will capsize into the ocean. It will then create a mega-tsunami some 600 to 900 meters in height that will affect not just the European and African continents, but the entire shoreline from Maine to much of the eastern length of South America. No coastline will be safe."

The coffee felt like acid in her stomach. How much worse could things be?

"And then we come to impact point four, a .9-kilometer piece that will be an ocean impact about 5 miles off the coast of Cuba. This will have limited initial destruction—we can easily evacuate Cuba and Florida through Texas–but there are hundreds of oil rigs there in the Caribbean, and the force of the impact could cause significant structural damage, even to long-capped and defunct rigs. The surrounding waters will suffer significant pollution."

"Christ," Madeline muttered, dread at what was coming for her world and her people more than she could bear.

Isa's face was pale. "And impact point five, a .5-kilometer chunk will slam into Greenland. This will vaporize the ice sheet and enter the atmosphere, creating a cascade of severe weather events, from torrential rains and snow depending on the location and the amount of other ejecta already in the atmosphere. Overall, we are looking at flooding as far inland as the Sahara Desert in Africa, much of the plains of North America, well, everywhere. And after that, well, at least five to ten years before the skies clear enough for people to grow crops. We're looking at a mini-Ice Age."

Madeline set her coffee down slowly. It was already cooling. She couldn't bear to take another sip, with her stomach churning like it was.

"Where do we send our citizens? What's

safest?" she asked, determined to find something she could work with, something she could help fix.

"For the impact? Or afterwards?"

"Both. Either."

He sat down at the table, resting his elbows on the surface, and covered his face with his hands. He sat there for a moment, saying nothing. When he looked up, his eyes were red, his skin blotchy, and his voice was bleak.

"Nowhere. There's nowhere that's safe. Not for long. And certainly not for the time it will take for the skies to clear and the temperatures to return to habitable levels."

"Christ." She sat down across from Isa. A silence descended between them.

A knock on the door, and Jack leaned in. "Ma'am, we need your authorization on the last group of refugees for the bunker in Russia and we have a situation developing in the South American refugee effort that will need your attention."

Madeline stood up. "Isa, run the numbers again. Get the rest of the team involved. I want everything double- and triple-checked. Also, try to get me some kind of survivability ratios for potential sanctuary areas. We need to give our people something."

Isa nodded woodenly; his eyes haunted. "Yes, ma'am."

She started through the door, then stopped and turned around. "And Isa, we can't save them all, but we can try to give them the best chance of survival. Focus on that. Nothing is for sure in this life, except that eventually we all must die. We'll do what we can for as many we can."

It wasn't particularly inspirational. But it was the best she could manage in the moment. Isa said nothing, inclining his head in a small nod. Madeline nodded and left, the door shutting behind her with a small click.

The refugee authorization for Russia took seconds, but the refugee effort in South America, specifically the delayed launch of one of the last lifeships amid rioting, took longer. There were hours of back-and-forth negotiations between the TUPG troops and the rioters in Brazil. More and more riots were occurring worldwide as panic rose. Jack received an update on how the unrest near the approach to the Cheyenne Mountain Complex that had stopped the steady influx of approved refugees into the underground bunker.

Azrael was a dim, fuzzy light in the sky now, discernible to the naked eye, and with its appearance had come mass suicides, demonstrations, and violence.

A dozen more emergencies erupted as the day wore on, and Madeline forced a sandwich down, along with cups of strong coffee, and tried to ignore the heartburn. Their world was on the edge of destruction, but Madeline held on as they continued to wade through the issues. She would do whatever she could for as many as she could.

Night had fallen by the time she was trudging back to her quarters with Adam. The conference room door was dark. One of the cleaning staff was making her way slowly down the hall. Madeline nodded to her as she passed by. "Have a good evening, Donna."

"The same to you, Madame President," the older woman replied as she opened the door to the conference room. Madeline hadn't made it two more steps before Donna screamed. Adam reacted. He pushed Madeline down to the ground, his weapon in his hand. Seconds later, the hallway filled with security personnel.

Donna screamed again, ran out of the room, and was tackled by security.

"He's dead, he's dead, oh God!" The woman was hysterical.

One of Madeline's security detail glanced into the room before he waved his partner off of the sobbing woman. "Let her go, we've got a suicide here."

A few feet away, Adam helped Madeline stand up as he apologized, "Sorry, ma'am, reflexes."

He stood between her and the conference room. Madeline tried to step past him and he held out a warning hand. "Ma'am, I wouldn't."

More bodies streamed into the hallway, and Adam was herding her toward her personal suite. Madeline side-stepped around him and shook off his hand.

"Let me pass," she ordered, hoping they didn't hear the tremor. She needed to see what had happened for herself. The security detail made way for her, and she stepped into the doorway.

Afterward, she wished she hadn't.

He had shoved the long conference table to one side, freeing a space in the middle of the room. The walls were lit with a scrawled message in red that read,

"Nowhere Is Safe. All My Fault." Below it was a language that Madeline assumed was Hebrew.

שאלוהים יסלח לי

Isa Netanyahu, whose great-grandfather had led Israel for over fifteen years nearly a century before, was hanging from the light fixture. It creaked slightly, as if it might break. The body had a slow, inexorable spin. Madeline sucked a breath into her lungs and felt faint. She had seen him mere hours ago. Alive, drinking coffee, working the problem, every fiber of his being focused on the problem at hand. How could he be so alive in one moment and then gone the next? How could his mind have taken him to this place, this end?

"May God forgive me."

A medic had arrived, and she stared up at the corpse. There was no hurry. The Chief of Staff had been dead for an hour, possibly more.

"I beg your pardon?" Madeline asked.

The young woman did a double-take, realizing who she was standing next to. She was petite, but lithe, and her long, dark hair was plaited down her back neatly

over her EMT uniform. "Sorry, ma'am."
What she was apologizing for, Madeline
was not sure. The young woman pointed to
the scrawled words. "It's Hebrew. It says,
'May God forgive me.'"

Madeline felt tears well up in her eyes.
Isa had nothing to ask God forgiveness for.
He had done what he could, examined
every possibility. Of that, Madeline was
certain. That her friend and adviser had felt
this was the only acceptable outcome filled
her with dread. She turned away, walking
to her private quarters, Adam in lockstep
beside her.

It was past midnight before Madeline
could drop into a fitful sleep, her thoughts
and her dreams filled with that last
horrifying image of her friend and adviser
hanging from the light.

First Gary, her parents and sister, and
her nieces and nephew had fallen to the
ESH virus. Then Aiden, who had
consumed the poison intended for her. And
now Isa, wracked with guilt, as if anyone
could have done better than him in
heading Azrael away from its destructive
path. Her world felt smaller and more
hopeless with each passing day.

Last Call

Earth
08.02.2104

May woke to a set of curious eyes, blurry and indistinct: they were close. Silas' nose touched hers, and his sweet little face lit up with a grin. "Mommy, you're awake!"

May groaned and rolled away, flipping the covers back over her head. It was in vain, and they both knew it. Besides, she could smell bacon and the distinct sweet smell of maple syrup. Ryan had promised them breakfast this morning, and he had delivered.

Silas pulled the covers back off of her head, giggling maniacally as he did it. He was small for his age, inches shorter than average for his age, but he was full of energy and questions. May wondered how older mothers did it. Wasn't it exhausting for them? As it was, she was in her early twenties and Silas wore her out, especially since the last miscarriage a few months ago. She had been so hopeful this one would take, but at fifteen weeks the contractions had come, hard and fast, and she had lost it. That had been hard. Ryan had been so careful ever since. It felt as if he walked around on eggshells.

As if I'm any different from any of the countless other women who have endured miscarriage after miscarriage since the ESH virus.

It was because he loved her. She knew that. She loved him too, more than she had thought possible. A twist of fate had brought them together, him serving on her protective detail during her third trimester. If it hadn't been for Ryan, she and Silas might have died from the placental abruption. It was Ryan who had approached Ollie with the idea of helping break May and Silas out of the hospital before the authorities swooped in and took Silas into protective custody.

She had stayed clean. It had been easy, really. The drugs had been an escape from life, but now she had a reason for living. Silas. Ryan. Ollie. She wasn't alone anymore; she wasn't that unwanted foster kid that no one loved. And she had abandoned drugs the moment she had learned she was pregnant with Silas.

May pulled the covers back and Silas dug his way in, giggling. She reached for him and tickled him until he shouted for her to stop and threatened to pee the bed. She pulled him close, curving her body around him, amazed at how wiggly one little boy could be.

She'd been lucky. While small for his age, Silas was bright, talkative, and on track despite being exposed to drugs in the womb. He had initially shown a delay in speech and he still struggled with some enunciations, along with some trouble focusing, but other than that, he was a normal and happy young boy.

"Daddy has pancakes ready," he said, squirming. "Dere's a stack this high!" He turned so she could see his hands and held them nearly two feet apart. "Get UP, Mommy. Grandma Ollie's coming too!"

May opened her arms and Silas, kicking and rolling, tossed off the covers and rolled down onto the floor with a loud thump.

"Are you okay?" she asked, peering over the side. Her son just laughed, got up, and ran out the door.

She watched him go, amusement and dread filling her. Ollie was here to take him to the ship. The last lifeship would depart today, at noon. And Silas didn't know, couldn't know, because he was going on it without her.

May sat up, swung her feet over the side, and opened the drawer of the dresser that butted up to the bed. Here in this remote cabin, they had made a life for themselves, a place of their own. She thought back to the night that she had come here, on the edge of collapse, still recovering from the emergency C-section, terrified and weak.

Ollie had been true to her word, though. May and Silas had been safe here. Ryan as well, and Ollie visited regularly. There had been fallout, to be sure, and likely there would have been a bigger investigation, and legal trouble for Ollie and Ryan if it hadn't been for the announcement less than five weeks later that Ultima Thule, or Azrael as it was now called, was on a collision course with Earth.

As if humanity hadn't suffered enough.
It had overshadowed the pursuit of one

missing baby in an instant. Suddenly, the fear that humanity would go the way of the dinosaurs if they didn't act fast took precedence. They had diverted nearly all resources towards building the lifeships to take as many as possible away to the stars. There were also dozens of underground shelters, either for people to live in for the decade or more it would take for the Earth to recover, or simply to sleep in Cryo, suspended, waiting for life to resume.

Suddenly, a population of 14.5 million people wasn't too *little,* it was too *many.* The parameters that limited those vaunted spots in Cryo (whether on a lifeship to outer space or underneath a mountain) were strict. They had funneled only the most fertile of women, the children, and an elite, yet minuscule portion of the men into a lottery of sorts. May knew she didn't qualify. That they had been willing to take her child from her because of her drug use had made that clear.

Ollie had made the cut. This was surprising, considering her age. In her late forties, any pregnancy would be risky, but she had given birth successfully in the past and because of her career as a psychologist, as well as her work with ESH survivors, she had made the list to enter one of the last lifeships. Her success in the field had made this a logical choice, especially after a harrowing incident two years earlier involving a group of women brainwashed by the No Future movement into attempting suicide. She had talked them down off of the ledge of a building, all thirty women, many pregnant. She was awarded the Heroes of the Future award, the new, and highest, award given to an elite few.

May slipped on her pants and shirt. Ollie would fly away onboard the lifeship Vision, which was slated to hold the last fifty thousand refugees in the underground lunar base on the Moon. There, powered by the solar energy of the Sun, they would wait in Cryo until the Earth recovered from the devastating impact of the fragments of Ultima Thule. This meal was the last one May would ever share with Silas. Her hands trembled as she buttoned her shirt.

Will he remember me?

If she couldn't raise Silas, she knew with no doubt that Ollie could. Those first few months living with Ollie had proved that, as had the years since as they remained in the house in the woods and avoided New Athens. None of them, not Ryan, Ollie or May, trusted the government not to snatch him from them, even now, with the greatest threat humanity had ever seen looming on the horizon. But today, well, it was time to save her son. He would board the lifeship. Ollie had seen to it. She said she worked hard to pull the strings, flatly refusing at the same time to reveal Silas' location until the last moment. She had also done everything she could to fight for May to take Ollie's seat on board the lifeship, something May hadn't wanted. Not at the expense of leaving Ryan and Ollie behind.

Ryan, there was another hitch.

Ryan had behaved oddly for a full month before he had finally caved and told her, "The TUPG sent me an admittance letter. I'm scheduled to report to Cheyenne Mountain Complex on August 3rd. They said they didn't have our marriage on record and therefore could not guarantee a family spot." He had wrapped his arms around her. "I'm not going, May. I'm not leaving you here alone."

Tears gathered in May's eyes. The Terran United Planetary Government was ripping her family apart, all in the name of rules and best practices.

Where is it in best practices that it's okay to pull us apart like this?

The latest data stream forecast that the one-kilometer chunk would fall in the Gulf of Mexico. The predictions were grim. If IO219 hit at the sixty-degree angle that was being predicted, it would send a 100-meter-high wall of water racing up from the Gulf, destroying everything in its path and not stopping until it reached the middle of Canada. Here in the prairies of North America, the world would be scraped clean of plants, animals, damn near everything. And anyone in its path would die. And that was just the beginning.

New Athens was a ghost town now. Anyone still in the city was leaving tonight. Only basic services, such as the transports up to the lifeship waiting in orbit, remained.

Silas will go with Ollie. And somehow, some way, I need to get Ryan on the transport too.

If she couldn't get on board a lifeship, or down deep underground, at least the people she loved most in the world would. She had hours to get it done, to live this one last, perfect morning with her son and Ollie and Ryan. It was enough. It would have to be enough.

May wiped the tears from her eyes and plastered a smile on her face. The aroma of pancakes and syrup, along with the rich, meaty smell of bacon, hit her like a stormfront and her eyes filled up again.

"Mommy, are you okay?" Silas asked, perched on a stool at the breakfast counter, his mouth full of bacon. "Are you sad?"

May wiped her eyes again. "No baby. I, uh, I think I've got allergies or something, it's making my eyes water."

Ryan wrapped his arms around her, his lips kissing her neck. He smelled of soap and maple syrup.

"I've got pancakes here for you."

"I'm not hungry," she said, grabbing his arms and squeezing back. He was her lifeline. And Ollie and Silas. It was why they had to survive. If they were safe, if they survived, she'd be fine. She had it all planned out, the flitter that would take her to the Ozark Mountains along with a group of others who hadn't made the cut. It wasn't high enough to escape the massive wall of water that would barrel through, but it would be one hell of a view. The group was one of many that had formed as the countdown had formed a year ago, the day of their demise spinning in space at 47,000 miles per second towards Earth.

Some had formed suicide pacts. May wondered if her mind would change when the lifeship carrying Silas and Ollie flew away and they delivered Ryan to Cheyenne, however unwilling he was to leave her. Perhaps she'd pick up the Danake packages the TUPG had provided for all who remained, a cocktail of sedatives that would ease her out of consciousness and send her sailing over the river Styx into the afterlife, if she were to follow the line from Greek mythology.

"You can't *not* eat my pancakes," he whispered, his breath tickling her ear. "I made them irresistible. A little magic, a handful of sexy thoughts, and a sprinkling of mystery."

May laughed as Silas screwed up his face. "Ew. You guys are gross."

A knock on the door and Ollie breezed in, an enormous bottle of orange juice in her hands. "Hello, my darlings!"

She swooped in and gave May a peck on the cheek, and a one-arm hug to Ryan before settling in the chair next to Silas. Ollie opened her mouth as he maneuvered a maple syrup-soaked bite of pancake towards his mouth, cheeping like a baby bird as she begged for the bite. He chortled and shoved it into her mouth.

Ollie rolled her eyes in ecstasy as she chewed the bite of pancake. "Mm, your daddy makes the best pancakes, but they taste even better from your plate, Silas. What do you do to them?"

Silas laughed and shrugged. "You're silly, Grandma Ollie." He looked over at Ryan. "I think Grandma Ollie is silly, don't you, Daddy?"

Ryan nodded dutifully.

"I brought some fresh-squeezed orange juice, the last bottle at the market today. I hear its extra sweet, just the way you like it."

Silas clapped and bounced in his seat; his mouth full of another bite of pancake.

May caught Ollie's eye. Ollie had said she would bring something that Silas would like, something he would easily eat or drink that would contain the sedative. Ollie gave a small shake of her head in the negative.

So, not the orange juice. What could it possibly be, then?

Ryan pulled out three glasses, and May

suppressed a smile. Silas loved orange juice, and so did May and Ollie. Ryan, however, hated it with a passion. He apparently felt the same about lemonade and grapefruit juice and instead kept a jug of grape juice in the fridge that he could consume by the gallon if given the chance.

She reached for two of the glasses of juice, passing one to Silas and the other to Ollie, and sat down on the far side of Silas.

"I'm glad you are here."

Ollie smiled up at her. "Me too."

May sat down and dug into the plate of pancakes Ryan had pushed in front of her. Part of her felt ill, her stomach in knots at the thought of saying goodbye to the people she loved more than anything else in the world. When she had come to Ollie with her plan, that of drugging Silas and Ryan as well, in order to get her son off of Earth in Ollie's capable hands and Ryan to Cheyenne, Ollie had resisted. There was still time to find a way into the lifeship, or see if the extra spaces in Cryo or there in the general population in Cheyenne opened up.

Ollie had argued with May, told her not to give up hope, but May had remained resolute. It was the only way. Nothing would sway the TUPG to accept a loser ex-junkie. Her darling son, yes. Her husband, an upstanding officer and soldier who had served in the Narine conflict with distinctions, absolutely. But her? They would never agree to it.

No matter, Ollie had eventually relented and come up with a plan. She could get the sedatives through the hospital where she still worked, and together they would find a pilot to take Ryan, unconscious from the sedatives, to Cheyenne while May watched Ollie and Silas leave Earth bound for the Moon.

So, it's not in the orange juice.

May took a large gulp of it. Ollie was right, it was sweet. She drained it and Ryan made a face, as if the very sight of the orange juice offended him, and poured another glass for her and topped up Silas' glass as he alternated between stuffing his face full of pancakes and chugging orange juice.

Ollie lifted her own glass of orange juice to her lips and then stopped. "Oh, my goodness, I almost forgot. I found those chocolates you love so much, Silas." She set her glass down and made a show out of digging in her bag. "Here, sweetheart, I know it's breakfast, but honestly, what breakfast isn't complete without a little chocolate?" She winked at May and followed it with a slow nod. "Drink your orange juice first. Little boys need their vitamin C!" She kissed his head.

"And I have enough for you too, Ryan." She placed a small bar of chocolate in front of him and then handed May one.

She drugged the chocolate? *I would have thought it would be the orange juice. Easier delivery system.*

Then again, there had been a massive spike in sedatives and other related drugs in the past few months. The last gasp of humanity's drug production facilities.

She caught Ollie's eyes and smiled. "I'll save this for later, I think."

"Of course."

Ryan loved chocolate. He grinned at Ollie. "Thanks Ollie, you remain my favorite." He popped the piece of chocolate in his mouth and began washing the dishes.

Silas leaned back and belched.

"Silas! Manners!" May said. Even now, in these last few hours with her son, she still took her job seriously.

"I was making room," he said and then

chugged the rest of the orange juice.

Moments later, Silas slumped in his seat, his eyes slipping closed. May reached to catch him, slipping as she did, her arms and legs windmilling as she listed to one side. Her arms and legs refused to listen to her. Somehow, Ryan had moved like the wind to her side and she felt his powerful arms wrap around her and pick her up. A blurry glance over and she could see that Silas was limp in Ollie's arms.

May tried to speak, to say something, anything, but her eyelids felt as if she'd attached them to weights. She spun away into the ether, darkness closing in on her as she surrendered to unconsciousness.

Her mouth felt gummed up, full of grit, her eyes still heavy. She dragged them open, confused by what she saw, struggling to understand where she was.

"Silas?"

Ryan's face swam into view. "He's safe, May. By now, they've got him in Cryo. In a few more weeks, he'll be on the Moon and safe in the underground tunnels."

They were moving. She was on a gurney, and Ryan walked beside her. Above was rock and lights.

"Wait, where are we?" May asked, her

words slow. They slurred somewhat, as if she were drunk. Or drugged.

Ollie drugged me. She drugged the orange juice, not *the chocolate.*

Overhead, the lights flashed by, and then they paused and moved through a doorway, Ryan disappearing momentarily from view before reappearing seconds later.

"All right, these are your assigned quarters," an unfamiliar voice said near May's feet. "Ma'am, let's get you upright." He came into view now, and May recognized his face. This was Anthony, the same guy who had helped Ollie break May and Silas out of the hospital four years earlier.

Shortly after they had made their escape, Ollie had told May the story of Anthony and her son Silas. The two men had fallen in love in college, married, and were planning to adopt a child when Silas died in the first few months of the ESH virus. He had carried the AB negative blood type, like Ollie, but that hadn't saved him when the pilot of the plane he was on entered the last stages of the virus on a flight from London to New York. Ollie had lost her only child, and Anthony the love of his life, when the plane plummeted into the ocean.

Anthony smiled at her. "They have closed the blast doors, but I would keep a low profile until impact. Ollie got you in under a false name. You are in Food Service. I hope you don't mind cooking."

With Ryan supporting her on one side, and Anthony on the other, she wobbled off of the gurney. The room was tiny, claustrophobic. But it was a lifeline, one she hadn't expected.

Anthony nodded to them both and wheeled the gurney out of the room. The door shut behind him with a soft click.

"I don't understand," May said as they made their way to the bed. "Ollie drugged *me*. But if there was a spot in Cheyenne, why not just tell me that?"

Ryan sat down next to her, silent.

"Ryan? What's going on?"

"It was the only way, May. And she didn't tell you because she knew you would never agree."

"Damn it, Ryan. I don't understand. Why would Ollie not tell me? She's safe with Silas. You and I are safe now, it's a win-win. We actually have a chance of surviving this, all of us! So why wouldn't she tell me?"

Ryan avoided her gaze, stared at his hands. He sighed and said, "She came to me when you first approached her with your idea. It was the day after they had notified me that I was to report to Cheyenne, which is where we are now. She told me she had an idea that could make everything better. Well, almost."

"Almost?"

"The TUPG was so eager to cram women and children on the lifeships that it was breaking up families. And Ollie knew of one couple in which they slated for the woman and their daughter to leave on a lifeship, but the husband was staying behind, headed for Cheyenne. A Michelin-level chef, no less. Ollie got Anthony to switch the assignment and get the husband in Ollie's spot on the lifeship with his wife and kid, and open his spot up here in Cheyenne. Then she gave it to you. It was the only way. We already registered Silas for the lifeship, and she knew that due to the increased security, they would stop you from getting on that ship with him. The underground bunkers, though, they have less security because it isn't a sure thing. We could still die during the bombardment, but at least we would have a chance.”

“But Ryan, Ollie isn’t here, and she isn’t on the lifeship. She’s…” May couldn’t move past the horror rising to choke her throat.

“She stayed at the cabin, May. To save you, to save us. A devil’s bargain, she said, and a price she was ready to pay.”

“No,” May whispered, her throat closing tight. Tears swam in her eyes. “Not Ollie. Not for me.”

Ryan turned away from her, digging through a rucksack. Clothes spilled out. He set a tablet in her hands.

“She left a video for you.” He stood then; eyes cast down. “I have to report in and get the assignments, review the duty roster. I’ll be back in a few minutes.” He put his hand on her shoulder. “She wanted this for you, May. She loves you.”

The door closed quietly behind him. May could hear others moving along down the corridor, their voices chattering as they passed by the door. She stared at the tablet for a few minutes, not willing to accept the reality she found herself in. Finally, she pressed the power button, unlocked the tablet, and pressed the icon waiting there on the screen.

The tablet's screen flashed and it showed Ollie, dressed in her standard scrubs, sitting at her desk in the New Athens hospital. She smiled, and May felt the tears trickle down her cheeks.

"May, my darling girl. I know this is not what you expected or planned for, but here we are. When you came to me and asked for my help in making sure that Ryan and Silas survived, even if you did not, I remembered the wild-eyed girl I met for the first time over four years ago. A girl who did not know her own worth, or of the beauty and art she was capable of. It has been an honor and a pleasure to have spent the last four years with you, first in my home, and then, in the home I raised my own Silas in."

"May, my sweet girl, you are more than a friend, but a daughter in my mind and heart and I would give anything for you, for little Silas, and for Ryan."

"I made sure that Anthony found a way for both of you to be together, there in one of the safest underground bunkers on the planet. You will survive, of that my heart is certain. And at the end, however long that might be, Silas will return to you. I know

you will forgive the subterfuge, for I can think of no better ending to this. A light at the end of an endless tunnel."

"Thank you, May, for showing up in my life. For allowing me to be a grandmother to your son. I am forever grateful for your presence in my life. In loss I found hope, and it is with hope and joy that I send you away to your future. For it will be a beautiful one. After all that the Earth and humanity have suffered, let there be love waiting for you at the beginning and end of it all."

"I love you. Thank you for letting me be a part of your family. Live your life well."

The video ended. May leaned back against the smooth, hard stone wall and wept.

Impact

Earth
08.09.2104

Half Moon Bay, California

In the distance came an enormous boom, and the sky lit up as a column of fire burned its way through the atmosphere. It wouldn't be long now. A few hours at most.

If I want to run like hell, now would be the time to do it.

Madeline stared out at the ocean. It was threatening to storm. She smiled and slipped off her shoes and dug her toes into the chilly dampness, felt the water flow over her and then pull back, the sand under her feet slipping sideways as the tide drew it out to sea.

The beach, except for her, was deserted. There was no one in sight as far as the eye could see. She looked north, examining the rocky cliffs. Then south, to the unending stretch of sand that disappeared in the distance. Her family had owned this entire stretch for more than a century and some of her earliest memories were of building sandcastles and running along the shoreline searching for shells. The smell of the sea, with its briny scent of fish and seaweed and life, filled her nostrils. It smelled like home. And she had been away from it for far too long.

Adam had been the hardest to convince. When the lottery had listed his name, he had tried to ignore the email. Would have ignored the email, if it hadn't been for her instructions that she be notified when any of her staff qualified for the lifeships.

Adam had stayed by her side, faithfully, all of this time. His role changed from protecting the spouse of the RUSA President to leading her security detail for the past five years. *He would be here now if I had not insisted. But what good would it serve? My work is complete. Now I can count my future in mere hours.*

She had exchanged her silk business suit for a simple, pale-blue summer dress. It was one she had purchased shortly after Gary's re-election and never worn, the hopes of stealing away to Camp David lost to the chaos of a virus that had threatened humanity. She found the gauzy fabric freeing after years of wearing suits, day in, day out. Madeline had done what she could. She had saved as many as possible. She had made decisions she regretted, but now it was over. Madeline watched the waves rise to meet the low, gray clouds.

"Mind a little company?" A familiar voice intruded on her thoughts. She turned, smiling, to see Jeff. He wore khaki pants and the loudest, brashest Hawaiian shirt she had ever seen. He leaned down and slipped off his shoes and socks and tossed them away as he squinted, staring at the growing gloom offshore. "I think you picked the wrong beach for viewing the end of the world."

"You had a space," Madeline said, tilting her head. "I made sure of it."

"Yeah, well, there was this crazy, tattooed, dread-locked girl with fiery eyes at the gates and her smart-mouthed teenage boyfriend determined to get her in. True love, what could I do?" Jeff said, digging his toes into the sand. "You know, I can't remember how long it has been since

I dug my toes in sand."

"Jeff…"

"Madeline…"

Grief bubbled up in her. "You need to live, Jeff. Of all the people…you are one of the good ones. You, Jack, Aiden." Saying Aiden's name still hurt, even after three years. "You shouldn't be here."

Jeff leaned down, scooped up a handful of sand, and watched as it ran through his fingers, coating his fingers with a fine layer. "I think I'm exactly where I need to be." He reached into the pack slung over his right shoulder. "I even brought snacks. Contraband. Hell, I even brought a couple doses of Danake, if we don't want to wait for the wave." He pulled out a cellophane-wrapped bag of Twinkies, wiggling his eyebrows as he did.

She laughed, even as the tears ran down her cheeks.

"Hell, I even found some Twix. Some damned factory has been generating junk food for the past few months and I can't help but indulge. My A1C is likely through the roof." He tossed one towards her and she caught it.

"I didn't think they even made these old candies anymore. Not after the Healthy

Bodies Act." Madeline winced at the memory of pushing through legislation that had banned foods using high-fructose corn syrup and sugar in response to a report on how obesity affected fertility. It had caused more protests than banning contraceptives had.

Jeff grinned. "Take a bite."

"I haven't eaten something this sugar-filled in more than a decade."

"All the more reason." He nudged her hand, and she unwrapped the Twix and bit into the bar, her eyes closing as the flavors of chocolate and caramel and cookie exploded in her mouth.

"Cue the diabetic coma," she said wryly, once she had finished chewing and swallowing.

"I think that, somewhere along the way of trying to save humanity, we forgot what it means to live," Jeff said, biting into the Twinkie.

"So, junk food is what it means to live?"

He raised his eyebrows, smiled, and gestured around them. "Look at where we are, Madeline. Here, where you grew up. Your fondest memories, perhaps. A simple beach, with sand and surf, and the salt air. Tell me your eight-year-old self wouldn't have wanted this, along with a Twinkie," he said as he handed the second one over. "And a sandcastle. We have to have a sandcastle."

A week before, they had finally received confirmation of the impact point. Hawaii, the main island, was ground zero. None of the island paradise would remain, and the resulting crater would quickly fill with water. There would be nothing left. Nothing but human memory and old maps to show that the island chain had ever existed.

Here on the beach, they wouldn't experience the shock wave or corresponding fireball, but the mega-tsunami would reach them in four hours, a wall of water a thousand feet high. They had time. They could still run, and with Jeff standing there, Madeline was tempted, briefly, for his sake. Of all of her advisers, he had been the lone voice of reason, outvoted, but never wavering. He'd been her conscience, her very own Jiminy Cricket. Madeline smiled, remembering Loren calling him that, and how it had stuck in her mind.

"You want to build a sandcastle?" she asked him, bemused.

"Yeah. I really do."

Hours later, a wonky sandcastle stood near the edge of the surf. "I remember being better at this," Madeline said, brushing the sand from her knees.

"Well, it's my first sandcastle. So, I think we did great." Jeff winked at her.

The moment between them vanished as the surf, so close to the edge of the sandcastle, now fled at an alarming rate, racing down the beach. The edges of rocks, a sharp drop-off they hadn't seen suddenly exposed, and fish and other sea creatures littered the way, caught off-guard by the sudden disappearance of the sea. The wind blew, not from the ocean, but towards the ocean, buffeting them. They could see a black wall of water forming in the distance.

"Azrael…" Madeline whispered. "Jeff, I tore apart families. Forced women to have babies they didn't want. Took their right to choose away from them."

Jeff reached for her hand, and she could feel the gritty layer of sand on his skin. "I've told no one this. Once, when I was twelve, I stole a neighbor kid's bike. I stole it and I never gave it back."

Madeline choked and then laughed at the thought of her adviser, her friend, actually stealing a bike. "Hoodlum."

"Fascist."

He gripped her hand tighter. "Time for our souls to be weighed."

In the far distance, lightning flashed, illuminating a massive darkness rising higher and higher into the sky, roiling black clouds combined with ink-black ocean water until there was little distinction between where the sky ended and the water began. The light breeze was now a gale-force wind that snatched their words away. It didn't matter. Nothing mattered any longer.

The maelstrom that was ocean and impact and force took them then. Their bodies disappeared into the wall of water that moved over the land with a force unseen in millions of years.

Casa Oceano–the Mediterranean Ocean Spiral

Lexi Santfeli, the mayor of Casa Oceano, was not ready for the flotilla that had arrived at the doors of her underwater city. Looking up from her fifth-level office, the boats cast a pall of darkness on an otherwise pleasantly greenish-blue-tinted water. There were far too many to count, and she regretted ever having mentioned that they had room to spare. Most of those people floating on the boats above were families with small children. Worse, these people weren't seasoned sailors, or researchers, or those with any specialties at all.

All the best, the tens of tens, those were already on the lifeships, promised a life after all of this destruction and chaos. Those who remained were without skills or a future–in more ways than one. Only people crazy enough to stay, like Lexi and a few dozen others here on Casa Oceano, were the exception to the rule.

There were no certainties that the spiral underwater city was any better of a fate than that of the surface above. The dire news, just two weeks ago, that at least one fragment, some 1.2 kilometers in size, would impact somewhere in the Strait of Gibraltar some 1,600 kilometers away had caused plenty of debate and second-guessing. Between that impact and the other that was heading for the Swiss Alps, their region would likely suffer enormously from both a tsunami and the dual-force waves. Here, under the waves, Casa Oceano should weather the initial impact easily, as long as the predictions held true. It was the aftermath that concerned her most. The main impact of the largest piece of Azrael would have world-spanning, long-term effects. Lexi's lover, Tamara, had studied the charts, noting that the ejecta from the impact would be at least five magnitudes worse than the volcanic eruption of Krakatoa in the late 19th century.

In some ways, being at sea would be safest. There would be a massive change in air temperature, and that would in turn affect the sea temperature. But Casa Oceano was well-suited for this, as long as the spiral made it through the short-term effects of the initial impacts.

Lexi's radio squawked. The transmissions sped up in frequency, and she could hear shouting in the background. She hurried up the five flights of stairs to sea level. The scene that greeted her was one of utter pandemonium. It rocked Lexi to the core. As far as the eye could see, there were boats, rafts, flotation devices, and people. Small children crying, women screaming, as the sky lit up with the fiery contrails of the asteroids entering the atmosphere. The blasts of two sonic booms as the asteroid fragments entered the atmosphere created panic in the already frantic refugees. Her men were not only overwhelmed, they were unprepared. There were only two who had any military experience, and one of them, Olanti, looked as if he were courting a coronary. The melee overwhelmed his booming voice.

Lexi felt a current of fear run through her. Casa Oceano had no police—none had been needed for the three-dozen staff currently living in the spiral city. In fact, to call it a city would be stretching the truth. At most, Casa Oceano could hold two hundred souls, and that was with everything at full capacity. Instead, the spiral was 75% complete and the living quarters still under construction. They couldn't allow all of these people in. There had to be at least five hundred, maybe more.

Tamara appeared at her elbow, out of breath from her climb. Considering she worked on the 20th level, in the deep-sea mammal observatory, that she was here as quickly as she was spoke to the urgency of the situation.

"Ah, Christ, Lexi," she managed

between labored gasps, "Call Olanti and Demall in. We have to close the doors and retract the deck." Trust Tamara to be ruthlessly pragmatic. The architect designed the deck to retract a good twenty feet below sea level. This allowed their spiral city to move in cadence with a stormy sea, with no damage.

"But the people, Tamara, the babies, we…"

Screams interrupted Lexi as a second sonic boom hit, and this one felt different, stronger than the others. The surrounding air vibrated and Lexi watched in horror as a woman clutching her infant dove off of a sailboat that listed sideways and began swimming, her baby wrapped against her back but taking in water as the woman fought to stay afloat in the water.

"Oh God, Olanti!" Lexi screamed at the tall hulk of a man. "They are going to drown!"

He turned, saw the woman's head disappear beneath the water, and took two long strides to the edge of the platform and jumped into the salty surf. Within seconds he had taken hold of the woman and was scissor-kicking his way through the waves, back to the platform. As Lexi and Tamara fought to pull him and the woman and baby out of the water, a group of three men shoved Demall to the ground and ran to the opening and down the stairs into Casa Oceano. A ragtag family of five followed their lead, along with couple in their sixties. The boats had formed an impenetrable armada and continued to stack up in rings around the platform. Other refugees were jumping from boat to boat, making their way to the much sought-after entrance to the spiral city. Others weren't so lucky. Plenty slipped and fell in between the boats. Swimming in the Mediterranean Sea was not the same as swimming in a local pool. Those without flotation vests tired quickly and disappeared beneath the water. The sky to the west had taken on a dark, purple-black hue. Roiling clouds sparked with lightning and the wind had picked up.

They needed to get inside. Tamara was right. There was no way to save them all. And if they didn't retract the platform, the spiral city risked being ripped apart by the boats as they crashed into the platform. The waves were rising, changing from a gentle roll to dark-crested leviathans. The force wave, or the tsunami, would be here soon.

Olanti sat on the platform, struggling to catch his breath. The woman, half-drowned, had found her voice. She was currently screaming, a seemingly unending keen as her hands clawed at Tamara's shirt while Tamara hunched over the tiny baby, fighting to clear its tiny lungs and breathe oxygen into it.

An eternity of seconds later, a thin wail issued forth. The baby, red-faced and miserable, returned to its mother's arms.

By now, at least twenty refugees had bulldozed a path through to Casa Oceano, disappearing down the stairs and out of sight.

Tamara lurched to her feet and grabbed Lexi's hand even as she used the other hand to yank on Olanti's shirt. "Come on, Lexi! Olanti! Now! We have to close the doors and retract the spiral. There's no more time!"

Another five refugees, maybe more, shouldered their way past. They could hear a roaring sound and the wind had suddenly ratcheted up to a level that Lexi would normally consider the beginning of a storm. The sky, however, remained clear.

Olanti raced to reach Demall, who was

now on the ground, bleeding from a gash in his head. As one, they turned and ran for the door as Lexi barked into her radio, "Close it down, NOW!" Demall, in the rear, was knocked off his feet in the melee. The access door began closing and Olanti lunged forward, pulling Demall up and deeper into the spiral, just in time. The doorway closed, forming an impenetrable wall. The screams of the people as they threw themselves against it faded away as the platform retracted beneath them. The section they were in was solid, no glassteel to see out into the water at the people left behind in the choppy waves.

Mere seconds later, the entire facility creaked and groaned, surging, buckling, as the tsunami passed overhead. Lexi and Tamara wrapped their arms around each other as it did, hoping and praying the facility would hold. In theory, they had nothing to worry about.

The spiral held, and Lexi and Tamara followed the others down below, Olanti's breaths coming in harsh rasps. As they descended, the opaque chute turned to glassteel, but it wasn't the gentle blue green of the Mediterranean. Far above them, the sky and the ocean were pitch black. The boats had vanished, along with what had to be hundreds of people. The wave moved on, black as night, lethal. It carried with it scores of people who did not know they were already dead.

By the time they did the tallying, fifty-three refugees had made it on board before the spiral had retracted. They clumped together, docile enough now that they were safe from the wave outside. They stared silently out of the windows into the dark waters of the Mediterranean Sea in shock.

Demall glared at the men who had pushed him aside. His forehead dripped with blood.

Olanti had pulled off his sodden shirt and shorts, stripping down to his swim shorts. And the young woman whose infant Tamara had resuscitated sobbed in one corner of the cafeteria. She rocked her child back and forth.

"She lost her husband. He fell overboard and couldn't swim," Olanti rasped, his voice raw. He had taken on a gulp or two of seawater during the rescue effort.

"What the hell are we going to do with them, Lexi?" Tamara whispered. "Do we even have enough food stores to spare?"

"We live in the sea, love. We'll find a way," Lexi answered her lover, before stepping forward to welcome the refugees to Casa Oceana.

Cheyenne Mountain Complex
The massive doors were closed, but the nightmare of seeing the people outside, screaming, clawing at the fences, holding out their children, had left Ryan shaking. Aiming a gun at a horde of desperate people had felt wrong, no matter what his training had taught him. The cold fact was, they were at capacity, likely beyond capacity, and if command hadn't called it, they would have been overrun. Still, it was the stuff of nightmares. As if they hadn't all suffered enough from the virus, here was fate come to deal yet another soul-crushing blow.

He had ushered in the last of them, a teenaged boy and girl. The girl was covered in tattoos. Her dreadlocks hung over her eyes on one side, while the other half was shaved, although not recently. There was perhaps an inch of growth. They clung to each other desperately, and with good reason. He had seen the boy arguing for the girl to be let in, but only the boy had the Ident tag necessary for entry. Clutching each other tightly enough to bruise, they disappeared into the milling mass of people in the enormous cavern that served as a meeting room. Whatever intake system they had for the refugees; it was in tatters now in these final moments. As if everyone had lost their minds as the urgency of the situation increased and the moments to impact ticked down.

The massive mega-tsunami currently washing across the Pacific Ocean was over 1.6 kilometers in height. The massive television screens showed it over and over as it turned the sea first black and then filled with debris. Houses, buildings, autocars and more showed on the screens and the refugees inside of Cheyenne cried, swore, prayed, and some even stood in silence as the world died outside.

The instruments that had measured it were destroyed in a blink of an eye, but Cheyenne had been home to NORAD, and they had at their fingertips a vast array of satellite images. They painted a horrifying picture of what was happening to Earth. The largest piece, just under 10 kilometers in diameter, had impacted the island of Hawaii at approximately 6:05 p.m. GMT.

Mere moments later, three more impacts appeared, just as the late Isa Netanyahu had predicted, as three significantly smaller pieces impacted one after another. A chunk approximately nine-tenths of a kilometer slammed into the ocean 5 miles off of the coast of Cuba, creating only regional destruction. Another piece, just one-half kilometer in diameter, slammed into Greenland. The 2-kilometer chunk that impacted the Alps just outside of the tiny hamlet of Zermatt, Switzerland had a plume of destruction that was quickly obliterating any views from space for most of Europe. The last major piece was a 1.2-kilometer chunk that slammed into the edge of Rabat, Morocco equal distance between the Canary Islands and the Strait of Gibraltar. The force of it destabilized La Palma and its long-watched western flank slid into the ocean, just as Netanyahu had predicted, sending yet another mega-tsunami racing towards the east coasts of North and South America and parts of Africa and the Mediterranean Sea.

The devastation played out on the large screens in the common halls and in what had been the center of the now-defunct NORAD. The views continued to switch from the feeds of hundreds of satellites that orbited above Earth.

The massive doors, now shut, would not be re-opened. Not for a long time. And suddenly, this massive mountain complex felt tiny. Ryan felt lost. Outside, millions were dying. He didn't want to think of Silas hundreds of thousands of miles away, his tiny body sleeping in Cryo on the surface of the Moon. He headed back to his and May's assigned quarters. The world was ending. All he wanted to do was hold his wife.

A Thousand Points of Light

The view from the Asimov International Space Station was spectacular and horrifying at the same time. And for the dozen men and women staring out at their beleaguered planet below, it seemed as if a thousand points of light were now streaking across the globe. The pieces of what had once been Arrokoth 486958, or the Kuiper Belt Object known as Ultima Thule, or simply Azrael, the angel of death—whatever they wished to call it— rained down on Earth, bringing destruction at a level unseen for over sixty-five million years. Some responded with tears, quickly bringing a small handheld vacuum wand to their faces so that their tears didn't turn into floating globules of saltwater in the zero gravity. Others were silent, grim.

A few turned away, especially as the lights from the coastal cities disappeared, snuffed out by a wall of destructive power as the mega-tsunamis, at least three separate ones, ravaged the coastlines on most of the continents. One by one, each continent went dark and the clouds from the impact regions continued to grow. The blue of ocean turned gray-black. As the cloud cover grew, more and more green disappeared until there was little left but cloud cover and the glow of volcanic activity all along the Ring of Fire.

Below them, far below, the ring of fire was alight, volcanic eruptions spewing forth. The tsunamis, at least three, had wreaked damage across the globe, and the clouds roiled with ejecta from the surface. Those who served as witnesses mourned as Earth burned, shook, and flooded.

A thousand points of light.

Each slammed into the planet and then winked out of existence.

The Impossible

Earth
12.24.2106

"TUPG Bunker 5HB, checking in, Cheyenne, over." The transmission was right on time, just as Syn had said it would be. Tobias leaned closer to the microphone. "Cheyenne acknowledging TUPG Bunker 5HB, over."

"Hey, where's Syn? Over." The girl's voice returned, breaking with protocol.

"Sick day. I'm filling in for her. Name's Tobias. Over," Tobias replied.

"Would you be Syn's Tobias? Over."

Tobias laughed. "Yeah, Syn's Tobias is pretty accurate. Over."

"I'm Julie. Nice to meet you, Tobias. I've heard a lot about you. Over."

Tobias grinned. "Thanks, Julie. Nice to meet you as well. Over."

"So, we had one death overnight. The engineer who got scalded by the busted steam pipe. And one of the preggers is about to pop. Any day now. Over."

"Sorry to hear about your man, 5HB. Any word on the water levels? How are they holding? Over."

Syn had kept him updated on all the bunkers she communicated with each day. Her shift ran Mondays through Wednesdays in communications, whereas his shift ran Thursdays through Sundays in the medical wing. Today was Monday, and she had been ill for days, tossing her cookies every morning and looking painfully thin.

The water levels in the 5HB bunker, which was located in portions of the Niagara Cave in Minnesota had dropped precipitously in the last month and there were concerns that their underground aquifer had some kind of leak, or fracture, in the bedrock. No water would mean a need to return to the surface, which was currently frozen solid with average temperatures holding steady at around minus 23 degrees Celsius in that region. The bunker had struggled through a string of problems, and Tobias and Syn had lived through them all, thanks to Julie's updates. Losing water was disturbing and with the surface uninhabitable because of extreme cold, 5HB was also struggling with maintenance issues that exceeded the population's abilities, especially now that the maintenance engineer had died.

"We are down by 10 meters still and holding steady. Looks like we will be on water conservation measures through the end of January and then re-assess. Over," Julie answered.

"Good to hear, Julie. We're keeping our fingers crossed over here. Over." With nearly 1,000 miles between them, keeping their fingers crossed was about the most that Cheyenne could do. And 5HB and the other bunkers knew it. Scattered across the continent, and across the world, there had been plenty of failures. Lack of foresight, poor site location, and so much more. The first year had been decent, with only one lost, a cave system in central Missouri with nearly two hundred people inside of it. But 2106 had seen five bunkers fail. With two, one in the ruins of Austin and another in the Black Hills in South Dakota, the transmissions had simply fallen silent. Whether they were still out there and their radio tower had failed, or something terrible had happened in the space of time between their twenty-four-hour check-in, no one knew. They were just…gone.

Tobias moved on to the next check-in, and the next, and the next. Hour by hour, transmission by transmission. He talked to them all and cataloged the information, just as he had seen Syn do. It was unlike her to be sick, and she frustrated him with her resistance over seeing the doctor. Jan Peters was petite and had a great sense of humor. On the days he helped the physician's assistant by working in the clinic, the patients clearly preferred Jan.

Not surprising, really. I'm cut out for research. I'd rather be in the lab, anyway.

He was getting close to replicating the cure to ESH. The information sent by the colony on Mars had taken some study and work. Whoever Antonia Antes Nix was, she was a genius, but it took all that Tobias had to deconstruct her work and findings on the virus.

Moving down the halls at the end of Syn's shift, Tobias nodded at the others as he passed them in the hall. He was used to being the weird kid who is too smart for his own good, but here at Cheyenne there were plenty of smart and capable people. They had invited the others to relax in Cryo, which had been far more appealing to most. The alternative meant walking stone hallways, never seeing the sun, eating MREs and breathing canned air for years on end.

Ryan flagged him down as he turned right and headed for the residential area. "Tobias, hey! What are you doing here?"

"I took Syn's shift in Comm; she's been feeling under the weather lately. Every morning it's hard for her to keep any food down."

Ryan raised an eyebrow. "Well, if it was May we were talking about, I'd suggest you get a pregnancy test. She gets morning sickness like you would not believe." He winced. May had been pregnant twice in the past two years, but both had ended in a miscarriage.

Tobias shook his head. "Syn can't have kids. They tested her; said it was impossible."

Ryan nodded, clapped Tobias on the shoulder. "Sorry to hear that. Hey, I'll let May know. She was coming by later with a little gift for Syn and you, anyway. If I don't see you again before tomorrow, Merry Christmas and all that."

The older man had always treated Tobias and Syn like adults, which had been a departure from some others, who not only viewed them as teenagers, but Syn as something less than human. Her eyes, with their limbal ring of fire, unsettled most.

"Thanks, man." Tobias continued on his way, thinking about the different bunkers. For some of them, for most, outside was a frozen wasteland. The solar panels were one hundred times better than they had been a century ago, but in this overcast, post-asteroid overcast winter world, they still struggled to keep up, even here in Cheyenne. If it weren't for the complete retrofit in the 2070s, which had included the installation of a nuclear reactor, they would be doing more than just struggling. There were hundreds of thousands of people here, most in Cryo, with only a few hundred, like Ryan and May, as well as Tobias and Syn, awake and monitoring. The halls were quiet, which would have been unusual except that it was Christmas Eve. Everyone was tucked away in their residential units. As he moved closer to the housing areas, you could see bits of decorations. Adorning one door was thin cardboard from a cereal box cut in the shape of a tree and painted green, complete with red balls and wrapped boxes at the foot of it. At another door, someone had stretched a garland out of bits of green, red, and white fabric across the doorway.

He entered the unit he and Syn shared and frowned. The lights were all off, except for the one in the tiny bathroom. She was curled on the floor of it, sleeping.

"Hey." Tobias crouched next to Syn and cleared a length of her hair away from her face.

Syn blinked, then groaned, one hand straying to her stomach. "Oh, boy."

After a moment of retching into the toilet, she leaned back against the fiberglass shower and groaned. Her lips looked cracked and dry and there were rings under her eyes.

"Let me get you some water."

She flapped her hand at him. "Don't bother, I'll just throw it up."

"Not even water is staying down?" he asked, worry rising. Syn shook her head in answer, closing her eyes.

"That's it, we're going to see Jan." He slipped his arms around her and picked her up with little effort.

Syn sighed, nestling her head against his chest. "Couldn't we just go to bed? I'm exhausted."

"Yeah, no."

Despite Syn's objections and requests to be put down, Tobias lifted her and carried her to the clinic. The waiting room was empty, but the lights were still on. Syn looked relieved. Tobias knew she avoided the times when the corridors were crowded. She hated being stared at. He deposited her in a chair and she slumped, turning sideways and drawing her legs up to her chest. Her hair was limp, lanky, her skin pale.

"I'll be right back." He walked through the staff door and called out to Jan.

"Tobias!" She was in her office, a notebook filled with notes next to her tablet. "I wasn't expecting you in the lab today. Why aren't you with Syn? It's Christmas Eve!"

"Actually, Syn's not been feeling well. Not for days. She's in the waiting room."

Jan Peters stood up from her desk and reached for her stethoscope. "Well, bring her back to Exam Room One, and we'll have a look."

A few minutes later, Syn curled miserably on her side in a hospital gown and answered Jan's questions, stopping twice to retch into a hastily proffered trash can.

"Syn, I want to take some blood and run a few tests, if you don't mind," the doctor said, a gentle hand on Syn's shoulder. Syn nodded, and Tobias prepared a tray of supplies, slipping into assistant mode. It took some doing to find a vein, and Jan finally used the top of Syn's right hand. "I'm also going to start an IV, since we're already in there, to get your hydration levels back up."

Tobias hated seeing Syn like this, so tired and miserable. Had she ever been sick before? If she had, he couldn't remember it. Not a single sniffle or bout of stomach flu, nothing. He couldn't say the same.

After the doc finished taking the samples of blood and he stepped in and hooked up the IV, they waited the handful of minutes for Jan to return. He stroked her hair and kissed her; her skin was cool to the touch.

When Jan re-entered the exam room, she smiled. "Well, I think I know what the problem is. I had a theory and wanted to verify it with that blood test, but it looks like we are dealing with hyperemesis gravidarum." Her eyes twinkled at Tobias.

Hyperemesis gravidarum.

"But that means…" Tobias voice faltered, stopping, as he gaped first at Dr. Peters and then at Syn. "She's, we're… *pregnant*?"

"That's not possible." Syn's voice trembled. "It's *not*. They tested us; they said our hormone levels prevented it, that we could never have children."

"And yet, here we are. The blood test verifies it and I can double-check with a pelvic exam, but I expect we would find that your uterus is already expanding to accommodate your pregnancy, Syn. I would say that your baby is at six weeks gestation, possibly more."

There was silence—a long one—before Tobias let out a whoop of joy. In another time, in another world, sixteen was far too early to become a father. And as for Syn, chronologically she was only five Earth years old, even if her body and mind were that of an adult. There had been a few raised eyebrows when they asked for a place in the couple's living quarters, instead of two of the Singles billets. More of that reaction was from others' discomfort around Syn more than anything.

Hell, I'll be nearly seventeen when the baby is born.

He turned to Syn, suddenly afraid. They had never talked about kids. At least, not in the sense of having their own. He had already known about her infertility. And, considering their ages, there was plenty of time as well. The first order of business had always been to survive long enough for the world outside to recover before they left the bunker. It was hard enough to imagine when that would be, or to make any plans for after. They had certainly talked about adopting children. But now, suddenly, if Syn's pregnancy continued, and that was a huge IF, considering the number of miscarriages still plaguing the survivors, they would be parents in just six or seven months. What if this wasn't something she wanted?

The look of growing wonder and excitement spreading across her face allayed his fears. In that moment, the fiery ring around her eyes had never looked more beautiful.

"I am going to give you some medicine to combat the morning sickness, as well as some prenatal vitamins, and the IV fluids should help as well. Hopefully, it will allow you to keep some food down," Jan said, her lips curving up into an infectious grin. "And I'd like to see you back here on Thursday. I'll need to do a full exam and ultrasound."

Syn nodded, her eyes wide, a giddy grin spreading across her face. Tobias' heart felt as if had expanded in his chest. His grin was so wide his face muscles hurt.

Then Jan Peters' smile disappeared. "I need to caution both of you, however. Post-ESH pregnancies are…well, we are all still struggling with the new normal. Miscarriages are common, far too common. I cannot make any promises, to either of you, that your baby will fare any better. I can tell you that attitude is everything. Stay calm, avoid stress, drink plenty of fluids, and eat as healthy as possible."

Syn's lips quivered as Jan spoke, and Tobias could see a sheen of tears in her eyes. "Do you think that the hyperemesis could have caused harm?" Her voice shook.

"No, not at all, Syn. No one has a simple answer for why some women suffer such an extreme form of morning sickness, but now that we know, we can take steps to stabilize you and keep you healthy. You will have every chance we can give you to carry your child safely to term."

Just hearing Jan's voice reassure Syn gave Tobias hope. He hugged Syn and listened as the doctor gave them a list of instructions.

They spent their Christmas in a haze of joy and wonder. In random moments, Syn would say, "They said it wasn't possible. They said we would never have children." He caught her staring at her flat stomach, appearing as much perplexed as she did hopeful.

The day after Christmas, they walked down to the clinic, hand in hand.

Inside the waiting room, Tobias could feel multiple sets of curious eyes on them, and he jumped up when the nurse called Syn's name, eager to escape to the relative privacy and isolation of the exam room.

"Now, I don't want you getting all excited. We won't be able to see much, but

I just want to take some measurements and make sure everything looks like it is developing normally," Jan said. She struggled to maneuver the ultrasound machine into the room. "Tobias, could you help me with the display? It's down the hall."

He nodded and followed her out the door, surprised when Jan pulled him into the lab. She leaned closed and pitched her voice low. "I ran the blood one more time, and the Beta hCG levels are higher than I would expect."

He frowned. "That's the exact opposite of what Syn overheard back before they shut the study down."

"It's a good thing, though," Jan exclaimed. "At least, it should be. I know Syn is unique, and that we don't have all the data, but typically it indicates…" She stopped and waved her hand impatiently. "No, I will not engage in 'what if' scenarios. The ultrasound will tell us what we are dealing with, and we will go from there, okay?"

Tobias could feel his throat closing, like a chunk of wood had wedged at the back, sharp, and he struggled to calm himself. "I just want Syn to be okay, to be healthy."

Jan stopped, reached out a warm hand, and gripped his arm firmly. "As do I, Tobias. Syn deserves nothing less."

They wheeled in the rest of the equipment and Jan grinned at Syn, winking. "All right, my dear, let's see this baby of yours, shall we?"

Syn nodded, her teeth catching on her lower lip. She clutched at Tobias' hand as Jan applied the warm gel to her flat abdomen and the image on the machine blurred, warped, and finally resolved to show a small space with a tiny mass inside of it, near the wall of Syn's uterus. Tobias squinted. It didn't look like the images he had seen before, and he frowned without realizing it.

"What's wrong?" Syn asked, panic creeping into her voice. "Is there something wrong?"

It was Jan who spoke first, delighted wonder filling her voice. "Not a single thing, Syn. Your babies are perfect, and…" Her fingers flew across the keyboard at the base of the monitor. "Perfectly on track at six and a half weeks gestation. Shared amniotic sac, from the looks of it." Her mouth curved into a broad grin. "They're doing well."

Tobias blinked, the words hitting his brain slowly, as if he were wading through molasses. "Wait. Did you say babies, as in…" His mouth worked but nothing came out. "Babies?"

Next to him, Syn looked just as confused and shocked as he did.

Jan nodded, her eyes sparkling. "Twins. Identical, in fact. Two boys, according to the report I received this morning." She pressed more buttons and a small printer whirred, a grainy color image emerging from the machine. "Believe it or not, the fact that you are having twins improves your odds exponentially. In 75% of the cases of post-ESH twin pregnancies, both have survived to term. We will want to check on them weekly, of course, but yes, your little boys are doing well!"

"And the high hCG levels?" Tobias asked, clutching the photo, his eyes locked on the image of his unborn children.

"Normal with twins. Something I suspected but didn't want to speculate on." She clapped her hands together. They both jumped in surprise, and she held up her hands in apology. "I'm so excited for you both. This is our first set of twins here in Cheyenne!"

The next six months were full of challenges. Enclaves fell, while others kept struggling along. In the early morning hours of August 2nd, 2107, Luke and Daniel Travani-Price were born. They had their mother's eyes.

This Changed World

Earth
05.17.2115

"It has been ten years, nine months, and nine days since the Bombardment. The world outside has been scoured, reshaped, but finally the skies have cleared. We stand on the precipice of a new world, one that we must live on with care, peace, and humility. I know these years have been hard on you all. We've had our differences, our falling outs, our successes, births, and deaths." Ryan's voice rang out over the assembled crowd. "But we're here. We survived. That's more than can be said for countless others."

May stood near the back of the cavern, the press of the others wearing on her.

Ollie shifted restlessly, unimpressed that her father had risen in the ranks and was now giving the last speech of his career as Acting Director of the Cheyenne Mountain Sanctuary. When the massive doors opened, he would step down, or as he kept repeating, "I'll be an average Joe." And they would leave this place that had sheltered them so well.

Dinah Sterling, one of Madeline Chen's former advisers and Ryan's campaign adversary, was here, somewhere, but apparently keeping a low profile. Her bid to rise into a position of power in the vacuum left by President Chen had not gone well. Too many looked at her as an extension of the former TUPG president, and a part of the regime that had made so many unpopular decisions. Their feelings were well-founded. Dinah had pushed forth most of the bills and restrictions that President Chen had signed off on.

May had gone back and forth on the matter. She understood that Madeline Chen's actions as TUPG President were likely made with the best of intentions, but thanks to her Draconian measures, May had first had to break the law to escape with her son and then endure being separated from Silas for these ten long years. It was not something she could forgive easily. And after ample evidence had come out of Dinah Sterling's deep involvement in passing bills that had destroyed and controlled women's lives, she had been happy to see Dinah lose the election.

The shift in power, and Ryan's dive headfirst into politics, was first fed by the hard-liner tactics taken by the TUPG and later continued here in Cheyenne. While the world had alternately burned and flooded, the earth blanketed by massive storms—the heavy-handed rules and laws had taken their toll inside, until they had all had more than enough.

Nearby, Syn Travani held her newborn twins, one on her back, the other in a pack on her front, and the couple's seven-year-old twin sons were nowhere in sight. She didn't look worried, however, and May met her gaze and smiled.

The tugging of a small hand on her pant leg distracted May. She looked down at Ollie, who stared up at her. Ollie's brown skin was lighter than May's, thanks to Ryan's genetics. Their daughter's hair was dark and curly, like May's, and her eyes were like Ryan's, a startling blue. Oleander LaShonda Evers-Denning was looking forward to celebrating her third birthday outside and finally meeting her older brother Silas. May's heart ached at the thought of Silas. She had missed him, feared for him, alone in Cryo miles from Earth. For him, no time would have passed, while for her and Ryan, it had been nearly eleven years. Ollie was just fourteen months younger than Silas had been when the lifeship had carried his unconscious body away to the lunar colony.

"Mommy, when is Daddy gonna stop talking?"

May suppressed a smile. "Soon, honey."

"An den we gonna go see Silas? Outside? And have my berfday?" Time for a preschooler was hard to quantify. No matter how many times May had tried to explain, it hadn't really gotten through. Terms like "next week" and "one month from now" simply eluded the little girl's understanding.

"Soon, baby, I promise." She bent down and lifted Ollie up into her arms. Every night, after Ollie had brushed her teeth and listened to Ryan read her a story, May would sit by her daughter's sleep mat on the floor and talk about the two strong, kind women May named her after. She knew that her mother and Ollie would have both been proud, and happy, to see how well May's life had turned out.

"The drones have sent back reports of significant tectonic shifts across the world," Ryan's voice rang out, his speech continuing as the inhabitants of Cheyenne shifted impatiently in place. "We have also received communiques from several lifeships which have returned. The lifeship Vision has returned from the Moon and landed in the plains of the Midwest. The Esperanza and the Sana have both successfully achieved Earth orbit. And the Masa Depan Bumi should achieve orbit soon. The 3D printers are already hard at work preparing for the first of the new cities. And many of those currently in Cryo will remain under for at least six months."

A murmur ran through the crowd. Many of them had family and friends in Cryo or on one of the lifeships.

"Okay, okay, folks. I know you are eager to get out there." Ryan held up his hands. "Please understand that while the blast doors will open soon, and that they will stay open, we urge you to stay within a half-mile radius of Sanctuary for the next few weeks. Frankly, we are walking out into a world that can sustain us, but still has very limited resources. There are other sanctuary cities underway already on the surface and transport to those cities will be offered over the next few days. We held off until some major storms passed and the snows had melted. You have all received notice of the upcoming election, and I urge you to not forget to vote on June 1st. We have the chance to rebuild our society, to learn from our mistakes, and to treat Mother Earth with the dedication and devotion she so richly deserves." Ryan took a deep breath. "Go in peace, my friends."

The applause filled the hall, reverberating off of the granite walls. Ollie pushed her tiny fingers into her ears.

"Now can we go outside?" Her voice was overly loud and several people laughed nearby.

One man winked at her. "You and me both, kiddo! I'm ready to breathe fresh air again."

The lights above the outer blast doors blinked to life and the trilling alarm sounded, warning people to stand clear of the two twenty-five-ton blast doors as they slowly creaked open.

The crowd was loud, excited, and they jostled in place. When the first breeze hit, it was clean, and a touch on the chilly side. The thousands of voices grew in pitch as they waited, impatiently, for the doors to crack open enough for people to crowd through. May could hear one deputy on duty call over the loudspeakers, warning people to be patient and wait. May stepped back, not wishing to be caught up in the tide of humans.

I didn't survive the end of the world twice, only to be crushed to death by a bunch of impatient idiots.

Slowly the crowd flowed out, becoming sparse, and Ryan appeared in front of her and reached for Ollie. "Here, I'll take her. You need to take it easy, after all." His lips grazed hers, his free hand resting protectively on her rounded belly. The gene therapy, developed by Tobias in collaboration with Antonia Antes Nix over the past five years, had changed the future. It had successfully canceled out the damage wreaked by the ESH virus, and women's reproductive rates had soared.

She was overjoyed when she became pregnant with Ollie and then again, just four short months ago. It had been a shock to learn they were expecting twins, but a welcome one.

"Are you ready to see the world again?" Ryan asked, his eyes on May's.

"I put in a request for a flitter a week ago," she said. "I need to see if the woods are still there." Her lips trembled. "If *she* is still there. I know, I know," she said, waving her hand at the look on Ryan's face. "It's impossible, but still. I need to see it. The GPS will get us there and I'll say my goodbye, even if it is to an empty foundation."

"Okay." Ryan kissed her forehead.

The sun's rays blinded them temporarily as they made their way out of the walls of Sanctuary and into the great outdoors. It was pandemonium—women, men and children running, crying, and dancing, their first breaths of fresh air in a decade. For some, it was the first time. Cheyenne, which had simply become known as Sanctuary, had sheltered them while outside the world shuddered and struggled to recover from the terrible blows it had received. The islands of Hawaii were a distant memory, obliterated by the largest section of Azrael. As well, so was Indonesia, what little remained after decades of rising seas. The footage from the drones had shown that there was nowhere on Earth that escaped unscathed.

The Sahara Desert in Africa was now the Great Saharan Salt Sea. It would take thousands of years for the salty water from the Atlantic to drain away. As it did, however, it would be much like Salt Lake City, Utah, although on a far larger scale, nearly one thousand times the size of Salt Lake.

The drones had picked up images of what could only be survivors. They had been recorded waving frantically at the drones as they passed overhead. Many appeared clothed in skins and camped near the coastlines, there were already sorties planned to connect with them in the days and weeks to come.

Overhead, the sky was a pale blue with only the hint of clouds. The air was crisp, and May could feel the hairs on her arm rise as goosebumps formed. After spending a decade in a place where the temperature never changed, it was deliciously reminiscent of life before.

"Sir!" One soldier jogged up to them and saluted. "The flitter is ready and waiting, sir."

Ryan glanced at May and then nodded at the young man. Hale had just turned twenty-one, one of the few with an intact family, or close enough. He had come to Cheyenne with his mother and his stepfather as a gangly pre-teen and grown up inside of the mountain, joining the Corps the day he turned eighteen. May had taught him sculpture, painting, and more over the years, but he was especially talented at sketching.

Ollie was reticent to leave her friends, a handful of age-mates currently tumbling in the grass, but the promise of a view of her new world from above convinced Ollie to climb on board. May had packed enough food stores to last them a few days, just in case.

As the flitter took off, Ryan elbowed her in the side and leaned in to whisper, "Abuse of power much?"

"You never once took advantage of your status as president," May answered primly. "Not in lodging or meals or any favors. I think that qualifies us for a pass this one time."

Ryan laughed and pulled Ollie onto his lap so that she could see the landscape flying by. Their daughter pressed her button nose flat against the glass and squealed at the sight of a herd of buffalo being chased by what could only be a tiger, its orange and black stripes clearly showing.

During the ESH virus, many zoos had simply opened the cages and let the animals free. They rounded many animals up after the new post-ESH cities rose, creating a new skyline. The new zoos were scuttled in the last days before the asteroid struck, the zookeepers releasing the animals in the hopes that they would find a way to survive. And it appeared that some had.

There was little else to see on the way to New Athens. There were few, if any, trees and in most places, the highways, once so distinct, were gone, obliterated during the massive wave that swept over the land. There was some new growth, but it was sparse. Thin trees dotted the landscape and occasionally they would see a large battered and bruised tree far taller than the others. It went on like this for miles. Nothing remained. Nothing recognizable, in any case. On the East Coast it would likely be the same. From the impact reports at the time of the bombardment and in the transmissions from the satellites, it appeared that when the large 5.2-kilometer chunk nicknamed Nickel slammed into the Strait of Gibraltar, it had set off a chain reaction that included flooding the Sahara with a new shallow saltwater sea and leveling La Palma in the Canary Islands and sent a mega-tsunami racing for the East Coast of North America. The entire shoreline, from Maine to Florida, had been obliterated. Not even the massive high-rises in New York had survived.

Hale called out from the cockpit, "GPS shows we are getting close, maybe 2 miles out. I'm going to have it set down over there." He pointed to a wide swath of land at the edge of a line of trees.

Ryan gave the soldier a thumbs-up and the flitter dropped like a stone, earning Hale a small shriek of distress from Ollie, who had drifted off, already overdue for a nap.

May stared out of the window, desperate to find any evidence of humans, or anything that resembled the house she had spent the first four years of Silas' life in. She was counting the days until she could see Silas. All she wanted was to wrap her arms around her little boy again.

She blinked, something catching her eye as they descended. Had she seen a wisp of smoke from that small clump of trees?

The prairie that they landed on was open to the west, filled with wildflowers and prairie grass. In the distance were shapes, possibly deer, although it was hard to tell at this distance. The flitter jerked a little to one side as it landed with another thump. The machine was on autopilot, but Hale had to have messed with the controls.

He threw up his hands. "Sorry! My bad! I'm used to the drones. Keep forgetting these things fly themselves."

May smiled at the younger man. "Don't worry about it." While Ollie grumbled in distress and rubbed at her eyes, May sighed. "I should have thought this through; she should be napping right now back at Sanctuary."

Ryan rolled his eyes. "She would lose her mind. You've told her so much about the place where you and Silas lived. I'm sure she's expecting a castle instead of the pitiful remains of a house in the woods. Honestly, May, what do you hope to find?”

The doors to the flitter opened and the fresh air, far warmer and muggier now that they had left the mountains of Colorado behind, flooded in. And with it, a distinctive smell.

“Is that wood smoke?” Ryan asked, his tone incredulous, as if he couldn’t believe his own nose.

“It is!”

“Mommy, dere’s a boy over there!” Ollie pointed, and they looked just in time to see a young boy disappear into the trees. May jumped out of the flitter and jogged towards the tree line, her heart pounding. Was it even possible? What were the chances that Ollie could have survived? May could hear Ryan call to her, but she didn’t stop. She couldn’t. If there was any chance of survival, of reunion, Ollie would have returned here.

The trees were just thick enough to hide the rough shack. Not the house, although the shack looked as if they had assembled most of it from planed boards. It was rough; the roof was weathered and covered in lichen. There was a tarp tied across one corner. Right now, the weather was fine, but it must have been hard living through the bitterly cold winters. A thin, ruddy-faced woman came out of the opening. The boy who had run away from May peered out fearfully behind her.

"Hello there!" May gasped, out of breath from her run. She could hear Ryan and Hale crashing through the undergrowth. They would be here soon.

"My Lord, I thought Ethan was seeing things when he said there were people." The woman's hand rested on Ethan's bone-thin shoulder. "But you look damn real to me."

"I'm May, and that is Ryan and Hale," May said, pointing towards the two men who were closing the distance rapidly. The boy, Ethan, disappeared inside of the shelter.

"Lindsay," the woman said, closing the distance between them and grasping May's hand. She jerked her head in the shack's direction. "Ethan's never seen other people. At least, not since he was small. He'll come 'round soon enough."

"Did you make it to a shelter? Or have you been here since the Bombardment?" May asked, taking in the woman's tattered clothes.

"I didn't make the cut." Lindsay's face twisted. "I was a mess right after the virus, couldn't get my head on straight for a while, and then they said I was persona non grata for any of the lifeships or underground sanctuaries. But hell, I had a first-row seat to the apocalypse; would've drowned if it weren't for me stumbling across a group at just the right time."

Ollie popped out of the tall grass. "Who are you? Are you my grandma?"   .

Lindsay clutched her chest and yipped with surprise. "Goodness, child, I didn't even see you in the tall grass." She laughed as Ollie's question sunk in. "And no, I am not old enough to be a grandma to anyone!"

"This is our daughter, Ollie, short for Oleander," May said, resting her hand on Ollie's shoulder. She wiggled impatiently under it.

"Mommy! I see the boy!" She uttered the words as she flew away, her feet barely skimming the ground. She barreled away through the opening in the shack where the boy had vanished yet again.

"Ollie, now that's a name I never thought I'd hear again," Lindsay exclaimed, a grin stealing over her face as she watched Ollie disappear into the shack.

"Again?" Ryan asked, and Lindsay nodded.

"Yes, the woman who saved my life. Her name was Ollie. Pulled me out of the floodwaters, rounded up a handful of us, got us to a cave. She saved us." Lindsay hitched up her shoulders. "Well, most of us. More than would have lived otherwise."

"Ollie," May breathed, "Is she…"

Lindsay shook her head. "The second winter, things got bad." She laughed then, a bitterness in her voice. "Hell, who am I kidding? It's been a shit show since 2099; nothing much changes. Ollie fell, broke her leg, and was out in the cold for hours before we found her. She died two weeks later. Couldn't tell you of what, probably pneumonia, but whatever it was, it took what little she had left. Three more of our group died that winter and by the end of the fourth year, it was just me and Ethan alone in the world. We came back to this cabin Ollie had said was here. And it was…until a forest fire took it down. I built that mess over there with whatever I could salvage about four years back. And we've been here ever since."

May could feel the tears sliding down

her cheeks. "Two years. While we were safe inside, she was out here fighting for her life." She felt Ryan's arms surround her. "It isn't fair."

Lindsay gave a small snort. "Life isn't fair. Not one goddamn bit of it." She stared at them, her eyes widening. "Say, you wouldn't have any food with you, would you?"

Later, hours later, after Lindsay and Ethan had eaten their fill of the foods that May and Ryan had brought, Lindsay drew a map for them.

"You'll find her grave there, the first of eight. I couldn't tell you why we survived and she didn't. I only know I owe her my life."

They left her and her son with a locator beacon and half of the food stores. It would take some time, but the two would be reunited with other survivors soon. The sun was low in the sky when they found the location of the cave.

"I remember this cave," Ryan said, "from a book I read in high school." He stared at it for a moment and then pointed to one of the few larger trees still standing. It was bent at an odd right angle. "You see that tree there? It's called a thong tree."

May nodded. "Yes! I remember that book. It was by Jessica Farnsworth, wasn't it? Part of RUSA's history of the Collapse. She was a survivor of the second civil war."

"Yeah, Jessica survived here, with her infant son and several others over a winter." Ryan added.

Moments later, they stood at the graves, mere heaps of rocks in a landscape that, even ten years later, still showed the damage, massive wounds inflicted upon Earth. The trees were thin, young, and only a few, like the thong tree, were older. Only the massive, well-established ones had survived the blast wave and flooding in the region.

"This changed world. She survived in it for two winters while we sat comfortable inside," May whispered, her voice raw with anguish.

"She did it for you, May. For both of us. For Silas. And for Ollie, even if she never knew her," Ryan said, his voice as steadfast as his embrace. "She did it because she believed we were worth it. So now it's our job to prove her right."

May hugged him back, her heart breaking at the thought of Ollie dying all those years ago. Ollie had given them a gift, one that May intended to spend the rest of her life repaying.

All of Our Tomorrows

Earth
07.04.2115

May held Ryan's hand tightly as they approached the massive ship. It had landed the week before, and the message had come that morning, an innocuous message appearing on her tablet that had sent her heart leaping with joy.

OFFICIAL COMMUNIQUE FROM LIFESHIP VISION TO EVERS NEE DENNING, MAY FLOWER
/BEGIN TRANSMISSION
REVIVAL OF DENNING, SILAS SCHEDULED FOR 0945 THURSDAY DAY 04, JULY 2115. PLEASE CONFIRM ATTENDANCE AND RELEASE OF

MINOR INTO PARENTAL CUSTODY
/END TRANSMISSION

May had gasped, drawing Ryan's attention. "He's up for revival from Cryo!"

Her husband leaned in, his eyes reading the text with a smile on his lips. "I didn't think it would work, but I guess it did." He did a double take. "Is your middle name really Flower?"

"You didn't think what would work?" May asked, ignoring his question.

"You are always harping on how I don't ask for special treatment, so I…" He shrugged. "I asked for Silas to be expedited and it looks like it worked."

May squealed and hugged him.

"Seriously though, how did I not know your middle name is Flower?"

May rolled her eyes. "Oh my God, really? That's what you want to know?" She had kissed him then. "Thank you, Ryan, thank you so much for asking for Silas."

The initial timeframe had been another month of waiting and the days, despite being full of tasks, were dragging. She hadn't seen her little boy in nearly eleven years. She wanted Silas in her arms. She wanted him to meet Ollie, to have her son home.

"I have missed our son more than I thought possible," he said, meeting her eyes, his gaze steady on hers.

She felt a pang of regret for doubting it for a second. There in the close quarters of the Cheyenne Mountain Complex, shortly after Ollie was born, she had watched Ryan hold their newborn daughter. She had searched his gaze for some level of difference, some preference perhaps, for holding a child that was half his by blood and DNA. She had feared that once they returned to the surface, once Silas returned, that Ryan might love him less. It had kept her up at night, haunting her dreams.

May knew how it could be; she'd lived it, after all. Foster home after foster home, none of them willing to love her, to accept her. White faces, black faces, it didn't matter. She wasn't theirs. It wasn't until Ollie had helped her escape from the hospital with Silas, and she had found herself safe in the cabin in the woods, that she had finally felt a part of a family again. It had been the first time since Mom died that May had felt truly loved. Ollie's love had been steadfast, maternal, and just the thought of her left alone on the surface as Azrael had impacted Earth still brought her to tears. Her sacrifice had been that of a mother's. May knew that in her bones. She knew Ollie loved her. She knew too that Ryan loved her. Their love hadn't been full of fire. He hadn't swept her off of her feet. Instead, it had been a friendship, a bond that strengthened, grew. First on the surface, there in Ollie's cabin, in the woods, and later, through her grief at losing a second mother in Ollie and missing Silas, their love had continued. May knew she had clung to him as a drowning man clung to a buoy in the storm, desperate to survive. And when they had learned, after so many years, that they were expecting a baby girl, well, there was no other name that fell from either of their lips. Ollie, of course it would be Ollie. Still, the fear that Ryan would love his own child more than Silas filled May with dread. Little Silas, he would wake in what would be to Silas mere moments after falling asleep. And instead of a world filled with forest, and Grandma Ollie, his world would be entirely different, including his family. He would need Ryan. He would need his father.

"May, I miss him too." Ryan's voice jogged her from her thoughts. "I know it is nothing like the love a mother has, but he is my boy, my firstborn son, and I love him and can't wait to see him again. You know that, right?"

May nodded, tears slipping from her eyes. How had she gotten so lucky? Ryan was a good man. He was a kind man and an amazing father. He had proved his love for Silas, over and over, and she was a fool for doubting him. He hadn't predicated that love on DNA, but on dedication and devotion. He wasn't like those foster families she had lived with after her mom died. He was like Ollie, steadfast and committed.

She had returned to Ollie's grave, taken little Ollie there, and they had built the cairn up with stones, added a headstone, and she had planted an oleander bush at the head of it. She would return there with Silas when the time was right. And when he was older, far older, she would explain the sacrifices that Grandma Ollie had made so that May, little Ollie, and the twins would survive.

May wiped the tears from her eyes.

"You're coming with me. When Silas opens his eyes, he needs to see both of us."

Her husband smiled at her and her heart fluttered. He was handsome, and her love for him was deeper and stronger than any partner she had ever had.

"That sounds perfect."

May barely slept, her dreams filled with images of the wrong Cryo unit, or Silas lying there and not waking up, or not recognizing her and Ryan. So many nightmares. The sun rose early, and she groaned, her eyelids crusted, and her eyeballs felt dry, aching. The smell of coffee spurred her to sit up, which she did with another groan, joints aching. The bed was not comfortable. Some supplies were plentiful, others not so much, and new mattresses would wait for another six months until the factories were printed and assembled. Meanwhile, everyone was using worn-out mattresses or worse, blankets on the ground, until they re-established production.

"Hey." Ryan's frame blocked the light from the window, a cup of coffee in his hand.

"Is that for me?" May croaked, and he nodded and placed it in her hands. "Thank you.”

“You tossed and turned all night.”

May ran her hand through her hair and groaned. “Shit, I forgot my bonnet. This is going to take forever.” Her hair was a rough mass of frizz. She slurped the coffee and felt the heat of it trickle down her throat and warm her stomach. Not that she needed warmth–it was well over 26° Celsius and predicted to top 40° Celsius by noon. The caffeine would help, and Ryan made it strong. Another few minutes and she would feel it kick her system into gear, despite her fragmented night of sleep.

Ryan pressed his lips against her forehead. “Mayflower, we’re getting our son back today.”

“You’ll never let that go, will you?” she asked, her voice smoother now that she’d managed a few sips of coffee.

Ryan’s low laugh rumbled in his chest. “Nope. I think I really would have liked your mom.”

May’s lips twitched, a pitiful attempt to hold back a smile. She failed. “Oh my God, you do not know the number of jokes kids made when I was young. Pilgrims and turkeys and sailing on the Mayflower.” The smile slipped. “When I went into the system, they asked what the F stood for and I said Fiona. That wasn't much better, unfortunately. Some damned vintage Disney movie with a troll princess of the same name in it." She drained the coffee cup and Ryan took it from her, threaded his fingers through her hair, and reached down to capture her lips with his.

She returned his kiss with no small amount of ardor. Despite the twins already pushing her stomach out and changing her center of balance, her libido had been at an all-time high recently and it had pleasantly surprised Ryan. It was as if being out of Cheyenne, with fresh air and the world around them, space to breathe, to live, had woken up a lust for living that had seemed almost impossible for the past ten or more years. Their kiss intensified, and he ran his hands down her back, dipping into the elastic waistband of her sleep shorts. How long had it been since they had a morning quickie? A few seconds later and May was sure it would not be today.

"Mommy! Moooommmmeeeee!" Ollie called from her bedroom. Her voice was distressed. The doorknobs differed from the easy handle on their lodgings in

Cheyenne, and Ollie was stuck more than once in the past week since they had moved into their newly printed home. All around them, the streets were still bare, just dirt and straggling weeds and the other houses were identical to theirs. It had been quite a change for Ollie, who was used to having all of her friends around her to play with. May hoped that Syn and Tobias ended up moving into the house nearby; the two families had grown close over the years.

Ryan groaned. May flapped her fingers at him. "Go rescue our daughter." He leaned in and gave her a kiss that promised they would revisit the passion later, once the children were in bed, and headed for Ollie's bedroom.

An hour later, they were dressed, combed, and fed and it was time to drop Ollie off with one of the Group One mothers. They had handled childcare through communal agreements, and a small group of five or six children met at different houses on a rotating basis. This allowed other mothers time to work. Everyone was necessary in the rebuilding of their world. It had its frustrations and inconsistencies, but over the last eight weeks, they had all made significant progress. The spires of the new city on the plains outside of the ruins of what had once been Kansas City, Kansas, were rising once again.

The sounds of the new city were constant in the daylight hours. The 3D printers chugged along, creating the houses the survivors would need. Everywhere she looked there were people doing whatever the machines could not. Factories were starting up, and the number of on-ground survivors continued to grow as flitters crisscrossed the continents, finding pockets of humanity sprinkled through the destruction. Last week there had been over two hundred survivors discovered in the remnants of New York—men, women, and children who had somehow found shelter in the subways as Azrael rained down upon them and later flooded the same tunnels with a mega-tsunami that had decimated everything in its path, bringing seawater all the way to Ohio.

People had survived in tunnels, fallout shelters, caves, and, in one instance, one of the spiral underwater cities. When May thought of it, she couldn't help thinking that humans truly were a lot like cockroaches. Come what may, humanity found a way. The tales were harrowing to be sure. There were areas close to some of the impact sites that had seen temperatures so hot the metal melted. And most of the surface had endured up to a decade of winter, the atmosphere so filled with particles that no sun rays made it through, chilling the surface and covering it with a gray snow.

May was working part-time assisting with refugee intake and interviews. Those who had survived were at turns angry, despondent and happy—and it was challenging as she tried to help them through their traumas. They had all lost so many people, both in the years before, thanks to the ESH virus, and now in the long decade since Azrael's impact. Many were unfit to work—their bodies had been at starvation level for years as they scrabbled in the remains of a world fundamentally changed by the asteroid and the deadly virus before it. May had wondered if any of them, including herself, would ever be okay. The news that she would soon have Silas back had wiped her thoughts clean of her work, however, and the smile on her face at the thought of holding her son again left her cheeks aching for relief. Her baby, her boy, her firstborn son.

As Ryan and May approached the gates of the revival center, a soldier held up his hand and pointed to the fingerprint register. The guards were necessary, unfortunately, after several incidents in recent days had devolved into fighting over the order of Cryo revivals.

"Name?"

"Ryan and Mayflower Evers here for Silas Denning's revival," Ryan answered, a grin on his lips. May sighed. Her husband was going to milk this to the very end.

There was a pause as the system chimed and then beeped in turn.

"Ma'am, you can proceed but you will have to wait here, Sir. We can only allow the custodial parent on file inside." The soldier was young, and his face showed no recognition of Ryan's name. He scanned the list. "I see that the custodial parent is May Evers?"

May felt ill. Of all the times for bureaucracy to interfere in a reunion. She opened her mouth to say something, anything to argue. Before she could, a familiar voice called out from the entrance.

"Ryan! May!" It was Tobias, and his grin

filled his face. "Today is the day! I saw Silas on the list for this morning's revivals. Come on back, you two!"

He beckoned, and May stared at the guard for a moment and then pulled at Ryan's hand, her heart pounding in anticipation. *Silas. Daddy and I are on our way, my love.*

The guard shrugged and let them pass. May interpreted the shrug to mean if one of the head scientists insisted, who was he to argue? She wasted no time, practically dragging her husband to the double doors, and hugged Tobias, tears forming in her eyes. "Thank you; he would not let Ryan in."

Tobias hugged her back. "I've missed having dinner with the two of you. Hell, I miss my wife and kids; they practically have me living here right now as we process all the revivals."

"Is it as crazy as I've heard?" Ryan asked.

"Worse; we had two fights last night and then one revival didn't make it." Tobias paused, and quickly added, "Underlying conditions, mind you, extremely rare."

May felt Ryan's arm slide around her. "Silas will be so happy to see us both."

"Ah, yes, sorry. I feel like all I do is say the same thing over and over these days to muzzy-headed revivals and anxious family, so it's nice to see a friendly face every once in a while." Tobias pointed. "This way. The process has already started and he should be awake in just a few moments. Keep in mind, nausea often comes with it, so watch out!" He led the way down the corridor, and Tobias ushered them through the two wide hospital doors into another corridor with a series of rooms on each side. "You are in Room 7."

"I heard the Masa Depan Bumi arrived in orbit last week," Ryan said, making small talk as they moved down the hall.

"Yes, we are already seeing revivees come down." Tobias grinned, "They are reviving them in orbit and let me tell you, I am thankful of that, I'm operating a week behind schedule as it is and working seven days a week."

They could hear raised voices coming from another room.

"And that's my cue," Tobias said, his voice neutral. "Good to see you two and I can't wait to meet the little guy!" He took off at a run.

"Room 7 it is, then." May felt Ryan's hand envelope her own and give it a gentle squeeze. "Are you ready?"

"More than you can imagine."

They stepped through the door into a darkened room. Lights illuminated everything in low lighting, and May's eyes focused on the tiny form of her son lying on the gurney. A nurse stood by his side, her eyes on the display that listed his vital signs. She looked up with a smile. "May Evers?"

"Yes," May whispered, her eyes on Silas, drinking in every detail of his face. His eyes were closed, his lashes dark, feathered, and still against his cheeks. She could see the tiny scar on his chin from when he had tripped and fallen on the trail outside of the cabin. How he had cried as May had wrapped him in her arms and rushed him back to Ollie and Ryan.

Tears pricked at her eyes. Ollie, he would want Ollie. And how would she ever explain to him that his grandmother was gone?

"I'm Jenny," the nurse whispered. "We keep the lights low. The revivees typically have light sensitivity for a day or two. There are special sunglasses here on the counter for Silas to use. He should wear them for the next few days until his eyes recover from his long sleep."

May nodded, but didn't look away from her son, drinking in every detail. How had she not remembered him being so tiny? Ollie looked bigger, or nearly as big as Silas. Would they get along? Would he accept his sister and the twins? Would he feel left out or wish it was just him?

"He should wake up any time now. Sometimes it takes a few minutes longer, other times less so. It just depends on their metabolism," Jenny added.

Ryan spoke, but May didn't pay attention. All of her was here with her son, her baby, her boy.

"May, you and Ryan can touch him. Sometimes that helps a revivee wake up, feeling touch and knowing their loved ones are close."

May nodded and took Silas' tiny hand in hers. It was cool to the touch, but she could feel his pulse, steady. His fingers twitched and his eyelashes fluttered.

"Silas? Baby?"

Ryan was by her side. One hand was in the small of her back, stroking, the other rested on Silas' leg. "Son, it's time to wake up," Ryan said, and May heard the catch in his throat. She glanced up and saw the tears filling her husband's eyes.

Silas opened his eyes then found hers, warbled a bit, blinked, and found Ryan as well. "Is it time to go on the ship now?"

"You're all done, son." Ryan sniffed hard, and May felt tears forming in her eyes. "And we can all go home now."

May looked at Jenny, her eyes questioning, and Jenny nodded. "He's fine to sit up, but he might be a little…"

Silas sat up on his own and retched, projectile vomit, covering a wide swath of Ryan's arm and shirt.

Jenny sighed. "Third one this morning, unfortunately." She turned away, reaching for towels and wipes, and pointed to a paper shirt neatly folded on the countertop. "You can wipe yourself off and then wear the shirt home, Mr. Evers."

"Sorry, Daddy." Silas wiped at his mouth with the back of his hand.

"It's okay, son." Ryan laughed and nudged May. "Why is it they always throw up on me?"

"You are just lucky like that, Babe."

Silas stood then, his legs clumsy and shaking, and May pulled him into her arms, her tears spilling over, wetting the top of her son's head. She had missed him. Feared for him, alone in Cryo on the surface of the Moon, feared an errant asteroid striking the ship, a failure in the solar collectors, or a half-dozen other catastrophes. They had woken her up at night, a scream on her lips, and only Ryan to comfort her. She hugged him tight and sobbed harder. "I missed you, Silas. I missed you so much."

"I missed you too, Mommy, but it was only a little while." His familiar scent enveloped her. She felt Ryan wrap his arms around both of them, his paper shirt crinkling, the scent of vomit fading.

"It felt like forever, Silas," Ryan murmured, his face buried in May's neck.

"Will we stay together now, Mommy?"

May's voice quavered. "Yes, baby. For all of our tomorrows. I promise."

"Okay, good. I wanna go home now."

An hour later, they stood in the doorway of the revival center and stared out. Dark sunglasses wrapped around Silas' face, and he stared out at the world. "It looks… differ'nt."

May looked out at the city rising around them. White spires of skyscrapers stood in the distance. Roadways were being added with each new day. Flitters and autocars filled the streets. All around them was a new life. She could see the robo-gardeners filling the last patches of tended earth with seedlings a block over, likely the last of the watermelon transplants before they began the fall crop planting. In this new city, housing blended with parks, workspaces, gardens and cropland—a reminder that each depended on the other intrinsically.

Their world would rise again. Earth had suffered an unimaginable loss. Despite this, they were still alive, and this next generation would be the first to walk upon a world devastated and reborn from the ashes. It was up to each of them to live their best lives possible. Not just to survive. But to thrive.

"All of our tomorrows, Mayflower," Ryan said softly, his hand warm on her back. Somehow, when Ryan said her middle name, she liked how it sounded. She felt the name roll over her. It reminded her of spring, and it reminded her of new beginnings. *Mom would have loved him.*

"All of our 'morrows," Silas agreed.

Ollie was waiting to meet her brother. It was time to go home.

It Still Stands

Earth
04.12.2116

Eaton stopped the flitter and stared at the washed-out road in front of them. It had taken nearly six months to revive everyone from the Masa Depan Bumi and Jia and Eaton had been one of the last batches revived and shuttled down to the Earth's surface.

It made sense when he thought about it. After all, there wasn't much need for art experts at present. As it was, Jia and Eaton had both pitched in to help with other far more mundane tasks. Rebuilding a world did not happen overnight. Nor did access to take a limited resource, the flitter, to unsettled parts of the world.

Resources were limited, and they chose to relocate to just outside of the ruins of

Lyon, to a new city rising from its ashes. They worked in the fields, planting crops, and in the distribution centers helping to organize supplies and food and more. When Eaton's Comm notified him that his request for a flitter was approved, he had called Jia.

"My request for a flitter. It's come through, we can take it to see if the house is still there."

"Oh Eaton, thank you!" Jia's voice sounded so happy and he was relieved. She had confessed just that morning that she felt out of place in this new city. It didn't help that they had received word that the world's artifacts would remain stored underground for at least five years. Their very livelihood was on hold.

"We'll be able to go tomorrow, we're both off work that day, anyway."

Now, here they were, almost there. Jia, who had lived in the area for four years with Willem recognized several landmarks.

"We're close," she said, staring at the tree, "I think that it might be the next road on the left."

Eaton nodded and eased the flitter higher in the air, allowing it to hover a few feet higher than the massive tree trunk. A mile down the road and the GPS pinged.

"Turn here."

The road that had been there was gone, obliterated by over a decade of severe weather and zero human occupation. The GPS, however, cared little for such things. It showed a clear line to their destination, and Eaton followed it.

As a clearing appeared, and the ever-shortening blue line indicated their journey was almost over, Eaton's heart rate sped up. There had been stories of survivors, there were new ones every day. Perhaps Willem had survived, perhaps his mother had as well. Anything was possible.

"It's the house! It's still standing!" Jia gabbled in shock, sitting forward and pointing to a roofline that Eaton had missed, seeing only the greenery.

The flitter stopped, descended to ground level, and Eaton turned it off and turned to help Jia out. She had already clambered out and was running toward the house.

Or its ruins. The closer he got, the worse it appeared. One side had caved in completely, the glass windows shattered and missing, and the green underbrush had firmly entrenched itself on one wall. It still stood, but not for long.

He caught up to Jia, in time to watch her fall to her knees. "Papa!"

"Jia, my love, he isn't here." His voice caught. He had wanted it to. So much. To find them both here. Sitting in the living room, their feet up, a stein of beer in hand, trading stories. Ma and Willem had become close friends the last two years before Impact. How many times had they both dreamed of returning and finding them, here, together, alive?

"I know." Jia's tears slid down her round cheeks and splattered onto her chest. "I just hoped and with the baby, I…"

A month ago, shortly after the retroviral treatment now available to all women, Jia had become pregnant with their child. After the years of sterility and miscarriages so many had suffered, it had felt like a miracle to wake up to a cure of sorts. It wasn't 100% effective, but it had increased the odds. The birth rate would soon be soaring and the cities rose from the broken and changed world would soon house a new generation, one that had never known the ESH virus or the Earth from before.

Eaton wrapped his arms around his wife and kissed her soft, wavy hair. "Me too. I miss Ma and Willem both so much. But we have at least found the house."

"I want to go inside."

He eyed the structure with distrust. "Jia, I don't think that's a good idea."

"It will be fine. I just need to find two things. We'll be in and out in no time."

Stepping inside of the moldering house, Eaton noticed the change in light. Everything was cast in gloom, and it smelled moist, rotten. The floor underfoot was soft and rotten. Despite this, the surface crunched, whether from glass or the bones of small animals, Eaton was unsure. Frankly, he didn't care.

They entered through the twisted remains of the French double doors that had led to the back patio, sidestepping a tree that had rooted into the ground at one side. The roof dipped even more inside than it did out, and at point, Eaton had only to reach his hand up to touch the spongy mass of drywall that hung directly above him.

He was relieved when Jia stopped and reached for a small picture frame. "Here, just this and the wood bear on the fireplace behind you."

Eaton peered into the gloom and saw the tiny carved bear covered in dust and debris. His hand closed on it and the house groaned.

They scrambled out, through the double door and around the sapling. Once they were clear, and Eaton's heart had resumed a normal pattern, he brushed off a large log and Jia sat, the picture frame clutched in her hands.

She wiped it off, used a portion of her tunic to rub the dirt and grime away and stared at it. It showed Willem, along with his wife and three children.

"Not one of the two of you?" He asked, surprised.

"I have hundreds on a memory stick." She answered, staring at them. "But I didn't have anything from before. They deserve to be remembered."

Eaton examined the tiny wood bear. "And this?"

"Jonas carved it." Jia answered softly.

"Jonas is a good name. A strong name. So is Willem."

Jia looked up at him, tears still sparkling in her eyes. She was so beautiful. He wished that Ma could see her now. Jia's face was filling out a little from the pregnancy, and her stomach had just begun to protrude. He could see the glow that so many described pregnant women as having. Ma would have fed her char siu and a dozen more delicacies. She would have hovered, and made a pest of herself, she would have been so happy waiting for the emergence of her first grandchild.

"Willem Jonas Ngai?" he asked, extending a hand to caress her belly, "Or Jonas Willem?"

"The first, I think. Yes," she said smiling. "Willem Jonas Ngai."

Eaton stared at the crumbling house. It groaned again and shifted. A section buckled inside and he could see the section of ceiling he had stood under collapse and fall to the floor.

"If you want, we could rebuild someday. If you want."

"Yes, I would like that very much." She leaned her head on his shoulder. "But for now, I think it is time to go home."

He kissed her hair again. "Yes. Home. Until we can rebuild *this* home. I love you, Jia."

"I love you."

The forest, mostly intact and familiar, soothed his soul. He could hear birds chirping, and the rasp of cricket song. The old world was gone, and with it, many of those they had loved most in the world. But they had the chance to make a new world, a beautiful one, in the ruins of the old. Their child, little Willem, would never know anything different except through their stories.

They stood and walked to the flitter slowly. Someday, perhaps in a few months, perhaps years from now, they would return here. They would build another house and fill it with children and love.

He believed it would be exactly what Ma and Willem wanted for them.

Acknowledgments

For Jeff Bonovich–It was a rocky start, but hey, you got some furnace filters out of it. Thanks for being a sport and letting me kill you with a huge wave. And I just have one question for you: Jeff, where's the guacamole you promised me?!

For my wonderful husband and two daughters–the eldest in the throes of teenage angst, the other entering Kindergarten in the fall. They are patient, supportive, and are always providing more fodder for my characters!

A shout-out to Dani, who always has a thumbs-up or supportive thing to say when I post. And great dog advice as well (can't forget that!).

To all of my friends and family who support my writing. You are all awesome! Thanks for being my ARC reader, catching the typos, and writing those reviews. You rock!

To my sweet little "min pit" Honey Nut Cheerios. You returned to me after two long years and I couldn't be happier. My house is now full of four wonderful dogs! And to the gentleman, David, who took her

in and loved and cared for her all of that
time, I am forever grateful.

Author Note

The Gliese 581 series began with a snippet of scene, I imagined a woman who drives up to the drive-thru stark-naked, parks her car, and eats until, well, until she dies. But this series has become so much more. In my research for *The Departure*, I learned how autopsies are conducted, and interviewed friends who were nurses and a virologist and professor at Washington State. I even reached out and exchanged emails with Steven Vogt, the astronomer who discovered Gliese 581g some 22 light years away.

I really wanted to get more in depth beyond the one chapter on the Mars colony in *The Departure*, and so I decided I'd jump in and write *Mars* and *Earth* and hopefully flesh out more of the stories behind the stories. While writing *Mars*, I learned more about regolith and terraforming than I thought was possible. And while I took a couple of leaps with nanite technology, I'd like to think it wasn't too unbelievable or far out there. And recently, when writing *Earth*, I learned plenty more about impact trajectories, and what their effects would be when impacting land or water.

Writing these books has often meant stepping outside of my comfort zone, but I hope that I did it with some modicum of grace and without too many glaring flaws. There are more to come—two more, in fact.

The next book, *Zarmina's World* will transport the reader to the Gliese system some 22 light years away to the Gliese 581g planet the scientists landed on in *The Departure*. The fifth book in the series will be an anthology of short stories, filling in even more backstories and details that my dedicated readers can dig their toes into. I hope to have both out sometime in 2022.

Thanks for reading. Please consider posting a review. Put simply, reviews are social proof. They tell a potential reader a few important things: 1) that someone, anyone has read the book, and 2) that they thought well enough (or not) to post a review.

And if you would like to know more about me and receive regular updates on my writing projects, you can find me on Facebook here: https://www.facebook.com/Christine.D.Shuck or at my author website:

https://www.christineshuck.com/

Other Published Works

Christine writes cross-genre, and her books can be found in e-book and in paperback through most book distributors.

Non-Fiction:
Get Organized, Stay Organized
The War on Drugs: An Old Wives Tale

Fiction Series:
War's End
The Storm
A Brave New World
Tales of the Collapse

Gliese 581g
G581: The Departure
G581: Mars
G581: Earth

Chronicles of Liv Rowan
Fate's Highway

Benton Security Services
Hired Gun
Smoke and Steel